Praise for
RAN: A Civilization in Hiding

Told entirely from the point of view of an incipient spacefaring reptilian race whose two Apollo-like astronauts were abducted by space aliens (Humans), *The Third Oort Chronicle* is hard, mind-stretching science fiction of the highest order. It centers on efforts to replace destructive reptilian tyrants with fair-minded leaders within an interstellar system. Thus, John Butler, Chairman of the Oort Federation, as well as lizard leaders of the planet Arcan, seek to oust Bopr Arclando, Leader of Ceffid and bring it into the Federation. It's no mean task, and the same applies to Lieutenant Dombit, whose use of clever strategy against General Klarot of The Geroptic Nation is worthy of a novel in itself. For those who like tribunals, especially when they involve despots like these, *The Third Oort Chronicle* features two fascinating ones which only superficially resemble trials on *Law and Order*.

The novel portrays three intelligent species besides Humans, all of them ingeniously characterized. For example, Jocara, a lizard from Arcan, expresses happiness in a distinctive way. At one point, her "pale green, finely shaped Saurian face scales rippled slightly with a faint lavender hue as she smiled joyfully…with no change in her mouth shape." With differences like these, it's understandable that achieving interstellar agreement and even peace would be difficult. To me, the novel's greatest strength is that it provides a sense of what governing contentious species in the vastness of space might really be like.

– Professor John B. Rosenman,
Norfolk State University
Former Chairman of the Board, Horror Writers Association
Author of *The Inspector of the Cross Series*

In *Ran: A Civilization in Hiding*, Robert G. Williscroft takes on the challenge of writing a novel where the viewpoint characters are not only not human, they aren't even mammalian. He does it convincingly.

Braxton Thorpe (whom we met in *Icicle* and revisited in *The Oort Federation*) and his team are on a voyage of exploration when aliens, on the brink of space travel themselves, stumble across them. The reptile-like aliens (they're not exactly reptiles, either) inhabitants of the Ran star system (also known as Epsilon Eridani), have kept their existence secret from the outside universe—until now. As if dealing with the surprises when the first crewed Ran spaceship encounters Thorpe's own ship weren't enough, Thorpe's old nemesis, Isidor Orlov, also makes contact and foments trouble trying to obtain exclusive trade deals. The resulting holy war between nations on the alien planet adds a disturbingly familiar scenario to an otherwise very alien world.

With plenty of Williscroft's trademark intrigue and action, backed by hard science, this tale sets us up nicely for whatever the next Oort Chronicle brings. I'm looking forward to it.

– Alastair Mayer
Author of *The T-Space Series*

THE THIRD OORT CHRONICLE
RAIN
A CIVILIZATION IN HIDING

Female Arcan astronaut Jocara Porovik

ROBERT G. WILLISCROFT

RAN: A Civilization in Hiding
The Third Oort Chronicle

Starman Press
Email: rgw@RobertWilliscroft.com
Website: RobertWilliscroft.com
Edition 2.0 2025

Cover art by Anik
Artwork by Robert G. Williscroft
Book design by Robert G. Williscroft
Covers by Stephen Geez

Names, characters, and incidents in this story are either products of the author's imagination or are used fictitiously. Any resemblance to actual events, locations, names, and people, living or dead, is entirely coincidental and beyond the intent of the author and publisher.

BISAC Subject Headings:
F1C028020 FICTION / Science Fiction / Hard Science Fiction
FIC028130 FICTION / Science Fiction / Space Exploration
FIC028090 FICTION / Science Fiction / Alien Contact

Library of Congress Control Number: 2023921486

ISBN-13: 978-1-968367-31-2 Paperback
ISBN-13: 978-1-968367-30-5 Hardcover
ISBN-13: 978-1-968367-15-2 Ebook
ISBN-13: 978-1-968367-32-9 Audio

DEDICATION

For the women in my life,
Margo, Kate, Ginger, Daphne…Jill.

Table of Contents

Acknowledgements

Several people contributed to the creation of this book.

Most significantly, my wonderful wife, Jill, pored over each chapter with her discerning engineer's eye. She kept my timeline honest and made sure that regular readers could understand fully the arcane details of the nuclear and quantum interactions that play a significant role in this tale. She also reviewed my celestial mechanics and made sure my recitation of Solar System exploration was historically accurate—not to mention keeping track of space battle participants.

Prof. John B. Rosenman, bestselling science fiction and horror author who taught science fiction writing at Norfolk State University, reviewed the manuscript and made several suggestions that significantly improved the story.

Hard science fiction author Alastair Mayer reviewed the manuscript and offered his scientific, engineering, and editorial insight.

Others have contributed with their comments and observations, and I thank them. You know who you are.

A tip of the hat to the incredibly courageous Russian cosmonauts and American astronauts who blazed the trail into space and first walked on the Moon. The starships in this story are named in their honor.

It goes without saying that any remaining omissions, errors, and mistakes fall directly on my shoulders.

Robert G. Williscroft, PhD
Centennial, Colorado
February 2021

Cast of Characters

MAIN CHARACTERS
(alphabetically by first name)

Braxton Thorpe—The Icicle from *Icicle: A Tensor Matrix*
Thorpe—The downloaded version of eThorpe
eThorpe—The original uploaded Thorpe
Binecot Katengi—Amred President
Braxton—The download version of eBraxton
 eBraxton— The original Braxton split from eThorpe
Dale Ryan, PhD—*Andromeda* research scientist
 eDale—Upload version of Dale Ryan
Dudengi Vrokhun—Prophet of The Geroptic Nation
Isidor Orlov—Russian oligarch head of Udachny Enterprises
Jocara Porovik—SPC Astronaut from Ceffid
Kenred Zlaxiz—SPC Astronaut from Amred
Nirurian Klarot, General—The Geroptic Nation
 Chief Military Officer
Spajo Boszut—Ceffid partisan leader. Later, President.
Sudaro Ferron—SPC Director from Arcan
Teynal Dombit, Lt.—General Nirurian Klarot's Aid-de-Camp
 (later, Capt., then Major)

SECONDARY CHARACTERS
(alphabetically by first name)

Blozok Garlan, Colonel—Ramden Geroptic Dragon Army Field
 Commander
Bopr Arclando—The original Ceffid Leader
Brad Kominsky, PhD—*Andromeda* Senior Scientist
 eBrad—Upload version of Brad Kominsky
Daphne O'Bryan, PhD—*Andromeda* Chief Scientist. Companion
 to Kimberly.
 eDaphne—Upload version of Daphne O'Bryan

Darflam Baxerd, General—Ceffid Chief Military Officer (replacing Garkid Sudajos)

Edoetti Kaylambo, General—Amred Chief Military Officer

Garkid Sudajos, General—Ceffid Chief Military Officer (replaced by Darflam Baxerd)

Gregory Dobson—*Andromeda* Chief Medical Officer

Holon Mavik—CEO of Roganian L2 Group.

John Butler—Chairman of the Oort Federation

Judhee Groklet—Teacher in the Geroptic Village of Cordan. Later, prosecutor at the Geroptic Tribunal.

Kimberly Deveraux—*Andromeda* Chief Information Officer. Companion to Daphne.

eKim—Upload version of Kimberly Deveraux

Klophut Gebala, Bishop—Dragon Bishop of the Ramden Sector.

Max—Daphne's tabby cat

eMax—Upload version of Max

Maxter—Cloned version of Max

Metajo Gwzon, Sgt.—Amred soldier

Olkklot Vulorn—Mayor of the Village of Cordan. Later Chief Judge of the Geroptic Tribunal.

Ostrrop Naoria—SPC Flight Director

Sally Nguyen, PhD—School of Mines—*Andromeda* Senior Scientist

eSally—Upload version of Sally Nguyen

Sergii Anatoly Borisovich, Academician—Udachny Enterprises Senior Scientist

Ustrun Strozid—*Andromeda* Chief Engineer from Rogan.

Spacecraft Roster

PHOENIX SPACECRAFT
PS Andromeda

PHOENIX M-CLASS STARSHIPS & PILOTS
(alphabetically by ship; callsign follows name)

PS Alan Shepard—Jocara Porovik (*StarChick*) and Kreax Nelgan (*Jock*)

PS Michael Collins—Nirlinn Odorbon (*GoGirl*) and Gloley Taced (*SlapTail*)

PS Neil Armstrong—Kenred Zlaxiz (*Bobcat*) and Neepons Kited (*Cupcake*)

PS David Scott—Klaaveola Nirhut (*Rainbow*) and Gzo Blubuts (*Slasher*)

PS Alan Bean— Jurkit Blibeks (*Snout*) and Darcat Janoi (*Tiptoe*)

UDACHNY SPACECRAFT
UZ Sergei Krikalyov (superluminal ABO craft)

ARCAN SPACECRAFT
Capsule Arcan-One

Author's Note

I have employed some non-standard language usage in this book. Four sapient races play significant roles. Their names are all capitalized: Human, Arcan, Asterian, and Oort.

The home star and home planet for each race is capitalized: Sol-Earth, Ran-Arcan, Aster-Rogan, and Sol-Earth, respectively. The home star system for Humans and Oort is the Solar System (capitalized).

Although Arcans and Asterians use an indigenous system of weights and measurements, I employ the metric system throughout the book. Both the Asterians and Arcans have six-digit hands and feet, so they naturally count and compute in the duodecimal system. I use the decimal system throughout this book.

The Arcans and Asterians have indigenous names for their suns. I used the Human name for Ran, and I created the name Aster for HD20367 in the constellation of Aries.

The Saurian race on the planet Arcan displays emotions as scale colors. This chart shows those colors and their equivalent emotions.

Arcan Color Shades	
Green	Normal
Light Red	Apprehension
Red	Fear
Pale orange	Irritation
Orange	Anger
Pale yellow	Hesitation
Yellow	Astonishment
Rainbow	Uncertainty/Discomfc
Pale Blue	Humor/Funny
Blue	Excitement/Pride
Pink	Sad
Lavender	Joy

The science and engineering behind the MBH and MERT Drives and portal technology is derived directly from current state-of-the-art physics research. Many of you reading this volume will likely see some form of MERT or warp bubble drive in your lifetime.

You saw it here first!

Robert G. Williscroft
November 2023

THE THIRD OORT CHRONICLE
RAN
A CIVILIZATION IN HIDING

PROLOG

Phoenix Starship Andromeda

PS Andromeda—a half-kilometer thick circular disk five kilometers across with an elaborate cityscape on one surface and an upside-down pastoral landscape on the other, complete with mountains, meadows, and streams. Transparent domes cover both sides. An artificial mini black hole inside the central disk supplies artificial gravity and powers the craft.

Andromeda is on the first leg of an open-ended voyage from the star Aster, pointed at the constellation Eridanus to investigate the Cosmic Microwave Background Cold Spot, six to ten billion lightyears distant, stopping along the way when things look interesting.

First stop: The star Ran—Epsilon Eridani.

PART ONE
FIRST CONTACT

CHAPTER ONE

Arcan-One Space Capsule—Space Push Consortium Mission, Circum-Lodan Trajectory

"Arcan-One, stand by for Lodan orbital injection burn!"

The announcement arrived at the capsule as an optical beam relayed by an Arcan geostationary satellite.

"Are you ready to do this, Jocara?" Kenred Zlaxiz asked off the circuit, turning to his companion.

"That's why we're here," she answered, pointing through the large, sapphire window to their moon, Lodan, hanging in space before them. "If we abort, it's the mines for me…for sure."

"You're jesting! The Ceffid government wouldn't do that."

"You're from Amred—I'm not sure you can understand. Should we abort back to Arcan, you'll be on the next capsule… but not with me. I'll be shoveling pitchblende or something equally noxious."

Kenred turned back to his console. *So glad I was born in Amred,* he thought and touched a control. "Roger! Standing by for Lodan orbital injection burn."

Mission Control—Amred City, Amred, Planet Arcan

"Attention, please!"

Flight Director Ostrrop Naoria stood behind his podium with raised arms. The room quieted. Individual technicians manned their stations, four curved rows deep, facing a wall completely covered with display screens filled with graphics except one, a direct visual color display of the view through the capsule sapphire window.

"*GO Check* for Lodan orbital injection burn," Naoria intoned.

One by one, the technicians gave "GO!" for their stations. Following the last "GO!" Naoria started the injection burn countdown.

The burn lasted two minutes.

"*Arcan-One*, status…"

"This is *Arcan-One*. Injection burn successfully completed. Capsule systems stable at zero-gee."

"Mission Control concurs, *Arcan-One* systems stable. Stand by for loss of communications in twenty-three minutes."

Arcan-One Space Capsule—Space Push Consortium Mission, Circum-Lodan Trajectory

"We're committed now, Jocara!" Kenred unstrapped from his seat, and floating, turned to face his fellow astronaut. Her pale green, finely shaped Saurian face scales rippled slightly with a faint lavender hue as she smiled joyfully—an open-eyed look with no change in her mouth shape.

"Our orbit takes us well clear of Lodan's three moonlets," Jocara said. "We may actually see one of them on the farside, however."

"Not if *well clear* means what I think it means."

"Stand by for loss of communications!" the optical beam processed through *Arcan-One's* non-emitting optical system. "Four…three… two…one…zero!"

Mission Control—Amred City, Amred, Planet Arcan

"Okay, people, listen up!" Flight Director Naoria announced from his podium. "We've got a half hour. Take a short break and be back at your stations twelve minutes before reacquisition."

As the time approached, the technicians manned their stations. The room was as still as it ever got. At the moment of expected reacquisition, CapCom transmitted, "*Arcan-One*, this is Mission Control, over."

Silence…

"*Arcan-One*, this is Mission Control, over."

Silence still…

"*Arcan-One, Arcan-One*, this is Mission Control, Mission Control, over."

More silence…

CHAPTER TWO

***Phoenix Starship Andromeda*—Hovering Invisibly in
Nullspace Beyond Lodan, Operations Center**

Kenred slowly opened his eyes. He was no longer floating in the capsule but lay on the deck of some kind of operations center filled with monitors and control consoles. He felt a whiff of panic. His scales rippled, showing a hint of red. Lighting and temperature seemed normal, but he felt heavier. He took a deep breath, shoving down his initial panic. Jocara rolled over beside him, hyperventilating, her scales bright red. Kenred gripped her arm and whispered softly, "Easy, Jocara, easy!" They both sat up as her scales faded back to bluish green.

Several humanoid creatures stood in a loose circle around them. A strange-looking one stepped toward him, five-fingered hands on its hips. It was oddly thin and tall, with puffy lips and a pointed nose in place of a snout. It had long, spindly, two-sectioned legs, a short torso with articulating arms, and no visible tail. Two intelligent eyes peered from a hair-crowned, spherical head.

Clearly, some kind of mammalian ancestry, Kenred deduced. The humanoid addressed him in his native Amred with an oddly distorted accent.

"I am Braxton Thorpe, Commanding *Phoenix Starship Andromeda*. I represent the inhabitants of the stellar system you call Rodal—we call ourselves *Humans*. We are on a peaceful research mission passing through your system. We pose no threat to you."

A second, different humanoid joined Thorpe. Like Kenred, it displayed six digits on each hand and was shorter and stockier than the Human. Its hairy head was much like the Human's, but with flattened nose and slender lips. Its ears articulated, reminding Kenred of the small domestic felines kept as pets by his own people.

Another mammalian, Kenred thought as he looked around. *No Saurians.* The second offworlder addressed him.

"I am Holon Mavik, Chief of the Roganian L2 Group. I represent the inhabitants of the stellar system you call Dytom—we call ourselves *Asterians*."

"We need to stand and introduce ourselves," Kenred whispered to Jocara, stroking the fine scales on her arm. Their color had returned to normal. "I'll take the lead." He climbed to his feet, his stumpy legs quivering in the higher gravity, balancing with his tail.

"I am *Capsule Arcan-One* Commander Kenred Zlaxiz from the nation Amred on the planet Arcan."

"And I am Astronaut Jocara Porovik from Ceffid. We represent Amred's Space Push Consortium."

"What happened to our capsule, the *Arcan-One*?" Kenred asked.

"Unharmed in Lodan orbit," the Human answered.

"How did we get here?"

The Human's mouth opened, emitting a cackling sound. "We will happily share that with you, but first you will need to understand some advanced physics I suspect your scientists have not yet discovered. We'll get to that later." The Human swept its arm toward the other offworlders in the compartment. "We are the senior people on this starship. Hopefully, you will get to know us before too long."

"*Arcan-One's* orbit is ninety-six minutes," Kenred said. "How long have we been away from the capsule?"

The Human checked an instrument. "Seventeen of your minutes."

"How do your minutes and ours differ?" Jocara asked.

"Arcan's rotation, and thus your day, is slightly longer than our home planet," the Human answered. "Your numbering system is obviously based on twelve." It held up its splayed hands. "Ours is ten-based, but both we and you count time in twelves. Your minute is a fraction of a second longer than ours. In casual conversation, they can be considered identical."

Kenred did a quick mental calculation. "We had just lost comms with Mission Control when you snatched us. In about nineteen minutes, Mission Control is going to discover that the capsule is empty."

The Human's mouth curved upward, and it held up a palm-size, silvery disk. "This is a hyper-disk. We sequestered one in *Arcan-One* where your people are unlikely to find it. That disk will open a portal directly to *Andromeda*." The Human's mouth curved upward again—*A smile*, Kenred deduced. "Let me show you."

The Human manipulated a control on a console. A doorway appeared between them to Kenred's right. Through the doorway was the interior of *Arcan-One*. Kenred walked around the door to examine the other side. As he passed the plane of the door, it disappeared. He stepped back to the front; the door reappeared, looking as solid and real as anything else in the room.

"Step through into *Arcan-One*," the Human said. "It's like walking through any door on Arcan." It emitted a clucking sound through a smile. "Go ahead—it won't hurt you, but be mindful that you will go from our gravity here to zero-gee!"

Kenred turned to Jocara. She opened her eyes wide, indicating a tentative *Why not?*

"Okay," Kenred said, stepping through the door into *Arcan-One*. He floated across the capsule to the opposite side. He turned and looked back through the door at Jocara and the offworlders.

"May I join you?" the Human asked.

"Not a lot of room here, but sure, join me." Kenred watched the taller Human step through the door—the portal—and tuck its legs close to fit into the small space as it floated and looked about.

"Very much like our Apollo capsules when we first visited our moon," the Human said quietly. It looked at both seats, but there was no way it would have fit in one. It looked at what was probably a time piece on its wrist. "We still have a few minutes before comms are reestablished. Do you want your fellow astronaut…"

"Jocara," Kenred interrupted.

"…Jocara to join you here before you return to *Andromeda*?" It floated back through the portal and deftly landed on its feet.

"Yes, please send her through." Kenred hesitated, thinking about the vast difference between the offworlder and Arcan technology, and realizing that he and Jocara were totally at these offworlders' mercy. "Do you want us here to reestablish comms with Mission Control, or back on *Andromeda*?"

"After Jocara passes through the portal, both of you please return here. You may already suspect my reasons, but I'll explain fully as we move forward."

Jocara nervously stepped through the portal into *Arcan-One*, and Kenred took her arm as she coasted over to him. They both sat, and he told her in her native Ceffid language, "These offworlders seem benign, but consider for a moment the vast gulf between their technology and ours. All we have seen is the inside of a control room without knowing how we got there. This *portal* technology is beyond anything we have ever imagined. We must seem like swamp lizards to them. Why are they interested in us? What can we offer them? What is their real motive? I don't trust them and don't want to give them any reason to be anything but friendly." He smiled with wide open eyes and rippling face scales and squeezed her hand. "Let's go back and see what we can learn—but cautiously. Mission Control will just have to deal with our disappearance."

Mission Control—Amred City, Amred, Planet Arcan

When Arcan-One failed to respond, pandemonium broke out in Mission Control. Flight Director Naoria hissed through his snout and raised his arms. "Settle down, people! Quiet!"

As the noise quieted down, he pointed to the technician, who controlled the capsule internal camera. "Pan the interior," he ordered.

Lodan, visible through the capsule's window on Mission Control's primary display, shifted left as the camera panned around the capsule.

Nothing, Naoria thought, *my astronauts are gone. But that's impossible. There's no way to exit the capsule without releasing all the air.* He glanced at the internal pressure gauge near the primary display. *Normal internal pressure. Had they exited the capsule, there would be no internal pressure.*

One of the seated technicians raised his hand. "Sir, the oxygen and nitrogen percentages are wrong. They're twenty-one and seventy-nine percent, respectively. They should be twenty and eighty. This is impossible!"

"Are the reserves topped up?" Naoria asked.

"Yes, Sir! Two-blocked."

Another technician piped up, "Sir, the onboard clock is four minutes behind. I've checked and double checked. Four minutes are gone!"

"Troubleshoot your consoles," Naoria told them. "Then check again. The rest of you, find an answer, a solution to this dilemma." Naoria turned to CapCom. "Keep calling!"

Thirty-seven minutes later, *Arcan-One* passed behind Lodan.

❋

Naoria walked down a hallway and entered a door into a cleanroom airlock. He quickly donned a clean-suit, booties, head and face covering, and entered a large space containing a duplicate capsule that was intended to be an emergency backup. A group of engineers stood around a table discussing the situation.

"Well?" Naoria said to his chief engineer.

"No idea, but we just started an out-of-the-box approach." He beckoned Naoria to the table. "How many ways can we end up with our present situation?" He gave Naoria a worried look. "Nothing is off the table—even alien abduction. Give us a couple of orbits to work this out."

❋

Three hours later, Naoria stood once again at the table in the cleanroom, listening to his chief engineer.

"If, hypothetically, one of our future spaceships had returned from the future to our present, linked up with *Arcan-One*, and transferred our astronauts to their vessel, this, or some similar event, would explain their absence. Ridiculous, I know. But even this fantastical explanation cannot explain the difference in atmospheric composition." He sighed and spread his hands on the table. The other engineers and technicians would not meet Naoria's eyes. "We have exhaustively examined every possible way to generate the difference in composition. Everything we came up with, we confirmed didn't happen. The only way to remove the astronauts while retaining the atmosphere is to link to another spaceship—the only way. Now, if that other spaceship has an atmosphere ratio of oxygen to nitrogen different from ours, then the resulting capsule mix will be some combination of theirs and ours."

Naoria attempted to interrupt, but the engineer held up his hand. "Let me finish! We know that Rodal, some ten lightyears distant, has a spacefaring civilization. Ditto for Dytom, but it's about seventy-six lightyears away. We have gone to great lengths to hide our presence in the galaxy. Arcan does not emit electromagnetic radiation. We use lasers for communication and ranging. It is highly unlikely that either civilization knows about us. On the other hand, if the Rodal civilization has developed FTL travel, we are the obvious choice for a first visit because they would have detected Arcan in the life zone—not us, just our planet." The engineer sighed. "Even if they don't have FTL, we are only ten lightyears away—still the obvious choice."

"So, what are you saying?" Naoria asked.

"I think you know, Sir. An alien spaceship out beyond the moon has abducted our astronauts."

Phoenix Starship Andromeda—Hovering Invisibly in Nullspace Beyond Lodan, Conference Room

Kenred and Jocara sat side by side at an oval, polished wood table in a conference room—the only other part of Andromeda Kenred had seen. To Kenred's surprise, the offworlders had come up with comfortable chairs that conformed to his and Jocara's anatomy. The Human Thorpe occupied a seat at one end of the table. Asterian Mavic was at the other. Ten other offworlders, mostly Human, filled up the rest of the table. To Kenred's utter surprise, a small feline creature very similar to a popular household pet in Amred jumped to the tabletop, rumbling softly. With tail stiff in the air, it visited each individual at the table, including himself and Jocara.

"Meet Max," Thorpe said, with a clucking sound that Kenred interpreted as amusement.

Max pretty much ignored Kenred, but when he stopped at Jocara, she reached out and petted him. In response, Max arched his back and rubbed his face against her snout, much to everyone's delight.

The Human Thorpe began speaking, looking directly at Kenred and Jocara. "Your Mission Control has had about two hours to figure out where you two are and how the atmosphere in your capsule changed. You are an intelligent, resourceful people. Remarkably so. You are an incipient spacefaring species without ever announcing your presence to the galaxy. We live practically next door, and we were ignorant of your existence. We are here because your star is the obvious first stop on a lengthy journey we are undertaking. Otherwise, we may never have discovered you." The Human dropped his gaze and seemed momentarily distracted.

"We are monitoring Mission Control's comms. They have attempted to contact you each time *Arcan-One* came out from behind Lodan."

"That's normal protocol," Kenred said. "It wasn't set up for this scenario, but one remote possibility has always been that something might happen to both capsule occupants while transiting the farside of Lodan."

"Do they have a backup rescue plan, another launch vehicle and capsule, a way of getting you back?" the Asterian Mavic asked.

"Not really," Kenred said. "Jocara's people, Ceffid, were reluctant to join our space effort, the Space Push Consortium—SPC. Amred is a free-wheeling, free-market state. Ceffid is a top-down bureaucracy where everything is controlled. You people showing up will be a big problem for them. We pushed ahead with SPC without Ceffid, but they sent us several people to train as astronauts. One of them was Jocara. But no, we have no rescue system. We have a second capsule in a cleanroom, mission ready, but it would take some time to prepare it for lift-off."

The Human Thorpe held up his hand. "We're receiving a transmission from Mission Control. Listen!"

"Alien starship, this is SPC Mission Control, over."

"They figured it out," Thorpe said. "There was really no other plausible explanation."

Jocara turned to Kenred, her eyes filled with questions. Kenred said quietly, "The capsule is empty but pressurized with atmosphere slightly different from ours. The only way for this to happen, short of black magic, is a hookup to another spaceship. Since there are no other spaceships in our solar system, it has to be an alien starship."

Jocara's facial scales rippled in acknowledgment. "Makes perfect sense."

"Alien starship, this is SPC Mission Control, over."

"SPC Mission Control, this is *Phoenix Starship Andromeda*." The person transmitting used the Amred name for the Andromeda galaxy. "We are on a scientific voyage of discovery. We come in peace and pose no threat to you. Astronauts Kenred Zlaxiz and Jocara Porovik are unharmed. They are our guests for the moment."

"This is SPC Mission Control." The speaker hesitated before continuing. "Your presence and abduction of our astronauts obviously changes our mission goals. We are wary of strangers arriving unannounced. How do we know you come in peace?"

"This is *Andromeda*. We understand your reluctance to accept us at face value. Your presence was as much a surprise to us as was ours to you. We very much understand our relative positions. If possible, we would like to meet with your representative in Amred City. We wish to demonstrate our intentions. We have arranged for this meeting from our end, but will only follow through if you agree."

The transmission paused, and Thorpe addressed Kenred and Jocara. "We would like to show you some of *Andromeda* and give you a sense of who and what we are—perhaps build a level of trust. This should take about a day. Are you willing to remain with us for this time?"

Kenred and Jocara looked at each other. "Tour a starship that is perhaps a century or more beyond us, meet the other offworlders running her—are you kidding?" Jocara said, her scales rippling blue with excitement.

"My thoughts exactly," Kenred said, and turning toward Thorpe, he said, "If we were reversed, would you accept?"

"SPC Mission Control, this is *Andromeda*. We have invited your astronauts to remain with us for twenty-four hours. They accepted. Thereafter, we will call you again this channel to discuss a meeting. Over."

"This is SPC Mission Control. I wish to speak with both astronauts."

Thorpe said, "Kenred, Jocara, talk to Mission Control. Reassure them."

"This is *Capsule Arcan-One* Commander Kenred Zlaxiz…"

"And I am Astronaut Jocara Porovik…"

Kenred continued. "We were brought aboard the alien craft by means we do not understand. We have not been mistreated; in fact, we've been well treated."

"This is SPC Mission Control. How do I know I am speaking with the real Kenred Zlaxiz?" There was a brief pause. "When you and Jocara made an unauthorized excursion to a dive restaurant in Amred City, what did you have to eat? Over."

"This is *Andromeda*," Thorpe said, and looked at Kenred.

"It was the Kettle Kooker, and I had Bobcat stew. Over."

"This is SPC Mission Control. Did Jocara like it? Over."

"This is Astronaut Porovik on *Andromeda*. I most certainly did not! Over."

"This is SPC Mission Control to Astronaut Zlaxiz. Are you under duress? Did you agree to remain on the vessel an additional twenty-four hours? Can you leave any time?"

"This is Astronaut Zlaxiz on *Andromeda*. No…Yes…Yes, but we are not leaving until we have seen as much of this incredible ship as possible. Over."

"This is SPC Mission Control. We accept the astronauts' statements. Under strong protest, we will contact our head of state to see what we can arrange. Over."

"This is *Andromeda*. We will call you in twenty-four hours. We will monitor this channel should you need to communicate with us before then. Out."

Mission Control—Amred City, Amred, Planet Arcan

Flight Director Naoria hissed through his snout and raised his arms. "Security, secure the doors! Nobody in—nobody out!"

Naoria had a comm unit directly linked by laser to SPC headquarters. Naoria's hands shook with excitement and his scales rippled blue as he connected to the SPC Director Sudaro Ferron in the government complex. He wasted no time on preliminaries.

"Director Ferron, I have just concluded a lengthy conversation with offworlders on a starship from the Rodal system."

"What do you mean, a starship? Offworlders?"

"Like I said, a starship, apparently from Rodal. The starship is located beyond Lodan, so we cannot track it by laser. Both the astronauts are aboard the vessel."

"Have you spoken with them?"

"Yes Sir. They have chosen to remain on the starship for twenty-four hours. Then they will transfer back to *Arcan-One* for return to Arcan. The offworlders have requested a high-level meeting in Amred City after the astronauts' return. I agreed, under strong protest.

"The offworlders apparently were unaware of us. They just stumbled upon our circum-Lodan flight and took advantage of the situation to establish contact. They claim to be on a voyage of discovery. It has the ring of truth, but I don't trust them."

"I'll get back with you as quickly as possible."

CHAPTER THREE

***Phoenix Starship Andromeda*—Hovering Invisibly in Nullspace Beyond Lodan, Conference Room**

"Mission Control handled that pretty well," Thorpe commented, displaying an expression that Kenred had decided was the Human equivalent of a smile. "Are you hungry? Would you like something to eat?"

The two astronauts looked at each other, their facial scales rippling pale lavender. "We would, yes," Kenred said, "but can we safely eat your food?"

"We have accessed your national databases to gain an understanding of your biology and nutritional needs, and what kind of foods you enjoy. Our kitchen has prepared a snack that we can all eat."

Several offworlders from both species appeared with plates holding something that looked edible and smelled delicious, and eating utensils that were not unlike what Kenred was accustomed to. Then the attendants passed water glasses around the table. Thorpe didn't bother with the knife and the utensil that looked much like the forks Kenred knew. He picked up a bite-size morsel with his fingers and put it into his mouth.

Kenred turned to Jocara and whispered, "I think we can trust them. If they wanted to kill us, they would have done so, not waited to poison us now!"

Jocara responded quietly, "They have kept us safe thus far. If they didn't trust their machines to make food we can eat, they wouldn't serve it to us. I think it's safe."

The astronauts looked at each other, rippling their scales in agreement. Kenred picked up a piece. It was bread, spread with some kind of meat spread, and it was absolutely delicious.

"Try it, Jocara," he said. "You'll love it."

As she did, blue ripples of glee crossed her face.

Thorpe tapped his glass with his knife to get everyone's attention. "It's time to give our guests some understanding of the starship *Andromeda*."

Above the table center, a holographic image appeared like nothing Kenred had ever seen, a thick circular disk with an elaborate cityscape on one surface and an upside-down pastoral landscape on the other, complete with mountains, meadows, and streams. Transparent domes covered both sides. Floating arrows indicated its diameter was five kilometers, shown in Arcan units.

"This is *Phoenix Starship Andromeda*," Thorpe said. "It's probably not what you envisioned, but we designed and built her with great care. We expected to be gone for a long time and wanted to include as much of our home worlds as possible." A floating arrow pointed to a prominent building near the city center. "We are here right now." The arrow moved to the top of the building's central tower. "Normally, we would be enjoying a magnificent stellar view from here, but *Andromeda* is parked in nullspace right now to avoid detection by Arcan."

"Nullspace—what is that?" Kenred asked.

"It's a feature of our propulsion system that is beyond your current knowledge of physics. If our meeting in Amred City goes as we hope, you will learn more. You already experienced our portal technology. It is ubiquitous throughout the starship. In your culture, I'm sure you have sinks and faucets where you bring fresh cold and hot water to a basin, and drain the waste into a sewage system. We bring water to the basin by portal from a central reservoir, and send the waste by portal to a processing facility. No plumbing—no pipes."

"How is it we're experiencing gravity right now?" Jocara asked.

"Once again, it's a feature of our propulsion system. We can place a grid beneath any structure and adjust the gravity above the grid to virtually any level. For example, I imagine the SPC plans to put a manned station on Lodan."

"It will be a couple of years, but yes, we plan to do that," Kenred answered.

"If you were to install one of our grids beneath your station, you could have normal gravity inside. We have learned, at least for our two species, that low gravity is deleterious in the long run."

"That must take a lot of power," Kenred said.

"An almost unimaginable amount of power. A mini black hole occupies a significant part of the volume between our two disks. It is the heart of *Andromeda*." Thorpe smiled broadly. "Before we cut you loose to explore this vast ship with a couple of guides to explain things and answer questions, I want to introduce you to another element of who we are."

A Human sitting in a chair suddenly appeared next to Thorpe. He looked like Thorpe, but was dressed differently. Astonished, Kenred stared at the Human, and then realized that he was a holoimage of such quality that he could not distinguish the image from the live Human.

"I am eThorpe," the image said, looking at the astronauts. "I am an electronic upload of Braxton Thorpe, created long ago. I reside in an electronic matrix, and my presence exists throughout every electronic element of the ship. Virtually all our original research team uploaded themselves, so that now we have sixteen uploads like myself. We play important roles in the operation of this starship that a flesh-and-blood individual cannot handle."

"You would appear to be immortal in your electronic form," Jocara said.

"We die if our matrix is destroyed, but we are set up to generate continual real-time backups. So, yes, in principle, we uploads are immortal."

"There's more than that," Thorpe said. "Each of us has a built-in system that creates continuous real-time backup uploads. Anytime we choose, we can download our current backup into a new body so that we remain continuously young and vital."

"That means," Kenred interrupted, "that should one of you die in an accident or otherwise, you can rejuvenate yourself from the backup."

"You catch on quickly, Kenred." Thorpe said. "Our culture has always valued youth, especially in our females. This technology has enabled virtual eternal youth for whomever wishes."

"We are not that much different," Jocara said. "I would certainly enjoy keeping my youth indefinitely."

"You still haven't told us how we got here," Kenred said.

"That's true," Thorpe responded as an image of *Arcan-One* just passing behind Lodan appeared over the table.

An oddly shaped spacecraft approached, and suddenly a silvery sphere encased the capsule.

"This is a stasis field," Thorpe said. "Time virtually stops inside the field."

The view moved closer as two space-suited figures left the odd spacecraft.

"They are wearing special suits that allow them to enter a stasis field," Thorpe said.

The view followed them closely as they entered the sphere and approached *Arcan-One*. One of them opened the capsule hatch. To Kenred's surprise, there was no explosive decompression. Instead, the atmosphere inside the capsule looked like a spongy mass. One figure pushed his way into the capsule and shut the hatch. The view changed, showing the interior of the capsule. The space-suited figure moved through the spongy atmosphere to the astronauts in their seats. He discharged a weapon into each sitting figure.

"That is an Electro-Muscular-Disrupter stun weapon set to minimum intensity," Thorpe said. "It rendered each of you unconscious for several minutes."

The view moved back outside as the stasis field disappeared and the silvery sphere vanished. Then it moved back inside, where the space-suited figure crammed into the capsule activated a hyper-disk. He passed the unconscious passengers through the portal and then hid the hyper-disk inside the capsule. Then he pushed through the portal. Outside again, the view showed the other figure returning to the odd spacecraft.

"There you have it," Thorpe said. "We put *Arcan-One* in a stasis field, rendered you two unconscious, and removed you by portal to *Andromeda*. *Arcan-One* was in stasis for four minutes, and the entire process took ten minutes."

The image over the table vanished.

"Let's break this meeting up," Thorpe said, "so our guests can spend their remaining time exploring *Andromeda*."

✳

"*Andromeda*, this is SPC Mission Control, over." The call arrived in the twenty-second hour.

Following several minutes of negotiations, everyone agreed the astronauts would return to *Arcan-One* and the capsule would return to Arcan. The astronauts would meet with Amred President Binecot Katengi and SPC Head Sudaro Ferron in the president's office. Braxton Thorpe would arrange to be present in some manner. There was no agenda, just an agreement to meet and talk.

✳

"Are you two ready to return?" Thorpe asked.

"Not really," Jocara said. "We could have continued our exploration for days."

"I agree," Kenred said, "but we both are delighted to be part of this first contact."

Thorpe handed Kenred a hyper-disk. "Keep this with you and bring it to the meeting in the president's office. Please do not tell anybody about it until it's time for me to join the meeting."

Kenred accepted the disk, tucking it inside his flightsuit. *How do I feel about this deception?* he asked himself. *I am convinced these offworlders are peaceful. Obviously, they could wipe us out in a moment if they chose. Instead, they're reaching out. All I'm really doing is enabling Thorpe to be physically present at the meeting.*

Kenred and Jocara stepped through the portal into *Arcan-One*. Thorpe waved at them, and the portal collapsed. They had ten minutes before comms were reestablished. Kenred turned to Jocara after they strapped into their seats.

"I have given what we are doing a lot of thought. How do you feel about the offworlders?"

Jocara was silent for a few seconds. "I trust these people. If they had evil intent, why would they have treated us as they did? It's pretty obvious they could take out our entire planet if they wanted. But why? What do we have that they need to take? What threat are we to them? So, yes, I'm with you on this."

Amred President Binecot Katengi's Office—Amred City, Amred, Planet Arcan

Kenred and Jocara walked through the Capitol rotunda accompanied by an assistant and an unobtrusively armed guard. They took an elevator to the third floor. It opened directly into the president's personal offices. The assistant ushered them into a room nicely furnished with a large desk, two antique couches on either side of a low table, and two chairs strategically placed near the desk. The pale blue walls carried a portrait of Amred's first president and an image of Lodan, displaying its cratered surface to great advantage.

President Binecot Katengi stood and walked toward them, grasping one hand of each in his hands. His facial scales rippled blue with excitement. "Welcome to my office. What an exciting adventure you have taken during the last couple of days. We have twelve minutes before the SPC Director arrives."

Kenred took the lead, giving the Amred president a capsule summary of their time with the offworlders. Then Katengi turned to Jocara. "And you, my dear, let me hear your version."

It was an astute approach. From Kenred, he received an engineer's summary of their time on *Andromeda*. From Jocara, he got her impressions, the beauty, the strangeness, the common elements, her subtle impressions as she and Kenred explored the mighty starship. She ended by saying, "They seemed to go out of their way to be open and without guile. I became close to one Human female, surprisingly so for such a brief stay."

A hidden speaker softly announced the arrival of the SPC Director. Kenred held up his hand.

"An additional moment before he arrives, Mr. President."

Katengi gave his assent. Kenred laid the hyper-disk on the president's desk.

"This device," Kenred said, "will open a portal, a door between *Andromeda* and here. Braxton Thorpe, the expedition commander, will step through the portal to join us."

Katengi's face scales rippled yellow, registering his astonishment. "In any real sense, we are at their mercy. Are you certain of their intentions? What if this whole thing is a ruse to get to me? Am I about to be assassinated by an alien we worked so hard to keep out of our solar system?" He pressed a button on his desk, and a guard ushered in SPC Director Sudaro Ferron. He acknowledged the astronauts and warmly gripped both hands with the president.

"That," Katengi said, pointing to the hyper-disk, "will somehow open a door between here and the alien ship *Andromeda*. Commander Thorpe is supposed to join us by walking through the door this disk creates. Are you comfortable with this, Sudaro?" All Katengi's visible scales rippled between multiple colors and seemed to lose their luster.

"Not entirely," Ferron said. "The astronauts briefed me on their return. They seem to have accepted the offworlders' genuineness, but I'm not so sure." He turned to the astronauts. "You are our best. You met this Thorpe. Will his arrival in this room pose a threat?"

"I don't think so," Kenred said. "If they wanted to harm us, they could do it from space."

"No, it won't," Jocara added emphatically.

Turning to Kenred, Katengi said with a sigh, "I'm reluctant to do this, but activate the portal."

Kenred picked up the hyper-disk and rubbed its dull side. An ordinary door appeared in front of Katengi's desk, and Thorpe stepped through into the presidential office. He nodded at the astronauts and turned to Katengi.

"President Katengi, I presume." He turned toward the SPC Director. "Sudaro Ferron." He spoke an accent-free Amred, quite an improvement from when Kenred had first met him. "I am Braxton Thorpe, Commander of *Phoenix Starship Andromeda*. I am present in this room through a portal—technology new to you. We come in peace with outstretched hands in friendship."

"Amred welcomes you to our planet and to Amred's capital, Amred City," Katengi responded. He walked toward Thorpe, hands held out. "In our culture, we greet a friend by grasping both hands and squeezing, thus." He took both Thorpe's hands in his.

"I am honored by your show of friendship," Thorpe said with a broad smile.

"That's the Human equivalent of our smile," Kenred said softly.

✻

Katengi had an assistant place two wide cushions on the couch, subtly acknowledging Thorpe's anatomical differences, and gestured for him to sit. The astronauts joined him. Katengi and Ferron sat opposite on the other side of the table.

"I know you have gone to great lengths to keep your existence a secret from the rest of the galaxy," Thorpe said. "You were quite successful. Neither Humans nor Asterians knew you existed until we accidentally stumbled upon you when we made your system the first stop in our outward journey. Now that we've found you, we are loath to continue our journey without first establishing some links between your civilization and ours."

"There must be vast differences between our technologies, our capabilities, even our cultures," Katengi said. "Kenred and Jocara have described your vessel to me. I cannot honestly conceive of such an enormous structure." He shifted uncomfortably on the couch. "Our historical reason for concealing our presence was our fear that an advanced species like yours would find and exploit, or even destroy, us. We knew about Humans and Asterians from your unintentional broadcasts and even deduced some details about the conflict between your species. That caused us to be even more diligent in keeping our presence a secret.

"I admit you do not seem to pose a military threat against us, but how do we know that? I am deeply concerned about the impact the mere knowledge of your presence will have on our people."

Ferron raised both hands with fingers splayed at chest level; his scales rippled between multiple colors. "What do you people really want? To my ears, you sound like a used car saleslizard. You offer us a one-sided proposition. There's plenty we can learn from you, but what do you get out of it? Can you answer that honestly?"

"I understand your concerns, President Katengi, Director Ferron," Thorpe said. "We will impose nothing on you or your culture that you do not invite—you have my word. You are correct, of course, Director Ferron. You do have much to learn from us. What is not apparent to you is that we have much to learn from you. You have independently solved problems we faced in the past and may face in the future. Learning from you, working together with you, we both have a better chance of successfully solving future problems as they arise—and they will."

Kenred glanced at Jocara. They had been through a lot together and knew each other well. She nudged him slightly. Hesitatingly, Kenred spoke up. "I am not a statecraft-trained lizard. I'm just a boondocks lizard with an engineering degree who was lucky enough to be selected astronaut. Jocara and I have visited their starship. We've seen some of their science and technology." He came to his feet. "Speaking for myself, I don't want to return to what now seems like primitive capsule technology. I don't want to wait for my great grandchildren to develop portals. I've seen them and used them, and I want them now. I don't want to plod around Lodan, eventually construct a settlement on its surface, and maybe, someday, walk on another planet in our system. I want to explore the universe with my new friends." He resumed his seat.

Katengi spoke up. "Arcan has three significant cultures, ourselves, Ceffid, and The Geroptic Nation. Amred is a free-wheeling society with a limited government that is restricted to national defense and a police and court system. The SPC is a private effort with close ties to the government. Ceffid is a totalitarian dictatorship with top-heavy bureaucracy—they are unlikely to welcome your presence. The Geroptic Nation is a backward theocracy that worships the sun, which they call the Great Dragon in the Sky. Their Prophet's ultimate goal is to bring Amred and Ceffid under his rule and convert all of us to their bizarre religion."

"*Andromeda* is a privately owned starship," Thorpe said. "It has close ties to the Oort Federation around Sol—your Rodal, and it has loose links with several outfits on Rogan, one of two populated planets orbiting Aster—your Dytom. We maintain portals to our home worlds. I can literally step back through this portal," he pointed to the door, "and step through another into the office of my friend John Butler, Chairman of the Oort Federation."

"It's difficult to imagine such capability," Katengi said, his voice filled with wonder—and fear, his scales rippling faint red. "I want to believe your message of peace and cooperation, but it goes completely against Saurian nature—and human nature, I would guess. Before you became the Oort Federation, I am certain that Humans on Earth took advantage of other Humans with lesser capabilities. You waged war against each other, just as we did. And yet, the differences between you and us are astronomically greater than anything either of us has experienced in our own past. How can I trust your promise not to interfere, to honor our wishes?"

"I completely agree with President Katengi," Ferron said. "I just don't trust you."

"We are very much like you," Thorpe responded, "just with different toys. While we will respect your desire to remain isolated, realistically, the cat is out of the bag. Ten thousand people live aboard *Andromeda*. By now, several have told folks back home about Arcan and these two." Thorpe gestured toward Kenred and Jocara. "Eventually, you will have more visitors. Most will be like us, open and friendly, wanting to learn about you, meet with your people, establish trade, exchange knowledge, all the things that make a civilization function. But, like you, we have bad guys in both our systems. One of them will eventually find the way here. You will need to be prepared." Thorpe sat back quietly to let his words sink in.

Ferron leaned forward, his scales rippling faintly red in a repeating pattern.

"I mentioned John Butler," Thorpe continued. "My friend John is the wisest man I know. He would be happy to join you, offering you guidance and counsel as you move through these uncharted waters." Thorpe turned to the astronauts. "Kenred, Jocara, you are welcome to join us on *Andromeda*. We have more than sufficient room. You can be the nucleus of what I suspect will become a significant Arcan contingent. We will remain in the Ran system—what we call your sun, for the time being, hidden until you, Mr. President, decide the time is ripe to reveal our presence to all."

"Do I have a choice?" Katengi asked. "Do any of us? Like you said, the cat is out of the bag." He sighed deeply and sat, dejection clearly visible to lizard and offworlder alike, while pink rippled through his scales. "All our preparations, all our hopes, all our dreams…"

Ferron looked sharply at Thorpe, his scales still rippling. "You will remain hidden, no contact except through the president or me until the president says otherwise?"

"You have my word," Thorpe said solemnly. He handed Katengi a Link. "This is a communicator that you can use to contact me anytime. It is the same unit we used to keep in contact and to access our massive database. Only it is restricted to comms with me directly."

Amred President Binecot Katengi's Office—Amred City, Amred, Planet Arcan

President Binecot Katengi looked up from his desk to lock eyes with Space Push Consortium Director Sudaro Ferron.

"You don't much care for the offworlder, Thorpe, do you?"

"It's not so much that as that I don't trust him," Ferron answered. "What do we have that he could possibly want? I mean, they're so far advanced over us, we are just swamp lizards by comparison."

"I take your point, Sudaro, but I simply don't agree with you. I'm convinced that they arrived here by accident." He paused. "That's not what I really mean. They came here on purpose, alright, but they did not know about us—I'm convinced of that." He stood and started pacing across his office, tail sliding across the plush carpet. "They stumbled across Astronauts Zlaxiz and Porovik and decided to make contact."

"Okay," Ferron said, his scales rippling an angry orange. "So what?"

"Put yourself in their shoes, my friend. How would you have reacted? You stumble across an unknown sentient race virtually next door that has developed space travel, at least in its initial stages? What would you have done?"

"You've got a point, Mr. President," Ferron said grudgingly, "but who's to say Thorpe is telling the truth?" Ferron sighed as his scales faded to pale yellow. "I just don't trust them."

"In the meantime," Katengi said, "we need to keep close tabs on the offworlders. Kenred Zlaxiz trusts them, and they seem to trust him. What do you think about using him as liaison with the offworlders?"

"Astronaut Zlaxiz is one of the best we have. If anyone can handle this touchy situation, he can." Ferron's scales rippled blue. "I agree with your choice. In fact, I'm proud of Kenred."

"And," Katengi continued, "we have this." He held up the Link.

"Assume you are being monitored one hundred percent of the time," Ferron said.

"I know, you don't trust him. We'll just have to watch our conversation around this device."

✳

Several hours later, Ferron sat with Katengi in the president's office. "You know we can't keep the offworlder secret to ourselves," he stated matter-of-factly.

Hesitatingly, Katengi nodded agreement, his scales rippling slightly, showing pale yellow.

"The longer we wait to inform Leader Bopr Arclando," Katengi said, "the more trouble he will give us. You know how he rattles his saber every chance he gets."

"Do we have any reason to delay?" Ferron asked.

"You're right," Katengi said, and manipulated controls on his desk. A large monitor on the opposite wall lit brightly. A few moments later, the screen filled with the dark green snout of Ceffid Leader Bopr Arclando.

"It's about time you called." Arclando's harsh voice filled the room.

Katengi lowered the volume and opened his eyes wide—a friendly Arcan smile. "Leader Arclando, it's been a while since we talked face-to-face. We have had some developments in our space program, developments you have probably heard about already, but I wanted to inform you directly."

Arclando responded with a *harrumph*.

Katengi related the events to Arclando, beginning with their discovery that the astronauts were missing. He took about eighteen minutes for the entire story, but left out his growing personal relationship with Thorpe.

When Katengi finished, Arclando hissed, "I should have been in this from the very start. You are obviously using the offworlders to your own advantage—and you have abducted Astronaut Porovik. I want her returned immediately!"

"For the record," Katengi answered, his voice tinged with anger and his scales rippling orange, "Astronaut Porovik is her own lizard. She has freely chosen to remain with the offworlders for the time being, but I will pass your request on to her."

Arclando hissed and terminated the connection.

✳

Katengi looked at Ferron with frustration.

"It's only going to get worse, I fear," he said. "Perhaps the offworlders can help."

He activated the Link Thorpe had given him and shortly was speaking with the offworlder. "I just completed an unpleasant conversation with Ceffid Leader Arclando. Can you join us to review our options?"

Amred President Binecot Katengi's Office—Amred City, Amred, Planet Arcan

President Binecot Katengi and SPC Director Sudaro Ferron sat in the president's office looking expectantly at the hyper-disk. To Katengi it seemed to take forever, but actually only two minutes passed before the portal opened and Thorpe stepped through onto the rich rug covering the floor in front of the president's desk.

"Gentlemen," Thorpe said in perfectly accented Amred, reaching out with both hands, first to Katengi and then Ferron.

Katengi indicated a stack of cushions on the couch opposite him, designed to accommodate Thorpe's anatomy. The offworlder's face contorted in what Katengi had learned was the Human equivalent of a smile. He sat quietly for several seconds, and then quipped, "It's your dime, Mr. President." The monetary term he used was for a small Amred coin.

"I'm not sure I understand," Katengi said.

The offworlder let out a cackle that Katengi knew to be laughter. "When Humans occupied only one planet, they used an audio communications device called a telephone. The devices were hard-wired to a planet-wide network. At one point, the cost for a telephone call from a public device was a dime. Thus, the expression, 'It's your dime,' means you contacted me, so what's on your mind?" The offworlder cackled again.

"It's amazing when we compare our cultures," Katengi said, "at how much in common we have and have had. Your telephone, for instance—we have a similar device and even a similar expression." He smiled at Thorpe, opening his eyes wide. "But culture comparison is not why I asked to meet with you."

He then related to Thorpe their conversation with the Ceffid leader. "He claims that I'm hoarding you offworlders. He's right, of course, but I cannot admit that. I need to find a way to satisfy Arclando without losing the advantage you have brought to Amred." Katengi paused, looked at Ferron with an unspoken question, and then continued. "On your planet not so long ago, several equally powerful nations vied for control. If I understand your history correctly, the nation of your origin eventually prevailed—without a nuclear war."

"Essentially, yes," Thorpe answered, "although the rise of my company, Phoenix, had as much to do with that as anything else."

"So, your Federation is akin to a supra-national government over everything else in your solar system?"

"In a sense, although it really serves as a forum where individuals, entities, and even nations can resolve differences, I guess it is that. The Federation does not have any really useful enforcement mechanism. We've been lucky thus far. We have only one really negative player, Udachny Enterprises, run by Isidor Orlov." The offworlder emitted a very Arcan-like sigh. "Eventually, you will have to deal with him."

"That's for the future," Katengi said. "Right now, we need to deal with Arclando, and that's why I summoned you." He stood and walked to an ornamental wall hanging. He pulled a cord, causing the hanging to roll up, revealing a Mercator projection of Arcan, centered on Amred. Katengi pointed to a continental mass across a significant ocean east of Amred. "This is Ceffid, technologically our equal, but a harsh dictatorship—ruled by Leader Bopr Arclando. We both have nuclear weapons and the means for delivery. Any time we have a serious difference, Arclando threatens nuclear destruction. Because he knows we can retaliate, his threats may be empty, but obviously, we cannot ignore them."

Katengi returned to his seat. "This time, he insists on our returning Astronaut Jocara Porovik, something I obviously cannot do—even if I wished." His scales rippled a succession of colors. "It's a conundrum for us." He splayed his fingers in front of his torso. "Jocara wants to remain with Kenred and on *Andromeda*. In Amred culture, that's a choice she can make, but not in her own country."

Katengi rose to his feet again and commenced pacing in front of the map. "The risk is real," he muttered, his scales rippling light red. He turned to look directly at Thorpe. "Now you know why I asked you here." He turned to his SPC director. "Do you have anything to add, Sudaro?"

Sudaro Ferron, who had been mute until now, glanced at his boss and then addressed Thorpe. "I am still overwhelmed by your transportation technology, and I'm the scientist here. It seems to me, however, that using some of your technology tricks, we might be able to place Jocara in Arclando's presence without risking her life or freedom. Am I on the right track here?"

"To do anything at all," the offworlder answered, "we will need to get a hyper-disk into Arclando's presence. How can we do that?"

"You mean," Ferron said, "someone has to go there with the hyper-disk?"

"That's about it," Thorpe said. "We haven't yet figured out how to project a portal without a hyper-disk at the destination." He paused.

To Katengi, he seemed preoccupied. Ferron started to speak, but Katengi waved him silent. The two Arcans and the Human offworlder sat quietly for about a minute. Then the Human spoke up.

"I've been communicating with your astronauts. They'll be here shortly."

"That's something else you will have to explain to me," Ferron commented. "The list is growing longer and longer." He opened his eyes wide at the offworlder.

As he did, Kenred and Jocara stepped through the portal.

*

"Mr. President…Director," Kenred said, coming to attention. Jocara followed suit.

Katengi couldn't help but notice how attractive Jocara was. With very light green scales, she was slender, with a small snout and overall delicate features. He could also see that Kenred was very protective of her.

"Please sit," Katengi told the astronauts, pointing to chairs facing his desk. He looked at the offworlder. "Please, Mr. Thorpe."

The offworlder looked at the two astronauts seated opposite the president's desk and made an exaggerated smile that Katengi took to be the equivalent of an Arcan grin—wide open, blinking eyes.

"We've gotten to know each other over the past days—sufficiently so that I think of you as people rather than as alien intelligent lizards. I'm guessing you see me as people, too." Thorpe used the Amred term for *people*.

Both astronauts nodded with eyes wide open. Kenred blinked.

"Okay," Thorpe said, "glad we're on the same wavelength." He took a deep breath. "It seems we have a problem."

Thorpe explained the dilemma that Katengi had outlined to him. He finished up by saying, "It seems that to keep the peace, we need to turn you," indicating Jocara, "over to Arclando."

"That's not going to happen!" both Jocara and Kenred said simultaneously.

Jocara said, "He'll put me in the mines!"

"Or even kill her," Kenred added.

"I've got some tricks up my sleeve," Thorpe said, looking at Ferron.

CHAPTER FOUR

Phoenix Starship Andromeda—**Hovering Invisibly in
Nullspace Beyond Lodan, Thorpe's Office**

Kenred watched Jocara take a seat in Thorpe's office, high atop one of the tallest buildings on Andromeda. Pale green scales covering her delicate snout and facial features created an image finer than any female he had known. She could have graced the cover of any fashion magazine—in fact, she had, but she chose to be an astronaut and had the credentials and smarts to be one of the best. He knew she was special, and even thinking about putting her in peril really got his juices going. One aspect of him said, *She's an astronaut—one of the best! She can handle anything they throw at her.* The other part insisted, *I need to protect her, keep her from harm.* The mixed message was driving him crazy.

Thorpe sat at a desk, not unlike President Katengi's desk back on Arcan. Kenred sat next to Jocara on a couch and took her hand in his. *What has Thorpe cooked up?* he asked himself.

"You both have learned a lot since you arrived on *Andromeda*," Thorpe said, "but you have only touched the tip of the iceberg." He looked directly at Jocara. "We need to send you to Ceffid. Leader

Arclando has threatened a nuclear attack on Amred if President Katengi does not return you, a Ceffid citizen, to Ceffid. I rarely yield to such threats, but President Katengi believes the Leader is serious. We risk nuclear war if he doesn't return you."

"But…," Kenred protested.

"Hear me out." Thorpe raised his hand. "I think we have a solution that will satisfy Arclando without compromising President Katengi's and my own principles, and will keep Jocara from harm."

This was beginning to sound less threatening to Kenred. He squeezed Jocara's hand.

"During our first meeting, you learned about our upload technology and the virtual immortality it brings."

They both nodded, a gesture common to both species.

"We supplied you both with manual Links so you have had access to our ServerNet. I know they didn't work on Arcan except near an open portal, but here on *Andromeda*, you have had full use of the network. Has anyone briefed you on our internal Links?"

"Not yet," Kenred answered for both.

"Did you happen to look them up on ServerNet?"

They shook their heads, another common gesture.

"All of us on *Andromeda*, and most of our species have surgically implanted internal Links that are integrated into our central nervous systems. We can electronically download into our brains any information we wish—knowledge, languages, skill sets. This is how I could learn Amred so quickly."

Kenred's and Jocara's scales rippled yellow with astonishment.

"This is truly possible?" Kenred asked. "We have a species of small lizard that can learn a skill by eating the brain of another lizard that has already learned that skill, but I never imagined this concept could be applied at our end of the evolutionary scale."

"Learning by download—it seems incredible," Jocara said. "It took me a year to learn Amred."

Thorpe's eyes twinkled. "I learned it overnight," he said.

The door opened, and a female Human entered. She smiled at them both. Kenred recognized her as Daphne O'Bryan, the female that had escorted them around *Andromeda*. She was tall and slender with copper-red hair. She handed something to Thorpe and then sat near Kenred and Jocara.

"We have been analyzing your scans—you and Jocara," Daphne said. "My lab people tell me our internal Link system is entirely compatible with your anatomy."

"How is that possible?" Jocara asked. "There simply have to be biological differences."

"You're right, of course," Daphne said. "We evolved in entirely different star systems. Even so, Human and Asterian biologists believe biological life anywhere in our universe will be similar. Advanced living creatures, such as yourselves and us—even your house lizards—will be a symbiotic blend of multi-cellular structures and a microbiome consisting of billions of beneficial bacteria.

"To create an internal Link, we insert nanobots programmed to your biological specifications and those of your microbiome. They actually set up the internal Link and connections."

She showed them two capsules, each about 2.5 centimeters long, one blue and one red. Jocara picked up the blue capsule. It was light and smooth.

"That one contains the initial nanobot swarm," Daphne said. "The red one contains the raw materials the nanobots need to build out their own ranks and create the integrated Link." Daphne smiled broadly. "You swallow both capsules before going to sleep. During the night, using the supplied raw materials in the red capsule and material from your body, the nanobots in the blue capsule expand their numbers and install the Link circuitry. In the morning, you awaken already knowing how to use the integrated Link and are already linked to a real-time backup in your database here on *Andromeda*."

Kenred looked at Jocara, his eyes filled with excitement, his scales rippling between lavender and blue. "Do we do this?"

"Remember," Thorpe added, "with this internal Link, should something happen to you—what I mean is, should you die or be killed—your backup here on *Andromeda* will automatically activate, and your life will go on. The internal Link backs you up continuously in real time so long as there is a portal connection to *Andromeda*. If the link is interrupted, your backup will contain everything up to the moment of disconnection." He smiled again. "One more thing—any time you feel your current body is wearing out or you simply don't like how it looks, you can grow a new body, younger if you will, and download your essence into that body."

"You are a beautiful girl," Thorpe said, looking directly at Jocara. "You can remain so indefinitely."

Jocara turned to Kenred with sparkling eyes and scales rippling bright blue. "We need to do this," she whispered.

"We need to talk," he responded.

Phoenix Starship Andromeda—Hovering Invisibly in Nullspace Beyond Lodan, Jocara's & Kenred's Quarters

Kenred understood Jocara's enthusiasm for the internal Link. What beautiful female would not aspire to be beautiful forever? Nevertheless, he still had reservations.

"Look, Jocara," he told her back in their quarters, "Daphne *says* her scans show that the internal Link is compatible with our species, but how do we know this? The offworlders have run no lab tests we know of, no animal tests, nothing really except their scans."

"Why would they lie to us?" Jocara turned to a mirror over the dresser, examining her face. "There's no reason. Let's ask Daphne," she said, using her manual Link to make the call.

A few minutes later, Daphne entered their room along with a shorter Human female with long, blond hair. Both females had more delicate features and softer voices than Human males, and they had chest protrusions that Kenred thought might be mammary glands.

"This is Kimberly Deveraux," Daphne said. "She is my close friend and business partner. Along with several colleagues, we developed Human uploads and the internal Link system back before the Oort Federation was what it now is."

"We have so many questions about the internal Link," Jocara said.

"We understand two races occupy *Andromeda*," Kenred said, "Humans and Asterians."

"Three, actually," Daphne said. "We also have several Oort who existed in our Oort Cloud for eons in uploaded form only. They were dying out as a species. We offered them the option of downloading their essences into Human form or into their original biological form. Eventually, they chose to download into Human form. The downloaded Oort are indistinguishable from any other Human."

"How did you program the nanobots for the Asterians?"

Daphne called up a holoimage of an instrument that gave Kenred no clue of its purpose. "This is a Nanocosm," she said. "In plain language, you enter what you want orally or in writing here." She pointed to the machine's front. "The Nanocosm gives you feedback to ensure it understands your directions. Then it sources the raw material and finally generates what you ordered."

"That's absolutely amazing," Kenred said. "I take it you no longer employ traditional manufacturing."

"No need," Daphne said. "Nanocosms control all of our manufacturing needs. We even use Nanocosms to design and build other Nanocosms. They have become so complex that the average person really does not understand how they work internally. They are complex tools we use in every aspect of our culture. You could say that we use them for virtually everything."

"So, you gave a Nanocosm the internal scan information of Asterians, and it produced the nanobots. Did I get that right?" Kenred asked.

"In principle, yes, but it's much more complicated than that."

"And the same thing will work for us?"

"Basically, yes." She called up a holoimage. "We maintain adequate supplies of all the raw materials needed for Human and Asterian regeneration. As you can see, we go right down to the radioactive trace elements. Your scans include all these elements, although some in different proportions, and none that aren't on the list, so we're good to go." She collapsed the holoimage. "Any time you decide to go this route, we can accommodate you."

※

"We built a large station in our Kuiper Belt," Daphne said. "It was nearly as large as *Andromeda*. Our culture is a very free-wheeling one, as Thorpe may have told you. Mostly, we cooperate as people, businesses, and nations. Unfortunately, a powerful, terrible player arose in our solar system, and has been a thorn in our sides ever since. Although we can't prove it, we believe this player initiated the implosion of the mini black hole that powered our station. All of us were there when it happened, and we all died in the implosion, including Maxter. Without our internal Links, Kimberly and I would not be here talking with you."

Daphne smiled at them and reached for Kimberly's hand. Kenred noticed a tenderness between the two females, something completely foreign in Arcan culture.

"Let me tell you about another capability of our system," Kimberly said. "Daphne and I created Ogden Enterprises, the business that offers the internal Links, makes the uploads, and stores them in several huge space-based matrixes. It occurred to us early on that besides reviving clients who had died, we could also create clones, identical in every respect to the original. We experimented with several animal types and eventually cloned Max, whom we called Maxter. They were identical at cloning, but their lifelines diverged after that."

Kimberly and Daphne glanced at each other, but Kenred could not decipher any meaning.

Kimberly continued. "Thorpe started out as a living Human back before either of us was born. Before he died of an incurable disease, he arranged for his head to be cryogenically preserved. When the technology became available, Daphne and her colleagues revived Thorpe into an electronic matrix, naming him eThorpe. Eventually, we learned to upload anyone, and both Daphne and I uploaded ourselves as eDaphne and eKim."

At this moment, two holoimages appeared—virtual duplicates of Daphne and Kimberly.

"I am eDaphne…"

"And I am eKim…" the holoimages said.

eDaphne and eKim appeared to be standing together next to Daphne and Kimberly, holding hands.

"It's a bit overwhelming, I know," eDaphne said. "Both of us exist throughout *Andromeda's* electronic systems, just like eThorpe, and we have entirely separate timelines from Daphne and Kimberly. We can localize ourselves inside a matrix box, and we can distribute ourselves throughout a ServerNet—and we live indefinitely long."

"What if the matrix box or ServerNet you occupy is destroyed?" Kenred asked.

"Like our flesh-and-blood sisters, we generate continuous, real-time backups of ourselves. Should the worst happen, we are automatically reconstituted. We'll awaken at a designated location and carry forward."

The holoimages looked at each other and emitted sounds that Kenred now immediately understood as laughter.

"It should be pretty apparent by now," eDaphne continued, "that we can create an electronic or physical clone of anybody. We don't normally do this, because things can get rather complicated with flesh-and-blood duplicates of living people walking around. Case in point: Kimberly and Federation Chairman John Butler fell in love, but Kimberly was committed to me, our company, and to our space explorations. On the other hand, she didn't want to leave John—so we all agreed to clone her. One copy remained with John, and one is here with us. Which copy is which is irrelevant. Initially, they were identical. Their lifelines diverged immediately following cloning, and especially when one remained with John and the other joined *Andromeda.* They are now two entirely different people, although they understand each other better than sisters."

Phoenix Starship Andromeda—Hovering Invisibly in Nullspace Beyond Lodan, Jocara's & Kenred's Quarters

Flesh-and-blood Daphne and Kimberly left and their e-version holoimages disappeared. Kenred was alone with Jocara. Jocara looked at him and tenderly nuzzled the side of his snout with hers.

"It's almost too much to grasp," she said quietly.

He took her in his arms and returned the nuzzle. Part of his mind focused on her, the other part wondered, *How do Humans express this kind of intimacy? No snouts, no scales…* He felt an urgency in his loins, but pushed it aside. It wasn't time. Jocara had not indicated that she was about to lay eggs. Her pouch was empty and would remain so for some time. For the thousandth time, Kenred wondered why Nature had made males always ready and females ready only with eggs in the pouch.

Pulling himself back, he whispered, "So you aspire to be forever young and beautiful?"

"Of course! You like how you are, too," she retorted. "I don't see a downside."

"Truthfully, neither do I." Kenred gave her a squeeze.

Jocara sighed. "More than one of me, even as an upload—that I don't see. But remaining as I am, how can a girl turn that down?"

"The internal Link seems to be a permanent change," Kenred said. "Once done, you can't reverse it."

"Daphne and Kimberly are obviously happy with their internal Links. Who knows how long they have had them? They could be a hundred years old for all we know."

*

"If I understand all this, with your internal Link, there's really nothing Leader Arclando can do to you," Kenred said gently. "Should he kill you, you will awaken in the bio labs here on *Andromeda*, remembering everything right until that moment."

"It scares me," she said. "But if it can prevent war between our nations…" Her eyes overflowed. "I don't know if I'm brave enough."

"The girl chosen to be the first female astronaut to round Lodan…?" Kenred looked at her with astonishment, his scales rippling through a range of colors. "You've got to be kidding!" He placed his hands on her shoulders. "You're the bravest female I know. No… cancel that. You're the bravest *lizard* I know!" He took her in his arms, nuzzling the side of her snout with his.

*

Kenred contacted Thorpe via his manual Link. "We've decided. We're ready to do it—to get cinternal Links."

Several minutes later, Kenred opened their chamber door to a beaming Daphne. "I'm so happy you've decided to join us," she said, stepping into their room. "Now, I'll never have to attend a funeral for my newfound Arcan friends."

She handed each of them a small box. "These are ILKs—Internal Link Kits. I explained them to you earlier. The blue capsule contains a nanobot swarm, the red one necessary nutrients and raw materials. Swallow both capsules before going to sleep. While you sleep, the nanobots will expand their numbers, build the circuitry and integrate it in your nervous system, and connect you to your database. You will waken already knowing how to use the Link and will be completely familiar with *Andromeda's* ServerNet." She smiled, a gesture that by this time seemed completely natural to Kenred. "Questions?"

"Will we have the entire *Andromeda* database in our heads?" Jocara asked.

"Not exactly," Daphne answered. "It will be just like the manual Link you have been using, except you access it internally by thinking about it. And, because it's internal, you can download a language packet from ServerNet and integrate it into your own knowledge set, or any knowledge package. Your brain still will have its normal capacity, and its short- and long-term memory, as before." She smiled again, first at Jocara and then at Kenred. "You'll get used to it quickly, I promise."

✳

Kenred held the blue and red capsules in one hand, a glass of water in the other. "This is irreversible," he said. "Last chance to change your mind."

Jocara stretched up on her toes to nuzzle the side of Kenred's snout with hers. Then she popped the capsules into her mouth and washed them down with half a glass of water.

Taken somewhat aback, Kenred followed suit.

Hand in hand, they crawled into bed. Jocara nuzzled Kenred as they drifted to sleep.

He heard her whisper softly, "Forever young and beautiful!"

Phoenix Starship Andromeda—Hovering Invisibly in Nullspace Beyond Lodan, Thorpe's Office

The following morning, Kenred and Jocara awakened and looked at each other with wide open blinking eyes.

"What do you feel?" Kenred asked.

Jocara nuzzled the side of his snout, whispering, "It's as if I always had it. You?"

"Same," he answered. "It's going to take a while, though."

For several minutes they sat side by side in bed experimenting with their internal Links. Kenred tapped into *Andromeda's* ServerNet, randomly moving from topic to topic. *What is the population of Arcan?* he asked. The accurate answer, so far as he could tell, included an error range for the Geroptic Nation, with an explanation that getting accurate information from that closed society was difficult. *Give me my ancestor tree* brought up a detailed holoimage that even included ancestors he had not known about.

Kenred glanced over at Jocara. She was intensely focused on the inner workings of the Ceffid government, judging from the holoimages in the air before her.

"Preparing yourself, I see," he said with wide open eyes.

She nuzzled the side of his snout in return.

They left their bed and dressed. Then they departed their chamber and stepped through a portal in the hallway that took them to Thorpe's office.

There they met again with Thorpe. Kenred quietly explored his Link and its connection to *Andromeda's* ServerNet, while he watched Jocara revel in her expanded capabilities. He called her Link.

"Focus, Girl!" Kenred said to her by internal Link.

Jocara turned and looked at him with wide open blinking eyes. "I think I like this," she whispered back—by Link.

"Well?" Thorpe asked as they took their seats.

"I love it! I love it!" Jocara said, her scales rippling blue.

"What she said," Kenred added. "It opens an entire universe."

"Indeed. In time, it will just be part of your existence," Thorpe said. "Now, let's talk about Ceffid."

With some difficulty, Kenred shifted his focus to Thorpe. He reached over and took Jocara's hand in his.

Thorpe held up a small disk. "This is an E-disk. We all carry one. It senses our vitality and, to some extent, our surrounds. In extremis—and it's pretty good at sensing this—it pulls you back to your designated home portal. If you depress this," he showed them a recessed button, "it also pulls you back." He handed the E-disk to Kenred. "Another function is that so long as you have an E-disk on your person, your internal Link will continue live, real-time updates."

"How?" Kenred asked, handing the disk to Jocara.

"The E-disk is a hyper-disk with special sensing capabilities. Any hyper-disk links to its Locus continuously, so long as the available Locus power can span the separating distance. If your E-disk link to its Locus is intact, your Link backs you up in real time. Your E-disk Locus receives its power from the massive mini black hole that powers *Andromeda*. It spans back to our solar system and even to Aster. We have yet to discover its limits—which I'm sure it has. As we move away from Sol, we will continuously test it."

"Whew," Kenred said. "This boggles the mind!"

"Your E-disks take you to our Central Docking Station." He handed each a disk. "These are your personal E-disks. Let's try them." He held up his E-disk, pointing to the recessed button. "At three on my count, press the button."

Kenred and Jocara held their E-disks in one hand, finger poised over the activating button.

"One…two…three…"

All three pressed their buttons.

✳

With no sense of transition, Kenred found himself standing upright in a medium-sized chamber lined completely with labeled doors. Jocara and Thorpe stood beside him.

"Remarkable!" was all Kenred could say.

"Kind of like walking through the portal into our *Arcan-One* space capsule," Jocara said.

"One significant difference," Thorpe said. "With the E-disk, there is no visible portal. Whatever you are escaping from cannot follow you." He headed toward a door labeled *Thorpe* and opened it.

Kenred took Jocara's hand, and they followed Thorpe back into his office.

Amred President Binecot Katengi's Office—Amred City, Amred, Planet Arcan

President Binecot Katengi sat at his desk, deep in thought. The Ceffid threat was on his mind. Sending Jocara into Arclando's clutches seemed a terrible solution. Even with the threat of nuclear war, he wasn't at all sure he could follow through with it. Sending anybody there was an uncomfortable thought, but sending this young, beautiful astronaut seemed a crime beyond comprehension.

The portal to *Andromeda* opened; Thorpe, Jocara, and Kenred stepped into his office.

"I was just contemplating our situation," Katengi said. "I cannot send Jocara to that monster. I'm willing to risk nuclear war before that happens."

"I don't think that will be necessary," Thorpe said with a facial expression that Katengi understood to be the Human equivalent of a smile. The offworlder turned to Jocara and said, "Activate your E-disk and then return here through the portal."

Katengi did not understand the offworlder's instructions to Jocara, but a moment later she disappeared—vanished into thin air. Thorpe and Kenred waited patiently, and several minutes later, Jocara stepped through the portal again, smiling at Katengi.

"What happened?" he asked.

Thorpe pulled a disk from a pocket. "Jocara used a variation of a hyper-disk we call an E-disk—an Emergency-disk. It transported her to a safe place on *Andromeda*. Then she simply returned here via portal."

Thorpe took a seat.

"If Jocara will carry an E-disk when she visits Arclando, he will be unable to harm her."

"What if she can't activate her E-disk?" Katengi asked.

"It senses her environment and even her physical state. Any significant change in either will cause it to bring her back."

"I still don't like it," Katengi said.

"Better than the alternative," Kenred said softly.

"I'm going…period!" Jocara said. "It's my choice, and I'm going."

The three males, one an offworlder, looked at her.

"I'm going!" she emphasized.

"I guess that's settled," Katengi said, feeling a deep sense of pride for the young female. "I admire your courage." His scales rippled blue.

✳

"What are the options for getting Jocara to the Ceffid capital?" Thorpe asked.

"We have regular diplomatic relations," Katengi said. "She could join a diplomatic party and fly there."

"Or I could fly her off a carrier," Kenred said.

"That's risking your capture and our fighter falling into Arclando's hands. I cannot allow that."

Thorpe lifted a hand. "As I have explained to you, Mr. President, I am reluctant to interfere in Arcan's internal affairs and disputes. On the other hand, I dislike Leader Arclando's tactics as much as you. I may help get Jocara into his offices without seriously affecting your relative positions on Arcan."

"And those would be what?" Katengi was astonished, his scales rippling yellow.

"I see Amred as the world's only superpower, with Ceffid close behind—near superpower status."

Katengi's scales returned to their normal green.

"I'm not sure why you are reluctant to lend Amred a hand," Katengi said. "Amred culture is much like yours—you told me this. Ceffid embodies everything you hate—you told me this as well. You can end this standoff permanently, giving all our peoples peace and prosperity. In your place, I would!"

"I take your point. With your permission, Mr. President, I would like to continue this discussion later. Right now, we have an immediate, pressing need. How do we get a hyper-disk into Arclando's presence?" Thorpe paused and then looked directly at Katengi.

"You already know," Thorpe continued, "that your ranging equipment could not track *Andromeda*. The starship is hovering in what we call nullspace. In this mode, it cannot be detected. We have smaller craft that we call M-Class craft. They, too, travel through and can hover in nullspace. One of these craft can hover invisibly five hundred meters above Ceffidia and launch a drone carrying a hyper-disk." Thorpe smiled. "You can contact Leader Arclando, informing him of this, telling him what he needs to know. If you are sufficiently persuasive, I think he will assent to this plan. Once the hyper-disk is in his office, we can activate it from here, and Jocara can join him."

"But…" Katengi started to interrupt.

"The E-disk will keep her safe," Thorpe said. "We'll place several sensors on Jocara—a couple of holocams, and several other devices. I will personally know everything that happens near her." Thorpe paused and took a deep breath.

Katengi had learned that this typically preceded new or startling information. This time was no different.

"I need to explain another piece of our technology," Thorpe said.

Thorpe told Katengi about his past and how he first became an uploaded electronic individual, and ultimately both upload and flesh-and-blood. He did not mention the cloning of his upload into eThorpe and eBraxton, nor did he mention the flesh-and-blood existence of Braxton.

"So, the bottom line is that eThorpe is an integral part of *Andromeda*, although he can place himself into a physical electronic matrix for transportation anywhere."

To Katengi's surprise, another Thorpe appeared beside the one talking to him. He examined the second Thorpe carefully and decided it was a holoimage.

"I am eThorpe," the image said. "Because I appear as a holoimage, I cannot use your traditional greeting—sorry."

Katengi clasped his hands together, using the traditional greeting for one unable to grasp both hands. eThorpe followed suit.

"I do not have to project a holoimage to be present," eThorpe explained, "but it helps—it's better than talking to a disembodied voice. I will be with Jocara from the moment she steps through the portal—invisible, but present. I will ensure that she suffers no harm."

Katengi struggled to maintain his composure. He felt nearly overwhelmed by the developments of the past few minutes, but was determined to show nothing. Slowly, he nodded his assent, his scales rippling several colors.

A nod is a nod, he told himself, for Arcans and Humans. A new thought struck him. What if Arclando kills Jocara the moment she steps through the portal? He still wasn't ready to buy into this scheme.

"Arclando is a devious lizard," Katengi said with a hiss. "What if he kills Jocara the moment he sees her? Your E-disk will return a corpse."

Thorpe sighed again, and Katengi presumed he had opened another door.

✳

"You have met eThorpe," Thorpe said to Katengi. "You know how he and I came about. Now put it all together. I think you will begin to see possibilities."

Indeed, Katengi thought, *that is so. Electronic matrixes can be backed up, duplicated, restored…* He let his thoughts take words. "An upload can make a backup of itself, even do so continuously…" His voice trailed off as the implications hit him. "eThorpe is immortal!"

"It goes beyond that, my friend. I have an implanted Link that transmits a continuous backup of myself to a database. Should something happen to the flesh-and-blood me—should I die or be killed—I will be reconstituted back on *Andromeda* with my memories intact right until the moment of death."

Katengi drew in a deep breath. Potential immortality—something he would not have dreamed possible a month ago.

"Both Jocara and Kenred have had internal Links installed. For Jocara, this means there is nothing Arclando can do to her, nothing at all."

CHAPTER FIVE

***Phoenix Starship Andromeda*—Hovering Invisibly in
Nullspace Beyond Lodan, Hangar Bay**

Kenred walked into Andromeda's hangar bay with Jocara. Fifteen M-Class craft occupied the hangar deck space, spacecraft like nothing he had ever seen.

To Kenred, the craft looked like saucers topped by upside-down saucers, twelve meters wide and three high. An eight-meter-long square tube ending in a silvery meter-wide sphere projected from each front end. Two twelve- by three-meter vertical wings bounded the main craft bodies.

Kenred and Jocara walked around the nearest craft.

"No jets," Jocara said. "What drives them?"

Kenred examined one of the vertical wings. "Watch out for these edges—they're razor sharp." He stroked his fingers across the smooth wing surface. "Have you ever seen anything this black?"

As they came around to their starting point, a hinged door near the back opened upward and a ramp slid to the bay deck. As they headed toward the ramp, Daphne approached them.

"What do you think?" she asked.

"Don't know enough to ask questions," Kenred said.

"Well, not exactly," Jocara said. "What drives them?" She tapped a wing. "What is this stuff, and for what purpose? Why the square tube and sphere?"

"I don't mean to denigrate your knowledge," Daphne said, "but you will need to absorb a lot of modern Human physics before I can fully answer your questions. Down there," she pointed to the bottom of the craft, "is a mini black hole. It powers everything in the craft, including weapons and any portals originating from the craft. The vertical wings are an alloy of exotic and normal matter."

Kenred interrupted, "By exotic matter, you mean non-baryonic matter, right?"

Daphne nodded. Jocara looked at Kenred with questions in her eyes.

"Protons and neutrons are baryons," he said. "They make up all normal matter—baryonic matter. We Arcans know virtually nothing about non-baryonic matter. Several theoretical physicists are experimenting with the concept, but mainstream physics still rejects their ideas."

Daphne continued. "That's pretty much how it happened in our own recent past. Look where it got us, though. Anyway, the wings create a Casimir field between them. You haven't discovered Casimir fields yet, so I am using our name for this effect. This field generates a wormhole the length of the vessel from here," she pointed to the ramp, "to the sphere." She smiled at them both.

"Now, here's where things really get complicated. The craft travels the length of the wormhole instantaneously, and repeats this for as many jumps the journey requires—divide the total distance by eighteen meters. The jump interval, the time between jumps, determines how long the trip lasts. We have reduced this to just a few picoseconds and expect to hit the femtosecond range soon."

Kenred ran a quick mental calculation. "That means that if your jump interval is five picoseconds, this little craft can travel from Rodal (your Sol) to Arcan in just under seven hours." He did another calculation. "*Andromeda* can do it in just over one and a half minutes." He let out his breath. "Whew…that's absolutely staggering!" His scales rippled pale yellow. "What I wouldn't give to fly such a spacecraft!"

"You'll have the opportunity soon enough," Daphne said, waving Kenred and Jocara up the ramp.

※

A control console occupied the space opposite and slightly to the right of the ramp. Two adjustable chairs were attached to the deck in front of it. A built-in couch bordered a recessed deck between the ramp and the console. Kenred stepped down to the deck and walked across to the console. To his pilot's trained eye, the controls were familiar, although the labels were in the strange Human script, and he didn't see window, screen, or monitor.

"How do you see out?" he asked Daphne.

She touched a control, and a holoimage of the area in front of the craft appeared at eye height above the console. She moved her hand over a section of the console surface, and the holoimage panned right and left, following her hand.

"You can also use verbal orders," she said. "Our resident Artificial Intelligence or AI—we call it *Mother*—actually drives the craft and controls everything, including weapons. Try it."

Kenred took one of the chairs, awkwardly adjusting his tail, and said, "Mother, show me a rear view."

The holoimage shifted to show the path he and Jocara had taken to the craft.

"Mother, change the control labels to Amred," Daphne said.

As Kenred watched, all the control labels on the console changed from the strange Human script to familiar Amred.

"How did it know Amred writing?" Kenred asked.

"It is hooked into *Andromeda's* AI, so it knows everything *Andromeda* does."

"Let me show you the rest of the craft," Daphne said.

They peeked into a pantry just to the left of the control console, then into two staterooms that shared a small bathroom. Another pantry was next to the staterooms, directly opposite the control console. The airlock and ramp lay between the pantry and another set of staterooms with a shared bathroom. Finally, they stepped into a small galley to the right of Control. It contained a table and chairs, a coffee and beverage maker, and equipment for preparing freeze-dried foods, should they lose the portal connection to their debarkation point.

"We'll have to modify the console chairs and a toilet unit to accommodate your anatomy," Daphne said. "Do you have any anatomical differences that would require separate toilet units for males and females?"

"Not really," Jocara answered, "but I thought you had access to all our databases."

"And we do, but sometimes reality differs from hypothetical—at least in our culture."

"You're right, of course. We have those differences as well, but males and females use the same toilet facilities." Jocara looked at Daphne quizzically.

"We Humans can use the same facilities, but typically, we don't." She motioned Jocara to the other console chair and supported herself between them, leaning her arms against the chair backs. "Try the holoimage controls."

Jocara played with it for a while. "How does Mother know whom to obey?"

"I can't really answer that," Daphne said. "Mother seems to get it right all the time. Keep that question in mind when you meet Brad and Sally, our chief scientists. If anyone can answer that question, they can. Between them and their people, they are responsible for most of the advanced technology you see around here."

Jocara and Kenred sat at the console for a while, playing with the holoimage controls. Jocara turned her head toward Daphne.

"So, without jets, how does this craft propel itself?"

"Now we're getting into the really advanced physics," Daphne answered. "You didn't ask about the craft's saucer shape…there's a reason for it. Around the edge of the craft are two contra-rotating rings of charged particles. Somehow, and this is way beyond my understanding, they grab hold of the fabric of the universe," she put air-quotes around the word *fabric*, and then had to explain what she meant, "and extract a minuscule amount of momentum that propels the craft and everything inside. It accelerates, turns, and stops instantaneously and can reach relativistic speeds very close to lightspeed. Passengers inside the craft feel no effects at all."

"How fast can it go?" Kenred asked.

"We call it an MBH craft (for mini black hole)," Daphne said. "We've tested it to ninety-nine point nine, followed by eight nines percent of lightspeed. That creates a huge relativistic effect. Subjective time for a trip from Rodal to Arcan would be just under four hours and seven minutes, but ten and a half years would have passed in the external universe."

"So, it's great for getting *there* quickly," Jocara said, "but it sucks for maintaining a reasonable timeline."

"That's about it," Daphne said.

"How do the wings fit into this?" Kenred asked.

"The MBH drive is good for short distances and tight, high-speed maneuvering, such as battle between spacecraft. Relativistic time dilation gets in the way for anything longer. We call the wings and associated equipment a MERT Drive, standing for Morris-Einstein-Rosen-Thorne, the scientists from our history who worked out the theoretical basis for the drive. We already talked about the Casimir field the wings create and the resulting wormhole. In an M-Class craft, the pilot tells the AI the destination, and it decides what combination of MBH and MERT is appropriate. For close-in battles, the AI and pilot develop a symbiotic relationship that gets better over time."

"You said we would fly one of these," Kenred said. "Did you mean that?"

"I did, but not this time out. We'll get to that later."

Daphne seemed distracted for a moment. Then she looked at Kenred. "I just called Kimberly. She's bringing the quadcopter and hyper-disk."

She stepped down into the central lounge area and sat. "Join me here while we wait for her."

Kenred and Jocara sat on the circular couch, but a bit awkwardly, since they had to sit forward to accommodate their tails. Daphne looked distressed.

"If we replaced the lower part of the couch back with a soft, compressible material, I think you would be more comfortable sitting."

"That would work," Jocara said. "Don't you think so, Kenred?"

Kenred hissed his agreement. In his mind, he was piloting the craft in a desperate dog fight with a Ceffid opponent. The character of the bench back was the farthest thing from his thoughts.

*

Kimberly walked up the ramp, carrying a drone about a meter across. Jocara stood and took it from her, admiring its structure and the four copter blades.

"It's beautiful!" she said.

A cover on the top opened, revealing the hyper-disk.

"Mother will take us into Arcan's atmosphere about five hundred meters above the government complex in Ceffidia, where we will launch this bird," Daphne said.

"What powers it?" Kenred wanted to know.

"A small portal in here," Kimberly pointed to the main body, "links to the launching craft supplying whatever power it needs. It can even be outfitted with energy weapons, although this one has none."

"When are we going to do this?" Kenred asked.

"As soon as Thorpe and President Katengi have set things up with Leader Arclando," Daphne said. She headed toward the ramp. "Come on, you guys, let's get something to eat."

Amred President Binecot Katengi's Office—Amred City, Amred, Planet Arcan

President Binecot Katengi sat at his desk looking at his seated guests, SPC Director Sudaro Ferron, General Edoetti Kaylambo, his senior military commander, Thorpe, and eThorpe, in some interconnected way commanding the Phoenix Starship Andromeda, and the SPC astronauts Kenred Zlaxiz and Jocara Porovik.

This may be the most distinguished group I have ever hosted in my office, he said to himself as he prepared to address them.

"First things first," he said, looking at Jocara. "Are you certain you want to go through with this?"

Jocara glanced around the group. She paused at Kenred and then looked directly at the president. "Yes, Sir. My mind's made up." Kenred squeezed her hand.

"Do any of you wish to comment?" Katengi asked.

General Kaylambo cleared his throat. He was bigger than average and projected a fierce look. "Why are we putting a young female's life at risk when we have many military options?"

Thorpe spoke up. "General, excuse me. I command the starship *Andromeda*. Although we haven't met, President Katengi has told me of your accomplishments and competence. I do not question them and am honored to meet you. Astronaut Porovik will not be in any danger."

Thorpe described her E-disk and internal Link connected to *Andromeda's* backup database. "The worst-case scenario," he concluded, "would be that they kill her, and her E-disk ports her to *Andromeda*, where she is rejuvenated."

"Difficult to believe—meaning no offense," Kaylambo said. His scales rippled multiple colors.

"None taken," Thorpe answered. "We employ this technology every day."

"I am an electronic upload," eThorpe said. "What you see is a holoimage I project to enable interaction with flesh-and-blood people. I am what you might describe as the original Thorpe. We cloned me, in effect made an electronic backup, and downloaded that backup into a flesh-and-blood rejuvenation we created from Thorpe's DNA. Thorpe is living proof of what we are telling you."

Kaylambo's scales rippled pale yellow. "It makes me feel a bit inadequate," he said with a hiss.

"Okay then," Katengi said. "Let's call Leader Arclando."

✳

Several minutes later, Bopr Arclando's stern features appeared on the large wall screen.

"Are you ready to accede to my demand?" His voice was a near bellow.

Kaylambo's scales turned bright red as he rose to his feet. Katengi waved him back.

"Leader Arclando, thank you for taking my call. As you can see, you are speaking to several of us at once."

Katengi then introduced each member of the group. He finished with Jocara.

"Astronaut Porovik is eager to visit with you to update you on the wonders she has seen on the alien starship. The offworlders have graciously agreed to let us use their transportation technology to facilitate this. What I am about to show you will seem impossible, but I assure you, it is entirely real." Katengi held up a disk. "The offworlders call this a hyper-disk. It opens a portal between itself and its origin Locus." He rubbed the disk back, and a portal to *Andromeda* opened. "This is a direct connection to the alien starship. No matter how unbelievable this may seem to you, I assure you it is true."

Daphne stepped through the portal, handed Katengi the quadcopter, and returned to *Andromeda*. The portal closed after her.

"This drone," Katengi said, holding it up, "was just delivered to me from the starship. With your permission, we will launch it over Ceffidia, carrying a hyper-disk. Once you have brought it into your office, the portal will open, and Astronaut Porovik will step through. She will be representing herself, but also the offworlders. She will, of course, be unarmed." Katengi paused for effect. "Be mindful that these offworlders are powerful and will take great offense if any harm comes to Astronaut Porovik."

Arclando hissed derisively.

"How will I know your drone does not carry an explosive device?" Arclando asked.

"We have trusted each other in the past. Trust me now. It is in everyone's interest for this transaction to happen, as I outlined."

Arclando muted his transmission and seemed to consult someone off screen.

He unmuted and said with a hiss, "I agree. How soon can I expect your drone?"

Katengi looked at Thorpe.

"A half hour," Thorpe said quietly.

"The drone will be over Ceffidia in thirty minutes, ready to land in your compound."

"That's not possible," Arclando hissed.

"I told you the offworlders are powerful," Katengi said. "Just be ready to receive it."

✳

"You didn't give us much time," Katengi said to Thorpe after Arclando's image vanished from the screen.

"More than enough,"Thorpe answered. He turned to Kenred and Jocara. "You two take the drone and hustle."

A portal opened, and they stepped into the interior of the M-Class craft they had previously visited.

Ceffid Leader Bopr Arclando's Office—Ceffidia, Ceffid, Planet Arcan

Ceffid Leader Bopr Arclando terminated the visual link to President Katengi's office with a flourish.

"What a swamp lizard," he hissed at General Garkid Sudajos, his chief military officer and closest advisor. "Just because he is friendly with the offworlders doesn't mean he can order me around."

Arclando came to his feet, his short, stout body out of proportion to his narrow snout and slender tail. His dark green scales rippled an angry orange.

General Sudajos stood, looking down at his much shorter but stockier Leader. "A swamp lizard he may be, Sir, but the offworlders are real. If half of what I hear and see is true, they are more than powerful. I counsel subtlety and forbearance. The offworlders may be more advanced than we technologically, but they are sentient beings like us. That means they make mistakes. If we remain vigilant, we can take advantage when that happens."

Arclando swallowed his anger, forcing himself to be calm. His scales returned to dark green. He glanced up at his military chief. Sudajos had lighter green scales than most Ceffids. *Must be some Amred in his ancestry*, Arclando thought. *Racial purity is important, but he's the best general I have. I won't let light green scales bother me—too much.* "Your counsel is wise, General," he said. "Place ceremonial guards in my office for the event, but make sure they are fully armed."

"Lethal?" the General asked.

"Both," Arclando answered. "We aspire to be ready for anything." He glanced at a clock on the wall. "We have twenty minutes. I don't see how they can deliver the disk in such a short time. I guess we'll see." He headed toward the door. "Let's watch the arrival in the Ops Center."

Amred President Binecot Katengi's Office—Amred City, Amred, Planet Arcan

"We have a few minutes before we need to concentrate on Ceffidia," Thorpe said, addressing the president, his SPC Director, and General Kaylambo. "I believe we are developing a genuine relationship with the Arcan people and with Amred specifically. Despite our physical differences, we seem to have much in common." He looked at Kaylambo. "General, the president, Director Ferron, and I discussed this earlier. The really big difference between us is our advanced technology. Director Ferron commented that while you can learn much from us, what can we learn from you?"

The general harrumphed, his scales rippled an irritated pale orange. "It's an obvious question," he said with a hiss.

"And I will address your concern. We are perhaps a century ahead of you in technology, much of which we intend to share with you. But you evolved completely separate from us. You have met and solved many problems we never saw or solved. You have developed music and visual arts completely foreign to us. You have what seem to us exotic plants and spices. Your scientists and engineers are highly creative people. They will be most interested in our technology. I look forward to what they do with it when they get the chance."

"What about advanced weapons?" the general asked. "Our enemy, Ceffid, is real, and it will pose a threat to you, too."

"You have a point," Thorpe said. "We'll address that later." Thorpe turned his attention back to the whole group. "I've asked Kimberly Deveraux to join us to explain her company, Ogden Enterprises."

A portal opened, and Kimberly joined them. "President Katengi and Director Ferron, you both are familiar with what I am about to present, but this will be completely new for you, General. eThorpe," she indicated the holoimage, "is the result of the original flesh-and-blood Thorpe dying from a terminal disease over a century ago. He had his head cryogenically preserved, and Daphne and her colleagues revived him into an electronic matrix when the technology became available. We have learned much since then. Eventually, we learned how to upload any living being into a matrix."

At that moment, Max ran through the open portal, looked around, and settled onto the general's lap, purring.

"Meet Max, the first living being we uploaded," Kimberly said.

"It appears he has judgment," the general commented with a chuckle and a hiss. The hiss caught Max's attention, but he remained where he was.

Kimberly explained the nature of internal Links and continuous backups.

"Kenred and Jocara have already undergone the treatment. The technology is ripe for all Arcans."

As he stroked Max, the general's features softened and his scales turned pale blue. He said softly, "But are the Arcan people ready for this technology?" He looked at the group members. "This technology implies immortality. I see females no longer laying eggs; family units disappearing; our social structure upending itself." He paused with apprehension, his scales turning light red. "What about Ceffid? Over there, only the powerful would receive the treatment. That would tear their nation apart. Just imagine an immortal Arclando. How would The Geroptic Nation fare? Would their religion even allow immortality treatments?" His scales rippled through multiple colors. "So far as I am concerned, we're just not ready for that."

✳

Thorpe motioned for everyone's attention. "The *PS Michael Collins* will soon launch the drone. Let's watch."

To Katengi's amazement, Thorpe called up a holoimage of the interior of the small spacecraft. "We can see and hear their activities," he said, "but they cannot see or hear us."

CHAPTER SIX

Phoenix Starship *Michael Collins*—Andromeda Hangar Bay

Kenred and Jocara stepped directly from President Katengi's office into the lower lounge area of PS Michael Collins, the same M-Class craft they had visited earlier. Kenred carried the quadcopter, the drone, in front of him with both hands.

Daphne met them. "We're on the clock," she said. "No hurry, but we want to arrive when we said we would." She handed the hyperdisk to Jocara. "Please put this into the drone well."

Jocara observed Daphne as she prepared for departure. "Do we exit through a lock, or do we evacuate the entire bay?" she asked.

"Neither," Daphne answered. "We'll enter nullspace right from here. Mother will set our vectors and adjust them between jumps and then maneuver to our precise position with the MBH drive." She walked toward the console. "Are you both ready?"

❋

Daphne sat before the left console, and Kenred motioned for Jocara to take the right seat. "It looks like you modified the seats," he said. "Thanks."

As he took position behind the seats, eThorpe and eKim appeared as holoimages.

"We aspired to be part of the fun," eKim said.

Thorpe poked his head through the portal to the president's office. "I'll remain here unless you absolutely need me," he said to Daphne. "We'll keep the portal open."

Thorpe turned to Jocara. "You will be safe, I promise."

Phoenix Starship Michael Collins—Arcan Cislodan Space— Ran Star System

Daphne addressed Michael Collins' AI resident. "Mother, take us to a point five hundred meters above the government compound in Ceffidia. Hover there in nullspace except for the time we need to launch the drone. We wish to launch the drone at..." She specified a time thirty minutes after Katengi's conversation with Arclando.

The screens blanked and remained so. Jocara presumed this was because they were in nullspace.

"We're in position," the AI said softly moments later. "Five minutes remain till drone launch."

Jocara knew the transit would be quick, but its suddenness amazed her. She looked at Daphne with her strange face and body, and yet somehow she felt a kinship that transcended species and gender, strengthening her resolve to remain with the offworlders.

Kenred picked up the drone and headed to the lock.

"At a half-kilometer altitude, there should not be much wind, but attach a safety line anyway," Daphne said. "Close the inner door, open the outer, and launch the drone on my signal."

"Do I have to launch it in any special way?" Kenred asked.

"Nope," Daphne said, turning toward him. "It will align itself automatically and follow the instructions it receives through the power portal." She turned back to the console and moments later gave the order to launch.

"Mother, take us out of the atmosphere and hover over the compound, moving in and out of nullspace so we remain invisible to radar while being able to assemble a composite image of events below."

It doesn't take a skilled pilot to fly one of these, Jocara thought, *just a detailed knowledge of how they work and how to issue orders.*

The space above the console filled with holoimages of the drone as seen through a telescopic lens and of the massive government building as seen through the drone's imaging. At the top, a terrace-like compound enclosed on all sides, filled one-half of the space, and Arclando's offices occupied the remainder. General Sudajos appeared in the compound with several uniformed Ceffids. Daphne zoomed in on them and determined that they were armed.

"If I were in Arclando's place," Kenred said, "I would send out armed personnel."

Jocara agreed.

The drone landed, and the top popped open. One soldier gingerly approached it. He retrieved the disk and handed it to the general. Then he attempted to grab one of the quadcopter arms. The drone slipped sideways and shot into the sky. The soldiers brought their weapons to bear and fired on the drone. The AI detected their action and maneuvered the drone radically so that all the shots missed.

"Head down and pick up the drone," Daphne ordered, "then return here." As an afterthought, she added, "Maintain visuals."

Jocara felt nothing during the radical maneuvers, but when Kenred opened the inner lock door, the quadcopter rested quietly on its supports. He brought it into the lounge area.

Thorpe stuck his head through the still-open portal to Katengi's office. "Well done, guys. Now the fun really starts." He looked at Jocara. "You have your E-disk, right?"

She held it up before placing it inside her clothing in her belly pouch. "It's as physically safe as possible," she said, patting her belly.

Kenred chuckled. "You got that right!"

"After the portal opens, wait for my signal," Thorpe said. "I want to scan his entire space before you step through. We don't want any surprises."

Amred President Binecot Katengi's Office—Amred City, Amred, Planet Arcan

A holoimage floating in the center of Katengi's office showed a disk view of a soldier holding the hyper-disk and handing it to General Sudajos. They picked up shots as the other soldiers tried to take down the drone. Then they moved with the general through a door, past several guards, and through another door into the Leader's office, where he placed it in the center of Arclando's desk. The room was large, with plush carpeting. The desk, placed three meters out from one wall, dominated that side of the room. Arclando sat behind the desk, his back to the wall. An armed guard stood in each corner behind him. A wide elevator door flanked by two armed guards occupied the wall opposite the desk.

"I count seven armed guards," Katengi said, "three outside the door and four inside."

"They appear to be carrying live ammo," General Kaylambo said.

"Who's the big fellow?" Thorpe asked.

"That's General Garkid Sudajos, Arclando's top military officer," Katengi answered.

"Both of them have side arms," Kaylambo added.

The comm screen on the wall flickered, and Leader Bopr Arclando appeared. "We're ready to open the portal," he said without preamble.

✳

At the sound of Arclando's voice, Max jumped from Kaylambo's lap.

"Watch him!" Thorpe said. "Max roams throughout *Andromeda* and explores every new portal he finds. The last thing we want is for him to jump through the portal into Arclando's office."

CHAPTER SEVEN

Operations Center, Government Compound—Ceffidia, Ceffid, Planet Arcan

Leader Bopr Arclando leaned over his radar operator's shoulder. His snout pushed past the operator's right eye, and his breath smelled of rotten meat.

"You should have something," he hissed. "If they're on time, you should have something."

"My screen is blank, Sir."

"Increase your power!"

"I'm at max power, Sir. If something is up there, we'll see it."

"Swamp-lizard-mentality Amred bastards," Arclando muttered to Sudajos, his scales rippling an irritated pale orange.

General Sudajos glanced at the bulkhead clock. "It's not yet thirty minutes."

Arclando walked over to the radar operator again. "Keep looking," he said, his voice cracking.

The operator hunched over his screen, intensifying his focus, his scales rippling red. Arclando walked back to the room center next to Sudajos. The clock indicated exactly thirty elapsed minutes.

"I got something!" the radar operator shouted, "at five hundred meters!" His scales rippled blue. "I got two blips—one dropping fast. It's small." He made an adjustment to his console. "Perhaps a meter wide." He strained over his console. "The other one is gone. I had it for just a moment. Then it just vanished."

"How do you explain that?" Arclando asked Sudajos.

"It could be anything—a bird, a spurious whatever-the-hell, even one of the alien spacecraft. They couldn't launch that drone from space. Something had to descend deep enough into the atmosphere to launch it. The thing is, we'll never know."

"It looks like it will land in the compound," the operator announced.

"Send some soldiers to retrieve it and meet me in my office," Arclando told Sudajos. "Capture the drone."

✳

Retrieving the disk was simple; the drone offered it up. Capturing the drone, however, turned out to be impossible. When it lifted off, Sudajos' best sharpshooters could not hit it. Carrying the hyper-disk, Sudajos returned to the Leader's office.

"I want four armed guards here," Arclando said, "each with a clear line to the front of my desk, and three outside the door."

General Sudajos briefed the guards. "Your job is to protect the Leader. Astronaut Jocara Porovik will come through some kind of door. Make sure she is alone, that no one follows her. If she produces a weapon—any weapon at all—shoot her. Be prepared to take her into custody, should the Leader so indicate. Questions?"

Ceffid Leader Bopr Arclando's Office—Ceffidia, Ceffid, Planet Arcan

Bopr Arclando sat at his desk facing the elevator. The office entrance door was to his right. General Sudajos stood to the right of his desk. Alert armed guards stood in the corners behind the desk and flanking the elevator door. All eyes were on the hyper-disk that occupied the center of the desk. Arclando glanced at his chief military officer.

"Are you ready to do this?"

"Yes, Sir," the general responded.

Arclando flipped a switch on his desk, opening comms to the Amred president. "We're ready to open the portal," he said.

Arclando didn't know what to expect as tension coursed through his body, and his scales rippled multiple colors.

Arclando and Sudajos focused their attention on the disk. Initially, nothing happened. Then the disk vanished, and a door appeared in thin air in front of Arclando's desk.

"That portal opens to an armed spacecraft outside the atmosphere hovering above Ceffidia. Are you ready to receive Astronaut Porovik?" President Katengi's voice sounded neutral and nonthreatening.

"We are ready, Mr. President."

With that, Jocara stepped through the portal. She wore her astronaut uniform with a small patch on her left shoulder, indicating that she came from Ceffid. She came to attention and saluted Leader Arclando and General Sudajos—right forearm across her chest, fist closed. The general returned her salute.

"Astronaut Jocara Porovik reporting as requested, Sir."

Her voice was neutral and her eyes showed no guile, but Arclando felt a rising rage at her words. As his scales rippled orange, he bellowed, "I did not request your presence, I ordered it!"

Jocara's scales remained pale green. She stood quietly, hands at her sides.

"How dare you decide to remain in Amred with the offworlders without consulting me first? I tell you where to go and how long to stay."

Jocara straightened and lifted her snout. "No Sir, you do not. I am an SPC Astronaut assigned to the offworlder starship. I take orders only from SPC." Her scales rippled orange with a tinge of red.

Arclando jumped to his feet, shouting, "This is outrageous! You will submit to my authority."

"No, Sir! I will not!" Her scales rippled full orange. "You are powerless to stop me."

"Arrest that swamp lizard!" Arclando ordered his guards. "Arrest her!"

The guards ran to her side and gripped her arms. As they did, Jocara vanished. They looked at their empty hands in astonishment.

"Where'd she go?" one guard asked.

"Fuck if I know," the other answered as the portal behind them closed.

✳

Arclando and Sudajos looked at each other in astonishment.

"Do you suppose she was just a holoimage?" the general asked. He addressed one of the guards. "Did you feel her? Was she real?"

"Sure was, General, as real as you and me."

Arclando picked up the hyper-disk that had reappeared on his desk when the portal closed. He rubbed his thumb across the shiny side. It was totally smooth. He turned it over and rubbed the deep black side. The disk vanished from his hands, and the portal reopened in its former position.

✳

To Arclando, it looked like Thorpe had walked through the portal. "Shoot him in the legs," he ordered his guards. "Don't kill him."

Nothing happened. The bullets slammed into the wall behind Thorpe without striking him. Before Arclando could issue any more orders, Thorpe held up his hand.

"Stop! I come in peace. I am eThorpe. What you see is a holoimage. I am an uploaded entity on the starship *Andromeda*. I am projecting my holoimage through the portal. I wish you no harm, but I will tolerate no acts of violence against my holoimage, or anything connected to *Andromeda*. Anyone initiating violence will die."

A holoimage of a chair appeared beside eThorpe. He sat down facing Arclando.

Arclando's scales rippled multiple colors as he evaluated the situation. He looked at Sudajos whose scales had turned bright orange. *This offworlder is usurping my authority. I can't allow that,* Arclando thought. "Take him out, General," he said. "A headshot."

Sudajos signaled the guard on his side of the desk. The guard fired a round through eThorpe's head…and dropped lifelessly to the deck. The second guard raised his weapon.

"I wouldn't," eThorpe said. "You'll die for no purpose."

With rippling red scales, the guard looked at General Sudajos, who shook his head slightly. The guard lowered his weapon and stepped back into his corner, scales fading to green.

"Now that's settled," eThorpe said, "let's talk."

※

"We need to establish a basis for future interaction," eThorpe said to Arclando. "I have a rapport with President Katengi and SPC Director Ferron. We are laying the ground rules for trade and technology exchange. It should be apparent that any input from our cultures to theirs will give Amred a material advantage over Ceffid."

Arclando felt the offworlder's eyes boring into his. *He is obviously right. Virtually any offworlder trade with Amred will put Ceffid at a disadvantage. But how to reverse things? The offworlders and Katengi are obviously in bed together. My instinct says the offworlders are not trading weaponry—at least not yet. This means that Ceffid and Amred are on par in any confrontation. Would the offworlders step in on Amred's side?* Arclando shifted in his seat, glanced quickly at Sudajos, and then locked eyes with the offworlder. He had an inspired thought. *These guys are no smarter than we are—they just have better toys.*

"I will leave our portal in place," eThorpe continued. "When it is open, you can speak into the portal, and one of us will respond. If you wish privacy, you can request that we close the portal. When it is closed, you can open it at will by rubbing the black side of the hyper-disk. Let there be no mistake, however. The portal is for our convenience, not yours. Anyone attempting to enter the portal will die. Anyone firing a weapon into the portal will die.

"I do not mean to threaten your sovereignty. We will not interfere with your internal workings without your express invitation, but we will respond vigorously should you attempt to interfere with us."

eThorpe's holoimage disappeared abruptly, and the portal closed, leaving the hyper-disk on Arclando's desk.

"What now?" Sudajos asked, scales rippling bright yellow. Arclando motioned the general to a chair.

Remembering his earlier thought, Arclando said, "Keep in mind, General, the offworlders are no smarter than us. They just have better toys."

※

Arclando looked at the lone guard still manning his station behind him in the left-hand corner and the two guards by the elevator.

"You're relieved," Arclando told them. "Remove your fallen comrade and set a normal two-lizard watch outside my door."

The guards dragged the body through the door, their scales rippling from red to green.

With just the two of them in the room, the general said, "Better toys, I agree, but what can those toys do to us? If we don't get a handle on this immediately, I fear Amred will overwhelm us."

"The offworlder said they wouldn't interfere…"

"And you believe that, Sir?" the general asked. "I don't—not for a minute."

"What are our options?" Arclando asked.

"With the offworlders gone, we can pressure Amred."

"So, how do we get them to leave?"

"How, indeed? Let me give that some thought."

Arclando watched his senior military officer settle back in his chair and close his eyes in contemplation. Normally, he would ask the general to do his thinking in his own office. But this was different, and time was critical. He stayed silent while the general remained deep in thought.

After about fifteen minutes, Sudajos opened his eyes and looked at Arclando with some hesitation. Then opened them wider as his scales rippled pale yellow.

"We need to gain the offworlders' confidence," Sudajos said. "We need to reach a state of cooperation so that they will invite several Ceffids as guests aboard *Andromeda*. We need to do this as quickly as possible. One of my most trusted lizards will join the guests. We will surgically remove part of his tail, replacing it with a small nuke—it will be indistinguishable from his original tail. Once onboard *Andromeda*, he will find the best place, go there, and detonate the nuke." Sudajos blinked his eyes while his scales rippled blue. "Even a small thermonuclear detonation should destroy *Andromeda*." He blinked his eyes again. "Even if it doesn't, the havoc it will cause should be overwhelming. If offworlders survive the blast, we can offer assistance that will further endear Ceffids to them. Then, when the time is ripe, we can hit Amred and take out the remaining offworlders. That will leave us in sole control of Arcan."

"What about The Geroptic Nation and the Prophet?"

"If we succeed in neutralizing the offworlders, the Prophet, and his ignorant hordes, they will pose no problem…Trust me."

✳

Arclando mulled over what General Sudajos had said. It's tempting, he thought, but what do we really know about the offworlders and their advanced technology? This portal transportation—I don't begin to understand even its basis. And what about electronic uploads? I think I grasp what they are doing, but the how is a mystery totally beyond any science I know. What killed my guard? I saw nothing—no visible shaft of energy, no…no nothing, and that's the problem. How did the offworlders get the drone here so quickly? Even without an engineering background, I know it takes time to get from here to there in space—and they launched the drone from 500 meters. They have better toys, alright, MUCH better toys. I like Sudajos' thinking, but it's much more complicated and involved than that.

Arclando turned to Sudajos. "I like your out-of-the-box thinking, but we have too many unknowns to implement your proposal. We need to pressure Katengi into severing his relationship with the offworlders. Like us, I'm sure he is overwhelmed by their superior technology. Things as they were before the offworlders arrived were much better than things as they are now. No matter our differences, I think Katengi feels the same way. We need to nudge him in that direction."

"I don't think nudging will work," Sudajos said. "Katengi needs to know that with or without the offworlders, we will destroy Amred if he does not sever his ties with them." Sudajos paused and shifted his position in his chair. "We have another matter that needs our attention, Sir. That partisan rebel, Spajo Boszut, has taken out several southern power transfer hubs, disrupting our southern military command."

"Why don't you just eliminate him and get it over with?"

"We've tried. He's a slippery bastard, and the locals protect him at every turn. It's not like up here in the North, where we have firm control of everything. The southerners resent our rule, our presence, and they do everything possible to disrupt whatever they can."

"Put one of your senior people on it. You and I have to deal with Amred and the offworlders." Arclando turned his attention back to his main problem. "General, put our nuclear forces on alert, and target Amred City directly with several missiles. I want a fifteen-minute launch capability."

Amred President Binecot Katengi's Office—Amred City, Amred, Planet Arcan

A portal opened into President Katengi's office, and Thorpe stepped through. He greeted Katengi with a double-arm grip and then settled onto a couch where Katengi indicated.

"I came to talk with you privately about some information we have received from Ceffid," Thorpe said without preamble. "We have tapped into their communication system. We monitor it automatically, scanning for keywords and phrases. When these pop up, a specialist examines the text to determine any likely threat." Thorpe leaned back against the couch and looked directly at Katengi. "Leader Arclando has increased his launch readiness. He can launch his missiles in fifteen minutes. My people tell me he is preparing for a nuclear strike."

"I've got a country to run, Mr. Thorpe. True, because of the nature of the Amred culture, most things run themselves. My job isn't merely ceremonial, however. The government rarely interferes in the lives of its citizens—individuals or companies, but, my prime responsibility is as Commander-in-Chief of Amred's armed forces. Through the military, I keep the country safe. Your news really alarms me. In the past, Arclando's saber rattling has been pro forma—I just shrugged it off. This is different. We have an early warning system for incoming missiles, but unless my missiles are ready to go, it's pretty useless.

"We are so radically different from the Ceffid dictatorship. A citizen legislature writes our laws. Citizens vote legislators into office for three years, and they can only serve twice. The courts determine the validity of laws, adjudicate disputes, and mete out justice when people or companies break the law. Amred has a local police presence supervised by the judiciary, but my office is completely separate from both. When something like this happens, I can react, but the legislature needs to back me up within two weeks, or I have to disengage and withdraw any forces.

"Right now, the most I can do is increase our missile and troop readiness as high as possible."

"There may be something I can do," Thorpe said. "I can't stop Arclando from launching his weapons, but I can render them ineffective. *Andromeda* and the M-Class craft are armed with a suite of defensive and offensive weapons. We can detect a nuclear device on a planet by its neutrino emissions. Then we can disable the nuclear device with a narrowly focused neutrino beam. There is no obvious damage to the device. It just won't produce a nuclear or thermonuclear explosion. We can destroy missiles that rise out of the atmosphere with anti-matter particle beams or lasers. Anti-matter beams don't work in an atmosphere; lasers work, but clouds, water vapor, and other pollutants make them ineffective."

"That's a remarkable capability," Katengi said. "I understand nothing can shield neutrinos, so there is no way to protect a nuclear arsenal from such a weapon."

"Essentially, you are correct—short of destroying the source of the beam. Neither Arclando nor you have that capability."

That felt like a veiled threat, Katengi thought. With Ceffid not able to respond to a nuclear attack, we finally could gain the upper hand.

"Here's the thing," Thorpe said, interrupting Katengi's thoughts, "if we do this, under no circumstance will you initiate a preemptive strike against Ceffid." Thorpe leaned forward, speaking in what Katengi presumed was earnestly. "You and I, Amreds and we offworlders," Thorpe's face momentarily shifted to a grin, "have developed a certain degree of trust. If I were presented this opportunity in your circumstances, I would consider a preemptive strike. I am certain that crossed your mind. Don't! We can help bootstrap your people to heights you never dreamed possible, but we will withdraw in the face of an Amred preemptive strike to leave you to your own devices."

Katengi could feel Thorpe's intensity in the surrounding air. He did not doubt Thorpe's words. There would be no preemptive strike, he decided.

PS Alan Shepard, Cislodan Space—Ran Star System

Jocara occupied the left-hand pilot seat on PS Alan Shepard. Daphne sat beside her. Under Daphne's training, Jocara translated her jet fighter skills to this odd M-Class spacecraft. They were operating in cislodan space near Lodan.

"See that mountain peak?" Daphne asked, pointing to the holoimage in front of them.

"I do," Jocara said.

"Hit it with a laser and then with your anti-matter particle beam."

"Mother, hit this peak," Jocara pointed to it in the holoimage, "with the laser."

Moments later, the peak puffed briefly, and the tip was gone.

"Mother, hit the same peak with the anti-matter particle beam."

Another puff, and fifty meters of the peak were gone.

"It's that easy," Daphne said. "You can aim and shoot manually using these controls, but Mother is faster and more accurate."

"*PS Alan Shepard,* this is *PS Neil Armstrong.* What is your position? Over."

It was Kenred's craft. Jocara gave him her position. Shortly thereafter, *Neil Armstrong* appeared alongside. Kimberly was training Kenred.

"Shall we try a dogfight?" Kenred asked.

"Sure!"

Daphne had already walked her through the process. Jocara locked out both the particle and neutrino beams and set the laser to training mode.

"First," Daphne said, "we need to establish your callsigns."

"What do you mean?" Jocara asked.

"Human fighter pilots take on names that follow them throughout their careers—even their lifetimes. It's how they are identified when flying. Jocara, Humans call younger, pretty females *Chicks.* I suggest the callsign *StarChick* for you. Kenred, are you listening?"

"This is Kenred, I am."

"I suggest the callsign *Bobcat* for you. I think you know why."

"That works for me. StarChick, this is Bobcat, let's start one hundred thousand kilometers apart," Kenred suggested.

"This is StarChick, Roger," Jocara said, and they jumped to their respective starting positions.

"Now, remember what you've learned," Daphne said. "Your MBH drive will allow you to maneuver close-in at high speed, but your MERT Drive will take you out in a direction unknown to Bobcat and back from another. If you both just let the AI do the job, you will either both lose or come to a draw. The only way to prevail is to put your brains and skill into the equation. Kimberly will be telling Bobcat the same thing. Go Girl!"

Jocara transmitted an entangled particle sphere and fired a laser beam in Bobcat's direction. *It will reach him in point three seconds,* she told herself. She immediately used her MERT Drive to place herself 100,000 kilometers above Bobcat's position. She arrived before her laser beam reached Bobcat's starting position, which, according to her Entangled-Particle-Detector (EPD), he had just departed, also on MERT Drive. She fired her laser blindly at a position 100,000 kilometers above her starting position, believing Bobcat might do the same thing she had done. He didn't. Her EPD showed him 100,000 kilometers below her position. She fired her laser in that direction and then headed directly toward Bobcat on MBH at near lightspeed. Halfway there, about a half second later, she fired her laser at her starting position and jumped straight up on MERT for 200,000 kilometers. Her EPD showed Bobcat moving straight toward her on MBH at nearly lightspeed. She fired her laser at what was probably point-blank range, and dropped into nullspace as the AI told her, "Direct hit—you got him!"

They practiced dogfights against each other and other *Andromeda* pilots for the entire day. They each won about as many fights as they lost, but they increased their proficiency until Daphne declared them as good as any of the other pilots on the giant starship.

It was time to do some actual work.

✳

Thorpe divided the Ceffid continent into sectors and assigned one sector to each of his pilots. He assigned Jocara to the Ceffidia section, including the large harbor, and Kenred to the ocean between Ceffid and Amred.

"Mother, do a neutrino grid search of the Ceffidia sector. Identify any nuclear or thermonuclear devices," Jocara ordered from the pilot's seat in *PS Alan Shepard.*

The AI commenced the search and almost immediately identified a cluster of thermonuclear devices just outside Ceffidia.

"One by one," Jocara ordered, "irradiate each device with a concentrated neutrino beam."

After the AI neutralized the cluster outside Ceffidia, she continued her grid search of the sector. As it located each device, the AI informed Jocara and then hit the device with a concentrated neutrino beam. The AI located and deactivated 736 devices—700 in silos or on battlefield launchers and the rest on submarines moored in the harbor.

The others found 100 devices. Kenred on *PS Neil Armstrong* found fifty on submarines at sea, two others found fifty between them, and one found none.

By the end of the day, with no one in the country knowing about it, Ceffid had no functioning nuclear or thermonuclear devices.

CHAPTER EIGHT

Ceffid Leader Bopr Arclando's Office—Ceffidia, Ceffid, Planet Arcan

Leader Bopr Arclando sat at his desk mulling over his situation. He had decided to force Katengi's hand. This meant explaining the facts of life to him without alerting the offworlders. His nuclear arsenal was ready to go. All that was left was for him to lay out exactly what he would say to the Amred president, and then call him.

He pulled out a notepad and scribbled when his comm line to Amred signaled an incoming call. It was President Katengi.

"Leader Arclando, my sources tell me you have put your nuclear missiles on a fifteen-minute launch window. In response, I have placed my missiles on a short leash, and put my Navy and Air Force on high alert. Amred will not be intimidated. I will reduce my response readiness immediately after you lower your attack readiness." Flecks of orange rippled through Katengi's green scales.

"And I will lower my readiness as soon as Amred severs its ties with the offworlders," Arclando hissed, scales rippling bright orange.

"That I cannot do." Katengi said. "The offworlders contacted me. There's no upside to my abandoning them."

"There is one distinct advantage. Sever ties with the offworlders, and Ceffid will not attack you."

"That won't happen," Katengi said and severed the connection.

✳

"Launch a three-missile attack against the government complex in Amred City," Arclando ordered.

Fifteen minutes later, three nuclear-tipped missiles rose from the complex outside Ceffidia and left the atmosphere. Moments later, all three missiles lost propulsion and crashed back into the ocean between Ceffid and Amred.

"Launch three more," Arclando ordered.

Fifteen minutes later, the second set crashed into the water. Arclando issued another order, and out in the ocean, three submarines surfaced several hundred kilometers from each other and launched missiles at Amred City. As soon as they left the atmosphere, they, too, crashed back into the sea.

A furious Arclando called General Sudajos. "What's happening to my missiles?"

"They're failing the moment they leave the atmosphere," Sudajos told him. "And, Sir, I've just received a disturbing report. A nuclear technician was making a routine check of the missile warheads assigned to him—all were disabled."

"What do you mean, *disabled?*"

"Something had disrupted the firing mechanisms. They were working when he last checked them a week ago."

"How does something like that happen?"

"I don't know, Sir. This has never happened before."

Ceffid Leader Bopr Arclando's Office—Ceffidia, Ceffid, Planet Arcan

Leader Bopr Arclando sat at his desk, staring at the hyper-disk the offworlder had left. His scales rippled through multiple colors, ending with pale red. He was afraid, not out of cowardice, but from knowing how powerless he was against these offworlders. He had considered disposing of the hyper-disk or even destroying it, but the uncertain consequences stayed his hand.

While he contemplated his options, the portal opened, and eThorpe stepped into his office. Arclando jumped to his feet as his guards lifted their weapons. He signaled them to stand down. They relaxed, but kept their weapons at the ready.

"We come in peace," eThorpe said without preamble.

Arclando felt frustration and a bit of fear. His scales rippled multiple colors, ending with a pale red, as he lifted his hands.

"Sit!" eThorpe ordered in a commanding voice. "Listen!"

Arclando resisted his impulse to launch himself at the unprotected offworlder and slowly took his seat, arms resting on his desk, hands folded defiantly. eThorpe remained standing.

"You need to understand, Leader Arclando, that the most powerful starship in the galaxy is hovering above Ceffidia. In the blink of an eye, we can destroy every living thing in Ceffid. Had we wanted to do that, you and I would not be here talking." eThorpe leaned over and seemed to place his hands on the front edge of Arclando's desk.

"I understand your desire and Amred's desire to remain undetected by Sol and Aster. You were aware of our conflicts. You knew the potential risk of either race discovering your existence and location. Despite your internal differences, you went to great lengths to keep your existence a secret. Unfortunately, through no fault of you or us, we stumbled on SPC's space venture. The proverbial cat is out of the bag, and there is nothing you or we can do to change that.

"We have zero interest in subjugating anyone, certainly not Ceffid or Amred. We're interested in knowledge and trade, and in bringing peoples like yourselves into our advanced universe. Here's the thing. I want to work with individuals and independent firms, not governments, and especially not dictatorships. I have developed a relaxed relationship with Amred President Binecot Katengi, because his government is a representative government that works closely with SPC and guarantees individual rights and a stable business environment. These are nonexistent in Ceffid.

"You attempted to coerce Amred to abandon its relationship with us. You threatened them with nuclear weapons to enforce your demand, and when President Katengi refused, you actually launched them. We stopped your missiles and disabled all your nuclear weapons.

If you attempt to reactivate them, we will destroy your entire nation, starting with its leadership.

"We will continue to work with Amred, its citizens, and its firms. We will assist them with technology, engineering, and science as they move into our universe. You and Ceffid will be left behind in the backwaters of history. I offer you one way out: Give up your dictatorship, write a constitution similar to Amred's, and establish general elections throughout Ceffid. When you accomplish this, we will grant you the same access we have granted Amred."

Phoenix Starship Andromeda—Hovering Invisibly in Nullspace Beyond Lodan, Conference Room

Sudaro Ferron let President Binecot Katengi precede him through the portal to the conference room on Andromeda. He didn't know what to expect, but it was just like walking through any door. He felt no sensation at all.

This could be any conference room in my headquarters building in Amred City, he thought, *except…this room is four hundred thousand kilometers away on an alien starship.*

Thorpe and Kenred sat at the head of the table, and Thorpe gestured for them to sit nearby.

"I wanted to bring you here," Thorpe said, "so when we finish our discussion, Kenred can give you a tour of *Andromeda*."

Katengi's scales rippled blue, as did Ferron's.

"We're here to discuss technology transfer. I understand that you, Mr. President, have some reservations. Are you willing to share them with me?"

Ferron smiled to himself, wondering how Katengi would answer. *I know what I want*, he thought. *With spacecraft like theirs, we can explore our entire solar system during my lifetime. We can even visit some of the nearer stars, a dream I never expected to see happen.*

"My reservations," Katengi said, "stem from my understanding of people. Right now, we are on the cusp of becoming a genuine spacefaring race. We accomplished this entirely on our own. Every day on Arcan, we advance technology—Arcan technology. Since your arrival, I took the time to read about your history. One thing stood out over everything else. When one of your advanced peoples encountered a more primitive group, within a relatively short time, the primitive group ceased to exist, either by war or by being totally subsumed by the more advanced. In the end, nothing was left of the more primitive people." He looked sadly across the table at Thorpe, his scales rippling pink.

"How are we Arcans different from those peoples?"

The president's presentation impressed Ferron. Furthermore, he had no solid counter argument. He glanced at his president and then at Thorpe. *How will the offworlders respond?* he wondered, his scales rippling multiple colors.

"I am pleased that you have learned something of our history," Thorpe said quietly. "I take no issue with your conclusions. That's exactly how it happened…over and over throughout our history, across many lands and nations. Some in our society take the approach that each generation, each new species, each offworlder contact, should be left to its own devices, to discover things independently. This may sound noble and generous, but the real result of this approach is that those new generations, species, and offworlder contacts get left in the dustbin of history.

"Your people have made tremendous progress, but now they know there is something better out there, something they will want. A famous leader in our past, Winston Churchill, once said, 'Those that fail to learn from history are doomed to repeat it.' I firmly believe that I and my people have learned from history. If you give us the chance, we will assist your move to our technology level. Your scientists can work alongside ours, your engineers can design alongside ours, and your artists can work with ours to make the universe a more beautiful place."

"That sounds too good to be true," Katengi said, "and in our culture, when something sounds too good to be true, it usually is."

"Again," Thorpe answered, "I don't disagree." He placed folded hands on the table and leaned forward. "If you choose to withdraw into your shell and try to ignore our presence, I will respect your decision; however, I will welcome anyone who wishes to join our expedition and has something to offer." He turned to Kenred. "Kenred and Jocara have already made their choices. As the word gets out, so will others. Remember, Ran is just a stop on our journey. When we leave, you will have whatever you learned from us during our stay, but nothing more should you choose to withdraw."

"I understand," Katengi said.

"On the other hand, if you choose to join our interstellar community, before we depart, I will introduce you to John Butler, the current Chairman of the Oort Federation, the central coordinator for our interstellar community. John is the wisest person I ever knew, Human or otherwise. He will assist you in establishing your place as a co-equal in the Federation."

Out of deference to his president, Ferron did not speak out, but inside he cheered loudly and enthusiastically for Thorpe's words.

✳

"You have just returned from a meeting with Leader Arclando?" Ferron asked, directing the conversation to a new topic.

"Not me—it was eThorpe, actually. He will join us shortly." As Thorpe spoke, eThorpe's holoimage appeared, sitting in a chair in an empty slot at the table. He greeted President Katengi and Ferron and nodded to Kenred.

"My conversation with Leader Arclando was not very fruitful, although it went as I expected. There is no chance that he will step down from his dictatorship to establish a democratic government in Ceffid. I sensed no remorse for his launch of nuclear weapons. He was resentful and perhaps a bit frightened at how easily we thwarted his intentions. I am certain even now he is looking for a way to circumvent my nuclear weapons sanctions."

Katengi spoke up. "There is a robust resistance movement in Ceffid. I understand your reluctance to interfere in the affairs of planetary populations. It makes sense to me, but this might be an exception. You are involved with Amred. You thwarted their nuclear attack against us. Several of our people have joined you—even, I suspect, several from Ceffid. If you were to enable the resistance—not take up their cause, but just enable their victory by giving them a strategic advantage…" His voice trailed off. "…Ceffid and Amred together could integrate your technology into our cultures so that we, as Arcans, could become part of the Federation."

Ferron was surprised at the president's audacity, but recognized this as an example of why he was such an outstanding leader. *If Thorpe takes him up on his proposal,* he thought, *there's a chance Ceffid can throw off its dictatorship. There's no downside to that.*

Phoenix Starship Andromeda—Hovering Invisibly in Nullspace Beyond Lodan, Jocara's & Kenred's Quarters

Kenred was unsure why Thorpe had asked him to join the discussion with President Katengi and Director Ferron. *And if me, why not Jocara, too? I think I was on display as his Amred advisor… or is that Arcan advisor? Thorpe has full confidence in Jocara, but perhaps he thinks President Katengi does not, even after her heroic confrontation in the Leader's office. Things are not always what they seem.* His scales rippled multiple colors as he walked to the room he and Jocara shared.

Once inside the room, Kenred nuzzled Jocara's snout and dropped into a chair, flipping his tail to one side, his scales rippling pale lavender.

"I think the offworlders are going to help the Ceffid resistance," he said. "President Katengi made a powerful argument, and I think Thorpe accepted it. I don't know how they will do it, but I think you and I will be involved."

They sat for a while quietly. Then Kenred asked, "Do you know who Spajo Boszut is?"

"Not really."

"He's the Ceffid who organized the underground resistance movement. I think Thorpe will find a way to assist his overthrow of Arclando. You and I will probably play a role."

"That swamp lizard tried to kill me," Jocara said, her scales rippling orange. "I'll be happy to help get rid of him."

CHAPTER NINE

***Phoenix Starship Andromeda*—Hovering Invisibly in Nullspace Beyond Lodan, Comm Center**

Kenred had met Dale Ryan several times, but didn't really know him. He knew Dale was part of the original team, and he had a long-standing relationship with Daphne and Kimberly. Kenred didn't understand that, because such a relationship was entirely foreign to his species. Even the relationship between the females, Daphne and Kimberly, was absent from his species.

Now, Kenred was assigned with Dale to locate the Ceffid partisan leader, Spajo Boszut. Dale was an electronics guy who had designed the original matrixes that the uploads used. They needed to develop a method of tapping into Ceffid optical communications—not just government, but all communications. Ceffid had Central Dispatch, a huge electronic and optical complex that received all comms and dispatched them to their destination along branching trunks. The only place one could access all communications was at Central

Dispatch. The government routinely tapped into private comms there to maintain control over everything throughout Ceffid.

Dale's idea was to locate the endpoint of an optical branch, tap into it, and insert an optical tensor. The tensor would traverse back to Central Dispatch, where it would set up a filter that could identify any desired communication.

Kenred grabbed Jocara, and they entered the hangar bay by portal. They mounted the ramp to Kenred's assigned M-Class, *PS Neil Armstrong*, and settled at the control console. "We're going to a spot above this village," Kenred said, pointing to a location on the holoscreen. "We'll remain in a nullspace loop except to launch a drone."

Kenred gave the AI the coordinates, and moments later, *Armstrong* hovered a hundred kilometers above the village.

"Make sure the hyper-disk is on the drone and launch it," Kenred told Jocara, while checking for a second disk in his pocket that would connect him to Dale.

Jocara guided the drone down to a wooded area just outside the village. Then she assumed control of the spacecraft, and Kenred activated the hyper-disk and stepped through to the wooded area outside the village.

"Okay, Dale, I'm on the ground," Kenred signaled. "I'm going into town to find the local comms terminal. I'll activate the hyper-disk to *Andromeda's* Comm Center as soon as I arrive and know I can operate for a while without bring disturbed."

Physically, Kenred looked like any other Ceffidian, although his clothing differed from the locals. *Hopefully,* he thought, *I can pass myself off as an official.*

He walked to the village center and located the comms terminal, a low, squat building that obviously was designed for equipment, not lizards on a regular basis. The building front was emblazoned with the government's OptiComm logo—a circle with a mouth and several trailing optical cables. A low door on the side granted access, if you had the key. The lock was a simple mechanical device that Kenred opened with one try, using an L-shaped tool from a lock-picking set he had brought along for just this purpose.

He glanced around, saw no one, and entered, locking the door behind him. Kenred activated the hyper-disk, and Dale entered the room carrying eDale's matrix. Dale had already made an appropriate adaptor. He plugged it into the matrix.

"Everybody ready?" Dale asked and connected the matrix to the optical comms terminal.

✳

eDale moved through the adaptor into the Ceffid optical termination unit. There are only so many ways you can terminate an optical signal. This setup, while not entirely familiar, was close enough that he found his way quickly to the central processor. From there, he followed the data stream back through increasingly large fiber bundles until he arrived at Central Dispatch, somewhere in the capital city, Ceffidia. Before he had departed *Andromeda*, eDale had structured a tensor that would filter all comms, isolate any originating from or directed to Boszut, trace their origin, and redirect a copy to the coastal village.

eDale returned and set up a Link through the portal directly to *Andromeda's* Comm Center. Then he exited the Ceffid optical termination unit into his matrix. Dale and Kenred passed through the portal to the Comm Center, and reduced the portal inside the OptiComm so it accommodated the Link but was otherwise invisible.

Kenred returned to *Armstrong*, and he and Jocara returned to *Andromeda*. They both joined Dale in Comm Center.

"Now all we do," Dale said with a hint of smugness, "is wait for Spajo Boszut to call."

✳

Several hours later, the coastal village Link announced an origin location for a short, encrypted call from Boszut. The AI quickly decoded the message. Although it was a routine dispatch, Dale now had a destination for an introductory message and an algorithm for their encryption protocol. He routed the message through a dozen internal transfer stations so that tracing the message's origin would be impossible.

"I am Kenred Zlaxiz, SPC Astronaut from Amred, partnered with Astronaut Jocara Porovik from Ceffid. We know who you are and what you are doing. We strongly support your activities and want to help. I wish to meet with you to discuss how we can assist. Please meet me here at one of the following days and times." Dale listed the hyper-disk location coordinates outside the coastal village and several successive days and times. "I will be at this location for five minutes each day and time listed until we make contact. I will understand any precautions you choose to take to protect yourself and your movement. Do not reply to this message. Just show up at one of the days and times listed."

Ceffid Coastal Village—Ceffid, Planet Arcan

Kenred stepped through the portal at the Ceffid coastal village on the first designated day and time. No one was visible, and no one arrived within the five-minute window.

Back in the Comm Center, Kenred told Dale, "I saw nobody, but if I were he, I would have been out of sight, observing."

"Do you think he saw you pass through the portal?"

"Don't know, but if he saw me, he likely thought he had just missed me during his first scan. Let's see what happens this afternoon."

The next time slot was three hours later, in the early afternoon. Kenred passed through the portal, waited five minutes, and returned.

"Nothing," Kenred said, "but I felt him watching."

"You guys have some telepathic sense we don't know about?" Dale asked, his eyes twinkling.

"Gotta keep some things to ourselves," Kenred answered, his scales rippling pale blue at the humorous exchange. "Next one's tomorrow morning. Perhaps he'll show then."

Rain was falling the following morning as Kenred stepped through the portal.

"Stop right there!" a male voice commanded. "I've got you covered."

The bushes parted as an Arcan pushed through to face Kenred, weapon in hand. He was early middle age, Kenred's height, with a better muscled body and stronger, thicker tail.

"Are you Kenred Zlaxiz?" the stranger asked.

"I am…and you are Spajo Boszut?"

"I am not, but I will take you to him." The stranger tossed Kenred a plastic poncho. "Put this on," he said. "It'll keep you dry." He tucked his weapon inside his poncho and started trudging through the woods. "We have a safe house in the village."

Twenty minutes later, the partisan walked to the back door of a house and knocked with a security pattern. The door opened partly, the partisan gave a password, and they entered a room that Kenred recognized as a simple kitchen. The partisan led him through a door into a larger sitting room. An Arcan came to his feet. He was somewhat shorter than Kenred, of medium build and tall, with rugged facial features that told a tale of hardship and sacrifice. He held out both hands in the traditional Arcan greeting. He gripped Kenred's hands.

"You must be Astronaut Kenred Zlaxiz…I am Spajo Boszut. We partisans operate without titles." He motioned to a couch. "So, you found me, and I couldn't trace your message. You must have some pretty sophisticated technology."

"It's a long, complicated story, Mr. Boszut, and I need to tell you all of it."

"Spajo, please, call me Spajo, and I'll call you Kenred, yes?"

They looked at each other with wide open, blinking eyes.

Kenred started with their circum-Lodan excursion, and related everything that had happened since.

"So, these offworlders of yours could dispose of Arclando with virtually no effort, but they won't do that. Why?"

"Any way I answer you will be just my opinion. They are a private venture, not subject to any government rules, except for those they impose on themselves. They see interference with other sapient species as a negative, although they are happy to expose another species to their technology and invite a partnership where one is possible. Obviously, they cannot do this for a stone age culture, but are happy to do so with us. They don't want to give one nation an advantage over its neighbors that it does not already have, but they hate dictatorships like Leader Arclando.

"I'm here to offer you access to technology that should enable you to overcome the Arclando dictatorship quickly. If you do this successfully and establish a representative government, the offworlders will be happy to include Ceffid in their cooperative technology plans."

"What kind of technology?"

"Three things. The offworlders have developed a spread spectrum communication technology that is undetectable, even by them. There is no way to track the sender or receiver. As much as possible, the offworlders want to avoid bloodshed. I already told them you were not interested in killing a large number of your countryfolk. They have a personal EMD weapon— Electro-Muscular-Disruptor. It is adjustable from a simple, powerful shock to a killing charge with an accurate range of a hundred meters. It gives your people the opportunity to take down opponents without taking them out.

"The lizard who met me at the rendezvous point never mentioned it, but I'm sure he wondered how I got there. This is perhaps the most important technology the offworlders are willing to give you. You do not have the background to understand the underlying science or engineering, so I will simply describe it to you. We call it a portal. It opens a shortcut between any two points. For instance, I stepped from the starship through a door to the rendezvous point. It's a bit like putting two spots on a piece of paper and drawing a line between them. That represents the normal path you would have to take to get from one point to the other."

He bent the paper, so the two dots touched each other.

"The portal makes this happen."

He displayed a hyper-disk.

"We call this a hyper-disk. It is one-half of a portal. We call the other half the *Locus*. A Locus must have a significant power supply at hand, and it takes up about the same space as a small suitcase. Rubbing the dull side of the hyper-disk opens a portal to the Locus. The portal can also be activated, shut down, or recalled at the Locus. The power draw is a function of the distance between Locus and hyper-disk and the size of the portal."

"To say I am astonished would be a great understatement," Boszut said, his scales rippling yellow. "The offworlders are willing to make these things available to the resistance?"

"They are," Kenred said.

"How can we possibly power the portals? Arclando's security forces would find us immediately if we were to make a large power draw."

"That's one of the beauties of portals," Kenred said, eyes wide open and blinking. "They will set up a power portal to any spot you wish, or even to numerous locations. These portals are nearly microscopic, and they supply unlimited power. You can tap into them and disappear entirely from the electrical grid. With secure comms and no power draw, you'll disappear, and can take over with the least possible bloodshed and disruption."

"In my experience, when something seems too good to be true, it usually is," Boszut said. "I want to meet these offworlders."

"Their leader, Thorpe, said you would want to." Kenred opened his eyes. "When would you like to visit them?"

"How about now? I presume you have the appropriate hyper-disk with you."

"I do," Kenred said, "but first, put this on." He handed Boszut a wrist Link. "This is a communication device that we all carry internally. This unit will let you communicate with me, Dale, whom you will meet shortly, and the captain. When it is fully activated, you can communicate with anyone on *Andromeda* and access its complete knowledge database."

Kenred showed him how to use the Link.

Phoenix Starship Andromeda—Hovering Invisibly in Nullspace Beyond Lodan, Thorpe's Office

Kenred and Boszut stepped through the portal into Thorpe's office. Thorpe sat at his desk and Dale occupied an easy chair facing Thorpe's right.

"Thorpe, Dale," Kenred said, speaking the Ceffid language, "this is Spajo Boszut, leader of the Ceffid resistance." He turned to Boszut. "Spajo, please meet my captain, Thorpe, and Dr. Dale Ryan, Senior Research Scientist, and *Andromeda's* Comms Officer."

Boszut held his hands together in front of him and said, "I am honored to meet you. Kenred told me about your portals, and I know I just stepped through one, but I really do not know where I am or how I got here." He opened his eyes wide, the Arcan equivalent of a Human smile.

"Please sit," Thorpe said, pointing to the couch. "It's not ideal for your anatomy, so use the cushions as necessary to get comfortable."

Kenred flipped his tail to one side and placed a cushion under himself. Boszut watched and then did the same.

"Tell me about your organization," Thorpe said.

"I'm sure you already know about Leader Arclando. He is a dictator of the worst kind. He came to power when I was young by overthrowing the current weak government. His army of storm troopers invaded every branch of government, killed all the supervisory people, and he installed his own lackeys. He rules with a harsh, brutal hand, and anyone who opposes him is summarily executed. I head a surreptitious like-minded group that wants to overthrow Arclando and his cohorts, and install a representative form of government like Amred. We live in the shadows with virtually no access to communications and weapons. We grow larger every day, but until you came along, we could not see our way clear to overcoming Arclando without massive loss of life on our side. My people have been willing to make that sacrifice, but what you offer may make that unnecessary." Boszut's scales rippled lavender.

"Dale and Kenred will work with you to get things set up. The spread spectrum comm system will require a swarm of mini-satellites in LEO. Dale will take care of that. Each of your people will need an earwig…"

"A what?" Boszut interrupted.

"A small earpiece that fits entirely inside your ear canal," Kenred told him. "Short of actually examining the inside of your ear canal, Arclando's people cannot detect it. The earwig will respond to whispered voice commands, and yet it does not hinder normal hearing."

"Okay, thanks."

Thorpe continued. "Kenred will supply the earwigs. Just let him know how many." He stopped and cleared his throat.

That was a Human gesture that Kenred still did not entirely understand. He knew the physiological function, but he had learned that Humans also used this to pause a monologue, perhaps to gather a thought.

"This brings us to EMD weapons. I know you have projectile weapons, some that function well over long distances. Unfortunately, they are noisy and messy. An EMD weapon will take down any living thing out to at least a hundred meters with no permanent damage to the target, unless you choose to inflict serious damage or death. The moving charge has no visible path, so the lizard using it can remain concealed. Dale will supply you with as many as you need. You can replace the charge unit with a fresh one any time. The charge units can be recharged as a batch in a recharger we will supply. The charge is good for five hundred medium shots. Dale will also supply you with extra charge units and chargers. Any attempt to dismantle an EMD weapon or look inside with x-ray will fuse the mechanism solid. This will keep them out of Arclando's hands." Thorpe smiled broadly at Boszut.

Boszut turned to Kenred, silently questioning.

"That," Kenred said, referring to Thorpe's smile, "is the Human equivalent of a smile." He opened his eyes wide, and Boszut reciprocated.

"The more time you spend with us," Thorpe said, "the more natural our expressions will seem. Since I have gotten to know Jocara and Kenred, I understand their expressions intuitively. Your changing scale colors," he added with a grin, "help a lot."

Thorpe shifted position in his chair. "Let's talk portals," he said. He turned to Boszut. "You experienced a portal when you came here. We use them everywhere in our daily lives. Portals bring hot and cold water to our sinks and carry away the wastewater—no pipes. Portals deliver electricity to wherever we need it—no wires. Portals supply cool or warm air, so we don't have piped-in air conditioning or heating. This starship is five klicks across and has two very different sides—a cityscape and a pastoral landscape. While it is possible to walk to any destination on either side, typically, crew members go to their destinations by portal.

"I believe if you and your resistance members can move anywhere in Ceffid quickly and safely, you are more likely to prevail. Distributing portals across a wide matrix is complicated and impractical. If we establish a hub somewhere in Ceffid, there is always the chance that Arclando's people will find it. Here is what I propose. We will establish a hub on *Andromeda*. All your Locuses will reside in the hub. You can establish as many portals as you need with hyper-disks. Every portal transit by your people will transit through the hub. Can you give me an estimate of how many portals you will need?"

"That's a difficult request," Boszut answered. "I'm not sure how to answer."

"I need a number, Spajo. You are the best lizard to give me that number. We can always add to it later, but I need something to start with."

"Okay—a hundred. That's a large number, but we…"

Thorpe cut him off. "I don't need an explanation, Spajo, just your estimate of what you think you might need." He smiled broadly again.

*

"Thorpe," Kenred said tentatively, "may I bring up E-disks and internal Links?"

Thorpe sat quietly for several seconds. "Do you think it wise?" he asked Kenred.

"Yes, Sir, I do. It will cement the relationship."

Thorpe turned to Boszut again. "Kenred asked me to discuss another topic with you." He turned toward Kenred. "Show him your E-disk."

Kenred pulled out his E-disk and handed it to Boszut. "Just look—don't depress anything."

Thorpe continued. "You are holding an E-disk, short for Emergency-disk. It senses the immediate environment of the holder, you. Should there be a significant change in your environment, a drop in pressure, sudden heat or cold, submersion in water, for example, the E-disk will transport you directly to our central hub, no matter where you are or where *Andromeda* is, so long as you are within range. Furthermore, you can purposefully activate it to take you away from any threatening situation. Let's demonstrate." He handed his E-disk to Kenred. "Kenred, please activate the E-disk and wait for Spajo."

Kenred activated his E-disk and found himself standing in *Andromeda's* Central Hub. A moment later, Boszut joined him, his face registering astonishment, his scales rippling yellow.

"Are you alright?" Kenred asked.

Boszut patted himself all over, opened his eyes and blinked them, and said, "I think so. What happened?"

"I am guessing Thorpe instructed you to press the activator on that E-disk, and I'm assuming you did."

"That's about it," Boszut said.

Kenred pointed to a door labeled *Thorpe*. "Let's return to his office."

They passed through the door into Thorpe's office that they had just vacated.

"A lizard could get used to this," Boszut said, blinking his open eyes.

They took their seats, and Kenred handed the E-disk back to Thorpe and accepted his from Boszut.

"Every one of our crew carries an E-disk," Thorpe said, "and we have supplied some of Amred's senior people with them as well." Thorpe held up his E-disk. "The E-disk has another function I want to tell you about." He leaned back in his chair. "I see Kenred fitted you with a Link. He probably told you we all carry a similar unit integrated into our bodies. One of its functions—and yours does not have this function right now—is to maintain a real-time digital backup of the wearer."

Boszut's scales started to ripple in various colors, indicating his uncertainty.

"I know this is a foreign concept to you, Spajo, but we developed the ability to upload anyone to a digital version, a backup if you will. We also learned to generate a new body from an individual's sequenced DNA and microbiome and download the digital version into that body." Thorpe stopped talking.

Kenred could almost hear Boszut's mental gears turning.

"Let me see if I understand you, please," Boszut said. "You create a continuous, real-time digital backup of everyone, and then…and then…" He looked at Kenred. "If you die, you are rejuvenated. Did I get that right?"

"In a manner of speaking," Kenred answered.

"So, if I have a Link and one of those," pointing to Kenred's E-disk, "if I am killed, I get whisked back to *Andromeda*, where my digital backup is downloaded into a newly created body?"

"Close enough," Kenred said. "You connected the dots rather quickly."

"That's why I lead the resistance and not someone else." Boszut looked around the room at Thorpe, Dale, and Kenred. "So, you guys are immortal!"

"In a manner of speaking," Thorpe said, "so long as we are in range of *Andromeda*. Our E-disks sense our physical condition. If one of us is seriously injured or killed, we are whisked to the Rejuvenation Lab, where the staff decides to repair or replace. It makes no difference from your perspective."

Boszut took a deep breath that ended with a sigh. "If I undergo that treatment, I will be immortal. What happens when you leave?"

"You lose your immortality," Thorpe said.

"Can we do the backup thing without the internal Link?" Boszut asked.

"We will need a sample of your DNA and make a onetime recording of your essence. After that, your Link will keep it updated. We won't need your microbiome, because we already have the Arcan microbiome in our files."

"This is a lot to process," Boszut said, scales rippling multiple colors. "You hardly know me, and you are offering me immortality."

"Not immortality so much as rejuvenation while you are using our help to overthrow Arclando. We'll readdress the topic when this is all over." Thorpe came to his feet. "Dale will take you to Medical for the DNA sample, and then you three will work out the details for our assistance."

Resistance Headquarters—Ceffid, Planet Arcan

Resistance headquarters was in a nondescript house in the capital city Ceffidia's suburbs. A resistance family actually lived there. An underground passageway provided member access. They entered the tunnel through a public restroom in a small park near the house.

Boszut returned to the coastal village safe house by portal. He carried his E-disk and a hyper-disk that connected to the Ceffid Hub on *Andromeda*. He briefed the resistance member at the safe house on portals and the new comm system, and gave him a dozen earwigs to distribute to members as they passed through.

Boszut made his way to Ceffidia. He avoided public transportation by hitching rides with a string of his colleagues. His final driver dropped him off at the park near headquarters. He had changed into running togs and jogged a lap around the park before entering the restroom. A full-length mirror responded to his triggering a hidden latch and opened inward. He stepped through and closed the mirror door behind him. Five minutes later, he climbed up through a floor hatch into the basement of his Ceffidia headquarters.

Boszut pulled out his hyper-disk and activated it. A moment later, Kenred and Dale stepped into his basement.

"I see you made it safely," Kenred said, scales rippling lavender. They gripped hands, and then Boszut took both Dale's hands in his in the traditional Arcan greeting.

"We are in the basement of a Ceffidia house several klicks from city center where Arclando has his headquarters. I keep a low profile and run resistance activities from here. I want to bring several dozen hyper-disks and a thousand earwigs here so my people can distribute them throughout the country. Once my people are familiar with portals and the new comms, we'll plan the next stage."

In two weeks, 100 hyper-disks sat in secure locations. Most resistance members could use the portals several times. People were getting used to entering a portal to the Ceffid Hub on *Andromeda*, and then passing through the destination portal. Everyone wore earwigs. Programming them was effortless. Tell your earwig your name—that was it. Call anyone by saying their name, or by saying the destination name—*Headquarters,* for example. Earwigs became ubiquitous within a few days of their introduction. Portals took somewhat longer.

Within three weeks, Boszut was ready for the next stage.

✳

"We are ready to receive the EMD weapons," Boszut told Dale by Link. "Can you send twelve weapons to each portal, along with seventy charge units and one charger? This will give each lizard carrying the weapon three full reloads, with the ability to replace the three charges and the operational load at one time."

"Do you have people standing by at each portal?" Dale asked.

"I do."

"Okay, we'll start passing them through in five minutes."

The guns were small, easily concealable, fit the Arcan hand perfectly, and were accurate out to 100 meters on stun or kill. Boszut tucked one under his belt and slipped three charges into his pockets. Kenred stood beside him.

"This will make a big difference," Kenred said.

"More than that," Boszut said, "it will give us the victory."

✳

Boszut called an online meeting with his lieutenants and Thorpe. Since holoimage projection was not available with the spread spectrum system, his people presented themselves audibly. He invited Kenred to be there in person, and Thorpe's holoimage joined them.

"The illusion of your presence is quite amazing," Boszut said to Thorpe.

"It's a technology we have developed for over a century, now," Thorpe said.

"Okay, Lizards," Boszut said, "we're going to pull off a remarkable subterfuge in which each of you will play a role. If we pull this off successfully, I expect the Arclando regime to fall.

"I want each of you to understand your role thoroughly. Should your part of this plan go awry, know your exit strategy implicitly and don't hesitate. We'll mop up those elements afterward."

Boszut then laid out the details of his plan and issued specific assignments to each lieutenant. When he finished, he said, "I'll give you a week to familiarize yourselves with the details and brief your people. Then I will set up my meeting with Arclando and will inform you of the exact date and time. You will need to have your piece of the plan in place and ready to go then. Should something go wrong at my end, enter a holding pattern as detailed in your instructions. If your judgment tells you to implement your exit strategy, do so—don't wait for instructions. If, for any reason, I cannot communicate with you, Astronaut Kenred Zlaxiz will be my spokeslizard. Follow his orders as if I were giving them.

"The offworlders have given us the chance of a lifetime. We're going to take it, and we're going to take back our country!"

CHAPTER TEN

Ceffid Leader Bopr Arclando's Office—Ceffidia, Ceffid, Planet Arcan

Resistance leader Spajo Boszut placed a regular call from his Ceffidia headquarters to Leader Bopr Arclando's offices. As received by Arclando, however, the call appeared to come from a small village in a remote corner of Ceffid, thanks to Dale's manipulation of the Ceffid communication system with optical tensors he had inserted into their system.

"This is Spajo Boszut," the resistance leader said, knowing that Arclando's comm people would initiate an immediate trace. He wanted the trace to locate the remote village. By the time secret police arrived there, he would have long since implemented the next step in his plan. "Please connect me with the Leader," he said.

Had any other caller made this request, Boszut was certain he would have been disconnected and perhaps traced and punished. He waited for several minutes while the wheels of dictatorial bureaucracy turned. Finally, Boszut heard a click.

"This is Leader Arclando. You are resistance leader Spajo Boszut, I presume." Silence filled the line for about thirty seconds. "Why have you called me?"

"I want to turn myself in," Boszut said matter-of-factly.

"You what?"

Boszut didn't answer that. Instead, he said, "But I have conditions."

"Conditions…?" Arclando's voice rose a notch.

"Let me explain, Sir."

"Conditions…what do you mean, conditions?" Arclando was close to shouting.

"I will turn myself in, Sir, and you can deal with me as you wish, but you must grant amnesty to every other resistance member."

"What?"

"And this amnesty must be completely public and without conditions of any kind."

"Why would you do this?"

"There has been too much fighting and dying—too much suffering. My people are tired of running and hiding. They want to settle down and raise their families. It's what they want, and the only way it can happen is if I take myself out of the equation."

"What if I say *no*, and make an all-out effort to capture and kill you all?"

"You can't do that, Leader Arclando. You are not strong enough. You can keep going like you are, and a lot of us will die, but so will your people. I am offering a much better solution. If we can make this happen, everybody wins."

"Except you," Arclando snarled.

"Except me, and I'm willing to make the sacrifice for my people," Boszut said.

"Alright," Arclando growled. "I accept your offer." Boszut could hear him hissing at the other end of the line. "Call me back in two days to work out the details."

✳

Boszut called Thorpe. "Arclando accepted the deal. I call him back in two days to formalize the arrangements."

"We follow the plan," Thorpe said. "Can you join me in my office for a few minutes? You need to meet someone."

Boszut passed through the Ceffid Hub into Thorpe's office. eThorpe's holoimage was present, apparently sitting in an easy chair.

"Spajo, this is eThorpe. He is a digital copy of my upload. The whole thing is a bit complicated, but think of eThorpe as an independent digital individual."

Boszut clasped his hands together and greeted eThorpe. The holoimage reciprocated.

"Arclando and I have already had a run-in," eThorpe said. "I am very much looking forward to your encounter." He gestured to the couch. "Please sit and let's walk through our plan."

✳

Two days later, Boszut placed another untraceable call to Arclando. Following a predictable wait, Arclando spoke.

"This is Leader Bopr Arclando. You are Spajo Boszut, I presume."

"Leader Arclando, I am prepared to present myself to you personally under the following conditions. First, I will present myself unarmed at the Capitol entrance, where I expect to be searched for weapons. Other than weapons, the contents of my pockets will be left alone. Second, when your security people announce my arrival, you will publicly proclaim amnesty for all resistance members without conditions. Third, your security people will escort me to your office, but will not touch me or manhandle me in any way. Fourth, when I enter your office, I will surrender to you personally, signaling the end of the resistance.

"Are these terms acceptable to you, Sir?"

For the plan to work, Boszut had to enter Arclando's office unshackled with access to the E-disk and hyper-disk sewn inside his clothing.

Following a pause, Arclando said, "I accept your terms."

Boszut drew a deep breath. "I will present myself at the Capitol in three days at noon."

✳

"I present myself in three days at noon at the Capitol," Boszut told Thorpe by Link. "I have someone with a hyper-disk at every significant Ceffidia government office and the main military stations. I will put EMD armed people in the hub and several people to direct traffic. Have I left anything out?"

"You've covered it. Mother calculated the odds for events when you enter Arclando's office. Mother says there is a fifteen percent chance he will talk with you, a ten percent chance he will shackle you, and a seventy-five percent chance he will kill you."

"What?"

"That's why you are wearing a Link and making a continuous backup. Here, I'll step in to maintain the status quo while we rejuvenate you and put you back in play."

"I guess I didn't really think my way through this," Boszut said with a hiss. "You're certain the rejuvenation process works?"

"I've been through it several times personally," Thorpe answered. "On the grand scale, we have done it several billion times back in the Solar System and here on *Andromeda*. You need not fear the process."

Boszut took a comfortable chair in the resistance headquarters and gave the matter some thought. I think I understand bravery. I have witnessed bravery in many of my lizards—several sacrificing their lives. I lead because my lizards see me as brave and are willing to follow. I never set out to be brave, I've only done what seemed necessary. Perhaps that's all bravery is—doing what has to be done. Thorpe says I have one hundred percent survival odds. It still seems like twenty-five percent to me, but I guess, he sighed deeply while his scales rippled light red, it's something I gotta do.

✳

On the appointed day and time, Boszut presented himself at the Capitol entrance. The building was a massive tiered concrete structure veneered with pale red sandstone. It gave the viewer a sense of permanent massive power. Arclando had it built in his first year as Leader. The entrance was thirty meters of bullet-proof glass with nine double glass doors that opened automatically upon approach. Tough-looking armed lizards guarded both sides of the glass entrance.

Boszut approached the glass doors with a confident stride, but feeling less certain inside than what he projected. He walked past the guards, through the door into the atrium, and stopped as two burly guards approached him.

"Hands where I can see them," one guard ordered.

Boszut complied. They searched him thoroughly.

"What's this," a guard asked, pointing to his wrist-mounted Link. "Just my watch," Boszut said.

"Fancy," the guard said. "Leading the resistance must pay well."

Two plain-clothed security people approached them. "We'll take him from here," one said.

The speaker led, the other followed. "Stay between us," the guard in front said. They didn't touch him.

Boszut remained between them with hands in his trouser pockets while he worked the specially designed small hyper-disk through a seam into his left hand. They passed two armed guards and entered a specially designated elevator, where his guards placed him between them against the back wall.

The elevator took them straight to the top level of the massive building. The wide doors, flanked by two armed guards, opened into Arclando's office. Two more armed guards occupied the corners behind Arclando's desk. As he crossed the threshold, Boszut activated the hyper-disk and dropped it through a hole in his pocket. It slid down his pants leg onto the lush carpet. Boszut flicked it under a chair with his toe, where its internal camouflage mechanism caused it to become nearly invisible. Its design allowed it to be activated without showing a portal until it received a command from the other end.

"So," said Arclando, "you are the infamous Spajo Boszut, the resistance leader who has plagued my life for so long." He gestured to his guards. "Shoot him!"

Phoenix Starship Andromeda—Hovering Invisibly in Nullspace Beyond Lodan, Rejuvenation Lab

Spajo Boszut opened his eyes and cautiously looked around. He distinctly remembered Arclando say, "Shoot him!" And now he lay here with no conscious perception of time passing between the two events. Doc Gregory Dobson hovered over him.

"Spajo…Spajo, can you hear me?" Dobson asked.

His scales flashing yellow with momentary irritation and then back to green, Boszut said, "I hear you, Doc, I hear you fine."

"Listen, Spajo, Thorpe and Kenred are here with me. We created your new body before you entered Arclando's office, because the odds were very much in favor of your getting shot. The moment you arrived here, we downloaded your essence into your new body."

"How long ago was I shot?"

"Three minutes," Thorpe said. "We need to return immediately to gain control of the situation. Follow me."

They stepped through a portal into Thorpe's office.

"How many armed guards are there?" Thorpe asked.

"Four. One on each side of the elevator doors and two in the opposite corners, behind Arclando's desk."

Thorpe handed him an EMD pistol set to stun and gave him instructions. "Can you do that?" Thorpe asked.

"Piece of cake," Boszut responded.

Ceffid Leader Bopr Arclando's Office—Ceffidia, Ceffid, Planet Arcan

Thorpe and Boszut walked to the portal side by side, weapons drawn.

"Activate," Thorpe said, giving the signal that opened the already activated portal. They walked through.

Boszut immediately dropped to the floor, taking out the corner guard as he fell. Then he twisted and took out the closest elevator guard. Out of the corner of his eye, he saw Thorpe do the same on his side. He sat up in time to see Arclando draw his sidearm. Boszut struck his chest with a bolt from his EMD, and the Leader dropped to the floor. It was over in fifteen seconds.

"Are you alright?" Thorpe asked.

"I am, but the Leader is down for the count." Boszut got to his feet. "I need to check the status of my people."

"Before that, you need to neutralize General Sudajos. Can you locate him?"

Boszut got on his new comm circuit. "This is Boszut. I have control of Arclando. I need to know the location of General Sudajos."

One of his lieutenants answered, "I've got him sedated in the Ops Center, along with most of his operational staff. We're three floors below you."

"Take him to the Ceffid Hub. Someone will meet you there with further instructions." On open circuit, Boszut said, "Give me your status by the numbers—*Okay* for accomplished, *Partial* for less than accomplished, and *Not* for failure."

He listened to their responses, checking them off on a mental list. He got ninety-five *Okays*, three *Partials*, and two *Nots*. The *Partials* were remote and involved one or more people escaping from the point of control. The *Nots* were at two southern military posts where the partisan made the operational decision to take no action because of what was happening at the post. None of the five incomplete operations affected the general operation. Boszut turned to Thorpe.

"We have operational control of the government and the military. The only things we don't control are the navy ships. That is one of the first things we will address."

Boszut sat down in Arclando's chair behind his desk and drew in a deep breath. *We've pulled it off,* he thought. *Ceffid is free, but we have to consolidate our victory.*

"Thorpe," Boszut said, "I need to speak with Dale. He can assist me to broadcast our accomplishment to the country."

Thorpe called Dale, who entered the office shortly thereafter.

"Congratulations, Buddy," Dale said to Boszut, "you did it!"

"Not *Buddy* anymore," Thorpe chuckled, "it's *Mr. President.*"

✳

It took about an hour before Dale returned to the president's office.

"We're ready to go, Mr. President."

"Knock it off, Dale. I'm your friend, Spajo, and that's what you'll call me unless protocol dictates something else for a specific situation." Boszut's scales rippled pale blue.

"Right…Spajo, but with you in that chair, things really have changed." Dale grinned at him. "These three cameras will record you live. My techs on *Andromeda* will select which image to broadcast at any moment. We have usurped Ceffid's optical broadcast and cable system. Your message will appear on every screen in the nation. Just tell me when you are ready to start."

Boszut had prepared for this moment ever since he joined the resistance as a young lizard barely out of his teens. He needed no prepared statement. He was ready to go.

Boszut placed his forearms on the desk, folded his hands, and nodded to Dale. Dale grinned and slashed his arm down.

"My fellow countrymen," Boszut began, "my name is Spajo Boszut. I have led the resistance movement in Ceffid for the past several years. This morning, my people seized control of Leader Arclando's government, his secret police, and the military. Bopr Arclando and General Garkid Sudajos, and other senior members of Arclando's government, are in custody awaiting trial. I have assumed the title of President, pending open and free elections we will hold as soon as possible. As part of that election, you will select representatives who will write a new constitution that will become the basis for law in our country. During the next few weeks, we will look closely at every part of our country, especially the police and courts. We will remove anyone not willing to swear allegiance to our new representative government. As citizens, please continue to obey the law and carry on your lives as you have. Thank you very much."

Although Boszut could not know it, in bars and taverns across the country, people lifted glasses toasting the new president, cheering, and wishing the new government well.

Boszut turned to Dale. "I need to address the military. Please adjust the broadcast so it includes only military receivers."

Shortly, Dale indicated the setup was ready and dropped his arm again. For military viewers, the broadcast would appear to have been continuous.

"Now I address the military, and specifically our navy warships. The resistance has assumed command of every aspect of the military. Every senior military position has either a senior resistance member in charge or a cooperating senior officer. Within twenty-four hours, every warship commanding officer must swear allegiance to Ceffid's new government or be relieved from command. Affirmation documents are being sent to you electronically. You must complete and return them by the deadline. When our new constitution is written, the military's role in our society will be fully spelled out. No matter what form it takes, one thing is certain. Elected civilians will control the military. In the meantime, carry on, but be sensitive to changes coming down the pike."

Capitol Building—Ceffidia, Ceffid, Planet Arcan

The assembly hall was spacious with tiered seating for a thousand people; every seat was occupied. A modified judge's courtroom bench dominated the platform that stretched the width of the hall. The Chief Judge's seat was raised above the other twelve seats, six on each side. A wood desktop ran the length of the bench. Each station, including the raised station of the Chief Judge, had a computer monitor and a microphone.

On the left side of the Judges' Bench, as seen from the bench, an enclosed witness stand of polished wood sat on the auditorium floor. A set of steps led to a waist-high door and a raised platform. The stand had a microphone, but no seating. The prosecutor's stand, opposite the witness stand, was similar, but had seating and a built-in desktop. Like the Judges' Bench, the prosecutor's desktop had a computer monitor and a microphone. In the center, on the floor in front of the Chief Judge's seat, stood the accused dock. Like the witness stand, it was polished wood with steps leading to an internal raised platform. Above a waist-high wall, bullet-proof glass enclosed the entire dock, including the top. The dock had a microphone, but no seating.

A hushed murmur rose from the seated crowd as it awaited the tribunal commencement. Spajo Boszut passed through the curtains stage left dressed in normal business attire and mounted the steps to the Chief Judge's seat. The crowd burst out in spontaneous applause. Boszut raised his hands.

"Thank you," he said, his voice amplified throughout the hall, "but please maintain a quiet, respectful attitude. I ask for no further outbursts or demonstrations of approval or disapproval. This is a solemn occasion that is being broadcast throughout the nation and recorded for posterity. Let history know that we, the people of Ceffid, gathered to administer fair and impartial justice to those individuals brought before this tribunal today and the days following."

Unobtrusive holocams strategically placed in the hall recorded the session. In every bar and tavern throughout Ceffid, Arcans crowded around video receivers to watch the proceedings. In every home that could afford a receiver, it was tuned in to the proceeding. Even in Amred, as many people as possible watched the tribunal proceedings. In *Andromeda's* main auditorium, a life-size holoimage of the proceedings played out live to a fascinated audience.

As Boszut took the Chief Judge's seat, twelve individuals wearing business attire approached the bench and took their seats. Boszut's six most senior lieutenants sat to his right. Six citizens chosen by lot from a pool of volunteers sat to his left. The resistance members would remain for the entire tribunal. The citizens would change out for each new defendant, so that as many volunteers as possible could participate as judges in the tribunal.

A side door opened, and the prosecutor crossed the floor to the prosecutor's stand. He was dressed in business attire and carried a sheaf of documents. Boszut called the tribunal to order.

"We are here to sit in judgment over senior members of the Arclando dictatorship, including several high-ranking military officers. In compliance with our nation's long legal tradition, except the time of Arclando's dictatorship, each accused will hear the charges, examine the evidence, listen to witnesses and may cross-examine, and may present impeaching witnesses and evidence. In the end, we thirteen judges will decide on the truth of each accusation and will impose sentence. There is no appeal of the verdict from this panel. Sentence will be carried out immediately." Boszut sat quietly following his presentation, hands folded on the desk in front of him. After a full minute, during which each judge assumed a similar stance, Boszut commenced the proceedings.

"Bring the accused Bopr Arclando to the dock."

A uniformed marshal brought the former dictator forward. The large Arcan held his shackled hands at his waist and shuffled because his feet were shackled with a short chain. He held his head high in arrogant disdain for the procedure. He mounted the steps to the dock and the waist-high door was locked behind him. Bullet-proof glass protected him on all sides. A quiet hissing rose from the crowd as Arclando took the dock. Boszut raised his hand to stop it.

The prosecutor, who was a former district judge widely known for his fairness and adherence to the law, began. "Bopr Arclando, you are accused of crimes against lizardkind, crimes against Arcan, crimes against Ceffid, high treason, sedition, rebellion, murder, extortion, bribery, and theft of public property and monies. Should other crimes be disclosed during this proceeding, they will be added to the indictment."

Boszut, as Chief Judge, asked, "How do you plead?"

Shouting into the mike, his scales bright orange, Arclando bellowed, "I am the rightful leader of Ceffid. I do not recognize the jurisdiction of this fool's tribunal. I demand to be released and returned to my rightful rule!" He slammed a fist into the glass barrier. The crowd hissed in response.

Boszut lifted a hand. "I enter a plea of not guilty on all counts for the defendant."

✳

The prosecutor meticulously laid out each count, supplying the tribunal with evidence and witnesses to corroborate every detail. When he called the first witness, Arclando hissed and bellowed, slammed his shackled fists against the glass, and threatened the witness, the witness's family, and even the witness's house lizard.

After the first intimidating outburst against a witness, Boszut said to Arclando, "You will be silent during a witness's testimony. You will refrain from threatening the witness or anyone else here. If you fail to comply, I will have you bound and gagged."

When Arclando verbally attacked the second witness, Boszut ordered him bound and gagged. Arclando was so large, however, that the marshals, who were resistance members, could not subdue him. Boszut ordered the senior marshal to stun Arclando at low power with his EMD. The marshal complied, and Arclando collapsed on the dock platform. The marshals bound his arms to his waist in addition to the shackles already around his wrists and tied each leg to an eyebolt in the dock floor. They stuffed a rubber ball into his mouth, held in place with a strap around his head. While this took place, several judges and audience members took short refreshment breaks.

As Arclando recovered from being stunned, he found himself virtually immobilized. He hissed and snarled and started banging his head against the thick glass. Boszut ordered the senior marshal to stun him a second time. Then he announced, "We'll take a thirty-minute recess while the marshals install further restraints in the dock."

Boszut called the senior marshal to his chair. "Install four eyebolts at waist level. Locate a strong collar. A good house lizard collar will suffice. Restrain his waist and neck four ways to the eyebolts. Move the mike so he can't reach it with any part of his body and make sure it is on. Then remove the gag and get out of the dock before he revives. And send an electrician to install a control switch for the dock mike on my desk."

At the end of the recess, Boszut called the tribunal to order. Arclando was just reviving. When he discovered his new restraints, he bellowed loudly and hissed fiercely. His scales roiled bright orange.

Boszut told him, "Your mike is muted, so we cannot hear you. If you quiet down, I'll turn on your mike so you can participate in the proceedings. If you insist on bellowing, I will keep your mike off, and the trial will proceed without your input. The choice is yours."

When the next witness took the stand, Boszut turned on Arclando's mike. He growled and hissed quietly, but not enough to disrupt the witness. Then the testimony got very specific. Arclando yelped, but when Boszut glanced directly at him, he quieted down, and glowered fiercely at the witness. The witness's scales turned red with fear, and he started stuttering.

"Let's take a fifteen-minute recess," Boszut ordered, "while we adjust the dock." He called the senior marshal. "Rotate the dock so the accused faces the prosecutor, and the witness can only see his back. Then anchor the dock so the accused cannot tip it over by rocking."

When the proceeding recommenced, the witness had composed himself and no longer felt intimidated by Arclando, since he could see only his back. The trial continued as the prosecutor presented each charge, went through each piece of evidence, and interviewed each witness. Arclando occasionally bellowed and hissed, but Boszut quickly muted his mike, and eventually, Arclando submitted to

Boszut's requirements. By the third week of the trial, Arclando asked that his restraints be removed, and promised to behave. Boszut removed the restraints to the sides and floor of the dock, but retained the hand and leg shackles. Arclando proved true to his word and remained docile during the final week of his trial.

On a sunny morning, the final witness answered the last question posed by a citizen judge about Arclando's embezzlement of public funds. The prosecutor closed the volume lying on the desk before him, and said, "If it please the Court, the prosecution rests."

A quiet buzz filled the hall. Boszut raised a hand and announced, "This tribunal is in recess for the rest of the day. We will reconvene tomorrow morning."

✻

Boszut and the other twelve judges spent the rest of the day and into the evening past midnight, comparing notes and discussing the matter.

The following morning, every tiered seat in the hall was occupied, and for the first time, Boszut allowed standing observers at the back of the hall. The low buzz filling the hall quieted as the twelve judges filed to their places at the bench. Then Boszut entered and took his place as Chief Judge. When the thirteen judges were seated and ready, two marshals escorted a shackled Arclando to the dock, where he was allowed to stand without further restraint.

Boszut opened a folder on the desk before him. He spoke quietly into the mike, "This tribunal is in session. In the matter of the People of Ceffid versus Bopr Arclando, on the first count, crimes against lizardkind, we find the defendant guilty. On the second count, crimes against Arcan, we find the defendant guilty. On the third count, crimes against Ceffid, we find the defendant guilty. On the fourth count, high treason, we find the defendant guilty. On the fifth count, sedition, we find the defendant guilty. On the sixth count, rebellion, we find the defendant guilty. On the seventh count, murder, we find the defendant guilty of four hundred thirty-nine instances of this count. On the eighth count, extortion, we find the defendant guilty of three hundred seventy-two instances of this count. On the ninth count, bribery, we find the defendant guilty of one thousand six hundred forty-four instances of this count. And on the tenth count of theft of public property and monies, we find the defendant guilty of ten thousand nine hundred seventy-eight instances of this count."

Boszut closed the folder and opened a second. "As to punishment in the matter of the People of Ceffid versus Bopr Arclando, for count ten, this court sentences the defendant to twenty years' incarceration plus return of all properties stolen and a tenfold restitution of monies taken. For count nine, this court sentences the defendant to twenty years' incarceration plus return of all properties received and a tenfold restitution of monies received. For count eight, this court sentences the defendant to twenty years' incarceration plus return of all properties and a tenfold restitution of monies extorted. For count six, this court sentences the defendant to incarceration for life. For count five, this court sentences the defendant to incarceration for life. For count seven, this court sentences the defendant to death by firing squad. For count four, this court sentences the defendant to death by firing squad. For count three, this court sentences the defendant to death by firing squad. For count two, this court sentences the defendant to death by firing squad. For count one, this court sentences the defendant to death by firing squad.

"Given the nature of these sentences, the defendant forfeits his entire estate to the Ceffid government, which will do everything in its power to reinstate the possessions of those affected by the defendant." Boszut closed the folder and looked directly at Arclando. "The sentence will be carried out forthwith!"

Arclando stood silently during reading of the verdicts and sentences. At the conclusion, he hung his head for several seconds and then bellowed loudly and fiercely. "This is a sham proceeding! You have no right to judge me or sentence me! I am the absolute ruler of Ceffid, and I will make you all pay for your transgressions against me!" He began pounding on the glass enclosure, finally cracking it in two places.

Boszut signaled the senior marshal, who stunned Arclando and trussed him to a gurney. The marshals rolled Arclando into an elevator that carried them to the courtyard that shared the top floor with the presidential offices. Under the watchful eyes of cameras broadcasting the event to the entire world and *Andromeda*, the marshals strapped Arclando to a frame in a corner of the courtyard. As Arclando awakened, a squad of rifle-bearing soldiers stood at attention, ten meters distant, facing him.

Boszut arrived, and facing Arclando, formally read the five death sentence counts. Arclando howled in anger and frustration as Boszut turned away and signaled the officer in charge of the firing squad.

In a single motion, the squad members shouldered their rifles and fired.

*

The trial for Chief Military Commander, General Garkid Sudajos, lasted two weeks. He was sentenced to death. Two other senior government officials and one high-ranking military officer also received death sentences after a week's trial. Fifty government officials and twenty senior military officers received life imprisonment following short trials. One hundred fifty government officials and fifty military officers received twenty-year sentences following their short trials. One thousand lower-level government people, secret police members, and judges received five to ten-year sentences following their trials.

It took six months, but the tribunal was done. While it was happening, resistance members built the infrastructure for national elections—first for the constitutional convention representatives. They wrote the constitution in two months and sent it out for confirmation to the various subunits of Ceffid. They quickly confirmed it.

In outline, the new constitution provided for an administrative division with president, vice-president, and law enforcement, a legislative division with a peoples' house and a senate representing the country subunits, and a judiciary to adjudicate personal matters, criminal matters, and to oversee legislation passed by the legislative division for compliance with the constitution.

With passage of the new constitution, the resistance members set up a national election for the various offices defined in the constitution. When the dust settled, Spajo Boszut was the newly elected president, backed by an enthusiastic legislature and senate, ready to establish Ceffid as a legitimate player on the Arcan world stage. All the Ceffid elected offices were for four years, limited to two terms. The constitution had provisions regulating how elections could be run. It was impossible for a wealthy individual to purchase an office for himself or for someone else. The playing field was as level as lizardly possible.

※

One of the first things Boszut did as president was to issue an executive order requiring all government agencies to divest themselves of any business assets or anything else that could be considered property, except for land on which government buildings stood and various things needed to run the agencies, such as vehicles, computers, weapons, etc. The properties were placed with several select committees whose job was to auction off the properties to private interests.

The constitution prohibited an income tax, and established a permanent value-added tax of ten percent on non-essential items. Food, rent, and other essential items were exempted from the tax. The tax was collected by businesses and submitted to the government monthly. The government was required to live within its income. The legislature was specifically prohibited from allocating funds the treasury did not have.

Government agencies were constitutionally self-funding, requiring fees for services they rendered. All non-constitutional government agencies and functions were up for renewal every five years. Legislators could not become judges, and judges could not become legislators.

Police and fire protection were local government functions, paid for by constitutionally limited local value-added taxes. Roads, utilities, sewer, and waste collection were regulated by local boards and contracted to private businesses.

Cross business labor unions were constitutionally prohibited. Labor for any individual business or corporation could organize a union and would receive board representation. There was no government subsidy of any business anywhere.

Basic schooling was mandatory, but all schools were privately run with curricula set by joint school-parent committees. All schools were paid for by a voucher system funded through local property taxes.

Phoenix Starship Andromeda—Hovering Invisibly in Nullspace Beyond Lodan, Thorpe's Office

Newly elected Ceffid President Spajo Boszut arrived by portal in Thorpe's office. Shortly after his arrival, Amred President Binecot Katengi and SPC Director Sudaro Ferron entered through another portal. Dale, Kenred, Jocara, and eThorpe were already there.

Thorpe smiled and said, "Thank you all for coming. I know you are busy, especially you, President Boszut, as you get your government up and running. I have two major topics I wish to discuss with you. The first centers on the Space Push Consortium." Thorpe passed a smile to each of his visitors.

"Since its inception, SPC has, in principle, been a joint effort between Amred and Ceffid. In reality, except for the loan of some personnel as astronauts, Ceffid has done nothing. Things should be different now. Speaking for myself and my starship colleagues, we have already shared a significant amount of technology with Amred. President Katengi has been reluctant to participate fully, and while I don't agree with him, I support his decision.

"Now that Ceffid has joined the civilized community of nations on Arcan, I want to offer Ceffid what I have already offered Amred. The thing is, I don't really want to deal with two independent governments. I am suggesting, therefore, that SPC, as a joint operation, take the lead in dealing with *Andromeda* and what we offer. I understand national independence. In no way am I suggesting that your nations merge. With Ceffid's new status, I think you both have more to gain by close cooperation than by any alternative."

"We are still privatizing our industries," Boszut said. "This will still take some time. Our firms will be at a disadvantage when competing with Amred businesses."

"Not so much as you might think," Ferron said. "SPC doesn't care who runs a business so much as how well do they run it. If a Ceffid firm can successfully bid on an SPC contract, that it is currently government owned makes no difference, especially since ownership will go private in the relatively near future."

"That works for me," Katengi said, "so long as the Ceffid firm is not receiving government subsidies."

"Those stopped when I assumed the interim presidency," Boszut said.

"Can we agree," Thorpe said, "that *Andromeda* will work through SPC?"

"There is the matter of The Geroptic Nation," Katengi said.

"Tell me about them," Thorpe asked.

"The Geroptic Nation is a closed theocratic society ruled by Prophet Dudengi Vrokhun. They worship the Great Dragon in the Sky—the sun. Their technology is borderline, almost nonexistent. They use wheels, steam engines, spinning and weaving mills, small printing presses, telegraph, and other borderline technology. Long distance transportation is by rail. Short distance and local transportation is donker-pulled carriages, donkerback, or on foot."

Kenred interrupted, "A donker is the Arcan equivalent of a Human horse." He blinked his wide-open eyes.

Katengi continued, "They have primitive smelters and produce a limited amount of copper, iron, and even steel, but they import their locomotives and rail cars, and their rails, from us. Their agriculture consists of small family farms organized into co-ops. In their schools, they teach *The Book of the Great Dragon*, which they believe was delivered to lizardkind by the Great Dragon, but was probably written by some long-forgotten prophet. They also teach basic arithmetic to facilitate mom and pop commerce and language skills to a level necessary to read and understand their *Holy Book*. They have a vast army that uses cutlass, spear, and bow and arrow—nothing more advanced. They have a navy of wind-driven ships with boiler assistance.

"The Prophet's stated goal is to subjugate Ceffid and Amred, bringing our peoples into the Great Dragon's lair."

"Is everyone at such a primitive level?" Thorpe wondered.

"Probably not," Katengi answered. "Prophet Vrokhun certainly has a broader, more sophisticated understanding of the world, as do some of his senior advisors. We have limited contact with them, even at the ambassador level. They tolerate one representative and a small staff. They must remain inside their compound unless escorted. They have no domestic help and cannot even purchase provisions locally."

"It seems a shame to allow an entire nation of people to be left behind as Amred and Ceffid move into the future," Thorpe said.

Boszut agreed, but kept his counsel for the time being. He was delighted with how things were going and didn't want to do or say anything that might hinder progress. In the long run, he was certain that The Geroptic Nation would pursue its stated goal. Under his leadership, Ceffid would be ready.

"We've gotten somewhat afield," Thorpe said, "so I want to address the second topic. My ten-thousand-member crew consists of Humans, Asterians, Oort, and two Arcans—Jocara and Kenred." He smiled at them both. "I want to offer Arcan one thousand berths aboard *Andromeda*. I want capable people—anything from pilots to chefs." He turned to Ferron. "That will be your job, Sudaro. Find me nine hundred ninety-eight qualified Arcans—and be sure to include ten fighter pilots."

PART TWO
THE GREAT DRAGON

CHAPTER ELEVEN

The Great Assembly Hall—Dragon Temple, Dragon City, The Geroptic Nation, Planet Arcan

Prophet Dudengi Vrokhun shifted position on his carved marble throne on a raised dais at one end of the Great Assembly Hall in the Dragon Temple at the center of Dragon City. Overhead, the splendid dome depicted in detailed relief the Great Dragon in conflict with Night, the Demon of Darkness. It reflected his own thoughts. He believed in the Great Dragon and His power over lizardkind, but the Dragon seemed trapped in His eternal path across the heavens— not a desirable characteristic of an omnipotent god. This conundrum had plagued him throughout his days as Prophet. Vrokhun would rather have been in his private quarters, comfortably ensconced in his personal overstuffed easy chair, reading a favorite poem from his collection of Geroptic poets.

Vrokhun pulled his attention back to the Hall and the report his Bishop of Foreign Affairs was reading. "Our embedded spies in Amred report that beings not of this world have visited Amred, bringing powerful gifts that will enable Amred to spread its godless heresies across our world. Our Ceffid spies report an internal uprising that has overturned the Arclando dictatorship. Ceffid now appears to be in league with Amred and may be sharing the gifts from the offworlders."

Why would the Great Dragon allow beings to transit his realm? Vrokhun asked himself. *Is the Great Dragon's power limited to just Arcan? Are there powers beyond the Great Dragon to which even He must submit Himself?* These were questions that needed study. Vrokhun scanned the Hall with its twelve-member council that advised him on virtually every decision he made. Each was a Bishop of the Order of the Great Dragon, wise in the ways of the Dragon and a capable administrator of his geographic sector of The Geroptic Nation. Vrokhun did not know the degree of true devotion his bishops had for the Great Dragon. Some, he had learned, were skeptics who claimed the trappings of religion in order to exercise the powers of their offices. That description fit him as well, but he had not yet faced his doubts squarely.

Vrokhun stood and raised his arms, his pale green, nearly translucent scales rippling a nearly invisible lavender. Each of the twelve bishops dropped to his knees reverently and placed his forehead to the floor. In a monotone voice, Vrokhun intoned the Great Dragon's blessing and then lifted his eyes to the overhead dome.

"The Great Dragon has spoken to me, telling me of wonders to come, and of his increased presence among us."

That should keep them thinking, Vrokhun said to himself as he lowered his arms and remained standing. "May the Dragon be with you," he said solemnly as the bishops came to their feet and departed the Hall.

General Nirurian Klarot's Office—Dragon City Army HQ, The Geroptic Nation, Planet Arcan

General Nirurian Klarot was a large Arcan, a head taller than most, with dark green scales and a thick tail. His snout was longer than usual, which gave him a fierce look, and he was heavily muscled. As the Prophet's Military Chief, he handled everything military in The Geroptic Nation.

Klarot sat at his desk in the Army Headquarters Building on the outskirts of Dragon City. It was a squat, heavy building without adornment. This was the day and time of his regular meeting with the Prophet. They alternated between meeting at the Temple and in his HQ. He was more comfortable meeting his country's leader in his own office away from the trappings of religious power at the Temple.

So far as Klarot could tell, the Prophet actually believed much of the nonsense the Temple put out, but no rational, educated lizard could possibly believe the sun was a god who determined the outcome of Arcan events. He had no illusions for himself. He displayed the superficial trappings of the Great Dragon. His troops would refuse to follow him otherwise. Other than that, however, in his personal life, he believed in himself. He told himself he was the captain of his ship, no matter the circumstances.

The Prophet's entourage arrived fashionably late in donker-pulled carriages. Prophet Dudengi Vrokhun passed Klarot's two levels of security without challenge and entered Klarot's outer office. His adjutant, a major, escorted the Prophet into Klarot's presence. Klarot came to his feet respectfully and offered the Prophet a seat.

They went through a few pleasantries that social intercourse demanded, and then the Prophet got down to business.

"General, what do you know about these offworlders that seem to have penetrated Amred society? Are they real? Do they pose a threat to us? What can we do about them?"

It was a typical Vrokhun question, or was it questions? Klarot had anticipated it.

"The offworlders are real, my Lord. They come from a relatively nearby star called Sol. They carry two other species on their vessel, one from a more distant star, called Aster, and the other from their own system. As beings considerably more advanced than even Amred or Ceffid, they certainly pose a potential threat to us, but have done nothing threatening. As you know, my Lord, getting accurate information out of Amred is difficult and from Ceffid nearly impossible. Since the Ceffid revolution, they are more transparent. As time passes, we will know much more."

Vrokhun took a deep breath, his nearly transparent scales showing light pink. "The Great Dragon does not want advanced technology to corrupt the Geroptic culture. Especially, advancements the offworlders bring will turn our people away from the true religion and their reliance on the Great Dragon. We must do everything in our power to prevent this."

Klarot maintained his facial expression while opening his eyes wide inwardly. The Prophet was a shrewd operator.

They continued their discussion for another hour, each presenting topics important to themselves. Then the Prophet came to his feet, signaling the end of the meeting. Klarot accompanied him to the door, telling him, "Go with the Dragon's peace."

General Nirurian Klarot's Comm Center—Dragon City Army HQ, The Geroptic Nation, Planet Arcan

Shortly following the Prophet's departure, a messenger brought Klarot an urgent message from his Comm Center. "We need you there right now, Sir!"

The Comm Center and its imported Amred equipment were a well-kept secret from the Prophet and virtually everyone else in The Geroptic Nation. It received its power from a bank of lead-acid batteries that were recharged with a Leyden jar that received its charge from an electrostatic generator in the same way the national telegraph system was powered. Klarot hurried down the corridor to the far end and turned right through a solid door into the Comm Center. This contained the most advanced equipment anywhere in The Geroptic Nation. Only Klarot and several of his most trusted underlings knew about or had access to this room.

"What is it?" he asked Lt. Teynal Dombit, the young officer in charge of the watch section.

"Listen to this, Sir." He turned on a recording device Klarot had smuggled in from Amred. "We received this a few minutes ago." The message was in Geroptic.

"General Nirurian Klarot, this is the Great Dragon in the Sky. I have important news for you and The Geroptic Nation, but first you and I must speak privately."

"What is this?" Klarot hissed. "Is this some kind of joke?"

Dombit's gaze dropped to the floor as his scales rippled red. "No, General Klarot. We received this message a few minutes ago. I immediately verified its authenticity—I mean, that it arrived from off-planet."

"Relax, Son, you did the right thing."

Dombit's scales changed to light red. Klarot chuckled inwardly. *The kid will do fine*, he thought, *but he needs to get control of his emotions.*

"Notify me if another message starts. I want to be here to respond."

Back at his desk, Klarot analyzed the situation. *The signal is from off planet. I don't think the offworlders working with Amred and Ceffid did this. My spies tell me this kind of prank is not their style. But Dombit insists it's from off planet. Boszut and his people in Ceffid or Katengi and his SPC organization, they have a bunch of hotshot pilots, and this kind of tomfoolery is something they might pull off.*

He telegraphed one of his operatives inside SPC: "I've received a radio message from the Great Dragon in the Sky. Find out if this is a prank by some SPC pilots."

Several hours later, he received a response. "They think it's hilarious and wish they had thought of it, but they didn't do it."

With no further comms from the "Dragon," Klarot sat at his desk, musing. *On Arcan we have three major groups—Amred, Ceffid, and The Geroptic Nation. We have our own goals, sometimes we work together—more often we go our own ways. Why would the offworlders be any different? On the starship they have hidden, they are divided between three races. They have a large crew—who knows how many factions divide them? What about their home worlds? My spies tell me that these offworlders do not represent their home systems, just themselves. Could there be others out there? We Arcans worked together to keep our existence hidden from the rest of the galaxy. That has turned out to be a colossal failure. What if another group from one of their systems followed them here, a rival group?*

A messenger interrupted his musings. "General, the Great Dragon is calling."

Obviously, the lieutenant stayed on past his watch to handle things, Klarot thought as he rose and left himself a quick note to give Dombit a written commendation. He hurried down the hall to Comms. As he entered the room, he heard Dombit say over the circuit, "Stand by, Great Dragon, General Klarot is here."

"This is General Nirurian Klarot, head of The Geroptic Nation Military. With whom am I speaking?"

"This is the Great Dragon in the Sky speaking directly with you, General Klarot, through the magic of radio." He spoke an educated Geroptic, but it had a slightly odd inflection. He was to learn later it was an AI generated translation.

"Cut the bullshit! We both know you are…" Klarot tossed a quick mental coin, "…an offworlder from the Solar System. We Geroptics are a religious people, but we are not stupid."

In his peripheral vision, Klarot watched Dombit do a double take. He could imagine what the young officer was thinking, but he didn't have time to dwell on it.

"Good guess, General Klarot. I come from the Solar System, just like Thorpe, Captain of *Andromeda*. The big difference is, I come offering you my assistance. I am Isidor Orlov. I head Udachny Enterprises, the third largest enterprise in the Solar System. I have learned that The Geroptic Nation is well behind Amred and Ceffid in technology. I can fix that in exchange for exclusive access to your markets. I know your manufacturing capability falls woefully short of the rest of Arcan. I can fix that, too. And your military—you have no modern weapons, no navy to speak of, no air force. We can address these together."

"I am interested," Klarot said. "You should know that Prophet Dudengi Vrokhun is The Geroptic Nation Head of State. I do not know his inner thoughts, but outwardly, he believes in the Great Dragon in the Sky's existence. I think he has his doubts and knows more than he lets on about the real world. But he rules his theocracy with an iron hand."

"Does he know about your communication capabilities?"

"He suspects, but doesn't know, at least not officially. I tell him what he needs to know to rule. I handle the infrastructure."

Klarot turned to look at Dombit. His youthful face was ashen. He clenched his fists. His scales rippled light red and orange.

"Is anything the matter, Lieutenant?"

"You just blasphemed the Great Dragon and mocked the Prophet." Dombit's scales went to deep red. He was badly frightened and stepped back away from Klarot.

Klarot chuckled. "Has anything happened to me? Are you expecting a lightning bolt to punish me for my blasphemy?"

Dombit's face dropped.

"Come now," Klarot said, "you're a bright, young officer. Despite what you learned in Dragon School, there is a real world out there. Did you study navigation at the academy?"

Dombit said he had.

"Did you learn to take sun shots?"

"Yes, Sir, but we called them *Dragon shots*. Our instructors told us that the Great Dragon has purposefully followed a regular path across the sky so Arcans can navigate."

Klarot cringed inwardly. "Sit down, Dombit," he said, pointing to a chair at a table. He sketched a rough picture of the Ran system and walked the young officer through it. He pointed to Ran. "This is our star, our sun, what you call the Great Dragon. It is one of billions of stars in the universe—those twinkling lights you see in the sky at night." He pointed to Arcan. "This is Arcan, our planet that revolves around Ran once yearly. In fact, this is how we define a year. Arcan rotates on its axis every twenty-four hours, so every part of the planet sees Ran once daily. This is why Ran—the Dragon—appears to follow a fixed path. Think about this for a few minutes."

Klarot moved away from the table to give the young lieutenant some space. Now that he had a link to the offworlders, he needed a gofer who understood what was really happening.

After several minutes, Dombit looked up. "General…"

"What is it, Lieutenant Dombit?"

"If what you say is true, if the Great Dragon is really just another star in the universe, then our entire religion is based on a falsehood. What I learned, what every child learns, in Dragon School is…" his scales rippled light red, "…is bullshit!" He spit the last word out, as if trying to get it out of his mouth.

"That's pretty much how it is, Son. *Bullshit* is an apt word." He smiled inwardly, his inner eyes wide open. *This is going better than I expected,* he thought.

Just then, the comm receiver crackled. "General Klarot, are you alone?"

"I am here with my trusted assistant, Lieutenant Teynal Dombit. You can speak freely."

"General Klarot, I want to meet with you face to face."

"How is that possible unless you land nearby—and that would alert everybody?"

"I can see that you have an inner courtyard—perhaps where your predecessors communed with the Great Dragon. I will send a drone, a small flying machine, that will deliver an object we call a hyper-brick. Have Lieutenant Dombit retrieve it and deliver it to you. Notify me when you have it. It will arrive in your courtyard in an hour."

✳

An hour later, Lt. Dombit stood in the small courtyard looking at the sky. He didn't actually see the drone until it seemed to appear right above him. He stepped aside, and it landed on the courtyard deck. The drone was about a meter across, with four radial arms extending from a central body. The arms ended with horizontal propellors. Dombit knew they were propellors, because they resembled the auxiliary ship propellors he had studied at the academy. He undid the latch on the top of the central body and removed a small brick-like object about ten centimeters long that weighed about a kilogram. He closed the lid and stepped away from the drone. The propellors started spinning, and it rose swiftly into the sky and disappeared.

Dombit carried the hyper-brick gingerly into the Comm Center.

"Isidor Orlov, I have the hyper-brick," Klarot announced over the circuit.

"On one side is a sliding cover," Orlov transmitted back. "Move the slide and depress the button."

Klarot complied, and a doorway opened in the air before him. He stepped back in alarm, startled despite himself, his scales rippling faint red with apprehension and then pale orange with irritation at himself.

"This is a portal, a doorway, directly from your Comm Center to my starship, *Udachnyy Zvezdolet Sergei Krikalyov*," Orlov said. "Do not be alarmed. The portal is harmless."

Klarot walked around the portal to the back. As he passed the portal plane, it disappeared from his vision. From the back, there was just empty air through which he could see Dombit. He continued around. At the plane of the portal, it was once again visible to him.

"Did the portal disappear when I walked to the back?" he asked Dombit.

"No, Sir. It remained just as it is."

"You walk around it, Lieutenant," Klarot ordered.

Dombit complied while Klarot watched. As Dombit crossed the portal plane, his scales rippled yellow in astonishment.

"Can you see it?" Klarot asked, while looking directly at it from the front.

"No, Sir. It disappeared. All I see is you looking at something in front of you that I cannot see."

"Okay. Walk straight toward me."

The portal blocked Klarot's view of Dombit, but as he walked toward the general, he seemed to materialize in front of the portal.

"Orlov, I do not understand what I am seeing," Klarot said over the circuit.

"The physics is way beyond you," Orlov said. "It's beyond me, too. My scientists and engineers designed and built it. Will you walk through the portal and join me?"

"How will it affect me?" Klarot asked.

"A portal doesn't affect anything passing through it. A portal is a door between two distant points. You walk through it like any door. It has no physical effect of any kind on you."

An oddly shaped humanoid appeared in the room beyond the door, gesturing for Klarot to enter. Klarot turned to Dombit.

"You stay here and keep watch."

Klarot stepped through the portal.

Udachnyy Zvezdolet Sergei Krikalyov—Flashing In and Out of Warp at Lodan L4, Operations Center

General Klarot stepped into a room somewhat smaller than his Comm Center. He panicked for a moment when he realized there was no gravity. His scales went from light red to yellow as he grabbed a handhold and oriented himself. A console filled one end of the space with windows looking out of the vessel. He assumed that was the front of the starship. Klarot later learned that they were screens, and that there were no actual visual ports to the outside. Behind him stretched a passageway that he presumed ran the length of the craft. Doors opened into the passageway from both sides. The starship was much smaller than he had expected. He estimated it could accommodate ten to fifteen people—no more.

"Welcome to *Udachnyy Zvezdolet Sergei Krikalyov*," Orlov said, extending a small transparent bag of clear liquid while speaking through a translating device. The bag had a nipple, although it was too small for an Arcan mouth. "Do Arcans drink ethyl alcohol?" Orlov asked.

"We do, although in The Geroptic Nation, our religion prohibits its consumption." The translator regurgitated his Geroptic into the Human's words.

"We call this *Vodka*. It is the national drink of my people, the Russians, one branch of Humans in the Solar System. We drink it in salutation when gathering with old friends and meeting new ones."

Klarot took the bag. Orlov curled his lips in what Klarot would learn was the Human equivalent of a smile, and squeezed the vodka down his throat. Klarot reciprocated—the nipple was unnecessary. The vodka was smooth and remarkably pleasant tasting.

He glanced at his host. Orlov was shorter than Klarot. His head was round, topped with hair. His eyes were at the front above a short protrusion that substituted for an Arcan snout. His puffy lips surrounded a smaller mouth than an Arcan's. His body was slender with spindly two-part arms and legs with five digits on his hands. He had no tail that Klarot could discern. His skin was naked and looked soft.

"As you can see," Orlov said, "Humans evolved from mammals. It appears that Arcans evolved from reptiles."

"And yet, here we are…" Klarot's voice trailed off.

＊

They moved into Orlov's cabin, first door on the left in the passageway. Orlov placed himself in a chair and secured himself with a strap. Klarot found he liked zero-gee, and simply remained floating.

"Tell me about Arcan and your place in the order of things," Orlov said.

This offworlder has to know the big picture, Klarot thought. I need to give him a favorable view of The Geroptic Nation and a desire to help.

Klarot began with an overview of Arcan and its three main subdivisions. Then he went into further detail. "*Andromeda* contacted Amred through SPC and set up a cozy arrangement. Ceffid rebels overcame the Ceffid dictatorship and established a government similar to Amred. They have a mutual defense pact and are working with *Andromeda* to further their space program. The Geroptic Nation has been held back by a long succession of Prophets who refused to introduce technology, and who kept the population cowering under the yoke of a vengeful Dragon in the Sky. I am emancipated as are most of my senior officers, but, sadly, the rest of the population remains ignorant of the modern world." His scales rippled pink.

"Is the Prophet aware?" Orlov asked.

"I do not know for certain. He practices the rituals and follows the teachings of *The Book of the Great Dragon*. On the other hand, he seems knowledgeable about the goings on in Amred and Ceffid. He has prevented advancements in steam technology, steel production, electronics—virtually anything that can move the population closer to the modern world."

"What about your military?" Orlov asked.

"I have a million-lizard army that fights well with saber, spear, and bow and arrow. I could not convince the Prophet to modernize our military. We had hopes of being able to conquer both Amred and Ceffid, but with the Prophet's recalcitrance and *Andromeda*, that seems impossible."

"Can you arm your forces with modern weapons without the Prophet's knowledge?"

"It all would depend on who would replace the Prophet. So long as Prophets rule The Geroptic Nation, we will remain a backward people."

"It is not my place to tell you, General, how to run your country, but I will say that I did not become the third largest enterprise in the entire Solar System by letting a pipsqueak religious zealot stand in my way." Orlov handed Klarot another vodka bag and opened one for himself. "To what could be," he said, holding his bag toward Klarot.

They squirted the liquid down their throats.

"What would you need, General, to become the effective leader of your country?"

Klarot closed his eyes and gave Orlov's question some thought. Finally, he said, "If the Prophet and his top advisors were removed, and if military officers I trusted assumed control of several strategic bases, I would control the country. Unfortunately, the million troops I mentioned earlier are simple and fight for the Prophet. They will rise against me unless I give them a reason to see me as the Great Dragon's choice to follow in Prophet Dudengi Vrokhun's footsteps. Then they will follow me as they do the Prophet."

"What do you need to get there?"

"Modern sidearms and rifles for my special troops—say, twelve thousand each and a million rounds of ammo for each. Troop movement ground vehicles, one hundred twenty field artillery, one hundred twenty thousand rounds of ammo. Once I've consolidated control of the country, we will need to discuss how we can move troops to Ceffid and Amred."

"One step at a time. In the Solar System, I have massive manufacturing capability, but Ran is near the limit of my portal capability. It will take me some time to manufacture what you require—two weeks should be sufficient. We'll need several days to move everything to you, and then you will need some time to train your people. I suggest a month.

"Have you given any thought to how you will bring about the actual demise of the Prophet and your elevation to Ruler of The Geroptic Nation?"

"If the bishops and the people see me as the Great Dragon-designated-successor to the Prophet, I think they will accept me, especially if we can devise a spectacular way to remove the Prophet."

"At the appropriate time," Orlov said, "we can set up a theatrical entrance for you that will convince believers of your connection with the Great Dragon."

"And cause the skeptics to believe in my power," Klarot added, his scales rippling blue.

CHAPTER TWELVE

Twelve Military Posts—The Geroptic Nation, Planet Arcan

General Nirurian Klarot called Lt. Teynal Dombit to his office. The young officer arrived, slightly out of breath, light red scales signaling his apprehension.

"Relax, Captain," Klarot said, sliding a set of captain's devices across his desk. "I'm promoting you to captain and assigning you as my aide-de-camp. I've already notified my adjutant and your chain of command. Move into the next-door office. Your job is to anticipate my professional needs and requirements, but you are not my servant."

Dombit came to attention and saluted, right forearm across his chest, fist closed. "Thank you, General. I am honored to be your aide-de-camp."

"Your first task will be to set up twelve portals like the one I used yesterday." Klarot gave him general instructions and set him to the task.

✳

Dombit couldn't believe his good fortune. He still felt somewhat ill at ease with his newfound knowledge about the solar system and the role Arcan and the Great Dragon played—*No!* he reminded himself. *Not the Great Dragon, but their sun, Ran.*

He went to the Comm Center and contacted Orlov. "I am Captain Teynal Dombit, aide-de-camp to General Klarot. He assigned me to establish a central location for the twelve Locuses and to coordinate distributing the hyper-bricks to their intended destinations."

"This is as I discussed with the general, Captain. I will notify you as soon as I have the Locuses and hyper-bricks available."

"One more thing, Sir," Dombit said. "Can you supply me with drones like the one that delivered the first hyper-brick? I could use them to deliver the hyper-bricks to our field people."

"That's easier said than done, Captain. You can do it with just one drone by sending it back through the newly established portal to commence the next delivery. The issue is programming the drone to travel to its destination. Right now, you are unfamiliar with programming and to further complicate things, our species uses base ten for counting and calculating, except for circles, where we use three hundred sixty degrees like you do. The programming keystrokes are set for base ten. You could learn it, but that won't happen in the next hour."

Dombit considered the problem. "I think I have a solution," he told Orlov several minutes later. "I will give you the Arcan coordinates for each delivery, and you or one of your people can enter the proper programming."

"Good thinking, Captain. We'll do it like that."

✳

For the next several hours, Dombit composed and transmitted twelve telegraphic messages to General Klarot's top twelve military commanders. The messages were cryptic, not revealing any specific information about the delivery of the hyper-bricks, except instructing the commanders to take the brick to a secure location and activate it.

Early the next morning, Orlov contacted Dombit. "I have twelve Locuses and hyper-bricks ready for you. Activate your portal and pass through it to *Udachnyy Zvezdolet Sergei Krikalyov*."

With his heart pounding and his scales rippling dark blue, Dombit pushed the slide back and activated the hyper-brick. The portal opened, and he stepped through. Even though he anticipated the switch from normal to no gravity, it still caught him by surprise. He thought he might lose his breakfast at first, but within a minute, his stomach settled, and he felt fine.

Orlov wasted no time with preliminaries. "Captain," he said, "glad to meet you." He pointed to twelve suitcase-size boxes lined up in the corridor. "These contain both Locus and hyper-brick. They mass about twenty kilos each. Moving into a gravity environment is a bit tricky, but you're young and strong."

Orlov's face crinkled, and his mouth opened, showing his teeth exaggeratedly. Dombit did a quick double-take, and then noted to himself, *Must be the Human equivalent of a grin—what else could it be?*

He gripped the handle of the first package and floated to the portal. He entered feet first, letting the package lag behind him. He stumbled as gravity took hold, but kept his grip on the handle. He set the case aside and reentered the portal. This time, he lined up the remaining nine cases, so they floated near the portal.

Turning to Orlov, he said, "Would you be willing to push the cases one by one within reach of the portal as I grab them from my side and pull them through?"

"*Da,*" Orlov said, which Dombit figured meant *okay* or *yes* in his native language.

They moved the remaining cases from Orlov's starship into the Comm Center in just a couple of minutes.

"Okay, now," Orlov said, "now return here. We have more to discuss."

Dombit returned to the starship and its zero-gee environment and joined Orlov in his stateroom. Like General Klarot before him, he preferred to float rather than strap himself to a chair.

"You understand power—I mean electricity, don't you?" Orlov asked.

"Yes, but only superficially. We collect static electricity in Leyden jars we use to charge lead-acid batteries for our telegraph system. We use the same method to power our comm system. As far as understanding what it really is, no, I don't." Dombit opened his eyes wide and blinked them, but he wasn't sure if Orlov understood an Arcan grin.

"Well, portals require thousands of times more power than all of your telegraph systems combined—probably millions of times more."

Dombit shook his head in amazement, his scales rippling yellow. "It's difficult to imagine such power."

"I'm going to establish what we call a power portal from here to your Comm Center. It will feed a manifold with twelve connectors. I'll give you twelve cables that you will connect between the manifold and your twelve Locuses. The manifold has a switch that shifts power to whichever portal you are using. When you use one of these portals, you make a huge power draw from my starship power system. Keep a portal open only as long as you need to."

*

Dombit set everything up as Orlov had instructed and then requested the drone. Orlov passed it through the portal and then closed the portal. Dombit loaded the first hyper-brick into the drone along with a sheet containing written instructions, took it out to the enclosed courtyard, and sent it on its way. The first post was relatively close, and Dombit figured it would take the drone two hours and several minutes to get there.

Two hours and fifteen minutes later, the field commander telegraphed he was ready. Dombit telegraphed back: *Go!* Moments later, a portal opened, and Dombit stepped through. He saluted the field commander, a colonel, and briefed him on the developments. With the reality of the portal right in front of him, the colonel spent no time arguing the facts. Dombit could see why General Klarot had chosen this Arcan.

"So, Colonel," Dombit concluded, "we will transfer five hundred sidearms and rifles along with sufficient ammo through this portal in a few days. We will also supply you with motorized troop transports and field artillery, along with shells.

"These portals are a huge power draw, so we will open them only when needed." He saluted again, picked up the drone, and returned through the portal to the Comm Center.

*

Dombit handled the other eleven posts like the first, except that the drone's transit was significantly longer. The entire process took several days.

The last field commander, Colonel Blozok Garlan, insisted on speaking with General Klarot. "Captain," he said, "I don't understand the black magic you are using, but I get that General Klarot is moments away using this contraption."

"Will you accompany me?" Dombit asked. "I'll take you to him."

"By the Great Dragon," Garlan swore with a hiss, his scales turning bright orange, "I'll not risk my life with your Night cursed doorway."

"Yes, Sir," Dombit said. "Stand by."

Dombit returned to the Comm Center and immediately went to Klarot's office.

"Sir, Colonel Blozok Garlan insists on talking with you personally, but he won't use the portal."

"He's the only one giving you trouble?"

"Yes, Sir. Your other commanders came up to speed fast. It's just Colonel Garlan."

"Okay, Son, let's see what the colonel wants."

They walked together down the passageway to the Comm Center. Klarot stepped through the portal first. Dombit held back a bit to see what happened. Col. Garlan came to attention and saluted. Klarot returned his salute and asked, "What's your problem?"

At that moment, Dombit entered the post and saluted the colonel. Garlan returned a cursory salute and then stammered, "Nothing, I guess. Captain Dombit overwhelmed me for a moment with this incredible technology. Sorry, General." He saluted again, and Klarot hissed softly, his scales briefly showing pale orange, and returned through the portal.

"That was intense," Dombit said. "Are we ready now?"

"We are, Captain, and thank you. Let's once again run through what you will require of me and what you will be delivering."

✳

Dombit waited impatiently for a full three weeks before Orlov contacted him with positive news about the troop transports and field artillery units. Orlov introduced Dombit to Academician Sergii Anatoly Borisovich, his chief scientist. Borisovich explained the process to him.

"The portals are large and connect back to an Udachny manufacturing facility in the Solar System. I can generate sufficient power there to keep a large portal open over the ten and a half lightyears. To keep the power draw as low as possible, at each post, make the transfers quickly, and then close the portal.

"Work directly with Udachny supervisory people at the facility. They don't speak Geroptic but will use translators like we do.

"The Geroptic Nation doesn't have powered vehicles except for steam locomotives, and you import them. You do use electricity for your telegraph system, and you generate the charge with an electrostatic generator. Now, imagine a similar machine where you feed it an electrical charge, and it produces rotation. We call that a *motor*. We use motors large and small throughout our society. The troop transports are motor driven—one for each wheel. The wheels are covered with a form of synthetic rubber. The motors are powered by a LANR—a Lattice Assisted Nuclear Reactor. Each transport carries one. A form of hydrogen, called deuterium, fuels the LANRs. Each troop transport carries two tanks of deuterium. These will have to be replaced from time to time, but they should last for several years.

"I have set up a training facility for maintenance and repair of the troop transports. You should send two people from each post to receive this training. Driving the transports is simplicity itself. The driver sits in the cab behind a steering wheel. A nearby lever changes direction from forward to back. One peddle on the deck, the accelerator, adjusts the speed. A second, the brake, stops the transport. A floor lever on the left is a handbrake to augment the foot brake and to keep the vehicle from moving when it is stopped. A swamp lizard can figure it out in two minutes." Borisovich did not actually use the term *swamp lizard*, but the translator converted the term he used, *idiot*, into *swamp lizard*. "I adjusted the gravity in our facility to match Arcan's gravity. This will simplify moving the transports through the portal.

"I've covered the main points. Do you have questions?"

"Not right now," Dombit said. "When they arise, I'll contact you."

"One of my people will be available any time the need arises," Borisovich said. "I'll have people standing by for when you open the portal."

✳

Transferring the troop transports was sufficiently complex that Dombit brought all the field commanders together. He visited each commander by portal, requesting their presence in Dragon City the next day. He explained the requirement for activating one portal at a time and set a schedule so none of the commanders would be kept waiting.

The following morning, Dombit started bringing the twelve field commanders to the Comm Center. He budgeted a half hour, but it took only fifteen minutes. When they were assembled, he asked General Klarot to join them.

"Commanders," Dombit said, "today, you each will receive twelve troop transports." He described the transport, its power supply, and how it worked. "The first delivery will be to Colonel Blozok Garlan at the Ramden Post. We'll gather at his post to observe the transfer. The offworlders will open a large portal. I will enter with one of Colonel Garlan's troops. He will observe me as I drive the first transport through the portal. He will take someone with him for the next transport, and so on, so we transfer all twelve quickly. I remind you that maintaining a large open portal over ten lightyears takes a power draw beyond imagining. Are there questions or comments?"

Colonel Garlan spoke up. "I will accompany you on the first transfer. Then you will accompany me on the second to ensure I understand how to do it. If all goes well, I'll take charge of the rest."

"As you wish, Colonel. I like your method better than mine." He looked across the group. "You all heard Colonel Garlan, right?"

Nods all around.

"Okay, we'll do it that way for everyone." He opened his eyes wide, blinking, scales rippling blue. "The general will now speak for a few minutes."

Klarot moved to the front of the group. "We are about to undergo a dramatic change in the governance of The Geroptic Nation and in the focus of its religious leaders. Each of you knows your sector bishop. They will gather in Dragon City for a special meeting with the Prophet following delivery of your equipment. When they return, each bishop will report directly to you as Field Commander. By then, you will have received detailed instructions from my office. What you will need to do and how you will accomplish it will be clear." Klarot opened his eyes wide and stepped away.

"Let's get this show on the road," Dombit said.

✳

At the Ramden Post, Dombit activated the special hyper-brick the Academician had given him. A four-meter-wide by three-meter-high portal opened. Dombit and his group could see the interior of a warehouse. Several Humans stood near the portal on their side. This was the first time any of the officers had seen a Human, and the first time any of the Humans had seen an Arcan. Dombit was amused by how carefully each species tried not to stare. He decided to take the raptor by its wing feathers. He stepped out between his officers and the portal so he could address both groups at once.

"I know we look strange to each other, so take a long look, and then let's get to work making the transfers so we can close the portal as soon as possible." With wide open, blinking eyes and pale blue scales, he turned to his officers. He could tell they got his humor. He glanced at the Humans. They displayed the open-mouth expression he knew was their equivalent of a grin—they got the humor as well. He turned to Garlan. "Shall we, Colonel?"

They entered the large portal and approached the transport. A Human stepped closer, saying through his translator, "I will answer questions you have."

Dombit climbed a short ladder into the cab. Garlan followed him. The Human climbed up the other side.

"You start the motors here," the Human said, pointing to a button on the console. "You steer like this." He rotated the steering wheel back and forth. "This lever puts the vehicle in forward or reverse. That peddle is the accelerator and that one's the brake." He put his hand on a lever sticking up from the floor. "This is the handbrake. It is set right now. When you are ready, start the motors, release the handbrake, and ease down on the accelerator. Be ready to hit the brake if you need to."

Dombit started the motors. He heard a faint whine. He released the handbrake, moved the direction lever to the forward position, and gently pressed down the accelerator. The transporter eased forward. He backed off on the accelerator, and the vehicle slowed. He touched the brake, and it stopped suddenly.

"Use the brake more gently," the Human said.

Dombit turned the steering wheel to the right and then left. The vehicle responded immediately. The vehicle was heavy, but steering took no effort. Dombit stopped the vehicle and backed for a few seconds. It took a moment to understand how to steer in reverse, but he caught on right away. He turned toward Garlan with wide open eyes.

"A swamp lizard could do this," he said, scales bright blue. He drove the vehicle through the portal and parked it to one side.

Dombit and Garlan returned on foot through the portal. This time, Garlan mounted first, and the Human remained on the deck. Garlan took the steering wheel firmly in his hands, started the motors, and eased off the handbrake. When he pressed the accelerator, the vehicle surged forward. He stomped on the brake so it stopped immediately, throwing them forward slightly.

"Gently," Dombit said, "like holding a fertilized egg."

Garlan opened his eyes wide and eased forward, this time without jerking. "Good analogy," he said, "about the fertilized egg, I mean." He parked next to the first transport.

"Are you ready to do it with one of your guys?" Dombit asked.

"Let's do one more, just to be certain," Garlan said.

After that, the remaining seven passed through the portal without incident. The Arcan soldiers took to driving like they had been doing it all their lives. Garlan and Dombit stood together, observing.

"Nice, Captain," Garlan said. "Smooth operation. I'll so inform the general."

⁕

The remaining eleven posts went without incident. All the Arcan soldiers took to driving just like those at the Ramden Post. By noon the next day, Dombit reported to General Klarot that all one hundred forty-four troop transports were delivered.

Dombit arranged to deliver two dozen field artillery pieces to each post. At the Ramden Post, he opened the portal to see all the weapons arranged for easy movement by hand through the portal. It took twenty minutes. Humans used a machine they called a forklift to transfer several pallets of field artillery shells to the post. Each unit had simple instructions in Geroptic embossed on its body. By the time Dombit closed the portal, Garlan's troops were already setting up one artillery piece to test it and learn how to aim it.

Before the day was over, Dombit had delivered two dozen artillery pieces and several thousand shells to each post. He reported to General Klarot.

"All twelve posts now have six hundred sidearms, six hundred rifles, twelve troop transports, two dozen field artillery pieces, and a thousand shells. Two troops from each post have received maintenance and repair instruction for the troop transports, and two dozen troops from each post are now trained drivers. We are ready to go to the next phase of your plan, General."

Prophet Dudengi Vrokhun's Private Chambers—Dragon Temple, Dragon City, The Geroptic Nation, Planet Arcan

Prophet Dudengi Vrokhun sat behind an ordinary desk in his private chambers. The Geroptic Nation's twelve senior bishops, dressed informally, occupied seats scattered around the Prophet's chambers. Vrokhun also wore informal business clothing, suitable for his bishops' eyes, but no one else.

"We have been hearing strange things coming from our twelve provinces," Vrokhun said. "Each of you has reported events taking place at the military post in your province. We need to get a handle on this before it corrupts the peoples' faith."

Vrokhun sat quietly, his nearly transparent scales revealing nothing at all. A quiet murmur spread through the chamber as the bishops discussed the events among themselves. There was no deep dogmatic belief among these twelve bishops. They were Arcans who respected power. The Prophet exercised power from his pulpit in the Dragon Temple, but the bishops held the real power in The Geroptic Nation. They controlled their people, the children's education, and collected taxes. Collectively, they kept the populace ignorant of anything except *The Book of the Great Dragon* and simple commercial arithmetic.

The twelve bishops lived lives of opulence behind closed doors. They were vigorous males with continuous access to females who had unfertilized eggs in their pouches. Where it made sense, the females were allowed to bring their eggs to term and raise the resulting offspring in establishments that resembled convents on ancient Earth. More often than not, however, the fertilized eggs were taken from the females and destroyed, and the females given a choice, become a religious acolyte inside the convent walls or die.

"I have invited General Klarot to meet with us here to explain what is happening in your provinces," Vrokhun said. "Be free with your questions. The general, like yourselves, has some issues with a rigid doctrinal interpretation of *The Book of the Great Dragon*. You should receive a sympathetic ear to any reasonable question."

"Please change into your robes for this meeting. I will see you back here in fifteen minutes."

※

General Nirurian Klarot arrived at the Dragon Temple in a troop carrier driven by Captain Dombit. Two dozen loyal troops occupied the carrier's belly, each in dress uniform and carrying one of the new sidearms that they had practiced using for the last several days.

"You know the plan," Dombit told the troops as they exited the carrier. They quickly dispersed through a Temple side door.

Klarot and Dombit, in full parade dress, mounted the sweeping steps to the Temple main entrance. A priest greeted them without fanfare and ushered them into the Prophet's private chambers.

The Prophet sat at his desk, dressed in his informal religious attire. A comfortable chair had been placed opposite the desk for Klarot. Someone quickly replaced it with two, the second a bit farther from the desk. Six bishops sat on either side of the desk arranged in quarter circles so they could see and be seen by the Prophet and the general.

Vrokhun and the twelve bishops came to their feet. Klarot and Dombit bowed deeply toward the Prophet. They remained standing.

"Welcome, General Klarot and Captain Dombit. We are eager to hear your latest report." Vrokhun closed his eyes and lifted his hands and head upward. In sonorous tones, he said, "Great Dragon in the Sky, we stand before you in reverence and awe, knowing that you control each of us and the universe in which we live. Extend to us your blessing during this meeting, and grant us courage to exalt your name above all else."

The Prophet spread his robes and sat. Klarot and Dombit took their seats, as did the twelve bishops.

"So, General, talk to me!"

※

"My Lord, I hardly know where to begin. Every day, I have been carrying out your wishes for the governance of The Geroptic Nation. Things went smoothly and without incident until, one afternoon, the Great Dragon spoke directly to me through the communications machines we use for our dealings with Amred and Ceffid. The Great Dragon told me, and I quote: *General Nirurian Klarot, this is the Great Dragon in the Sky. I have important news for you and The Geroptic Nation, but first you and I must speak privately.*

"My Lord, the Great Dragon opened a door into his realm. I passed through the door and met the Great Dragon's Archangel. We Geroptics have never before known the Archangel's name. I reveal it to you now: *Isidor Orlov*. He does not look like us, but he has two arms and two legs. His head is round with hair on top, and he has no tail. He can reach down into our individual lives and affect our behavior." Klarot smiled inwardly. "Archangel Orlov showed me much about your private behavior—each of you. I know about the girls, the convents, the opulent lifestyle."

A quiet hiss passed through the twelve bishops as their collective scale color rippled light red.

"The Archangel wants us to bring the true faith to Amred and Ceffid. He has given me a large cache of weapons every bit as modern as Amred's and Ceffid's."

Klarot glanced from side to side at the twelve bishops. Then he nodded slightly at Dombit, who extracted a ten-centimeter hyper-brick from a pocket and handed it to Klarot.

Klarot stood and raised his voice. "The Great Dragon has ordered me to bring you into his Archangel's presence." He placed the hyper-brick so the portal would be visible to the Prophet and all twelve of his bishops, and activated it.

A collective gasp rose from the bishops. Vrokhun remained stoic. Klarot reached out his hand.

"Follow me, Lord." He gripped the Prophet's hand. "The Great Dragon will remove your weight when you enter his realm. While you are there, you can fly, although I recommend you keep hold of me for stability."

Vrokhun walked around his desk and followed Klarot through the door.

Udachnyy Zvezdolet Sergei Krikalyov—Flashing In and Out of Warp at Lodan L4, Operations Center

Vrokhun had listened to General Klarot with a good deal of amusement. He did not know what his general was trying to accomplish. When Klarot started discussing weapons, Vrokhun perked up. He didn't believe for a moment that the weapons came from the Great Dragon. He was skeptical of His existence, anyway. He presumed the weapons came from Amred sources, but if his bishops wanted to believe the Great Dragon was the source, that was fine with him.

Then the door opened…to somewhere. Not the Great Dragon's realm, of that Vrokhun was certain. *Could this be offworlder interference?* he asked himself. *That would explain a lot.*

Vrokhun let Klarot lead him through the door and found himself floating with a falling sensation. For a few seconds, he thought he might lose his breakfast. *Not suitable Prophet behavior,* he thought as he consciously settled his stomach. Klarot floated to his right. Before him floated, not the Great Dragon's Archangel, but a bipedal being that matched the description of the offworlders who had contacted Amred, according to Vrokhun's sources.

"May I introduce…" Klarot started to say, but Vrokhun held up his hand.

"I am Prophet Dudengi Vrokhun, spiritual leader of the Geroptic people." Something picked up his words and translated them into an offworlder gibberish. "I am also head of the Geroptic government. You have already met General Nirurian Klarot, who heads my military forces. He informed me you have supplied him with weapons equal to those of Amred and Ceffid."

"Did General Klarot explain to you my role in the Great Dragon's realm?" Orlov asked, his strange sounding words made intelligible by the same machine that translated Vrokhun's words.

"Let's dispense with the charade," Vrokhun said sharply. "You are one of the offworlders, and we are aboard your starship."

Orlov shrugged at Klarot.

"Turn off your translating machine," Vrokhun told Orlov. Orlov did so. "Testing the translator," Vrokhun said. It produced no sound. He turned to Klarot.

"What in the Great Dragon's name are you trying to do?"

"My Lord, your intent has always been to bring the rest of Arcan under the rule of the Great Dragon. This is how I thought we could do it."

"Why the subterfuge? Do you really see me that stupid?"

"No, my Lord, naïve perhaps when it comes to the Great Dragon and the outside world, but definitely not stupid."

Out of the corner of his eye, Vrokhun saw Orlov point something at him. Then everything went dark.

✳

Klarot did a double take when Orlov rendered Vrokhun unconscious. He pointed at the translator. When Orlov activated it, Klarot said, "What did you do to him?"

"I used an EMD—Electro-Muscular-Disruptor. He'll be unconscious for at least an hour. You don't want to use a pellet firing weapon on a spaceship. It can penetrate the hull."

"Now what?" Klarot asked.

"I was just about to ask you the same thing."

"If we are to move forward, I need to assume complete control of the government," Klarot said. "I can do that by force, but the people will not follow me—even most of my troops would rebel." He hung in the air, thinking. "Do you have a facility where you can safely detain Vrokhun?"

"Back in the Solar System, yes. Why?"

"If you detain him, I can tell the bishops that as a reward for his faithfulness, the Great Dragon has decided to let the Prophet remain in his realm. The Great Dragon can name me as the Prophet's successor."

"Why not just eliminate him?" Orlov asked.

"I may need him in the future. I would want him properly cared for, with dignity."

"I can handle that, but if I am going to be your jailor, I will need several Arcans you trust to run the detention facility."

"Fine; you set it up, and I will supply the personnel. I think we can probably deal with that later. Right now, I need to handle the Vrokhun matter."

They worked out the details, and then Klarot walked alone through the door, back into the Prophet's chambers. As he walked through the door, a bright light surrounded him, projected from the starship's Control Center. A deep, resonating voice from the Control Center filled the chambers.

I am the Great Dragon in the Sky. As a reward for his good and faithful service, Prophet Dudengi Vrokhun will not return to Arcan and The Geroptic Nation, but will remain in my realm as my permanent liaison to The Geroptic Nation for the glorification of the Great Dragon in the Sky. I have chosen General Nirurian Klarot as his worthy successor, to rule The Geroptic Nation in his stead, and to carry out my greater plan for bringing all the peoples of Arcan under my rule as the Great Dragon in the Sky.

The bright light faded, and the portal collapsed. Klarot looked around the chambers. All twelve bishops had prostrated themselves on the floor.

"Gentlemen, to your feet! The Great Dragon has spoken. I am a military guy. I have read *The Book of the Great Dragon*, of course, but am not really familiar with its deepest meanings. Consequently, I will rely upon your wise counsel as we move forward. To facilitate this, you will immediately come together here in this chamber after I leave to select one of your number to be my personal advisor. Then you will agree on a successor to the bishop slot of the individual you choose."

Klarot turned, picked up the hyper-brick, and motioned Dombit to join him. They left by the main entrance and descended the broad flight of steps. A trooper standing watch hurried to the side door, and several moments later, the troops who had entered the Temple surreptitiously returned to the carrier.

The Village of Cordan—Southeastern Corner of The Geroptic Nation, Planet Arcan

The small village of Cordan sat on the coast several dozen kilometers north of Sogard, the third largest Geroptic city located on the southeastern corner of The Geroptic Nation. Cordan was home to 2,500 lizards—farmers, fisherfolk, and tradesfolk. The tradesfolk serviced the needs of the farmers and fisherfolk, and the local families. Cordan was self-sufficient, importing from Sogard things impossible to make locally. The Bishop rarely visited, except annually around harvest time when he could collect tithes that the villagers did not have at other times.

The local Dragon School served the entire village. Classes started at 8 am and the children left around 4 pm. There was just one classroom where all the students attended together. They learned to read *The Book of the Great Dragon* and learned to write by copying passages from the *Holy Book*. Half the day was spent on this. In the afternoon, the children learned numbers and arithmetic—just enough to calculate sums for business. Their teacher of thirty years had died. The village elders looked far and wide for a replacement. Nobody wanted to live in their remote village, far from the attractions of a big city. For several months, the children went without a teacher. The local lay-minister tried to substitute, but he lacked training to do the job, and ended up just reading passages from the *Holy Book* and having the children recite their numbers. Finally, they found Judhee Groklet, who had a reputation for thoroughness and was popular with his students, and didn't seem to mind Cordan's remoteness. There were things they didn't know about Judhee Groklet, but that didn't matter. He was a teacher willing to come to Cordan, and they badly wanted a teacher.

❋

Judhee Groklet closed *The Book of the Great Dragon* and addressed his working-class students.

"We have learned together for some time now. We have looked beyond the world of Cordan to glimpse a bit of the universe in which we live. I have asked you to be careful how you present these ideas to your families. If your parents are deeply religious, you might want to avoid sharing with them, and instead, talk with your classmates. I will be happy to speak with any parent who has questions. Please tell your parents to give you a message for me, and I will visit them whenever they wish." He gave them a wide-eyed Arcan smile.

"Let's pull out our private notebooks and pick up where we left off yesterday. Who can define a quadratic equation?" Every hand in the room went up, from the youngest to the oldest. "Let's ask our youngest lizard. She seems eager to share her knowledge with us."

The other hands dropped, and the little female lizard got to her feet. "A quadratic equation is a second-degree polynomial equation that contains at least one squared term."

"Very good, Bethpage. Can you tell us what that means?"

"May I come to the chalkboard?" she asked.

Groklet handed her a piece of white chalk. She went to the board and said, "The general form of a quadratic equation is…" and wrote: $ax^2 + bx + c = 0$, "where a, b, and c are variable coefficients, and x is an unknown variable." She returned to her seat to the noisy approval of her classmates.

By the time General Klarot had sent the Prophet to his heavenly reward, Groklet had taught three generations of Cordan children. In Cordan, most young and middle-aged lizards had a good understanding of basic science, including physics, chemistry, biology, and astronomy. They were familiar with the Amred and Ceffid classics, and several had become writers. Out of necessity, they kept to themselves, lest the strong hand of the Great Dragon's Bishop descend upon their village.

Udachnyy Zvezdolet Sergei Krikalyov—Flashing In and Out of Warp at Lodan L4, Operations Center

General Klarot floated freely in Isidor Orlov's cabin aboard *UZ Sergei Krikalyov*. Orlov had strapped himself to a chair.

"That went better than I expected," Klarot said. "All the bishops have accepted me as their leader, and they are working closely with my field commanders." He opened his eyes wide and let his scales ripple faint lavender. "I think it's time for our next step."

"Are you sure you know what you are requesting?" Orlov asked. "I don't think you really understand the immense power of a thermonuclear explosion."

"I understand explosions, since we have exploited them with our field artillery units."

"Yes, I know, but this is so far beyond artillery that it is difficult to explain. One of these bombs exploded above a million-occupant city will destroy the city and kill all its inhabitants. Just one bomb.

Exploded at ground level, it will still create a lot of destruction, but less than an aerial blast."

"Can you make them in smaller sizes?" Klarot asked. "Something that will take out the government complex?"

"We can scale them down," Orlov said. "What is your battle plan? If you hit all the cities with nukes, you won't have many people left to rule, and my trading options will be severely limited."

"I plan to take out the governments of Amred and Ceffid simultaneously by striking their government compounds with the scaled-down nukes you described. Then I will hit their major military installations. This should leave them without an effective government or military. I'll flood troops into remaining critical areas using your portals. Before the populace understands what has happened, my troops will control every major section of both countries."

Orlov contemplated Klarot's plan for several minutes, while Klarot floated patiently, watching the emotions passing across Orlov's face. *These Humans show their emotions, too,* he thought. *One must simply spend enough time with them to interpret their faces.*

"Overall," Orlov said finally, "your plan is not bad. It has some significant flaws, however. Amred certainly has nukes. Ceffid had them, and I suspect they do again. Furthermore, since they both are close allies now, you will face their combined forces.

"We're talking about weapons that use principles you don't understand," Orlov said. Klarot's scales flashed pale orange with irritation, and Orlov held up his hands. "I'm not saying you cannot learn the science and engineering that make these weapons work. As smart as you are, and you Arcans don't take second seat to anybody in the smarts department, you won't learn this in a few days or even weeks. Many of we Humans never learn the intricate details of rockets and nukes—including me."

Orlov called Academician Borisovich to join them. "Academician, can you give General Klarot a simple explanation of a rocket and a nuclear explosion?"

"Give me a moment, please," he answered.

A few minutes later, Borisovich joined them in Orlov's cabin. With three occupants, it was crowded, but still doable.

"General Klarot," Borisovich said, producing a rubber balloon. "This is a toy Human children play with." He inflated the balloon, squeezed the opening, and handed it to Klarot. "Be sure to keep the opening tightly shut," he said.

Klarot held the inflated balloon, examining it closely.

"Now, let go of the balloon completely," Borisovich said.

Klarot did and watched the balloon zoom around the cabin until its air was exhausted.

"That is how a rocket works," Borisovich said. "Force something out the back of a vehicle, and it will move forward, especially in space, but it works in an atmosphere, too." Borisovich smiled. "Going from here," he held up the flattened balloon, "to transporting a weapon thousands of kilometers between continents is a very big step, but the principle is the same."

Klarot retrieved the balloon, inflated it, and released it. "What an elegant concept," he hissed.

"Now, let's talk about nukes," Borisovich said. "You understand fire, and to some extent, I presume you understand explosives. Our world is ruled by chemistry. If we look at solid objects closely enough," he used his Link to create a holoimage between them, where the view zoomed in from the macro to the molecular level, "like you see here, they really consist of extremely small particles we call molecules. The molecules consist of even smaller particles called atoms." The holoimage zoomed in even farther. "Atoms consist of a nucleus surrounded by a swarm of electrons."

Klarot focused on the holoimage—something new for him—and listened carefully to the Academician's words.

"Everything in your normal life—growing plants, the birth, and death of animals and Arcans, storms, smelting metal, all these things—involve rearranging the swarms of electrons around these nuclei. Everything, except your sun, the Great Dragon, Ran."

Klarot looked at Borisovich in astonishment, his scales turning yellow. "Let me guess," Klarot said. "The sun involves the nucleus, not the electron swarm." He paused. "And nukes," he continued, "somehow use the power of the sun."

Borisovich lifted his eyebrows at Orlov, an expression Klarot did not understand.

"Do you know how large the sun is?" Borisovich asked.

"Not really. I'm still getting used to these ideas."

"Fair enough. Arcan is about thirteen thousand kilometers in diameter and some forty-one thousand kilometers around. The sun is so large that it would contain the volume of one million three hundred thousand Arcans. Since Arcan is spherical, more or less, the sun could hold about a million spherical Arcans."

Klarot floated in astonished silence, his scales remaining yellow. "It's really difficult to comprehend," he said finally. "And if I understood you correctly, the sun's fire involves only the nuclei, nothing else."

"Of certain atoms, yes," Borisovich added. "And a nuclear explosion recreates that environment in a small, confined space."

Orlov spoke up. "We make a vehicle that works similar to the balloon, but millions of times more powerful, we add guidance electronics, and stick a nuclear bomb on top."

✳

Klarot sat at his desk, reviewing what he had just learned. The Geroptic Nation is far more primitive than I ever imagined, he thought. Night—I'm more ignorant than I had imagined! I need to learn as much as possible from these offworlders, and I need to get Dombit in on the learning process.

Klarot called his aide-de-camp to his office. "Captain Dombit, I just returned from the alien starship. I learned a great deal that I want to pass on to you before it fades."

Klarot brought out the balloon Borisovich had used to demonstrate rockets. Deliberately, he walked Dombit through his entire conversation with the Academician.

"Questions?" he asked at the end.

"Many," Dombit said, "but I don't think you can answer them."

Klarot stood up. "Let's go to the Comm Center. I have some questions for Orlov."

In the Comm Center, Klarot called Orlov. When Orlov acknowledged, he laid out his proposal.

"If we Geroptics are to take full advantage of what you are offering, some of us need to climb out of our ignorance. This morning, I had a glimpse of what there is to learn. I would like to send Captain Dombit, whom you already know, to spend a half day every day with some of the Academician's people, learning as much as possible as quickly as possible. Can we do that?"

"Let me talk with the Academician. I'll call you back shortly."

Klarot remained in the Comm Center talking with Dombit about what this might mean. "As your knowledge increases, you will rise to the highest levels of our society. You will be equal to any Amred or Ceffid, and you can pass on your knowledge to those below you. You can become a beacon of enlightenment for The Geroptic Nation."

Orlov announced himself. "The Academician was most impressed with your quick learning today, and remembers Captain Dombit's rapid comprehension of the complexities he placed on the captain. He will be delighted to set up such a learning path, commencing tomorrow."

CHAPTER THIRTEEN

***Phoenix Starship Andromeda*—Hovering Invisibly in Nullspace Beyond Lodan, Thorpe's Office**

Ceffid President Spajo Boszut stepped into Thorpe's office. "I'm really beginning to like this form of transportation," he said to no one in particular.

Amred President Binecot Katengi arrived a moment later. The two Arcans grasped hands, greeting each other in the traditional way. Others arrived—SPC Director Sudaro Ferron, Astronauts Jocara Porovik and Kenred Zlaxiz, and Amred General Edoetti Kaylambo and Ceffid General Darflam Baxerd.

Thorpe walked through a portal behind his desk. "Sorry," he said, "I was dealing with a Bridge matter." He settled in his desk chair. "Please, everyone, make yourselves comfortable."

To his delight, Boszut noticed that every chair in the room could accommodate a Human or Arcan. He sat on the couch next to the astronauts, the attractive female, specifically.

"I've asked you here," Thorpe said, "because something important has come up, and I thought working on it as a group might produce a better response.

"The Geroptic Nation is undergoing a major change. Their military head, General Nirurian Klarot, seems to have usurped the Prophet and his theocratic government in a bloodless coup. I don't have the details yet, but the Prophet has disappeared, although my source believes he is still alive. From somewhere, Klarot has received modern weapons, at least at the infantry level. We have captured several of the small arms—they carry the earmarks of Udachny Enterprises, a rogue operation in the Solar System that ranks third in size behind Phoenix and Ogden. They have FTL and portal transportation, but less advanced than ours. The head of Udachny Enterprises, Isidor Orlov, caused a lot of lethal mischief in the Aster system a while back. We can presume he is here now, although we have not located him nor any of his vessels."

"What is the threat?" Katengi asked.

"In the Aster system, he fostered rebellion on one of the system's planets. His purpose was gaining exclusive trading rights. That may be his goal here."

"What should we do about it?" Boszut asked.

"The Geroptic Nation is an independent entity," Thorpe said. "It has every right to arm itself, especially if it feels threatened."

"That's not happening here," General Kaylambo said.

"Not from us either," General Baxerd added.

"There is another issue," Katengi said. "The Geroptic Nation Prophet has long stated his goal of bringing all Arcans into the rule of the Great Dragon in the Sky. General Klarot has never, so far as I know, disagreed with the Prophet on this matter. If he's running the show now over there, we may be looking at a surprise attack against both nations."

"They certainly don't have nukes," Kaylambo said.

"If they're getting weapons from this Orlov fellow," Baxerd said, "why not?"

"We've got to remember," Katengi said, "that the Geroptic population is virtually preindustrial. I can see no ethical way for either or both of us to conduct a preemptive strike against them. I, for one, will not be responsible for wiping out millions of innocents."

"I think we are all with you on that," Boszut said, "but we can't wait for Klarot to hit us with nukes."

Katengi looked pointedly at Thorpe.

"This is where we might play a role," Thorpe said. "We can detect the presence of nukes, and we can permanently disable them. We can locate conventional explosives, but can't do anything about them remotely." He turned to Ferron. "Sudaro, I want you to organize our M-Class spacecraft and pilots, and set them to patrol all of The Geroptic Nation, but especially the military installations. Each M-Class craft is equipped with a neutrino projector that will allow your pilots to disable the nukes they find."

The conversation mostly went over Boszut's head. He was a soldier turned reluctant administrator. The world of science had always meant less to him. As he listened to Thorpe brief Ferron, however, he gained a sense of just how much further advanced these offworlders were. They had enabled his liberation of Ceffid, and now they were helping the free people of Arcan retain their freedom in the face of almost certain attack by Klarot's forces. *But not all the offworlders*, he reminded himself. *That Orlov fellow seems bent on setting some of us against the rest of us.*

"This Orlov offworlder," Boszut said, deciding to vocalize his thoughts, "seems to be a real problem for you." He looked at Thorpe. "Is he Human like you?"

"He is," Thorpe answered, "but that doesn't make him like me or my crew on *Andromeda*. I have a much closer and more cordial relationship with Holon Mavik, the Asterian head of the Roganian L2 Group, than I ever could with Isidor Orlov."

"Then why is he still around?" Boszut asked, frankly confused, his scales rippling through several colors.

"I wish I could give you a satisfactory answer," Thorpe said. "It isn't through lack of trying. Orlov is a slippery, brilliant character. He has evaded our clutches several times. Back in the Solar System, he has skirted the line many times, but always kept his operations barely legal. The Federation has warned him and even sanctioned him, but he can bring to bear a force nearly equal to the Federation's, which means a virtual standoff. In the Aster system and here, it's a different question. We bring to any confrontation a far superior force, so Orlov has turned to subterfuge. Stated, we *know* he's here—we just can't find him. The Ran system is a very large place. We could search for years without ever spotting him. He has the capability of slipping into and out of warp, so he is virtually invisible. We know his tactics—we will find him, eventually. In the meantime, however, we need to focus on his mischief, keeping the Amred and Ceffid people safe."

✻

Katengi listened carefully to Thorpe's answer to Boszut's question. He had been wondering himself. He recalled one of his earliest conversations with Thorpe. Thorpe had said, *We are very much like you, just with different toys.* Katengi mulled that over. *I've watched these offworlders tackle several issues. They're smart and thoughtful, and they definitely have better toys, but I've seen no evidence that says they are superior to Arcans. In fact, I've seen several indications that we Arcans grasp concepts more quickly. Does that make us smarter, more intelligent? Maybe, but like Thorpe said, they have better toys, and that puts them on top.* He looked around the room, his eyes coming to rest on Jocara and Kenred. *Those two have integrated so completely with the offworlders, that they are almost part offworlder themselves. It's obvious that they and the Humans see them as full equals.* He chuckled quietly to himself. *If that's how it goes for all of us, in a century, Arcans will occupy many, if not all, senior positions on* Andromeda. *But it won't matter because nobody will distinguish between Arcan, Human, and Asterian. Is that really possible?* he wondered.

A conversation between the two generals pulled Katengi back to the present.

"The way I see it," Amred General Edoetti Kaylambo said, "if the SPC M-Class fighters can eliminate the nuke threat, we will face troops armed with modern weapons, troops that probably will swarm through strategically placed portals."

"You have a point," Ceffid General Darflam Baxerd responded, "but there is no way Klarot's million-lizard army will all be carrying modern weapons. Even an offworlder like Orlov has to manufacture them, and the troops need to train—I'm thinking Klarot will use the modern weapons to keep his regular troops in line."

"How do you see the Geroptic troops engaging us, General Baxerd?" Katengi asked.

"I would bring them through a portal as fast as possible." He turned to Thorpe. "Thorpe, do you have an estimate of how wide Orlov can make his portals?"

"It's entirely power dependent. He will place Locuses at the debarcation point or points, and power them in some manner. If he uses onsite LANR power, he probably can maintain a twelve to fourteen-meter-wide portal."

"LANR?" Baxerd asked.

"It's a power source that produces energy similar to how Ran produces power, but without all the heat and radiation. We used to use them until we adopted the Asterian mini black hole. Orlov still uses them."

"So, we're talking twelve abreast," Baxerd said. "That would be twelve every two seconds, three hundred sixty a minute—so, he can pour forty-three hundred twenty troops through a portal in twelve minutes."

"They'll probably be wielding sabers and spears with archers in the rear ranks," Kaylambo added. He turned to Thorpe. "Is there any way we can detect the troop portals before they open?"

"I'm afraid not," Thorpe answered. "That's where your military expertise will come into play. Where would *you* place the portals—you and General Baxerd?"

Thorpe paused and then added, "Theoretically, we can detect an opening portal. We've just never had the occasion to do so. I'll put Sally and Brad on it right away." He turned to Kenred.

"Kenred, please meet with Sally and Brad and brief them on this matter?"

✳

Kenred sought out *Andromeda's* scientific brains and told them what Thorpe wanted. Kenred remained in the lab, keeping out of the way, curious about how these Human geniuses went about their business. Ignoring him, Sally and Brad huddled together, looking at the portal detection problem.

"A portal is a dipole, right?" Brad said. "The negative charge is at the Locus and the positive charge is at the hyper-disk, so the electric field it produces is proportional to the dipole moment, the product of their charge and separation."

"When you open the portal," Sally said, "you suddenly collapse the dipole to a distance of just a few centimeters. This collapses the field associated with the dipole moment from very large to almost nonexistent."

"That would generate a very large signal," Brad said.

"Not one signal," Sally said, "two—a positive pulse from the hyper-disk end of the dipole and a negative pulse from the Locus end."

"Good point. I agree," Brad said, giving Sally a hug, "something we could detect and pinpoint from out here."

"If it's on our side of Arcan," Sally said with a smile.

"We'll place a hovering detector on the opposite side of Arcan with a line of sight to us," Brad said. "All we need now is to identify the pulse frequency of a collapsing dipole." Brad grinned broadly. "Then, if someone opens a portal anywhere on Arcan, we will immediately know exactly where the portal was opened."

"The way you describe it," Kenred said from his corner, "it sounds obvious and simple."

"It is, really," Sally said. "It's just something we never addressed before."

Phoenix Starship Andromeda—Hovering Invisibly in Nullspace Beyond Lodan, Bridge

With Andromeda hovering in nullspace beyond Lodan, but with a clear line of sight to Arcan, and there being no potential threats, Thorpe had set a more relaxed Bridge watch. He showed up daily at random times to keep the watchstanders on their toes, but he didn't require the focused attention that would otherwise have been the Bridge norm.

Thorpe came to the Bridge accompanied by the guests who had been in his office earlier. Except for Kenred and Jocara, none had seen the Bridge before.

Thorpe announced to the watchstanders, "We have some important visitors on the Bridge today—the presidents of Amred and Ceffid, their chief military officers, and the head of SPC, the Space Push Consortium. Should one of them approach your station, please introduce yourself and give him a general description of what you do."

Kenred wandered over to the EPD console. The watchstander was a young Asterian tech. Entangled-Particle-Detectors had fascinated Kenred since he first learned about them.

The EPD showed Lodan, Arcan, Ran, the other planets, and their moons, the two asteroid belts in any detail the operator wanted, and random space junk scattered throughout the Ran system. Arcan-Lodan L4 and L5 showed an accumulation of space junk. Items spotted by each passing wavefront displayed a persistent point in the EPD.

As Kenred watched, a bright point appeared at L4, but the next wavefront didn't see it, nor the next two, but then it showed up again. He watched it through two cycles.

"What's that?" he asked the operator, pointing to the bright spot when it next appeared.

"Space junk at L4. What else could it be?" the operator said.

"Then why isn't it a persistent point?" Kenred asked.

They watched it for several minutes, appearing and disappearing with a measurable frequency.

"Captain," the operator announced, "we got something on the EPD."

Thorpe walked to the EPD console. "What do you have, Son?"

The operator pointed out the bright spot that appeared and disappeared periodically. "Kenred spotted it. I thought it was just space junk at L4."

Thorpe called his guests to the console. "This is an Entangled-Particle-Detector," he said. "*Andromeda* pulses a continuous sequence of concentric entangled neutrino spheres where one entangled neutrino rides the expanding wavefront and the companion remains behind. The wavefronts expand at nearly lightspeed. When the wave passes something hiding, anything at all, the entangled companion back on *Andromeda* senses it instantly, and the holodisplay shows its location in three-dimensional space." He turned to the EPD console and pointed at the bright spot. "This object is something that is present sometimes for a passing wave and not present for others. Normal matter cannot behave this way. Either it's there or it isn't. It can't be both.

"There is one exception to this rule that we know about. We have discovered two ways to travel FTL—faster than light. *Andromeda* and our M-Class spacecraft use the MERT Drive. Here, one portal passes through another, that then passes through the first, and so on, moving the distance between the portals instantaneously. When the jump interval is sufficiently short, *Andromeda* can travel between our star systems, ten and a half lightyears, in one and a half minutes.

"The second FTL method was developed by Orlov's scientific team. They call it the ABO Drive. The drive creates a warp bubble around the craft and lowers the pressure at the front while increasing the pressure at the back. At their current level of development, an ABO craft can travel between our systems in about twenty-nine hours. If they ever can harness sufficient power, they might make the trip in a third of a second.

"You might think that we should have powered *Andromeda* by ABO since it seems capable of faster speeds, but the warp drive has a theoretical size limit, and *Andromeda* is well over that limit.

"Now, back to the exception to the rule that normal matter is either there or not. When a spacecraft enters warp, it is no longer *there*. What we are looking at is an ABO craft jumping into and out of warp to conceal its presence."

"Do you want me to hit it with long-range radar?" the radar operator asked.

"Negative!" Thorpe said. "Right now, he does not know where we are or that we are aware of him. Let's keep it that way."

"Can we take an M-Class ship near him and hit him with a stasis field when he flashes out of warp?" Kenred asked.

"That's a good question, but we can't do that for two reasons. First, his ship is coated with anti-stasis material, like the suits we wear to enter a stasis field. Second, even if he did not have the anti-stasis coating, if we missed, he would see our radar pulse and warp away. Right now, we know where he is, and he is unaware of us. Like I said, let's keep it that way."

Phoenix Starship *Andromeda*—Hovering Invisibly in Nullspace Beyond Lodan, Hangar Bay

SPC Director Sudaro Ferron stood on the deck of the hangar bay, surrounded by a group of Arcan pilots. They were young, eager, and impatient to get things going. His job was to ensure they could fight their craft, and that they returned safely.

"You Lizards are my Astronaut Corps. You joined to fly around Lodan and eventually to land and set up a station. Well…things have changed. Just ask StarChick and Bobcat about that. You're about to become starship pilots. A year ago, you were jet fighter pilots standing in line to ride an SPC capsule. Now, you're going to fly and fight an M-Class fighter. Each of you has been assigned a callsign and a spacecraft—two per craft. Each craft will carry an experienced Human or Asterian pilot who will help you adapt your jet fighter skills to these new machines, except *Shepard* and *Armstrong*, where StarChick and Bobcat will supervise. Each craft will also carry an experienced Human or Asterian pilot upload. These uploads will be part of the crew, but will not participate in the exercises. In the event of a mishap, the uploads will assume piloting responsibilities while the rest of the crew solves the problem."

Ferron looked at each pilot, dressed in an alien-made spacesuit with callsign boldly written across the back, globe helmet snapped to the belt, feet shod in TBH boots. Somehow, they looked younger than he remembered, and that made him feel old.

"Bobcat will assign you to specific exercises. Verify that you have locked out both your craft's antiparticle and neutrino beams and set the laser to training mode. The last thing you want to do is vaporize another pilot."

A quiet murmur rose from the group.

"Listen, Lizard-pilots, I know each of you has been fitted with an internal Link and continuous backup. So, if you vaporize one of yourselves, we can bring that lizard back, although I am told the process is not especially pleasant. We have only five M-Class spacecraft, however. We need all five of them. So, vaporize each other if you must, but spare the ships."

✳

Kenred took over and addressed the pilots. "Listen up! Each of you is a top-notch pilot or you would not have been selected as an astronaut. Your flying experience is with jets in an atmosphere. You developed an instinct for using the air around you to make your craft obey your wishes. It's all different out here. Your craft does the maneuvering, and Mother, your resident AI, does most of the thinking, shifting between MBH and MERT Drives as necessary to accomplish your goal. You got that—right? *Your* goal. You are the brains. You are the one trying to outthink the other guy. Listen to your instructors—they know what they are doing. What they teach you will bring you and your spacecraft back in one piece." He clapped his hands and slapped his tail on the deck.

"Okay, into your spacecraft, and let's get this show on the road!"

The Arcan pilots entered their spacecraft, joined by their Human or Asterian pilot instructors. One by one, the spacecraft vanished as their pilots took them to their designated start positions on MERT Drive. *PS Neil Armstrong* was the last to leave.

Becoming familiar with the onboard weapons was the initial part of the training exercise. With only five spacecraft to deal with, Kenred organized them in a single line flight with himself on *Armstrong* in the left-most position and StarChick on *Shepard* in the far-right position. Earlier, he had identified five mountain peaks on the Lodan farside that formed a line about halfway between the north pole and equator.

"Flight, this is Bobcat. Set your lasers to high power and unlock your antiparticle beams."

"Cupcake, Roger."

"GoGirl, Roger,"

"Rainbow, Roger."

"Snout, Roger."

"Jock, Roger."

Cupcake was his trainee, Neepons Kited, a female astronaut from Ceffid, cute as a house lizard. GoGirl was Nirlinn Odorbon, a female Ceffid astronaut assigned to *Collins*, the first to volunteer for any assignment. Rainbow was Klaaveola Nirhut, a female Amred astronaut assigned to *Scott*, whose scales frequently displayed multiple colors. Snout was Jurkit Blibeks, a male Ceffid astronaut assigned to

Bean, a tough lizard with a big snout. Jock was Kreax Nelgan, a male Amred astronaut assigned to *Shepard*, and StarChick's trainee; if he wasn't working, he was working out.

Kenred set up the flight so the five spacecraft would approach the peaks on a broad front. Each craft was assigned a peak to hit with laser. On the next pass, they used antiparticle beams. Kenred regrouped the flight, and they examined the results of their onslaught.

"This is Bobcat. You Lizards removed the top fifty meters from each peak. That's fifty meters of solid rock. Keep this in mind as you employ these weapons in actual combat. You wield enormous destructive power."

Inside *Armstrong*, Kenred turned to Kited. "You want to do the next run, too, Cupcake?"

"Sure, if I can. That was great!"

"This is Bobcat. Shift trainees, and let's do another run. Report when ready."

"Cupcake, Roger."

"Tiptoe, Roger."

"Slasher, Roger."

"SlapTail, Roger."

"Jock, Roger."

Tiptoe was Darcat Janoi, a female Amred astronaut assigned to *Bean*, the quietest of the Arcan astronauts. Slasher was Gzo Blubuts, a male Ceffid astronaut assigned to *Scott* who had distinguished himself in an unprovoked knife fight. SlapTail was Gloley Taced, a male Amred astronaut assigned to *Collins* who frequently slapped the ground with his tail.

Kenred duplicated the flight's approach to the now truncated peaks with the same instructions as before. After the assault, they regrouped, and Kenred addressed them.

"This is Bobcat. You Lizards removed another fifteen meters of a much wider mountain section. Again, I remind you to remember this destructive power when you are in combat. Now we will enter individual dogfight scenarios that are programmed into your spacecraft memories. First thing, however, supervisors personally lock the antiparticle beams and set lasers to training mode. Report to me when done."

Once Kenred had set his own weapons and received personal reports from the other four supervisors, he instructed the flight to break up into individual units and begin combat training. For the next ten hours, every spacecraft in the flight was *vaporized* at least twice, and every craft achieved one or more tactical victories.

Tired but satisfied pilots returned to *Andromeda* for a meal and sleep.

✳

The training continued for a full week, with pilots shifting spacecraft and crews mixing until everyone had trained with every other pilot trainee and with each supervisor.

When Kenred was satisfied with the progress of each pilot, he assembled them in the hangar bay. Sudaro Ferron joined them.

"Bobcat informs me you all have passed his vigorous training and are ready to don starship fighter pilot wings."

The pilots interrupted him with whoops, hollers, and tail slapping, as dark blue and lavender washed across their collective scales.

Ferron called each pilot to the front by his or her callsign, and one by one personally pinned their starship fighter pilot wings to their jumpers.

Military Training camp—The Geroptic Nation, Planet Arcan

Halfway between Dragon City and the southern tip of The Geroptic Nation, General Nirurian Klarot stood on a low rise watching his troops train. His officers understood the purpose of this training, and most of them had communicated this to their senior noncoms. Not even he knew how the portals functioned, but he and his senior officers had worked out an effective plan that made full use of them.

His overall plan was to decapitate the Amred and Ceffid governments, and then flood every city and military installation with overwhelming lizardpower. The trick was to place portals where enemy troops weren't. He had considered using drones, but in wartime conditions, they probably would be shot down. That left surreptitious hyper-brick placement, and his lizards were working on that.

As Klarot watched, a block of 576 troops in forty-six rows of twelve armed with saber and spear, with two final rows of archers, ran twelve abreast down a slope through a pole-marked gap fourteen meters wide and fourteen meters high. The top of the gap was marked with a tight leather rope. The gap represented the battlefield troop portal. The downslope gave the archers clearance above the charging troops, and the high top allowed the archers to release their arrows at any angle from behind the portal. The troops ran through the gap and scattered left and right, while the archers rained arrows on the opposing troop positions, and designated archers took out obvious leaders. His goal was to get the entire troop block through the portal in one and a half minutes. Right now, they were taking five minutes, but the noncoms were urging them to move faster and not trip over their feet as they ran in close quarters. The key was placing the portals where they would not run into automatic weapon fire. Klarot left this decision to his field commanders, but kept himself in the loop.

✻

General Klarot wanted one nuclear-tipped missile for each major city in Amred and Ceffid. When he expressed his desire to Orlov, to his surprise, Orlov resisted.

"My friend," Orlov said, "you simply do not understand the destructive effect of these weapons. You don't need to destroy every major city in these nations, just decapitate their governments. Your massed troops will take care of the rest." Orlov heaved a sigh of frustration. "Nuclear weapons are high maintenance, not like conventional explosives. If you neglect routine maintenance of nukes, when it comes time to use them, all you get is a poof and a fizzle."

"I've got lizards who can learn the maintenance."

"I agree, but their learning will take months. It's not something that can be done by checking off boxes on a maintenance guide. I thought you wanted to overcome Amred and Ceffid before the offworlders have completely inculcated themselves into their cultures."

"Okay," Klarot said, "I concede your points, but I want four missiles, one for each capital and a backup."

The Village of Cordan—Southeastern Corner of The Geroptic Nation, Planet Arcan

Over the years, although Judhee Groklet was as isolated as one could be on Arcan, he kept abreast of current Arcan developments using a small satellite transceiver he had procured on a surreptitious trip to Amred. He powered it with a Leyden jar and generator he kept in the back of his school.

He learned of the developments in Dragon City and the apparent disappearance of Prophet Dudengi Vrokhun. He was uncertain whether this was a positive or negative development.

To the south, the military was showing a lot of activity and, according to several reports from Amred, had received modern arms from an offworlder. Now, that interested Groklet. Someone from out there had finally discovered Arcan despite everything they had done to keep themselves concealed.

CHAPTER FOURTEEN

***Phoenix Starship Neil Armstrong*—Cislodan Space, Ran Star System**

Kenred formed up his five-ship flight 100 kilometers toward L4 from Andromeda. They formed a V-formation with Armstrong on point.

"This is Bobcat, listen up, everyone. We are on a war footing. The Geroptics have been armed by Thorpe's long-time rival. We don't know what they have, but we're looking for nukes. Spread out in a line a thousand klicks apart—I'll take the center slot, a thousand klicks over the surface. We'll transit north to south. Have your AI maintain a focus on the neutrino detector. Note the geographic position of any hits, but keep scanning. Questions?"

There were none.

"On my lead, close V-formation until we form up in a line at the north end of The Geroptic Nation."

The five M-Class spacecraft performed a coordinated MBH transfer to their designated location over the north end of The Geroptic Nation. They spread out over 4,000 kilometers and commenced a southward sweep.

"This is Snout. I got four hits over Dragon City off my port."

"This is Rainbow. I got four hits over Dragon City off my starboard."

"This is Bobcat, Roger. Maintain the sweep until we hit the south end of the continent."

An hour later, the five craft had covered all The Geroptic Nation with only the four hits near Dragon City in the northeast corner of the country. Kenred pulled the flight away from Arcan.

"This is Bobcat. I'll disable the nukes. StarChick, hang ten klicks off my starboard quarter to back me up. The rest of you return to *Andromeda*."

✳

Kenred gave the nuke site coordinates to the AI.

"Cupcake, take us to the location five hundred klicks above the target."

Neepons Kited faced the control console, her scales rippling dark blue with excitement, and ordered, "Mother, take us five hundred klicks above the coordinates Bobcat just gave you."

Moments later, *Armstrong* was hovering over Dragon City. Kenred confirmed the presence of four nukes. "Cupcake, hit each target in sequence with a narrow-focus neutrino beam."

"Roger that."

The occupants of the spacecraft noticed nothing. Any outside observer would have noticed nothing. Technicians near the warheads would have noticed nothing. A warhead technician actually conducting preventive maintenance on the weapons might have noticed a passing transient, but Klarot had no one trained for such maintenance.

"Okay, Cupcake, take us home."

Udachnyy Zvezdolet Sergei Krikalyov—Flashing In and Out of Warp at Lodan L4, Operations Center

Once again, General Klarot floated mid-air in Orlov's cabin aboard *UZ Sergei Krikalyov*. Orlov, as usual, had strapped himself into his chair.

"Orlov, I'm here to report the completion of our troop training and our readiness to proceed. The missiles you supplied are at the ready in the Dragon City Military Compound. Your technicians have set the missiles to launch ready and verified their targeting information.

I have strategically placed lizards in locations throughout Ceffid and Arcan with hyper-bricks set to open fourteen-meter-wide portals."

"When will you launch operations?" Orlov asked.

"How long can the missiles remain at launch ready?"

"Three days. Then they need to stand down to undergo another launch check. That takes about a day."

"I want to run through our complete plan one more time with my field commanders before we launch the operation. That will take me a day, leaving us a two-day margin."

"Remember," Orlov cautioned, "when the two bombs explode, both countries will be without central governments. You will have a relatively short time to invade unopposed, before someone takes charge and organizes an effective resistance. Give it a day for the realization to sink in that their governments are gone, then hit them with everything you've got."

✳

Back in his Dragon City Headquarters, Klarot reached out to Dombit, and together, they hurried to the newly established missile compound. Ran shone brightly in a nearly cloudless sky on that cool morning. It had taken Dombit several days of diligent design and construction supervising to create the launch facility so close to the HQ.

Guided by Academician Borisovich, his troops dug five-meter-deep pits under each launch pad, curving to horizontal, and then twenty-meter tunnels opening through the face of a small rise. They piped seawater to fill the pit below the pad with sufficient water to flash to steam on launch, but keeping the horizontal tunnels open to exhaust the steam and flame.

Both missiles sat launch-ready above the flooded pits. A hundred meters distant, a blockhouse-style control room completed the launch facility. It contained two countdown timers and launch switches, nothing more. The ballistic missiles were programmed to launch, orient themselves regarding the target, and drop the first stage as soon as the fuel was spent.

Launch time for missile one was arbitrary. When it launched toward Ceffidia, the second timer started so missile two would launch to bring its warhead over Amred City when the Ceffidia warhead exploded.

Klarot and Dombit completed their inspection of the launch facility. "You did a great job installing the blast pits and deflectors," Klarot said. "Tomorrow, we'll see how well they work."

✳

Klarot called his field commanders to his Dragon City HQ. They arrived one by one, following Dombit's protocol for cycling the portals.

"This is our final meeting before we commence hostilities," Klarot told them. "Each of you has received a Locus and its accompanying small LANR that will power your troop portal. I know these portals seem like black magic to you, but you all have seen them work. LANRs power your troop transports, so you know they work as well. I want to emphasize to you that the LANRs powering your troop portals are very small. They pack more power than anything you've ever known, but the troop portals consume more power than anything you've even known. You need to get your troops, your carriers, and yourself through the portal as quickly as you can. When your LANR runs out of power, your portals will collapse.

"You have trained your troops hard. Captain Dombit tells me that each of you can push a five hundred seventy-six troop block through a portal in ninety seconds. I'm impressed. That means that you can field three hundred eighty-four dozen troops in twelve minutes. Your LANR will keep the portal open at fourteen meters wide and fourteen high for seventy-two minutes so you can pass your troop transports, field artillery, and additional troop blocks. After seventy-two minutes, the portal collapses to a small pipe that will accommodate the comm lines Captain Dombit supplied you with. The LANR will maintain this small portal for several weeks. When you need ammunition or other supplies, the portal can open to door-size long enough to pass through the ammo and supplies. Try to keep this mode as short as possible, since every time you go to door size, you decrease your total comm line time.

"We have two days remaining to launch the missiles at the capitals. After that, the missiles require a full day's maintenance, followed by another three-day launch window. Each of you has a comm line that connects to my Comm Center through a comm portal. When you return to your posts after this meeting, review your troop movements and logistics with your lizards. When you are confident extra time will not significantly improve your performance, let Captain Dombit know, and I will set the date and time for commencement of hostilities. Sooner is better, but not at the expense of our ability to prevail."

✳

Dombit pushed hard, but he couldn't get every commander's go-ahead inside the remaining two days of open launch window. A part of him was frustrated, knowing that he could not report success to General Klarot. On the other hand, he reasoned, if the commanders go into battle and fail, then…

When it was clear they would miss the window, Dombit met with Orlov on *Krikalyov.*

"I need your maintenance tech to recertify the missiles for launch," he told the offworlder. "The field commanders could not guarantee readiness in the remaining time for the last launch window."

"I'll have him at your HQ tomorrow morning. He will take all day for the four missiles, but you already know that." Orlov paused, and then asked slyly, "Are you sure your commanders are up to the task?"

"I can't answer that, Sir. The commanders have way more experience than I do."

"Really? When did they last fight a war?"

"Not in our lifetimes, Sir."

"So," Orlov said with a wide grin, "your commanders have more experience parading troops, inspecting barracks, and other meaningless tasks. Do they have the balls to pull this off?"

"I don't understand, Sir?"

Orlov gave Dombit a short course in Human anatomy and the source for the expression. Dombit opened his eyes wide, blinking them.

"I get it. We have an equivalent expression in Geroptic—Are their snakes long enough? I really cannot address that. I've watched them train their troops. From what I saw, they did an excellent job.

They adapted to motorized troop carriers quickly and smoothly. They appear to be ready for a successful campaign."

"So why do they seem reluctant to move forward? Is it *balls*—er, *snakes?*"

"Let's see what happens tomorrow evening when the missiles are once again ready to launch," Dombit said, his confidence shaken by Orlov's skepticism.

✳

As the missile tech finished prepping the fourth missile the following evening, Dombit took another survey of the field commanders. To his delight, they all declared a *Go!* on Klarot's orders, their schedules coordinated with the time the bombs would explode over the capitals. Dombit reported their readiness to Klarot.

General Klarot met Captain Dombit an hour later in the blockhouse launch center. Dombit reviewed the procedure with his superior.

"Flight time to Ceffidia is forty-seven minutes; time to Amred City is twenty-two minutes. The launch timers are set so the Amred City missile will launch twenty-five minutes after the Ceffidia missile. The field commanders will open their portals twelve minutes after the simultaneous blasts—fifty-nine minutes after the Ceffidia launch. As soon as the first missile launches, you should return to the Comm Center to give the order through the portal lines to open the troop portals at the fifty-nine-minute mark. I will remain here to ensure the second missile launches properly."

"You've done well, Major, way beyond my expectations!"

"Sir?"

"That's right, Son, I'm promoting you to Major. You've functioned at least at this level or even higher ever since we undertook this project." Klarot handed Dombit major devices. "I expect you to be in proper uniform when you return to HQ."

With his scales alternating between blue and lavender, Dombit clutched the devices in one hand and reached for the launch lever with the other, He looked at Klarot for confirmation. The general nodded.

Phoenix Starship Neil Armstrong—Hovering over The Geroptic Nation, Planet Arcan, Ran Star System

PS Neil Armstrong and the other four M-Class starships hovered high over The Geroptic Nation. Kenred knew the location of the four deactivated nuclear bombs, but none of the pilots knew what offensive arrangements Orlov might have made with the Geroptics. Missile delivery of the nukes was an obvious choice, but the Geroptics had no modern military infrastructure. Kenred could imagine no way they could mount an effective assault on Amred or Ceffid. Thorpe had explained that the offworlder Human, Orlov, did not have the physical resources to support any kind of large-scale operation by the Geroptics. And they were mostly preindustrial. To Kenred, the Geroptics seemed hopelessly outgunned and outclassed.

Nevertheless, he and his flight stood guard in space above The Geroptic Nation. When hostilities commenced, they were ready to do their part, whatever that turned out to be.

As Ran rose in the east, reflecting brightly off the ocean surface below them, Neepons Kited announced, "Bobcat, I've got radar activity near Dragon City."

"Be more specific, Cupcake."

"Mother, analyze radar imaging," Kited ordered,

"Ballistic missile launch," the AI said, "toward the west." Moments later, the AI continued. "Target is Ceffidia. Arrival time forty-seven minutes after launch—thirty-nine minutes from now."

"Cupcake, check the neutrino detector."

"It's carrying a nuke—one we deactivated," she answered.

On portal comms, Kenred said, "*Andromeda*, this is Bobcat. We have a missile launch from Dragon City to Ceffidia to arrive in thirty-five minutes. The nuke it carries is a dud."

"This is Thorpe, Roger. Splash the missile when it passes over the western ocean."

"StarChick, it's Bobcat. Splash the underway missile once it reaches the ocean."

✳

Jocara had been tracking the missile over The Geroptic Nation. "Jock," she said to Kreax Nelgan, "when it passes the shoreline, give it another minute and splash it with the laser."

Nelgan ordered, "Mother, target the missile with the laser. One minute after it crosses the shoreline, destroy it."

✳

As Kenred on *Armstrong* received the splash report on the missile from Jocara, Kited reported "Second missile launch. Mother, generate the specifics."

The AI responded, "Ballistic missile heading east. Destination is Amred City, time of arrival twenty-two minutes."

Kenred turned to Kited. "Cupcake, splash that missile now!"

"Mother," Kited said, "hit that missile with laser and destroy it now."

Dragon City Headquarters—The Geroptic Nation, Planet Arcan

Newly minted Major Dombit stepped out of the blockhouse to watch the missile rise into the sky. To his utter surprise, as it arched out over the ocean, it suddenly exploded. He hurried back to the Comm Center and queried the Northwest Post Commander. He had not personally seen the missile explode, but several of his lizards reported seeing an explosion in the western sky at about the time the missile would have passed. Dombit went to Klarot's office.

"General, both missiles exploded over the water, The Amred City missile exploded immediately after launch over the water. The Ceffidia missile crossed the continent and then exploded over the water."

"We need to talk with Orlov," Klarot said. They walked together down the passageway to the Comm Center.

Dombit explained the two explosions to Orlov over the comm circuit. He concluded with, "based upon my limited knowledge of these things, the Amred City missile exploding right after launch could have been a missile problem. But the Ceffidia missile exploding over the water after crossing the continent does not seem like a missile problem. And both missiles exploding over the water as they did cannot be a coincidence."

Klarot added, "The major has stated it accurately, and I agree with him."

"You're correct. We have an interference problem."

"What do you mean, *interference*?" Klarot asked.

"I mean, *Andromeda* has entered the conflict, however subtly."

"What can they do…subtly?" Dombit asked.

"You've already seen one thing. I suspect one of their M-Class craft shot your missiles down from space."

Orlov went silent as he conferred with Academician Borisovich. Klarot and Dombit looked at each other with questions, their scales rippling several colors as they showed their uncertainty.

"My Academician tells me he is unaware of any specific capability *Andromeda* has that we don't, but he knows they have done much neutrino research. This work could have produced capabilities we don't know about."

"Such as?" Klarot asked, his scales turning orange.

Dombit noted the color change, thinking, The general must be pretty angry for orange to break through his control.

"Borisovich tells me that under certain circumstances, neutrinos can affect nuclear weapons, but we have no evidence that *Andromeda* has anything that could do this."

From Dombit's perspective, they had all the evidence they needed. "Can you send a nuclear weapons tech to inspect the weapons atop the remaining two missiles?" he asked, working hard to keep his scales a neutral green.

"We'll send someone within the hour," Orlov said.

✸

"That was pretty gutsy," Klarot told Dombit.

"Ever since receiving my commission," Dombit said, "I've watched senior officers cover their tails in the same way, meaning no disrespect, Sir." He paused a moment. "I predict their tech will find both nukes inoperative." Dombit swallowed. "I also predict they won't be able to repair them. If this invasion is going to work, we need to find another way to deliver nukes to the capitals."

Klarot offered him an encouraging smile. "You will find a way to make it happen," the general told him. "I am very impressed with your resourcefulness."

"Thank you, Sir," Dombit said, but something inside raised a red flag. Dombit returned to the Comm Center and sat reflecting on the entire matter.

I'm a soldier, and soldiers fight. But why do we fight? The Geroptic Nation hasn't been attacked. We are facing no external threat—unless Orlov poses an implied threat. The only thing that has really happened is that Orlov assisted the general in displacing the Prophet. And now General Klarot is planning to attack Amred and Ceffid. But why? What have they done to us? This question weighed heavily on Dombit's mind as he reviewed all that had happened in the previous months.

"Major," the general signaled him through a recently installed voice tube, "arrange a meeting with the field commanders here in two hours, and meet with me a half hour before their arrival."

As Dombit set up the field commander meeting via portal comms, he asked himself, *What role am I playing in all this? I've been the facilitator in virtually every step, as we have armed our troops with modern weapons, set up portals for the invasion, and even prepared nuclear weapons for delivery. Do I want to be responsible for killing several million lizards in the capital cities? This is not the way of The Book of the Great Dragon, and it is not the Geroptic way.*

As this realization hit Dombit, he sat and heaved a deep sigh. *How can I extricate myself from this mess?* he asked himself.

The Village of Cordan—Southeastern Corner of The Geroptic Nation, Planet Arcan

The news from Amred was depressing. Judhee Groklet searched the available channels for more information on the failed Klarot nukes. Nothing specific.

Groklet had an Amred connection, but he rarely tapped into it for fear of discovery by the increasingly sophisticated Dragon City Headquarters personnel. With nuclear weapons in the wind, Groklet figured it was time to find out as much as possible. He spent a half hour on his electrostatic generator, charging up his Leyden jar so he could spend some time with his Amred connection.

"This is not known even at the highest levels," his contact said. "This is informed opinion from a connection I have with the SPC Astronaut Corps."

His contact then told him that there might be someone high up in the Klarot administration, someone close to General Klarot himself, who may be sabotaging the Geroptic nukes.

"Is there any way you can put me in contact with this individual?"

"We're not sure he exists, and we don't know who he is."

"Let's assume he exists," Groklet said. "Does your Astronaut Corps contact have access to the offworlders?"

"Probably."

"Put the problem to them," Groklet said. "I really want to talk with this lizard."

CHAPTER FIFTEEN

Phoenix Starship Andromeda—Conference Room

All the active players were present at the conference table, even Max, greeting his friends as he strolled the table's length.

"We're dealing with a serious situation," Thorpe said. "Kenred, tell us what you know."

Kenred knew everyone at the table, some better than others. He reached out and stroked Max as he walked by. Kenred still was not sure what role Max played in anything, but he always seemed to be part of anything important. He started speaking.

"The M-Class pilots did a thorough survey of The Geroptic Nation, looking for nuclear devices. We found four nuclear devices near Dragon City, and we took them out. Then we shot down the first two missiles they launched. We identified several concentrations of troops along with conventional weapons depots. We did nothing about them." He looked at Thorpe, indicating he was done.

Thorpe picked up the conversation. "Orlov is not stupid. He will have checked the nukes and knows they are not operational. Only we could have done that. He knows this. I think he has armed the Geroptics on their promise he will receive exclusive trade rights when they prevail.

"Orlov remained in the Solar System during *Andromeda's* construction. He probably received reports about the starship, but I don't think he realizes the extent of our project. In an open conflict with us, he cannot prevail or even inflict significant casualties on us. He probably knows this, which is why he has remained hidden.

"As we've discussed earlier, I think he intends to bring the Geroptic forces to Amred and Ceffid by portal. You Lizards," he indicated the two Amred generals, "have already selected the most likely spots for Klarot's incoming troops. The problem is, of course, that we are only guessing. We think they can pass five hundred seventy-six troops through a portal in ninety seconds. If you know where they are entering, you can greet them with withering fire, but if they land unopposed, they can establish a beachhead to become a formidable adversary. Sally and Brad have worked out something that should help here. Brad…"

Brad's broad face burst into a wide grin, something Kenred had long since learned to interpret instinctively. He had come to understand just how special the Sally-Brad team was at solving problems. Thorpe had told him they were responsible for nearly all the significant advances in his company. He wondered what they had concocted this time.

"The idea was to detect a portal when it opens," Brad said. "I won't go into the details, but it turned out to be an application of something we already understood. *Andromeda* now can detect and locate an opening portal anywhere on Arcan—directly for the hemisphere we see, and indirectly via a space-born hovering sensor for the other hemisphere." He spread his hands on the table in front of him. "That's it, I guess."

Thorpe picked up again. "We think Klarot will try to send nukes to both Amred City and Ceffidia by portal. Ideally, Orlov will send the nukes to Klarot by portal, we will detect and disable them, and when they send them to the capitals, nothing will happen. The problem is nothing ever happens ideally, especially during wartime. We need to be prepared to disable the nukes the moment they appear in Amred City and Ceffidia. We can allow for no delay—nothing at all. The moment a bomb appears in either or both capitals, we need to disable it instantly!"

Dragon City Headquarters—The Geroptic Nation, Planet Arcan

Major Teynal Dombit kept his private thoughts to himself as General Klarot and he worked out the details together for how they would repurpose two troop portals to act as nuke delivery portals. If he expected to accomplish any changes in how things were going, he needed to remain in the general's good graces.

The field commanders gathered in the Comm Center with Dombit, and Klarot joined them.

"We have run into a glitch," Klarot said. "The missiles that were to have destroyed Amred City and Ceffidia apparently were shot down by Amred and Ceffid spacecraft, probably aided by the starship *Andromeda*. Our intent was to cut the head off the snake by destroying both seats of government. We had two backup missiles with their own warheads. Major Dombit, out of diligent caution and a sense that things were not entirely as we thought with the offworlder Orlov, demanded that the offworlder send a technician to verify the nukes. They, too, were non-functional.

"Orlov's explanation is that somehow, *Andromeda* manipulated the environment around the nukes, rendering them useless. Major Dombit is inclined to agree with Orlov; I'm not so sure. Nevertheless, we needed to develop an alternative to the missiles carrying nukes. Major Dombit worked out an alternative arrangement with Orlov. Major Dombit…" He gestured to Dombit.

"I assume when Orlov's people transfer a nuke to Arcan by portal, somehow the Amred and Ceffid spacecraft, or even *Andromeda*, neutralize it immediately, or at least within several minutes. We are repurposing the two portals nearest the capitals from their troop transfer configuration to a simple portal. The field commanders responsible for these two portals will send agents through the portals. These agents will move the hyper-bricks into the center of each capital and return. They will receive another hyper-brick that they will transfer to each capital and conceal in a place that will accommodate a cubic-meter-size container.

"I have arranged with Orlov to deliver two small nukes configured on little wagons that we can wheel through the portals whose Locuses are here in Dragon City HQ. The nukes will be exposed to any spacecraft for a few seconds at most. They will be timed to detonate five seconds after passing through the portals."

"That still leaves more than five seconds of exposure," Colonel Blozok Garlan, from the southernmost command post, said. "Just how fast are these offworlders?"

"We don't know, Colonel," Dombit said, "but reason says that detection might take a second, followed by several seconds to analyze the signal, followed by two or three seconds to respond with whatever they use to disable nukes. It will take us at least that long to receive the nukes, open the portals to the capitals, push the nukes through, and close the portals."

"Let me get this straight," Garlan said, scales rippling yellow. "You will receive two nukes, set a timer in each for a few seconds, open a portal, push them through, and close the portal. Did I get that right?"

"Almost, Colonel. We'll open the portal and then set the timers. The last thing we want is a nuclear detonation at Dragon City HQ, because we couldn't open the portal." Dombit opened his eyes wide, blinking, his scales rippling pale blue.

✳

Klarot took the floor again. "When the nukes detonate in Amred City and Ceffidia, I'll give the order to open the troop portals. Without their central governments, the Amred and Ceffid armies cannot coordinate their actions. Remember to consolidate your entry points and reinforce them as soon as you are able. Communicate back through your portals and have your lizards forward all reports directly to me here in Dragon City. We will maintain the overall picture here and will direct your troops through you to wherever they are needed.

"Nevertheless, if you see an opportunity to gain a strategic advantage, don't wait for my input. Take it and report back to me through the portals. Whatever you do, don't let your advance stall. We have the lizardpower to push their armies into the sea."

Colonel Garlan asked hesitatingly, scales rippling pale yellow, "What if the nukes don't detonate?"

"They will," Klarot said, "but I will only order your troops through the portals if Amred City and Ceffidia are destroyed." He looked sternly at Garlan, his scales rippling pale orange. "If that actually happens, we'll deal with it then."

Phoenix Starship Neil Armstrong—Hovering over Amred City, Nation of Amred, Planet Arcan

Kenred checked his position for the dozenth time—one hundred klicks over the center of Amred City, hovering on MBH drive. The AI simultaneously scanned the dipole detector and was prepared to fire a concentrated beam of neutrinos at any nuclear device that might appear at the location indicated by the dipole detector. eDaphne backed him up from her matrix in the Armstrong console.

Jocara and eKim were similarly hovering above Ceffidia, their focus just as intense as his.

Logic said these two locations were the most likely destinations of the nukes that would probably arrive by portal. *That's two uncertainties,* Kenred thought, *each driven by a separate set of variables. It is pretty certain that the targets are Amred City and Ceffidia, given that's where the original missiles were targeted. It's not so certain the nukes will arrive by portal.*

Thorpe had placed several dipole sensors hovering over both Amred and Ceffid, with portal links to the AIs of the three other M-Class craft. Any opening portal would instantly and automatically move one of the craft by MERT Drive so its AI could disable any appearing nuke with her neutrino beam.

"Bobcat, it's StarChick. I'm a nervous wreck."

"Be strong, StarChick. We have the offworlder's best technology working for us."

"But if we're wrong, millions will die."

"I know, so let's make this work!"

Dragon City Headquarters—The Geroptic Nation, Planet Arcan

Major Teynal Dombit passed through a portal into the vast warehouse he had previously visited located somewhere in the Human Solar System.

Time was running out for Dombit to do something about the Saurian tragedy that was about to happen. He strongly suspected that the offworlders working with Amred and Ceffid had disabled the first two nukes. *In fact,* he thought, *I suspect the nukes on the two destroyed missiles were already disabled before they were shot down. This time, we've got things timed to the split second. Unless their capabilities are way better than I think, they will not have time to detect, pinpoint, and disable these last nukes.*

A Human met him and led him to the two nukes. They were small, not encased in anything, probably to make them lighter, taking up the space of a half-meter cube. Each sat on a small, four-wheel cart, much like the toy wagons used by young boys in his culture.

"Will you take them with you now?" the Human asked through a translator.

"No," Dombit said. "We need to minimize their exposure on Arcan. I intend to signal you, open incoming and outgoing portals, and then move the wagons as rapidly as possible from your portal to mine." He turned to look at one of the nukes. "Show me the timer."

The timer was a knob with a line that pointed to symbols Dombit did not understand. "What are these symbols?" he asked.

"One through ten seconds," the Human answered. He handed Dombit a marking stylus. "Add your own symbols," he said.

Dombit marked the dial with Geroptic numbers one through ten. "How does the timer work?" he asked.

"You set the dial and then push this button." The button was under a hinged cover to prevent accidental pressing. "You can set the delay now and press the button when ready."

"What happens if one of these exposed wires breaks?" Dombit asked.

"No detonation. They're all purposed. This isn't a puzzle like a hero solves on a holocast thriller."

"When the portal opens, how long will you take to push the wagons through?"

"Several seconds."

Dombit walked around each nuke, examining them, looking for any differences. They appeared identical.

"What are these wires made of?" he asked.

"Solid copper with a plastic insulating cover. They will withstand normal abrasion, but a sharp edge can cut them, so be careful with knives and other sharp objects."

Dombit handed the Human a hyper-brick. "This is a portal directly to my launch location. When you receive my signal, stand by the wagons. When I open the portal, push the nukes through immediately."

"Got it! How long till your signal?"

"A few minutes at most."

✳

Dombit returned to Dragon City HQ, where he verified everything was in position to execute the plan. He opened the portals to the capital cities. The portals looked like ordinary doors opening to a city street. He looked at the four troops selected for the honor of participating directly in the momentous event.

"When I open the portal to the nukes, Humans on their side will push them through the portal. You two," he indicated two troops, "move one nuke right up to this door. And you two," he indicated the remaining two, "move the other right to this door." He placed himself between the doors, concealing a small blade in his hand. "Concentrate on the other side of the portal. We don't want any interference when you push the nukes through."

Dombit looked at the first pair and opened his eyes wide. Then he turned to the second with the same Arcan smiling gesture. "I will set the timer and activate the sequence for the first nuke. When I say *Go!*, push it all the way through the door and collapse the portal by pushing this." He showed them a button on a hyper-brick and handed it to one of them. "Then I'll set and activate the second timer. When I say *Go!*, you Lizards push the nuke through the second door and collapse that portal." He showed them a button on a second hyper-brick and handed it to one of them. He looked keenly at the four lizards. "Are you absolutely clear about this?"

All four troops nodded.

"If we screw this up, Dragon City will be consumed in a nuclear blast!"

✳

Dombit steadied himself between the two portals, listening to city sounds coming through each. The small blade in his right hand seemed to weigh a ton. He opened the portal to the distant warehouse. Two Humans pushed the first nuke-laden wagon through where his two troops pulled it right to the Amred City door. The Humans pushed the second nuke through, and his guys moved it to the Ceffidia door.

Dombit reached out with his left hand and twisted the Amred City knob until it pointed to eight. Then he slipped his right hand under the strut that held the switch while flipping the cover open with his left. He threw the switch and simultaneously cut a wire beneath the strut.

"Go!" he shouted and reached for the second nuke.

While he set the Ceffidia timer, the first two troops pushed the Amred City nuke through the door and collapsed the portal. He set the second timer for eight seconds, flipped the switch cover, and threw the switch while groping under the strut for a wire to cut. To his horror, the blade slipped from his fingers and fell inside the nuke framework.

In just seconds, the nuke would detonate. Out of desperation, he grabbed a handful of wires and pulled with all his strength. He felt an initial resistance that suddenly released slightly and shouted, "Go!" as he pulled his hand out. He helped the troops push the wagon through the door, eying the timer all the while. As it reached *One*, the portal collapsed.

The four troops stared at Dombit's right hand. He looked down—a finger was oozing blood.

"Must have cut it on the underside of that strut," he said.

CHAPTER SIXTEEN

Phoenix Starship Neil Armstrong—Hovering over Amred City, Nation of Amred, Planet Arcan

Kenred started when the AI activated the alarm. "The dipole has detected an opening portal in the center of Amred City," the AI reported. "Nuke not detected…wait! Nuke detected. I hit it with a neutrino beam."

"Bobcat, it's StarChick. We just detected a portal opening in the center of Ceffidia, a nuke, and deactivated it."

"This is Bobcat, Roger. We did the same here. Stand by." He called Thorpe and explained the situation. "I will land near the nuke, inspect it, and leave a hyper-disk linked to *Andromeda* so you can examine it."

"Both of you do that," Thorpe said. "I'll send hyper-disks linked to the lab."

✳

Kenred dropped *Armstrong* to the pavement right next to the nuke. He grabbed the hyper-disk Thorpe had sent him and exited down the ramp. The device was a small open cage on a little wagon. It had a timer dial with Human numerals and Geroptic ones next to them. On a strut beside the timer was a switch with a spring cover.

The cover was open. He saw something protruding from under the switch. He looked more closely and found a cut wire. Kenred sent a holoimage to Thorpe.

"Thorpe, this unit was sabotaged before it was pushed through the portal."

"Bobcat, it's StarChick. I found several loose wires right beneath the activator switch. They appear to have been pulled free. Also, there's a small folding blade in the wagon bed. I think this unit was sabotaged before it left The Geroptic Nation."

"One more thing," Thorpe told them both. "Find the hyper-bricks they used for the portals and destroy them."

The Village of Cordan—Southeastern Corner of The Geroptic Nation, Planet Arcan

Judhee Groklet charged his Leyden jar and contacted his Amred connection.

"I have good news," his connection said. "My Astronaut Corps contact tells me he is positive there is a high-up lizard disrupting Klarot's nukes. He says this lizard is doing it at great risk to himself."

"Can he put me in contact?"

"He will talk with an offworlder friend—yeah, they're developing friendships with our people now."

Udachnyy Zvezdolet Sergei Krikalyov—Flashing In and Out of Warp at Lodan L4, Operations Center

Dombit notified General Klarot the moment the portals to the capitals closed. The general passed through a portal into *UZ Sergei Krikalyov*'s Operations Center, where Orlov awaited him.

"The two nukes should have detonated within the last minute or two," Klarot told Orlov.

"The transit time for light from Arcan to our location is about one and a half seconds," Orlov said. "No matter what Arcan's rotational position is right now, at least one of the capitals should be visible." He scanned the planet. "Ceffidia is cloud covered, but we should see the blast, anyway."

After a long five second pause, Orlov said, "Nothing, General, nothing at all."

"Did you supply me with duds?" the general hissed, his scales rippling bright orange with anger.

"Absolutely not, General. My techs verified the devices moments before we delivered them to your lizard, Major Dombit. I understand that within seconds, he set both timers, activated the switches, and transferred the nukes to the capitals. Your Major is good. I'm confident nothing went wrong at his end."

"But they did not detonate. Where does that leave us?"

"There would have been two or three seconds from when the major pushed the nukes through the portals and closed them, and the nukes detonated." Orlov shook his head. "I must conclude that *Andromeda* can detect a portal when it opens and, in less than a second, can zap that spot with whatever they use to kill nukes."

"So, where does that leave us?" Klarot demanded.

"We have to assume *Andromeda* can detect any nuclear device we place on or near Arcan," Orlov said.

"So, we have only non-nuclear options," Klarot hissed, scales flaming orange. "Can they destroy the new weapons you supplied?"

"Sure, if they find them, but how do they do that?"

"I don't know, but your people are the experts. I assume the offworlders will show our opponents how to detect normal advanced weaponry. That means no field artillery, no repeating rifles, none of the weapons you gave us. All we have left are saber, spear, and bow—carried by some of the fiercest fighting lizards on the planet." The general hissed loudly in frustration. "So be it! We're going to fight this war the old-fashioned way."

Dragon City Headquarters—The Geroptic Nation, Planet Arcan

General Klarot returned to his office in Dragon City HQ and called Dombit. "We need one final field commander meeting," he said. "Set it up for tomorrow morning."

Dombit contacted each field commander and arranged for all twelve to meet in the Comm Center the following morning. As he used the advanced equipment Orlov had supplied to contact the commanders, Dombit felt a deep inner conflict. When he cut the wires on the nukes, he betrayed his commander and his country. And yet, what General Klarot was doing was, itself, a far bigger betrayal of The Geroptic Nation. Dombit had lost his naïve faith in the Great Dragon in the Sky. The mere existence of Orlov and the weapons and advanced technology he had supplied belied the very existence of the Great Dragon.

Dombit was convinced the Geroptic theocracy had to end— the theocratic rule that had kept Geroptics at a primitive level compared to the other Arcan nations. What General Klarot was doing, however, was twisting the ancient faith to serve his own personal ends. Should he prevail, all Arcan would be strapped with a despot who used everything and everyone to serve himself. That was the ultimate treason, Dombit reasoned. His own betrayal served a greater need.

As Dombit completed his call to the last commander, he resolved, *Henceforth, I will dedicate my actions to serving the greater good of Geroptics. I will follow orders so as not to disrupt the current situation, but will do everything within my power to minimize military casualties and ensure the ultimate takedown of General Klarot.*

✳

The following morning, General Klarot stood before his twelve field commanders. "I'm not one to sugarcoat bad news," he told them. "The nukes we placed in Amred City and Ceffidia did not detonate. We think we are dealing with the offworlders that have been assisting Amred and Ceffid. Apparently, they can neutralize nukes and identify the location of other modern weapons. There is no way, however, for them to identify concentrations of troops and weapons like sabers, spears, and bows."

He paused and raised his hands, his scales rippling dark blue. "We have one option going forward. We will reset the capital portals to a location outside but near each capital, and then we will attack through all portals simultaneously." He took a deep breath and slowly glanced at each commander. "Each of you still has the field artillery and the rifles and sidearms. Arm your officers with sidearms. Hold the remaining weapons in reserve until your last wave of troops has passed through the portal. Then bring out the field artillery, protected by your trained long-gun lizards. To overcome a superior enemy, you must fight smart, and your troops must fight fanatically. They mustn't fear death, but welcome it. As soon as you return to your posts, meet with your bishops and tell them that the Great Dragon has revealed a great truth through me, the Prophet's successor. Every lizard who dies in battle fighting for the Great Dragon will receive unlimited access to willing nubile females in the afterlife. Have your bishops pound this into the troops several times daily until we launch the invasion. Make sure every soldier not only knows this, but believes it fanatically and wants a part of it."

Klarot singled out the two northern post commanders. "You two send someone through the portals and have them move the hyper-bricks to an appropriate location outside the capitals. As soon as that's done, notify me so I can coordinate the attacks."

Klarot left the Comm Center, and Dombit dismissed the field commanders. "Signal me as soon as you've moved the hyper-bricks," he told the two northern commanders.

✳

An hour later, the first northern commander called Dombit. "We have tried everything, but the portal won't work. The Locus doesn't even show it can see the hyper-brick. It's as if there never was one."

"Wait while I check with the other commander," Dombit said.

The story was the same. The Locus acted as if there were no hyper-brick.

"Stand easy while I notify General Klarot," he told them both.

The first thing Dombit did was go to the launch site and attempt to open the two portals to the capitals. The Locuses showed no connected hyper-brick. Dombit stood quietly, contemplating the problem.

Orlov said that portals work so long as the hyper-bricks are within range. That leaves two possibilities—either someone moved the hyper-bricks out of range, or someone destroyed them. In either case, someone was there, which means someone knows about the sabotage. Someone knows we're not all crazy. He turned and headed for Klarot's office.

When he reached Klarot's office, he wasted no time. "You said you don't sugarcoat bad news, General. Well, neither do I. The capital portals don't work. I checked the portals we placed for transferring the nukes. They don't work either." His scales rippled light red and then settled back to green as he got his emotions under control.

"What?" the general yelled. "How the Dragon could that happen?" His scales rippled bright orange.

"I think I know, General," Dombit said.

"Okay, tell me!" The general was still angry, but Dombit sensed the anger was not directed at him.

"We're dealing with offworlder interference, General. The only way the portals won't work if they have sufficient power is if the hyperbricks are out of range or destroyed. That means someone found them. That doesn't happen by accident, General. Neither the Amreds nor the Ceffids can do that. It has to be offworlder interference—there's no other way."

"What if some pedestrian or even a youngster found the bricks?"

"They're set to be activated at the Locuses, and they are way too tough for a little lizard or even an ordinary adult to break, and even if they removed them, they still would be in range." Dombit opened his eyes wide while wrinkling his forehead, the Arcan equivalent of a Human rueful smile. "No, Sir, either the offworlders got them, or our opponents got them using offworlder technology." He shook his head, his scales rippling varying colors for a moment. "That's how I see it, General."

"Has any of this affected our other portals—the troop portals?"

"Not so far as I can tell, Sir. I don't think they can detect a portal until it opens."

"Are the field commanders ready to deploy their troops?"

"They are, General. Your order will open five portals on each continent, sending thousands of troops on a two-front invasion like nothing ever seen in Arcan history."

Phoenix Starship Neil Armstrong—Patrolling the Skies over The Geroptic Nation, Planet Arcan

Kenred spaced his five-member flight in a straight line across the northern edge of The Geroptic Nation. He held the westernmost slot in PS Neil Armstrong with Neepons Kited. Jocara was at the eastern end in PS Alan Shepard with Kreax Nelgan. The Geroptic Nation was a rectangular continent. The northern end was rounded, with the northernmost point centered on the continental mass. The southern end came to a sharp point extending south from the western corner. Both the eastern and western sides bulged out near the equator, forming the widest part of the continent. The northern half of the continent held 70 percent of the population.

In his earlier survey looking for nukes, Kenred had identified several troop concentrations. The purpose of this survey was to pinpoint all the troop concentrations and identify what kind of modern weapons they had, if any.

"Flight, this is Bobcat. Maintain your line formation and spread out with StarChick maintaining herself over the continental eastern margin, and I will remain over the western margin. As the continent widens, you three middle Lizards spread your spacing, so the flight maintains an evenly spaced line."

"This is StarChick, Roger."

"This is GoGirl, Roger."

"This is Rainbow, Roger."

"This is Snout, Roger."

✳

Since The Geroptic Nation had no SAMs or even ground-based artillery that could attack an aircraft, the flight had no concern about being spotted from the ground. They flew at fifty kilometers, which gave their scanners excellent overlapping coverage. By the time they reached the equator, they had pinpointed eight military concentrations. Each had several thousand lizard troops and a cache of field artillery with a large supply of ammunition. They also got hints of small arms, but nothing definite.

They continued their survey through the southern half of the continent. The population was more sparse than in the north, most of it concentrated in two large cities on the southern coast and in the surrounding countryside. Sogard was at the southeastern corner of the continent. Ramden was near the tip of the large peninsula that extended south from the continent's southwestern corner. They found two military concentrations on the peninsula, one near Ramden on the western side of the peninsula and one near the top of the peninsula on the eastern side at the bend. They found two other military posts, one on the southern coast west of Sogard, and the other halfway to the equator on the east coast.

As in the north, the southern military posts had several thousand lizard troops and field artillery with ammunition. As they passed the southern tip of the peninsula, Jocara made a general call to the flight.

"This is StarChick on a general call. We have been closely examining the images we received from three military installations along the southern coast. Each has an identical structure, two markers fourteen meters apart. The markers could be poles. Troops were massed in block formations and appeared to be running between the posts. This is unusual. Any thoughts, Lizards?"

"This is Bobcat on a general call. Good catch, StarChick. I think the poles represent a portal. They are drilling to pass troops through a portal as efficiently as possible."

"This is GoGirl. I see the markers and troops on the military post I found."

"This is Snout. Me too, on two installations."

"This is Rainbow. We found three like that."

"This is Bobcat. We also found three. What about the modern weapons? We found them at the three installations we examined."

The four other flight members all reported detecting modern weapons. They grouped into a tight formation over the southern waters.

"This is Bobcat. Good job, Lizards! Let's return to the nest."

CHAPTER SEVENTEEN

Phoenix Starship Andromeda—Conference Room

Thorpe sat at the head of the conference room table on Andromeda. Jocara and Kenred sat to his right. eThorpe appeared to occupy the chair to his left. Although Kenred had been closely associated with Thorpe and eThorpe, he still reacted with a start when eThorpe, or one of the other uploads, was present.

"Tell me exactly what you saw and what you think you saw," Thorpe said.

"We did a linear formation flight over the entire country," Kenred said. He used his internal Link to create a holoimage of The Geroptic Nation. "We found twelve military concentrations." The military posts appeared on the holoimage. "Jocara first pointed out an unusual feature." The holoimage moved to one side and a closeup of a military compound appeared. It was an AI mix of all the available inputs.

"Notice the troops in block formation," Kenred said. "They are twelve across and running in formation through the gap between those markers. They appear to be poles fourteen meters apart. We believe, all of us, they demark a portal. The troops are practicing running through with the greatest possible efficiency. Note that the troops are not carrying modern weapons. Instead, they carry sabers and spears, and the last two ranks carry bow and arrow." The closeup view shifted to an area behind the troops. "This seems to be a cache of field artillery, with what we believe is a large supply of ammo." The closeup disappeared and the main holoimage of The Geroptic Nation took its place.

"That is a lot of troops, and they seem to be practicing running through a portal. I think that means only one thing—an attack on either or both Amred and Ceffid. I think we need to hit them before they hit us."

"This is a matter we cannot decide ourselves. We need to bring some other folks to the table."

✳

Several hours later, Kenred and Jocara once again sat to Thorpe's right at the *Andromeda* conference table with eThorpe to his left. This time, several more individuals sat at the table, SPC Director Sudaro Ferron, Amred President Binecot Katengi, and Ceffid President Spajo Boszut represented Arcan leadership. Amred General Edoetti Kaylambo and Ceffid General Darflam Baxerd represented the combined militaries of Amred and Ceffid. Holon Mavik, CEO of the Roganian L2 Group, represented the Asterians. Several more Humans and uploads from the *Andromeda* senior crew rounded out the group around the conference room table.

Thorpe said, "Kenred, please brief our guests about your survey of The Geroptic Nation?"

Kenred gave them the same brief he had given Thorpe earlier. He ended by saying, "It's obvious the Geroptics are preparing for a preemptive strike against one or both our nations. We must do something!"

eThorpe picked up the conversation. "We have several options. One is to do nothing. If they attack, you respond. Two, you nuke all twelve posts. This will stop the threat, but you will kill tens of thousands of Arcans. Is this worth the cost? Three, you use lasers on low-flying M-Class fighters to take out the modern weapons and ammo, leaving the troops substantially unharmed. This leaves you open to attack, but the attackers will be using primitive weapons. Many will die, but far less than if you nuked them. The fourth option is to use your lasers to take out the troops before they pass through the portals. This is, of course, a brutal preemptive attack that may justify whatever response the Geroptics can muster."

Humans, Arcans, Asterians, and uploads around the table sat silently, thinking about eThorpe's words. Finally, Thorpe spoke up.

"This is not an *Andromeda* problem. The outcome matters to us, but this has to be solved on Arcan by Arcans. We will assist by allowing your pilots to use the M-Class fighters, and we will supply you with intelligence. We hope you can solve this with minimal bloodshed."

The two generals looked at each other. "We expect portals to open any time," General Kaylambo said. "General Baxerd and I have identified where we think they might open, but these are guesses based on nothing more than intuition. We have quick response strike teams standing by to be flown to a Geroptic portal when it is identified."

"We can assist you there," Thorpe said. "The moment a portal opens, we will detect it. We can immediately give you the coordinates."

"That will help tremendously," General Baxerd said. "The sooner we can put troops with automatic weapons in front of the invaders, the quicker we can put an end to this."

Kenred spoke up. "We can assist in getting troops to a location. If you place Locuses at your deployment locations, my M-Class craft can deliver a hyper-disk to the invasion point within two or three minutes so you can open a portal and send your quick response team or even an entire battalion to the trouble spot."

"That will work," General Kaylambo said.

"Great thinking," Thorpe said. "I will have my people place the Locuses and hyper-disks. You will have them within the hour."

"Keep in mind," Kenred said, "that there will be a maximum of twelve portals—I presume six for each country. If we place twelve Locuses with each of you, you will have absolute coverage."

"That works for me," General Baxerd said.

"For me too," General Kaylambo added.

"This still leaves the modern weapons depots Kenred flight found," Thorpe said. "What do you intend to do about them?"

Both generals spoke up at once. Baxerd deferred to Kaylambo, who said, "We need to take out the weapons depots. We can't allow the Geroptics any advantage we can prevent."

Baxerd nodded his assent. "We should use the M-Class craft lasers," he added.

"I can't authorize that without approval from Presidents Katengi and Boszut," Thorpe said. "Our lasers will definitely destroy the weapons depots, but they will also take out anyone nearby. Their use could cause dozens of deaths." He looked at the two presidents.

They looked at each other and spoke quietly together. Finally, President Katengi spoke up. "We agree that this action is necessary, and the sooner the better. We don't want Geroptic troops pouring through their portals with automatic weapons and field artillery. Consequently, we authorize this action."

✳

Kenred had been working his Amred contact for several days. He knew about Judhee Groklet in the southeast section of The Geroptic Nation, and that this lizard wanted direct contact with whoever the lizard was that had sabotaged the two nukes. He called Brad.

"Brad, this may seem a bit strange, but here is what I need from you and Sally. I've got a lizard I don't know in Dragon HQ who is sabotaging nukes and otherwise doing what he can to slow Klarot's progress. I need to contact him surreptitiously. He has telegraph and twelve portal comm lines. It's a weird mix of primitive and modern."

"Give me a few hours," Brad said. "We'll come up with something."

✳

Four hours later, Brad called Kenred. "I think I've got something," he said. "I'll see you in my lab."

Kenred went through several portals and arrived at Brad's and Sally's lab. As labs go, it was simple. They did most of their development with Links and then Microcosms.

"This box," Brad said, putting his hand on a small box, "will send your lizard a signal to his telegraph, and each of his portal comm lines. It will appear as an anomalous element. If he is smart, he'll figure it out. He will receive a message to go to a specific location outside the compound where you will have dropped a hyper-disk. He knows about hyper-bricks but not hyper-disks. The original message will instruct him on what to do. When he opens the portal, he will receive a satellite transceiver with which he can communicate with your guy in the south."

The Village of Cordan—Southeastern Corner of The Geroptic Nation, Planet Arcan

As Judhee Groklet charged his Leyden jar, he thought, *There has to be a better way to do this. I know Amred and Ceffid have power distribution throughout their countries. I can't use an internal combustion generator because I don't have any fuel.*

Groklet knew about solar generators, but he didn't really understand their workings. He had not gained access to that material, but he knew they existed. He determined to acquire one on his next foreign outing—whenever that might be.

Groklet came up on his satellite transceiver and established contact with his Amred connection.

"I've been waiting for your call," his contact said. "We found a way to put you and the rebel in contact."

He described what they intended to do and what Groklet had to do to make it happen.

Dragon City Headquarters—The Geroptic Nation, Planet Arcan

Major Teynal Dombit sat at his desk filled with conflict. The nukes did not detonate, and he was uncertain whether he or the offworlders were the cause. But that didn't change the fact that he had committed treason. But had he? When he acted to prevent unnecessary atrocities for which General Klarot would have been responsible, was that treason or heroism? He didn't know the answer, and right now he was too busy coordinating the imminent troop portal transfer—the unprovoked invasion of two sovereign nations.

"Are all the field commanders ready?" Klarot asked over the tube com, his voice distorted by passing through the tube.

"They are standing by for your order," Dombit told him.

That's when he received an urgent call from his southernmost commander. "We are under attack!" the commander said. "Fire from the sky is destroying our armaments. I've moved the troops away from the weapons cache, but we took many casualties when the ammo cache exploded."

Dombit acknowledged and immediately informed Klarot. "I am ordering the commanders to move their troop concentrations away from the weapon depots."

"Why?" Klarot asked.

"Because I believe our opponents are taking preemptive action to destroy our weapons. They're not targeting the troops, just the weapons."

"Fine—carry on."

Dombit contacted each post, ordering the commander to move his troops as far away from the weapons depot as possible, and to do it immediately. He received two more calls about fire from the sky destroying weapons depots before he had notified everybody. In both cases, only the weapons and ammunition were targeted, not the troops. Dombit went to Klarot's office to discuss this.

"General, they have got to know what we are planning. I don't think they have any way of predicting where our troops will appear, but they can make shrewd guesses. They obviously know where our troops are massed. So why haven't they attacked the troops as well?"

"That's a good question, Major. You've clearly thought your way through this matter. I'm sure you reached a conclusion, so share it with me." The general's scales showed pale blue for a brief moment, informing Dombit that the general saw the matter as somewhat humorous.

Dombit didn't know quite what to make of this, so he chose his words carefully.

"General, I think we are dealing with offworlders like Orlov. I do not doubt for a moment that they are assisting Amred and Ceffid, but I believe they could wipe us off the face of Arcan should they so choose. Obviously, they haven't done this. Neither Amred nor Ceffid can do what we just experienced—launching focused fire from the sky to destroy something. Their avoiding killing the troops is a message." Dombit paused, composing his words carefully. "I think they are telling us to back off. By destroying the weapons, they are showing what they can do, and also protecting themselves by eliminating the modern weapons. By not killing the troops, I think they are saying they don't want to hurt us—they want us to give up our war plans and find another way to reach our goals." Dombit had presented his last words with greater intensity because he really believed this was the offworlder's message. His scales went light red as he tried to suppress his apprehension at being so straightforward with the general.

The general leaned back in obvious thought. Then he spoke with a slight hiss. "You are a courageous young lizard, Major, to speak so forthrightly, but that is what I admire about you. That's why you are a major so early in your career." He opened his eyes wide, his Arcan smile softening what might come next. "I think you are exactly right. I had concluded the same thing before you told me your opinion. I sense, however, that you think we should concede to their veiled demands, pull our troops back, and negotiate terms with Arcan and Ceffid."

Dombit said nothing, but was astonished internally at how accurately the general had read him.

"Well," the general continued, "I'm not going to do that, and I trust you will continue to be my loyal right hand."

Dombit's scales rippled multiple colors as his uncertainty got beyond his ability to control. "Of course, General Klarot. You are my Commander-in-Chief; I am your loyal aide-de-camp.

"If I may, General, we should call the field commanders for another meeting to ensure everyone will be on the same page now, since the weapons are no longer part of our plans."

"I agree, Major. Make it so."

✳

He's a good lizard and a fine officer, Klarot thought as Dombit left his office, but I need to keep an eye on him. He's smart and perceptive. I need him working with me one hundred percent.

Klarot opened his Battle Plan book on his desk and removed the weapons. He was planning to bring the field artillery through the portals immediately following the archers, and lob shells over his troops' heads into the enemy concentration. This would have given his saber- and spear-armed lizards a better chance at reaching the enemy troops for face-to-face, hand-to-hand battle, where his highly trained lizards could overwhelm the enemy troops.

He sat, thinking about various alternatives. One thing was absolutely essential. He needed to get his troops into hand-to-hand position as soon as lizardly possible. The Arcan and Ceffid troops had never trained to fight a saber-armed or spear-armed fighter, especially one trained to peak performance. The key was hand-to-hand.

Since he didn't have field artillery anymore, Klarot decided to increase the archers by two rows, so his troop blocks would have four archer rows. His idea was to fill the sky with arrows raining down upon the enemy troops, taking out as many as possible, and focusing their attention on the sky instead of the advancing troops. With a bit of luck, his troops could reach hand-to-hand range before the enemy knew what was happening.

Klarot added this to his battle plan and leaned back, waiting for Dombit to call him to the Comm Center to brief his field commanders.

Dragon City Headquarters—The Geroptic Nation, Planet Arcan

Dombit assembled the field commanders in the Comm Center and called General Klarot. Shortly, the general entered the room with his loose-leaf Battle Plan book under his arm.

"You all know," he said, "that your advanced weapons have been destroyed. The offworlders seem to be helping the Arcans and Ceffids. I won't paint a good face on this. It's hurting us a lot." His scales turned deep blue. "Fortunately, I have a plan that should get us around the problem."

He described his plan, answering questions and making sure his field commanders completely understood the urgency of getting their troops into hand-to-hand range as soon as possible.

"Get yourselves organized with the two additional rows of archers and spend as much time as possible training for this new mode. We will launch the attack in a few days, subject to your being ready."

*

On his own initiative, Dombit ordered the two northernmost commanders to distribute their troops south, each to the three commands to their south. He told the commanders to use their troop transports and to work with the other commanders to use their troop transports to facilitate the transfer. He visited the other ten commands to see how their training was progressing. He watched four rows of archers unleash their arrows into an area one hundred meters beyond their position. They let the arrows go two rows at a time. They filled the sky with arrows for a full twelve minutes. Dombit had seen nothing like it. He was impressed and reported this to General Klarot.

"The archers can saturate a block a hundred meters away. The block is twenty meters wide by ten meters deep. So long as they have arrows, they can keep this area clear of enemy troops sufficiently long for our troops to travel the hundred meters. The commanders have arranged signals, so the archers cease their onslaught when our troops have covered the distance." Dombit stopped for a moment to emphasize his next comment.

"It all depends on how distant the enemy troops are concentrated. The signaler estimates the enemy troop distance and shouts a number to the archers. They adjust their angle accordingly. We can effectively rain arrows at three hundred meters. Each command has several archers who can reach four hundred meters with killing accuracy, but they cannot saturate at that distance, so the signaler directs their attention to individual targets, typically officers or other obvious lizards in charge."

"What about gunners with automatic weapons?"

"The signaler identifies them as well and directs a distance archer to that target." Dombit paused again. Internally, he was appalled at how lethal the Geroptic troops appeared to be, but he saw no way around his reporting accurately to General Klarot. "I think our troops are as lethal as possible for the coming battle."

"Thank you, Major. How soon do you think we should initiate hostilities?"

"Virtually any time, General. The troops are impatiently ready. Too much delay will dull their edge." Dombit opened his eyes wide, blinking. "As soon as possible, General. As soon as possible."

✳

For reasons Dombit did not understand, General Klarot told *him* to initiate the attacks when he felt the time was right. As he left the general's office, he thought, *This is an opportunity to slow things down, lower slightly the troop efficiency, even add some confusion because of the delay.*

Dombit returned to the Comm Center where he arranged a visit to the southernmost post—Colonel Blozok Garlan. The colonel was cordial enough, but obviously eager to get the program underway.

"I'm here to look at the lethality of the arrows," Dombit said. "Our entire strategy depends on the archers being able to hold off the technically more advanced enemy troops until our troops can engage them face-to-face. Talk to me about your best archers, the ones in the fourth rank."

Blozok seemed irritated by Dombit's request, but he had learned that this major had General Klarot's backing. "My best archers can kill a lizard at four hundred meters. All the fourth-rank archers are of this class. We don't expect the enemy to be that far away, but one never knows. More realistically, the archers can saturate a twenty-by-ten-meter field with arrows for at least twelve minutes at any distance from fifty to three hundred meters."

"Some of the other posts have had trouble with the portal height… fourteen meters, isn't it? They needed to readjust their troop block position to give the archers a little more room closer to the portal. You seem to have solved that problem, Colonel. I will inform the general of this."

Dombit spent another two hours reviewing troop movements and archer displays—not so much displays as training exercises. To Garlan's obvious relief, Dombit finally departed for the next southern post to the north at the peninsula's great bend.

Dombit visited each post following the same pattern. All the posts were at peak proficiency, including the archers that were Dombit's reason for his visit, but he used every visit to slow down the process, to move the troops from their peak level. Halfway through the process, Klarot called him into his office.

"I just received a written note from a courier, a note written by Colonel Garlan. He complains you made an unnecessary visit to his post. He said you were conducting these visits to every post, and that this was delaying the attack. What's going on?"

Dombit had expected this question and was surprised it took so long. "We created fourteen-meter-high portals to give our archers enough room for high-angle shots. In my earlier visits, I saw way too many misses, with arrows flying over the portal tops. I discussed this with the commanders, and they seem to have corrected the situation. My visits are to ensure that this is no longer a problem. Out of necessity, I have had to make these visits before the attack."

If the general were to check, he would discover Dombit's deception, but he didn't, so Dombit felt safe. He had effectively slowed the invasion by several days, taking the troops off their peak performance, but now he had to give the order to commence the invasion. Reluctantly, Dombit issued orders to start simultaneous portal attacks three hours hence.

Dombit informed General Klarot and then went to the Comm Center where he outlined his next step in his plan to slow the invasion and, if possible, bring an early end to hostilities.

✳

As Dombit worked on his plan, the telegraph signaled. He didn't use the telegraph anymore, but it definitely signaled, and the signal was not a normal signal. He got up and walked over to the telegraph. As he did, all twelve portal comm units signaled with the same odd signal he got from the telegraph. He was at the telegraph, so he looked at the signal. *Strange* was the only word that came to his mind. He checked the signal out on one of the portal comm units. This was a signal he could decipher.

Dombit looked at the deciphered signal with astonishment. *Is it possible,* he asked himself. *Am I really receiving a signal from an Amred astronaut?*

The signal read: I am Kenred Zlaxiz, an astronaut with the SPC Astronaut Corps. We have been surveilling your Dragon HQ for some time. I carefully followed the portal placement of the two nukes to Amred City and Ceffidia. I personally found your cut wire on the Amred nuke, and my partner found the broken wires on the Ceffidia nuke. We wish to support you. Go to the following coordinates and activate the portal by rubbing the metallic side of the hyper-disk you will find there. It is an advanced version of the Hyper-brick with which you are familiar. The coordinates followed.

Dombit memorized the coordinates and destroyed any evidence of the signals.

Within the hour, Dombit gave General Klarot an appropriate excuse and left the compound for the hyper-disk. He found it lying on the ground in a meadow. He picked up the small disk and turned it over in his hands—one side deep black, the other dull metallic. He rubbed the metallic side with his thumb. The disk simply disappeared from his hands, and a small portal opened at chest level. Inside, he found two devices, one small with controls and the second larger, with a simple connection and a wire that obviously connected to the smaller device. He also found a set of instructions in Geroptic.

The smaller device was a satellite transceiver that he was supposed to use to contact a dissident in the southeast. Why not? He had nothing to lose. He was alone in the meadow, and the general did not expect him back for another hour. When the transceiver battery ran low, he was to connect the transceiver to the larger unit for a recharge. The larger unit contained a hundred recharges.

Dombit followed the instructions and activated the transceiver. "Hello, hello," he said. "Is anybody there? Hello?"

"Hello back. I'm Judhee Groklet. Who are you?"

Amred & Ceffid—Planet Arcan

Ten troop portals opened within seconds of each other, four from south of the Geroptic equator and six from the north. Two southern portals targeted the outskirts of Amred City and Ceffidia. Four portals opened across Amred near strategic cities or military installations. Four opened across Ceffid, as in Amred, near important cities or military locations.

Two portals to Ceffid found no opposition. They established well-fortified strongholds and moved toward their objectives. Three portals to Amred also found no opposition. As in Ceffid, they fortified their positions and moved toward their objectives.

The third and fourth Ceffid portals opened to intense machine gun and mortar fire. Machine guns took out the first several ranks of Geroptic soldiers. They didn't have a chance. At first, the mortars lobbed their shells over the portals, where they exploded harmlessly in the grassy fields. As deadly arrows rained down on them, taking out every second lizard, the Ceffids adjusted their aim and took out the archers. After that, it was wholesale slaughter. The Geroptics kept charging, screaming, "Dragon!…Dragon!… Dragon!"

At both portals, the dead piled up in front of the charging lizards, who leaped to the top of the body piles, only to be killed by a hail of machine gun bullets, collapsing where they stood to grow the piles, or rolling down the piles of bodies, coming to rest in the deepening pools of blood spreading from the base of the piles. When it was all over, both portals collapsed and the Ceffid troops counted 576 slaughtered Geroptics at each portal.

✳

Over in Amred, the fourth portal opened to machine gun and mortar fire. When mortar shells began to explode on the Geroptic side of the portal, the commander shut the portal, abandoning the troops already on the other side—about a quarter of the troop block. Then he lined up four troop carriers with four more behind them, they were three meters wide, at the portal line. He put archers inside the rear carriers with instructions to loose their arrows at the closest possible range. Regular troops filled the front carriers and closely followed the carriers on the ground with instructions to spread out rapidly as soon as they cleared the portal. The two outer troop carriers would also turn left and right to give the troops on the ground some protection from the machine gunners.

"Stay behind the carriers as they turn left and right and attack the enemy flanks," he ordered, and opened the portal.

When the portal opened, the machine gunners peppered the armored troop carriers without effect. As the outside carriers turned to flank the Amred position, the gunners shifted their aim to the carrier sides, but the armor stopped the bullets. The mortar troops had insufficient time to adjust their aim to the moving carriers as Geroptic arrows rained down on them. The carriers completed their flanking movement so the Amred troops found themselves surrounded on three sides with ferocious Geroptic warriors swinging sabers, shouting, "Dragon!…Dragon!… Dragon!"

It was all over in three minutes. The surviving Amred troops retreated in disorderly array as Geroptic warriors picked them off with saber and spear.

CHAPTER EIGHTEEN

Phoenix Starship Andromeda—Conference Room

Presidents Binecot Katengi from Amred and Spajo Boszut from Ceffid entered the Andromeda conference room. Generals Edoetti Kaylambo from Amred and Darflam Baxerd from Ceffid followed them. Thorpe, who was sitting at the head of the table, rose and gestured for the four lizards to sit on either side of him, Amred to his right and Ceffid to his left.

"It's good to see you, my friends," Thorpe said, as the rest of the team arrived, having waited for the two presidents and their generals to enter first: SPC Director Sudaro Ferron, Kenred, Jocara, Daphne, and Dale. Max strolled in and remained on the floor this time, rubbing legs as he greeted Humans and Arcans he knew.

Thorpe looked left and right at the two presidents. "You Lizards called this meeting," he said with a smile. "What's on your minds?"

Katengi spoke up. "Despite our advanced weaponry and trained troops, we are taking substantial losses. The Geroptics have developed effective techniques that neutralize our advanced weaponry. They opened five portals on Amred. Four were unopposed," he looked at General Kaylambo with a scowl, "and we were slaughtered at the one portal where our predictions were on the mark. At the four unopposed portals, the Geroptics spread out so that our machine gunners were ineffective. Their archer sharpshooters took out our sergeants and officers from four hundred meters. They hit our mortar units and machine gunners with a withering hail of arrows that effectively neutralized them until we developed an arrow-proof tarp we suspended over the mortars and gunners. By then, it was too late for several thousand Amred soldiers. The bottom line is we need help, or we will lose this war."

Boszut took up the narrative. "We were fortunate where we accurately predicted the location of two portals. Both resulted in a heart-rending slaughter of the Geroptic troops—five hundred seventy-six at each portal. I'm guessing that is a troop block of seventy-three rows of twelve. They marched through the portal to their deaths. We had no opportunity to take any prisoners. We lost a few mortar lizards and machine gunners to their archers, but we took them all out before they could inflict serious casualties. The three portals whose locations we did not predict are another matter. As Binecot described for Amred, the Geroptic tactics pretty much neutralized our machine guns when we finally encountered them. Our troops have performed better than Amred, possibly because of our former Leader, but we, too, are not winning. Like Amred, we need help."

✳

Kenred listened to the conversation with an incredulous sense of disbelief. Both militaries, he thought, have access to M-Class fighters armed with lasers. Any field commander could call in a fighter and wipe out the entire opposition. So, what's the problem?

"Excuse me for interjecting a comment into a high-level discussion," Kenred said, "but why don't you use the M-Class fighters and their lasers?"

"You're here for your expertise, Kenred. You are not interrupting anything." He turned to Katengi. "Would you care to answer Kenred's question, Mr. President?"

"Kenred," Katengi said, "both President Boszut and I greatly admire your dedication and accomplishments. I know you could end this conflict with your fighters and their lasers. But think of the carnage. We could have atom-bombed each of the portal Locuses before all this started, with even more death and suffering. We didn't start this conflict, but neither did the common Geroptic soldier. I understand the common soldiers believe that if they die in battle for the Great Dragon, they will have unlimited access to nubile females in the afterlife.

"I want to give these lizards a chance, and lasers will not bring that about."

He's a good Lizard, Kenred thought, but he will lose the war with that attitude.

"Even if we could interfere," Thorpe said, "all we have are weapons of mass destruction, nukes and other greatly lethal devices. None of these are suitable in your present conflict."

Dale had been quietly following the proceedings. He lifted a hand, and Thorpe acknowledged him.

"Our radars are fitted with a device that throws a stasis field around anything the radar detects. Inside this field, time virtually ceases to exit. Oh, it's still there, but moves so slowly that light would take several centuries to cross a medium-size stasis sphere. I think we can modify our fighter radars to project stasis spheres that would encompass a large group of Geroptic troops. Several of your troops could enter the sphere wearing anti-stasis suits we would supply. They could disarm the Geroptic warriors, shackle them together, remove their weapons from the sphere, and finally collapse the sphere once all the warriors inside are disarmed and shackled."

"You can do this?" Boszut asked.

"Yes, Sir—absolutely!"

"Well, that's what we'll do then," Katengi said, "just as soon as you can modify your fighters and supply us with the anti-stasis suits."

Phoenix Starship Andromeda—Engineering Spaces

Kenred sat down with Ustrun Strozid, the Asterian Chief Engineer in his office in the bowels of Andromeda's engineering spaces. Kenred didn't know exactly where, because he had come to the office by portal. Strozid would know where his office was located, as would Thorpe and several others on the first team, but Kenred was ignorant of much location information, because he had used portals almost exclusively since he had joined the crew.

"I am familiar with the stasis field," Kenred said. "I know a lot less about the anti-stasis suits and the material used to coat space craft to make them impervious to the field."

"It's pretty arcane stuff," Strozid said. "Asterian scientists developed the stasis field some time before the Humans, and we built *Andromeda*. They actually used it in their battle with the rogue Human, Orlov. His scientists ended up figuring out our anti-stasis material and manufactured bolts of it to cloak their spacecraft. It was too late to affect the outcome of the battle, but it definitely made a difference in future contacts with Orlov. It turned out that we still could detect a cloaked craft with neutrino detectors. Because only we have these devices, cloaking remains an effective tool in space warfare." Strozid pursed his lips while opening and closing them, an expression Kenred knew was an Asterian grin.

"Let's talk about anti-stasis suits. The suits are made from a woven fabric consisting of a blend of the rare earth metals gadolinium and yttrium alloyed with indium to add needed malleability without reducing the anti-stasis characteristics of the rare earths."

"That's it?" Kenred asked. "Just a cloth made from some rare earths?"

"It may sound simple," Strozid said, "but they are called rare earths because they are—rare, that is." He pursed his lips, a smile, Kenred noted.

"Let's modify your craft. We need to adjust the radar sensor so sphere placement is half above and half below ground. We can do this by feeding the lidar return to the controller. The precise measurement from the lidar will give the controller the parameters it needs to place the stasis sphere accurately. My guys will create small modules that you can install into your radar transmitters. This will automatically give your radar what it will need to place the stasis spheres accurately."

"I presume you will use a Nanocosm to manufacture the modules," Kenred said.

"That's right. We will not actually know exactly what is inside the modules, but I guarantee they will function exactly." Strozid pursed his lips again.

"When will you have the modules?" Kenred asked.

"You will need five of them. Give me three hours. I'll call you if they are ready sooner."

✳

Kenred left the engineering spaces thinking about the Nanocosm. What an amazing device. They write specifications for something they need in plain language in one of any number of languages. The machine returns a verification in the input language, and then it programs nanobots to construct the desired device, literally molecule by molecule. I am really glad these guys are our friends and not our enemies.

Kenred returned to his quarters and informed Jocara about the meeting in the conference room and with the Chief Engineer. To his total surprise, an hour later, he got a call from Strozid.

"Your modules are ready. It took a lot shorter time than I thought it would. I'll have them delivered to the hangar bay."

Phoenix Starship Andromeda—Hangar Bay

Kenred assembled his Arcan pilots and their backups in the hangar bay. The rumor mill had preceded this meeting, and everyone already knew what he would say. Nevertheless, everyone listened with rapt attention.

"You Lizards are finally going to join the Holy War, as it is being called in The Geroptic Nation. I want you guys to understand our role. The presidents of both Amred and Ceffid are determined to keep casualties at a minimum—on both sides. We could go in there and totally take out the Geroptic troops, their installations, and even their command structure. Both presidents want to avoid this at all costs. We will be saving lives, not taking them."

Kenred stopped talking and scanned his pilots. They were young, capable, probably the best pilots on Arcan. Certainly, they were the best spacecraft pilots anywhere. He would put them up against any *Andromeda* pilots of any species.

"You will install these modules." He pointed to the five small modules at his feet. "The installation is an easy, two-wire job that should take no more than a minute. I'll give you five minutes. When you're done, we'll test the installations, and then we'll go into battle." He opened his eyes wide, blinking them. "Questions?"

"Where will we test them, and how?" Jocara asked.

"I will lead you to an open terrain area south of the equator in central Ceffid. We'll run the tests there."

✳

As Kenred predicted, the module installation was quick and easy. In ten minutes, all five craft were ready to deploy.

"This is Bobcat. Set your destination to these coordinates." He gave them a single set of coordinates south of the Ceffid equator. The AIs on each craft would coordinate their actual destinations so they would arrive in formation. Moments later, the five craft floated three kilometers above the empty Ceffid landscape.

"This is Bobcat…Okay, Lizards, listen up! You aim your radar at a specific point, adjust the width of the sphere you want, and activate. Once you have created a stasis sphere, you cannot change the parameters. Your only available action is to collapse the sphere. Also note, you can collapse any stasis sphere by focusing your radar on it and deactivating it.

"Okay…down the line. Each one of you create a stasis sphere. I'll go first."

On the plain below, five silvery hemispheres appeared, each a slightly different size.

"This is Bobcat. You will notice that sphere three is right against sphere two—they look like two soap bubbles against each other. They don't merge, but maintain a single layer between them. That layer—and the skins of all the spheres—is infinitely thin. Don't ask me how that works, I haven't a clue.

"Okay, Lizards, collapse your spheres."

Down below, the silvery spheres disappeared.

"This is Bobcat…Once again, this time, larger distances."

Once again, five large hemispheres appeared below. They reflected everything and sparkled brilliantly in the bright noon light from Ran.

"Okay, Lizards, collapse the sphere of the craft to your right. StarChick, you collapse my sphere. Go for it!"

Like soap bubbles bursting, the stasis spheres disappeared, leaving the sunlit plain as untouched as it was before.

Later, Kenred commented to his team over drinks that the plain where they practiced creating stasis spheres really was not the same following their exercise.

"The plants and bugs captured inside the spheres were in stasis for the time the spheres existed," he said. "This extended their lives by the same amount."

"Do you think," Jocara piped up, "these minor extensions could have a world changing consequence—you know, the Butterfly Effect?"

Kenred chuckled. "Okay, Lizards, stand by for immediate orders. You will be on individual assignment. I suspect you will be zipping all over the planet."

He got to his feet and grabbed Jocara's hand. "Good luck to you all!"

Amred President Binecot Katengi's Office—Amred City, Amred, Planet Arcan

Amred President Binecot Katengi sat at his desk talking with Spajo Boszut, newly inaugurated President of Ceffid. Over the last few months since the inauguration, they had become fast friends. Katengi, older and more experienced, had guided Boszut as he set up his administration following the removal of the dictator, Leader Bopr Arclando. Ceffid was well on its way to becoming a free and prosperous republic.

On this morning, the two lizards were solving a joint problem, the apparent military successes of The Geroptic Nation in its campaign against both nations.

"There's no need," Katengi said, "to remonstrate over our losses. I deeply regret the loss of life on our side, but also on theirs. Of all the wars I know about, this one seems the least meaningful. I know we were attacked, and we must respond, but I will not go down in history as the lizard who used atomic weapons to take out primitive fighters."

"You know I agree with you," Boszut said. "So, let's set up the gift we have received from *Andromeda*."

❋

It turned out not to be complicated. Field commanders from either Amred or Ceffid who found themselves facing a superior Geroptic force or even one they could overrun, pressed a button on a small console they each carried, supplied by *Andromeda*. The console transmitted a signal on a specially designated frequency that gave their exact coordinates. All five M-Class craft received the signal, and their interconnected AIs autoselected a craft and sent it by MERT Drive to a kilometer above the position.

The crew then evaluated the situation and placed a stasis sphere around the Geroptic troops. Sometimes, they would use several spheres to cover the maximum number of enemy troops. Several times, the sphere captured a shower of arrows in flight, freezing their motion until the sphere was collapsed.

The Village of Cordan—Southeastern Corner of The Geroptic Nation, Planet Arcan

Judhee Groklet grabbed his satellite transceiver. Fortunately, it was fully charged. He activated it. The transceiver beeped and then Groklet heard: "Hello, hello…Is anybody there? Hello?"

Groklet pressed the transmit button with a shaking hand and said, "Hello back. I'm Judhee Groklet. Who are you? Over."

"I am Major Teynal Dombit of the Dragon Forces. I was told you wish to speak with me. Over."

"That is so. This line is secure, meaning that no one can intercept our conversation. I am a schoolteacher in the village of Cordan. For three generations, I have been teaching outside the Dragon parameters. My students learn math, physics, chemistry, biology, and astronomy, and they read the Amred classics. Cordan has twenty-five hundred inhabitants, most educated by me. All of them can be a resource for you, either now, if we can work out a way, or later, when this stupidity is done. Over."

"Fascinating! I know of nothing your people can do right now, but please tell them that as soon as the conflict is over—and you know how it will go—I will contact you again on this channel. If I need to speak with you in the meantime, how can I do that? Over."

"Call on this channel. Your call will be recorded, and I will hear it the first time I activate my transceiver. In your message give a time for a live call. Over."

"Okay, that works. I need to get off this call right now. Over."

"Okay, I look forward to our next contact. Out."

CHAPTER NINETEEN

Amred Battlefield—Outside Amred City, Planet Arcan

Sergeant Metajo Gwzon carried a sword as a badge of authority. He knew how to use it, but had never used it in battle—until now. Twelve minutes ago, he had bloodied it for the first time when a squad of Geroptics had charged his position. He lost three lizards in the exchange, but the Geroptics lost three dozen to his bullets and his one sword thrust.

Runners brought up ammo, ducking arrows as they ran. Gwzon had found a way to outfit his ninety troops with flat metal plates welded to their battle helmets that protected from arrow showers. He had purchased them at a local hardware store in the Amred outskirts. Otherwise, all the troops wore flexible armor that protected their torsos, arms, and legs. They were not impervious to a saber chop, and far too many Amred soldiers had lost their heads when they failed to protect their necks with their rifle stocks.

Before he and his squad went into battle, Gwzon had studied the Geroptic tactics. Since they had no guns, they were forced into hand-to-hand combat, and they were good at it. The obvious counter tactic was to keep them at bay, but this did not always work. The body armor that protected his troops had four vulnerabilities—face, both hands, and neck. The Geroptics invariably went for the neck. Before his troops went into battle, Gwzon drilled them in a counter tactic until they could do it without thought. When face to face with a Geroptic warrior swinging his saber, hold the bayonetted rifle vertically on the side where the saber was, to catch the cut. Then, swing it horizontal to thrust and fire simultaneously. In battle, where his troops actually used this counter tactic, they survived, and the Geroptic didn't. It was brutally effective.

Gwzon's squad was good, and the Geroptic field grade officers figured this out fairly quickly. They threw more and more troops against Gwzon's position.

Gwzon had lost his machine gunners early in the conflict and had received no replacements. As the onslaught against his position increased, he set his squad up in three rows of thirty for a modified retreating countermarch volley fire—the front kneeled, the second squatted, and the third stood, all with automatic rifles at the ready. This was a maneuver they had practiced until they could do it sleeping.

With Geroptics rushing at sixty meters, Gwzon held his sword high and then dropped it, yelling, "Fire!"

The back row fired a burst of three automatic rounds and stepped back six paces while the middle row stood and fired a burst of three automatic rounds that followed the first volley so closely it seemed like continuous fire. The second row dropped back and squatted as the first row stood and fired in what again seemed like continuous fire, and dropped back six paces to kneel in front of the middle row. As they kneeled, the back row took up the fire again, maintaining the continuous fire.

As the squad used up its ammo, runners kept them supplied from the rear. The maneuver worked well, and they killed hundreds of Geroptics, but they kept coming, and now they were only twenty-four meters away.

Gwzon knew an officer was watching the slaughter and the advancing Geroptic warriors. His faith in that officer's skill kept him focused on his own squad as they slowly retreated while pouring withering fire into the advancing Geroptic warriors, who were shouting, "Dragon!... Dragon!... Dragon!" as they advanced at a flat-out run. As the warrior front ranks succumbed to the withering fire, the next rank ran over their bodies, carrying the entire block forward several meters before themselves falling to the hail of bullets. The block was twelve warriors wide and moved ever forward over the bodies of the fallen, shrinking in size, but finally reaching hand-to-hand contact with Gwzon's squad.

Gwzon's lizards knew their stuff. They switched from their retreating volley fire to hand-to-hand combat, using the rifle-blocking technique they had practiced so often. Several Amred soldiers fell as the Geroptic block pressed against the squad. For every squad soldier felled, however, a dozen or more Geroptic warriors gave their lives.

Gwzon found himself faced with a warrior swinging a saber in each hand. Gwzon blocked one blade with his armored arm and the other with his rifle, and swung the rifle horizontal for the killing thrust, when suddenly, a silvery apparition was dragging him across the ground. His sword and rifle were gone, and he was encased in some kind of silvery suit.

To Gwzon's astonishment, the apparition unzipped his suit and stepped out in a major's uniform. Gwzon came to attention, but the major said, "Stand easy, Sergeant," and reached out and unzipped his suit. "You were just caught up in a stasis sphere. I put you in a suit and dragged you out. This is all new stuff, so listen closely, because you will explain it to your squad. Our friends up there," he pointed to the sky, "can somehow encase anything in what they call a stasis sphere. Inside the sphere, time effectively stops—not entirely, they tell me, but almost. These suits," he pointed to the crumpled suits on the ground, "called anti-stasis suits, allow a lizard to enter a stasis sphere without experiencing the effects of the sphere. You have to push the air aside to move around—you'll see what I mean."

The major pointed toward one part of the sphere. "As you can see, your anti-stasis-suit-encased lizards are being pulled out of the sphere as we speak. I will issue each of you an anti-stasis suit. You will enter the sphere, locate all the Geroptic warriors, disarm them—be sure to check for hidden knives—and bring the weapons out of the sphere.

Other lizards will handle the weapons from there. Then you will reenter the sphere and shackle the warriors together. When they are all shackled, we'll collapse the sphere. Remember what you experienced when I dragged you out? One moment, they are fighting or doing whatever they were doing, the next, they are shackled together and lying on the ground. They are going to be confused as hell—probably even angry, fighting angry. Make no mistake, a shacked Geroptic warrior is still a formidable opponent. Watch yourselves. Make them stand, and bring them to one of the obvious holding areas."

The major opened his eyes, blinking. "You've got quite a reputation, Sergeant. I know you will get this working quickly. We've got potentially several thousand Geroptics we need to handle." He gave another Arcan grin, eyes wide open and blinking. "Oh, the war is over."

Stasis Sphere—Amred Battlefield Outside Amred City, Planet Arcan

To say Gwzon was astonished would be a monumental understatement. His scales turned a solid yellow, and he worked hard to control his astonishment as he watched his lizards being dragged from the sphere. He gave a loud whistle and pulled them together—all remaining ninety-seven. The three fallen troops had been removed in body bags by the field medics.

"This is important, Lizards, really important," Gwzon said, his scales rippling multiple colors, telling the world of his uncertainty. "You Lizards will wear those shiny suits. They will protect you from the effects of the inside of the spheres. They tell me time stops inside. That means ain't nothin' movin'. It's completely black. You open your suit inside, you stop movin' till someone rescues you. We will form a line right at the edge of the sphere, all ninety-eight of us—yes, that includes me at the center. We'll be connected with a comm cable that is insulated like our suits. Without that insulation, comms won't work. So be careful of it. Don't tear it or anything, or we lose our comms. We'll step through the sphere together. Once inside, the air will be thick and spongy and it will be black as coal. We'll push our way through it. Keep the chatter on the comm line to a minimum.

"We'll walk forward together, arms linked, peeling lizards off the sphere side as we move forward. As this happens, you will be pushed outward by the line. Just keep contact with the sphere and move forward with the line, keeping it as straight as possible in the darkness. When one of you runs into a frozen warrior, inform me by comm. You will know who found the warrior. Two lizards on each side mark your spot with a marker and crawl toward the warrior. First thing, you disarm him completely. Now remember, it's pitch black, you can see nothin'. Be sure to locate his hidden knife or knives. Place the weapons on the line between the markers. We'll deal with them later. Then shackle the warrior's hands and feet, and lay him on the ground."

Gwzon whistled to get the attention of a couple lizards in the back who were not paying attention. "Listen up, Lizards, this may save your life."

He continued his brief. "Now we reform the line by crawling back to your position. During this process, be sure to give the comm line sufficient slack. Then move forward with the line like before until we run out of sphere. We will continue to stop as we find warriors and deal with them. Once we reach the middle, the last lizard at each end will be free of the sphere. Let me know by comm. While we are on the middle line of the sphere, we will do our best to straighten the line. Then we move forward as before, stopping for warriors. The end lizards will remain close to the sphere wall when they reach it. Adjust your position as needed and hold it until the rest of us reach the sphere. When we all reach the sphere, everyone move along the sphere to my position. Then we will form a single line and walk toward the center. I know how far it is. When we reform, our line should cover the width of the sphere."

Gwzon walked along the front rank. "That's a lot of info, Lizards. Questions?"

For fifteen minutes, Gwzon fielded questions from his troops. Some were thoughtful, some were less so, but he patiently answered all.

"Okay, Lizards, form up on me along the edge of the sphere."

They did.

"Count off, right and left."

The troops counted off to forty-four on the right and forty-three on the left.

"Now, remember your number, Lizards. It will matter inside."

 Robert G. Williscroft

Stasis Sphere—Amred Battlefield Outside Amred City, Planet Arcan

Sergeant Metajo Gwzon was a tough, accomplished noncom. He had earned his chops during the Ceffid conflict and was recognized as one of the best noncoms in the army. He had seen a lot, but nothing like this. His troops seemed to think he had done this before and knew how everything worked.

If they only knew, he thought. *This thing scares the shit out of me, but I'm the only one who knows that.*

He squared his shoulders and gave the order, "Lizards, enter the sphere."

Gwzon had been told what to expect, but this was really strange. It was like walking into a room filled with soft bubbles. They moved away when he pushed, but otherwise surrounded him completely—almost like a cocoon.

"This shit is weird, Lizards," he said over the comm. "Everyone okay?"

"Crazy shit!"

"Wild!"

"Fucking unreal!"

"Knock off the chatter, Lizards!" Gwzon said. "Okay, move forward on me, peeling off the sphere when the line reaches you."

A few seconds later, someone shouted, "Got one!"

"Stop the line," Gwzon said. "What's your number?"

"Six-right."

"Okay, Four- and Five-right, move to your right…Seven- and Eight-right, move to your left."

"This is Six-right. They're here."

"Alright, you Lizards, disarm the warrior completely and shackle him."

"This is Seven-left. I just reached out in front of me and touched a warrior."

"Okay, Eight- and Nine-left, move to your right…Six- and Five-left, move to your left."

"This is Seven-left. They're here."

"Okay, Lizards, disarm and shackle him."

And so it went for five hours. They found several troop carriers, but Gwzon told them to leave the carriers. Removing the warriors from the carriers was a real challenge, but they got it done. By the time Gwzon's lizards had downed the shackled warriors and separated the weapons, their suit air supplies were nearly empty, and the troops were exhausted.

※

The warriors' reactions when the sphere collapsed were something to behold. From his own experience, Gwzon could sympathize with them. From their perspective, one moment they were in full charge with a combat mindset. The next, they were shackled to each other, hand and foot, lying on the ground. It was undignified. At worst, it was horrifying.

The major spoke to them in Geroptic, a language Gwzon had acquired somewhere along the line.

"Geroptic Lizards, to your feet!" The major's voice was loud and firm, but even-tempered.

The Geroptic soldiers responded, although several shouted arrogant insults. The major ignored them.

"Walk to that truck and climb aboard. Help each other as necessary," he ordered.

The bewildered Geroptic warriors shuffled toward the truck and did as told. Even the belligerent ones seemed to grasp their impossible position. They were prisoners, and their war was over.

※

After the sphere near Gwzon collapsed and the shackled warriors were removed, ten empty troop carriers stood in the field. The major sent ten of his lizards to drive them to a holding compound next to a temporary pen holding the warriors, who were still shackled, but not to each other.

Gwzon launched a drone and flew it over the battle area. Three spheres still shone in the afternoon sunlight, and he spied five troop carrier groupings that he assumed marked the location of earlier spheres. Soldiers drove trucks full of shackled Geroptic warriors toward the holding compound, and others drove the now empty troop carriers to their holding area.

Although he didn't have direct information, Gwzon assumed that the same kind of activity filled each of the other portal sites in Amred and Ceffid. The major was right—the war was truly over!

Amred President Binecot Katengi's Office—Amred City, Amred, Planet Arcan

Thorpe stepped through a portal into President Binecot Katengi's office in the government complex in Amred City. Ceffid President Spajo Boszut sat in one comfortable chair near Katengi's desk. Thorpe took the other. Katengi took a deep breath and let it out slowly. His scales rippled somewhat but remained green.

"Thank you both for coming. This is an informal meeting. I am making no recordings and taking no notes." Katengi gave them a big Arcan smile, wide open eyes.

"That's fine by me, Binecot," Boszut said. "You have been a friend and mentor ever since I assumed the presidency of Ceffid. If you want to be off the record, I have no problem."

"As for me," Thorpe said, "I'm not sure how history will treat my presence on Arcan, but any time you want to be off the record, it's fine by me."

With that established, Katengi wasted no time coming to his topic. "The Holy War is over. Between us, Spajo and I have tens of thousands of prisoners. We can handle them fine. Within a few months, all of them will be repatriated. Our joint problem, however, is General Nirurian Klarot. We are holding him under house arrest, but we simply do not know what to do with him."

Both Katengi and Boszut turned to look at Thorpe. Katengi smiled inwardly as Thorpe struggled to answer. He had come to know the offworlder quite well. Answering questions like this was not his forte. Unfortunately, he and Boszut were at loggerheads on this issue. Boszut wanted to imprison the general. Katengi wanted to execute him. Hopefully, Thorpe could find a way.

Thorpe looked back at both Arcans. "You two have boxed me in," he said. "We have a *Holy Book* in our culture that tells of a king confronted with a similar problem. Two women each claimed a baby.

The king, Soloman, offered a solution. He would cut the babe in half and give half to each woman. One woman agreed. The second reacted with horror and said to give the baby to the other woman. Of course, the king gave the baby to the rightful mother, the woman who did not want the babe killed." He grinned widely.

"General Klarot is not a baby, and the situation is not really similar. Still, I really don't have the wisdom to solve this for you. But, I know someone who does. I have mentioned him earlier—John Butler, Chairman of the Oort Federation. Are you willing to have him arbitrate the matter?"

Katengi and Boszut looked at each other, their scales rippling yellow in astonishment. *I should have thought of that,* Katengi thought. "Yes!" he said. "Let's go for it."

"That works for me," Boszut said. "I want to get this shit behind us." He looked at Katengi, eyes wide open. "If John Butler can pull this off, we'll have an entire planet at peace."

Neither Katengi nor Boszut had paid much attention to Thorpe during their exchange. When Katengi looked at him, he was astonished and pleasantly surprised, because John Butler had just entered his office quietly, unannounced. Butler walked to Katengi, both his hands extended in friendship. Then he offered his hands to Boszut, who had come to his feet when he realized Butler was in the room.

Katengi pulled up another comfortable chair and gestured for Butler to take it. Katengi sat on the couch.

Butler smiled. "Let's have a conversation," he said. "But first, with all due respect to you, President Katengi, we are sitting in your office in the Amred center of government. Intended or not, this is a bias with which I am uncomfortable. Would you all be willing to join me on *Andromeda*, where we will have impartial neutrality?"

CHAPTER TWENTY

***Phoenix Starship Andromeda*—Conference Room**

Sergeant Metajo Gwzon peeked through the Andromeda conference room door. The room looked like any other conference room he had seen. If Kenred hadn't told him he was on a starship, he would not have known. He was still getting used to the idea that the major had picked him to represent all the Amred and Ceffid troops at this important conference. He knew he was good at his job, but so were a lot of others, including sergeants senior to him. But here he was, on a gigantic starship taking part in a crucial conference that would determine the fate of The Geroptic Nation. He didn't quite know what to make of the offworlder, Thorpe. It was obvious he ran things. The offworlder, John Butler, seemed to be the most important individual in the room. Gwzon was still getting used to how strange the offworlders looked.

Several lizards waited with Gwzon. He recognized General Edoetti Kaylambo, his ultimate boss. Kenred told him that the other general was General Darflam Baxerd, head of the Ceffid military. Gwzon was certainly surrounded by some high-level brass. Kenred pointed out SPC Director Sudaro Ferron and introduced him to Jocara.

The offworlder John Butler sat at the head of the conference table and the offworlder Thorpe chose the other end of the table. President Katengi sat on Butler's right and President Boszut on his left. Gwzon recognized President Katengi, but Kenred had to identify President Boszut to him.

Kenred Zlaxiz stood near one door. Thorpe spoke up, and Gwzon was surprised that he could understand the offworlder. "This is a momentous discussion that will go down in Arcan history, and I thought it would be appropriate to have the major participants at the table with us." He turned to the offworlder Butler.

"I have no objections," Butler said, turning to both presidents. "Do either of you object?" This time, Gwzon recognized a translator putting his words into Amred.

"Of course not," Katengi said, his scales rippling pale yellow before fading to dark yellow briefly and then back to green, showing his brief astonishment and then momentary irritation.

"I'm fine with the rest being here," Boszut said, his scales remaining green.

The offworlder Thorpe nodded to Kenred, who opened the door. SPC Director Sudaro Ferron entered, followed by Generals Edoetti Kaylambo and Darflam Baxerd, Jocara, and finally Sergeant Metajo Gwzon.

The offworlder Thorpe continued. "I've included Sergeant Metajo Gwzon at Kenred Zlaxiz's urging because of his exceptional performance on the battlefield and to represent all the Amred and Ceffid troops who participated in the Holy War." He turned to the newcomers. "Please take a seat, but leave an empty seat by each president."

The two generals sat near their presidents. Jocara and Kenred sat together near Thorpe. Ferron sat next to General Kaylambo, and Gwzon sat next to Kenred, the only lizard in the room he knew.

Gwzon did not know where all this was going, but he paid close attention. The offworlder Butler started to speak through the translator.

"Thank you for agreeing to meet here on *Andromeda*. As I consider the reason for our meeting, I see this as the most momentous conference in Arcan's long history." His face took on an odd distortion. Kenred whispered, "That's a Human smile."

"Let's put our cards on the table," the offworlder Butler said.

"His words are in English, his native language," Kenred whispered to Gwzon. "The translator makes it Amred, but changes his allegories and local references to their Amred equivalents."

"Simply stated," Katengi said, "I think we should execute General Klarot."

"And I think," Boszut countered, "we should imprison the swamp lizard for the rest of his life. Death is too good for him."

That is an impasse, Gwzon thought. *Where do I sit?* Gwzon pondered that question, and then a thought bubbled into his mind. His mouth took over, and he said without thinking, "What about the Geroptic people? Do they get a say?"

Both generals looked at Gwzon with irritation, their scales rippling bright yellow. President Katengi gave him a slight Arcan frown, eyes squinting. The offworlder Thorpe smiled, a facial gesture Gwzon now recognized. The offworlder Butler smiled at him quizzically, a gesture Kenred explained quietly.

"From the mouth of babes," the offworlder Butler muttered.

The translator had trouble with this allegory. Kenred explained softly, "He means that sometimes we hear real wisdom from the least expected sources—he means you, Gwzon. That's high praise, especially from this Human."

"How about that?" the offworlder Butler asked.

"We held a tribunal in Ceffid," Boszut said. "I think it worked out very well. Ceffids are satisfied with the outcome, and I believe so are the Amreds."

"We are satisfied," Katengi said.

"Then," the offworlder Butler said, "I propose a tribunal made up exclusively of Geroptic citizens, who will hear the evidence against General Klarot and anyone else complicit is his rule, and will judge them, and set appropriate punishment."

✳

As John Butler made his proposal, President Boszut looked at his friend and mentor, President Katengi, and said, "Why didn't we think of that? Does it really take an offworlder to point us in the right direction?"

Butler overheard them and said, "No, it doesn't. I know both of you. Given a bit more time, I'm certain you would have come to the same conclusion. We Humans are no different than you, except for our outer trappings. We are both intelligent, sapient species who have managed to find each other in this vast universe. We are friends, and colleagues, and dare I say it, often confidants.

"We Humans and Asterians are no smarter than you Arcans. In fact, something tells me that your species may outclass us in that department. Our only real difference is that we have advanced more along the path of technology. Because we have already blazed that path, you can catch up with us as rapidly as you wish."

Butler reached out and took one of their hands in each of his. "I am deeply grateful you chose to put your confidence in me. I am certain as you work out the details, you will determine this is the right path for everyone."

Butler dropped their hands and gave them a broad Human smile. Boszut was deeply impressed. *No wonder the others admire this Human so much,* he thought. *If there is anyone I really wish to emulate, it's this Human.*

✳

"We need to take General Klarot into physical custody," Katengi said to Boszut. "Even though he doesn't have modern communications, he will hear about his total defeat soon. When that happens, he will disappear, perhaps even with Orlov. We need to act immediately."

They both approached Thorpe, explaining the problem.

"You have not yet put any military posts in The Geroptic Nation into stasis, have you?" Thorpe asked.

They said they had not.

"I suggest you do that immediately."

✳

"The Geroptics have twelve military posts," Kenred told his flight team, "eight north of the equator and four south. Each of you has been given coordinates for two posts. Head to the first and await my signal.

When you get my signal, put each entire post in stasis—everything. If you see anything outside your spheres that even looks military, put a smaller sphere around it, too.

"StarChick and I will each take three outposts. Including the two northernmost ones. My first target will be the central military compound in Dragon City. As soon as it is secure, I will send the signal." He gave them an eye-blinking, wide-open eyes Arcan grin. "Hop to it!"

Kenred entered *PS Neil Armstrong* and set up the coordinates for the central military compound in Dragon City.

"You got the coordinates, Mother?"

"I do."

"Take us there!"

He turned to Neepons Kited. "Are you ready to plant the sphere, Cupcake?"

"Yep."

"We're there," Mother said.

"Do it," Kenred said.

"It's done," Kited said.

Kenred signaled the other members of his flight. "Go for it, Lizards!"

Twelve minutes later, all twelve Geroptic military compounds were safely in stasis, and the central military command, including— presumably—General Nirurian Klarot, was in stasis.

Kenred dropped a hyper-disk outside the sphere in Dragon City and signaled SPC, and it sent an inspection team with anti-stasis suits to retrieve the general.

A half hour later, Kenred received a communication from SPC. "The Dragon City team did not find General Klarot. He must have gotten word and fled the compound."

"I'm on it," Kenred said.

"Wait," SPC said. "We did collect a Geroptic officer, Major Teynal Dombit, who claims he has been working against Klarot and his invasion. Says he disarmed two nukes."

"He may be important," Kendal said. "Get him to headquarters right away."

Then Kendal turned his attention back to his flight. He wanted to start a search for Klarot before the general had time to disappear.

"Flight, grab my coordinates and join me in linear formation."

Three minutes later, his five M-Class fighters were lined up to his right.

"We're looking for General Klarot. He escaped the central military compound about an hour ago. He will almost certainly be driving a troop carrier. He may have his special troops with him. There's nowhere to go to the north or west, so we will find him somewhere to the east or south. StarChick, you take GoGirl and scan everything south of Dragon City to a forty-five-degree angle from the compound. Rainbow, you and Snout head east from the compound to a forty-five-degree angle south. Both you teams, use everything at your disposal. We MUST find this swamp lizard! Go!"

Kenred dropped to 500 meters and started a semi-circular scan around the military compound, using radar and lidar at their most sensitive settings, and visual across all visible spectra and ultraviolet and infrared. Kenred figured Klarot was a devious lizard who might just move a short distance from the compound and hide in the city.

Eighteen minutes of searching brought him the unmistakable image of a troop carrier with twenty-four troops, a driver, and another lizard—almost certainly Klarot. They were huddled inside an agricultural enclosure at the edge of the city. Kenred dropped a stasis sphere over the carrier and the surrounding area. Then he called SPC.

"SPC, it's Bobcat. I need you to send Sergeant Gwzon and a team of twenty of his squad to the hyper-disk I just placed at the edge of a stasis sphere containing General Klarot and twenty-four of his finest troops. Have them enter the sphere and disarm the troops and extract the general and the weapons. Then collapse the sphere, and collect the troops and the carrier."

Dragon City Headquarters—The Geroptic Nation, Planet Arcan

Sergeant Gwzon was notified to report to his commanding general shortly after Kenred put Dragon City HQ and surrounds into stasis. He didn't know about the stasis, but receiving a call from the top boss was top priority. When he arrived, General Edoetti Kaylambo sat in a chair behind his desk, looking almost friendly.

Gwzon came to attention and saluted, closed fist with right arm across his chest.

"Relax, Sergeant, and take a seat," the general said, very much to Gwzon's surprise.

"We have captured General Klarot inside a stasis sphere near Dragon City Headquarters. I have chosen you and your squad to go inside and bring him out. We know he is inside a troop carrier with twenty-four crack troops and a driver. They are inside an agricultural shed close to the military compound. That's all we know. We don't care if others are inside. When we collapse the sphere, they will continue on with no knowledge of the time lapse. Assemble your squad and report to Astronaut Zlaxiz."

"Yes Sir, and thank you for the opportunity."

"My pleasure, Sergeant, now go get that slimy swamp lizard."

✳

Gwzon called his squad together, chose thirty lizards, and reported to Kenred. Kenred took them to a Locus.

"The hyper-disk is just outside the sphere I put around the agricultural compound. Find the carrier and bring his troops out. I'll have lizards there to take the weapons and warriors. When you have secured the general, bring him to the inside edge of the sphere, but leave him inside." Kenred handed Gwzon an odd-looking hand weapon. "This is an EMD—an Electro-muscular Disruptor. As you can see, it is coated with anti-stasis material, so it will work inside a stasis sphere." He showed Gwzon how to set the intensity of the bolt. "Hit the general with a medium charge. It will keep him out for several hours. Then suit him up and bring him out. A special team of lizards will be there to take charge of him."

By this time, Gwzon and his lizards were old hands at entering a stasis sphere and removing its occupants. He and his reduced squad donned anti-stasis suits and clustered where the trail entered the sphere.

"We're doing something different this time, Lizards. Instead of a sphere search, which you Lizards do better than anyone, we will enter where this trail penetrates the sphere, and follow it to the shed containing the carrier. Following the trail will be tricky, but the edges seem pretty obvious." He pointed back along the trail, where the edge formed a mud ridge. "I'll pound a post into the ground where we enter and attach a line. As we progress, I'll place further posts as necessary to keep the line taut. Follow this line. Are we clear?"

"What do we do when we get to the carrier?" one lizard asked.

"There are thirty of you. Split up in pairs down the line and pull the warriors out of the carrier. Then you can disarm them and shackle them. They'll get picked up when they collapse the sphere. Leave the general to me. You two," Gwzon pointed to the nearest lizard pair, "help me with him. Unlike the others that we leave where they are, we will bring him just to the inside sphere edge." Gwzon looked over his thirty lizards. "Anyone else got a question?"

No one responded.

"Okay, let's do this."

Gwzon entered the sphere and pounded a post into the ground. Keeping one foot against the mud ridge, he moved forward, stopping from time to time to place another post. His troops followed closely, maintaining a rapid pace. They took twelve minutes to find the shed and open its doors. An hour later, all twenty-four warriors were lying on the ground beside the carrier, shackled in threes, hand and foot. They shackled the driver by himself, and Gwzon, with his two assistants, pulled the general from the cab, and disarmed and shackled him.

The rest was easy. The lizards moved the weapons out of the sphere. As always, when the sphere collapsed, the warriors reacted with a startled lack of comprehension, and some with rage. But that was a problem for the lizards waiting outside the sphere. The squad members assembled to the side and watched.

When his troops had removed the weapons from the sphere, Gwzon and his two lizards dragged General Klarot along the trail to the inside sphere's edge. Gwzon drew the EMD, checked the setting, and placed the nozzle right against the general's skin. He pulled the trigger. So far as he could tell, nothing happened. He stuffed the general into an anti-stasis suit. He suspected that the moment the suit closed, the charge took effect.

Gwzon exited the sphere. The special team was waiting several meters away. They identified themselves, and Gwzon told them to wait for a few minutes. He reentered the sphere, located the inert general and his two assistants, and together, they dragged the encased general out of the sphere. As they unsuited him, Gwzon watched Klarot's face closely for any reaction. He thought he might have seen a brief eyelid quiver, but nothing more.

The special team took custody of the general, and Gwzon watched him leave, figuring he would never see him again.

Phoenix Starship Andromeda—Conference Room

John Butler met with Thorpe and Presidents Binecot Katengi and Spajo Boszut in Andromeda's conference room. They wanted to create a tribunal that would be a Geroptic function. They specifically did not want to give the appearance that Amred and Ceffid were running the show, and they wanted to hide the offworlder presence entirely.

"Do you have any idea whom to use as judges?" Thorpe asked. "And what about the Chief Judge? He needs to be someone known to the populace, someone absolutely not complicit in the invasion, someone who will not be an accused."

"We don't know much about The Geroptic Nation," Boszut said. "We have some spies in Dragon City and down south, but I already queried them. They had no suggestions."

"I may have something," Katengi said. "We just captured a Major Teynal Dombit at Dragon City HQ who claims he has been acting against Klarot—he even claims he deactivated two nukes destined for Amred City and Ceffidia. This could be an important break." He looked at Butler, who nodded slightly.

"I think we should bring Major Dombit to this table so we can question him," Thorpe said, looking at both presidents.

"A major doesn't carry a lot of responsibility," Katengi said.

"You said he was captured at Dragon Headquarters?" Boszut asked. Katengi nodded.

"Then he may be the most knowledgeable lizard we have captured other than Klarot," Boszut said. "Yes, I agree. We should bring him here."

"I'm convinced," Katengi said.

*

With shackles on his hands, Dombit followed his guard through a portal into a conference room. Four individuals sat at the end of a large table. Two he recognized as the presidents of Amred and Ceffid. The other two shocked him, although he tried not to show it as he stifled the yellow that crossed his scales. They had to be the offworlders he had heard about but never seen. They looked like the Human Orlov, with round heads and scrawny necks. Their noses stuck out from their faces and their mouths were small and surrounded with pudgy flesh. Groomed hair covered the tops of their heads, and he noted again with interest that they had only five digits on each hand. An odd thought passed through his mind. *They count by tens, not twelves!*

One of the offworlders spoke to him in perfect Geroptic with proper accent and tone. That was impressive.

"You are Major Teynal Dombit."

It was a statement, but Dombit answered anyway. "Yes, Sir, I am Major Teynal Dombit, formerly Aide-de-Camp to General Nirurian Klarot, head of The Geroptic Nation and Prophet of the Dragon in the Sky." Dombit felt a bit silly making that statement, given that he was talking with offworlders who certainly knew better.

"Guard," Thorpe said, "remove his shackles and leave us."

"Are you certain, Sir? This prisoner is a trained soldier…"

"I am certain, but thank you for your concern. Please unshackle him and take your leave."

And thus, Dombit found himself unshackled in a room with the presidents of the two nations he had helped attack, and two offworlder Humans about whom he had insufficient evidence to draw a conclusion—except that they came to Arcan from another star.

Dombit came to attention and saluted, tight closed right fist against his chest. "Thank you, Sirs."

"Relax, Major," the offworlder who had spoken earlier said. "Take a seat at the end of the table so we can all see you directly."

Dombit sat.

"I am a Human named Thorpe, and this is John Butler, Chairman of the Oort Federation, the largest governing unit in the star system that is our home. I am captain of the starship *Andromeda*, where you are presently sitting. You obviously understand portals, since you used them for your unprovoked attacks on Amred and Ceffid. You are in a very large starship hovering in space out beyond your moon, Lodan."

The Human's face contorted with its mouth extended across its face, slightly open, showing white teeth. Since the offworlder did not seem to be aggressive at the moment, Dombit assumed it must be the offworlder equivalent of an Arcan smile, something he had seen with Orlov. He smiled—opening his eyes wide. He figured the offworlder had been briefed and knew he was smiling back.

"I understand," the offworlder continued, "that you worked directly with General Klarot, but that you took actions to undermine his war efforts."

Dombit took that as a question. "Yes, Sir. I was a lieutenant in the communications division at headquarters when we received a call from the offworlder Orlov."

"But your nation had no electronics nor any kind of modern communication equipment," Thorpe said. "How did that work?"

"I don't know the details, because at the time I was a lowly lieutenant, but I understand Amred supplied General Klarot with the equipment and training."

"He speaks the truth," Katengi said, and then he turned to Dombit. "I am Binecot Katengi, President of Amred." He turned to Boszut. "This is Spajo Boszut, President of Ceffid." He turned back to Thorpe. "Amred supplied basic electronic equipment that allowed General Klarot to communicate with us. This made possible the sale of locomotive engines, steel rails, and some other basic technology that The Geroptic Nation desperately needed." He turned back to Dombit.

"Please continue," Thorpe said.

"In that call, Orlov pretended to be the Great Dragon in the Sky. He had me convinced at first, but the general set me straight. In a few short days, I went from a naïve, young lizard to a somewhat confused but significantly more knowledgeable officer. Then I met Orlov. The general worked with him to arm his forces with modern small arms, field artillery, and troop carriers. General Klarot promoted me to captain and assigned me to moving the arms, ammo, and equipment to our twelve military posts.

"I knew that Prophet Dudengi Vrokhun had a long-term goal of bringing Amred and Ceffid under the fold of the Great Dragon. However, I didn't connect General Klarot's activities with the Prophet's goals. Then General Klarot staged a coup, displacing the Prophet with himself. He and Orlov rigged some kind of light show that convinced the bishops that the Great Dragon had taken the faithful Prophet to his just reward, and had then assigned General Klarot as Prophet."

"What happened to Prophet Dudengi Vrokhun?" Thorpe asked.

"I do not know. The general escorted him through a portal into Orlov's spacecraft, and that's the last I saw him."

"Did they kill him?" Boszut asked.

"I don't think so," Dombit answered. "I sensed that Orlov greatly feared you, Thorpe, and may have thought you would do something dreadful to him should he kill an Arcan, especially the Prophet."

The two presidents looked at each other and then at Thorpe. Through all of this, the Human John Butler sat quietly, saying nothing.

Thorpe looked at him. "Please continue your narrative, Major."

Dombit considered his options. Never in my life did I imagine I would be facing something like this. At the far end of this table sit the presidents of the other two great nations on Arcan, the captain of a powerful starship, and the Human who heads a government so vast that it encompasses every planet in a star system. And at my side of the table…I am a poorly educated Geroptic promoted ahead of my time, and who facilitated a war against the presidents I am looking at. Sure, I tried to stop it, but it was too little, too late. Lots of Arcans died for nothing, and I was partly at fault. So, how do I tell this story?

At the other end of the table, the two Arcans and two Humans waited expectantly for him to speak. He decided to tell it straight, without spin. Dombit detailed what he did to prepare the troops for the invasion, the actions he took to slow things down, and how he disabled the two nukes so they wouldn't detonate when they passed through the portals.

"Had I been more alert, had I been smarter, had I been more effective, perhaps the invasion would not have happened. Perhaps all those lives could have been saved— on both sides." He hung his head in shame, his scales rippling pink.

"Major," the Human John Butler spoke for the first time, his words coming through a translator device that astonished Dombit with its clarity and—he assumed—its accuracy, "I think I speak for all of us when I say we hear you loud and clear. I realize you chose honesty over spin. I am grateful for that."

Thorpe picked up the conversation. "Major Dombit, we need your help. We are setting up a tribunal to try the parties who perpetrated this war, and—yes—that includes you, Major. But with what you have told us here, I believe the tribunal will go easy with you. We want the tribunal to be Geroptic. We have several major hurdles before us." He held up his five-fingered hand, displaying one finger.

"One—Whom do we put on the tribunal?"

He held up a second finger.

"Two—How do we get around the fact that virtually every Geroptic is ignorant of modern technology like electricity, electronics, computers, and so on?"

He held up a third finger.

"Three—How do we retain control of the tribunal without giving the impression that it is just a puppet show? We don't want inexperienced judges throwing the book at each accused in an *I win—you lose* scenario."

He held up a fourth finger.

"And four—How do we bring the tribunal participants up to speed with the modern technology they will be using?"

"In Ceffid after the revolution, we had a similar problem to the first one Thorpe mentioned," Boszut said. "We solved it by setting up a twelve-judge panel and a Chief Judge. As the leader of the revolution, I was the Chief Judge. Six of the judges came from my senior staff. The other six were chosen randomly from a volunteer pool of citizens. We changed the citizen judges for each accused."

"We want to set up something similar," Thorpe said, "but unlike Ceffid, we do not know enough about The Geroptic Nation to choose the participants. This is where you come in."

"I have some thoughts on that," Dombit said. "But first, there is something I did not tell you because it was not pertinent, but it is now. On the Geroptic eastern coast north of Sogard lies the village of Cordan. A teacher there, Judhee Groklet, has been teaching his students math, science, and the classics for three generations. Virtually all twenty-five hundred residents of Cordan are well educated and are aware of the larger world around them. The only other Geroptics who are even mildly educated are military officers and the bishops. Putting the officers on as judges seems a conflict of interest. The bishops stood to gain a lot from the invasion, although they did not participate. When General Klarot took over, he placed the bishop in each section under the sectional field commander. The bishops took advantage of their positions both before and after General Klarot, and in my mind, that makes them ineligible."

Dombit sat quietly for several seconds. Then he continued. "The Cordan mayor, Olkklot Vulorn, could be the Chief Judge. He has executive experience, is not intimidated by the Great Dragon and the Temple minions. He will want to select the other judges. I recommend you let him select six. As for the remaining six citizen judges, we can scour the cities and villages for businesslizards who have excelled in business and tradesfolk who have excelled at their trades. Their reading skills will be marginal, because they only learned to read sufficiently well to read *The Book of the Great Dragon*. Their calculating skills will depend on how much calculating they need in their business or trade. The Dragon Schools will have given them the bare minimum. From them, we should be able to generate a pool of eligible lizards. They will take their responsibility seriously. Again, I cannot be seen as part of the selection process."

"Thank you, Major," Thorpe said. "We will keep you out of the selection process."

"As to your second point," Dombit continued, "Geroptics are intelligent lizards. Explain the facts and any of those I have mentioned, Cordans or business and tradesfolk, will catch on quickly. Put a computer in front of a Cordan and that lizard will master it in no time, and any of them, put an earwig and throat mike on them for guidance, and in no time, they will be experts." Dombit gave the bigwigs at the other end of the table a wide, Arcan grin, eyes wide open, blinking rapidly. "Trust me on this!"

"Major Dombit," Boszut said, "although I'm president of Ceffid, my roots are revolutionary opposition to the former dictatorship. You and I have much in common. I want you to know that I do trust you, and I will do everything in my power to get you through the tribunal unscathed."

"But you also need to know," Thorpe added, "we will not interfere with the tribunal unless it goes completely off the reservation."

"I understand and agree with you," Dombit said.

"On to your third point," Dombit said, raising his voice a bit, "you outfit each participant, judge, and prosecutor, with an earwig and throat mike. If a participant goes off the reservation, as you say, pull him back in no uncertain terms, including threats, if that becomes necessary. Be sure to use someone with a native Geroptic accent. After the fact, you may have some complaints, but they will be after the fact. We'll deal with it then. And speaking of prosecutor, I recommend the teacher Judhee Groklet. He will be aggressive and tough—as good a prosecutor as you can find in The Geroptic Nation."

Dombit looked at each face at the other end of the table. He began to understand that in some strange way, despite his relatively low major's rank, he was the equal of each person over there, Arcan or Human, except for the Human, John Butler. Dombit had not yet figured him out. The others deferred to him, and Dombit found himself doing the same despite himself.

"Thank you, Major," Katengi said, "for your frankness and informative suggestions. I think I speak for everyone here."

Everyone nodded their agreement.

"We are releasing you on your own recognizance," Boszut said. "We will try to have you be the first accused before the tribunal."

CHAPTER TWENTY-ONE

The Great Assembly Hall—Dragon Temple, Dragon City, The Geroptic Nation, Planet Arcan

The Great Assembly Hall in the Dragon Temple at the center of Dragon City had undergone some changes. Gone was the marble throne on the dais. The main auditorium now held a thousand seats on a tiered floor, so even the back row could easily see the dais. The overhead dome remained unchanged. It still depicted in detailed relief the Great Dragon in conflict with Night, the Demon of Darkness, but a large, decorative light fixture hung from the dome center that filled the entire auditorium with bright light.

The dais was extended to cover two-thirds the width of the auditorium. In the middle sat a raised judge's courtroom bench with lowered extensions stretching ten meters on each side. The Chief Judge's seat was in the middle, raised above the other twelve seats, six per side. Each station, including the Chief Judge's, accommodated two individuals and had a computer monitor and microphone.

Just like at the Ceffid tribunal, an enclosed witness stand of polished wood sat on the auditorium floor to the left of the Judges' Bench, as seen from the bench. A set of steps led to a waist-high door and a raised platform. The stand had a microphone, but no seating. Opposite the witness stand, the prosecutor's stand was similar, but had seating and a built-in desktop with computer monitor and microphone. In the center, on the floor in front of the Chief Judge, stood the accused dock. It was polished wood with steps leading to an internal raised platform. Above a waist-high wall, bullet-proof glass enclosed the entire dock, including the top. The dock had a microphone, but no seating.

Since The Geroptic Nation had no general electricity distribution and the Dragon Schools didn't teach science and technology, the average citizen was unaware of electric lights, sound amplification, and advanced electronics such as computers and holocams. The average Geroptic citizen, however, heard things about Amred and Ceffid, about machines more advanced than their own, so it was with great anticipation that lizards filled the Great Assembly Hall. Most knew their country had been at war. All knew the Prophet was with the Great Dragon, and that the new Prophet was General Klarot.

As the hour for the tribunal to start approached, the crowd quieted, focusing their attention on the bench that filled the dais. The lights in the Hall dimmed, something most of the crowd had never seen, and twelve Geroptic citizens, all from Cordan, walked onto the dais dressed in plain black robes, six from the left and six from the right. Once they were seated and the crowd had quieted, Cordan Mayor Olkklot Vulorn, dressed in a black robe with a golden neckpiece, walked slowly across the back of the dais. As he did so, a lizard in front of the long bench, dressed in business attire, spoke into a hand-held microphone, "All rise for Chief Judge Olkklot Vulorn."

The crowd reacted with surprise at the clerk's amplified voice throughout the Hall. Many thought it was an effect of the Great Dragon, but most just accepted it as new technology that had finally made its way into The Geroptic Nation. Vulorn walked to his raised bench and took his seat at the center of the dais.

The clerk announced, "Be seated, please. We understand this is a new experience for everyone here. We ask you to refrain from talking or demonstrations of any kind. This is a solemn occasion that will decide the fate of your fellow citizens."

Having been well briefed beforehand, Chief Judge Olkklot Vulorn picked up his gavel and rapped it twice. "This tribunal is now in session." He rapped his gavel again, its sound picked up by the judge's microphone and reverberating throughout the Hall. "Here is how we will proceed. The prosecutor will have an accused brought to the dock. Then the prosecutor will read the accusations against the accused, and if the accused wishes, allow him to make a statement. The prosecutor will present witnesses corroborating the accusations. The accused will then present his defense or his explanation of the events. He can present witnesses to testify on his behalf. The accused may be questioned by the prosecutor, and by any of the judges, including the Chief Judge. When there are no more questions, and the accused has nothing more to say, he will be taken back to holding. The judges may retire to deliberate this case, or they may wait for an accumulation of cases. When the judges have deliberated a case or cases, they will return to the bench to render their verdict or verdicts. Upon hearing a verdict, an accused may request that he be allowed to present further evidence and, if granted, ask the judges to reconsider their verdict. After rendering judgment, the judges will assign a sentence which will be carried out immediately."

The Tribunal Hall, Major Teynal Dombit—Dragon Temple, Dragon City, The Geroptic Nation, Planet Arcan

Teynal Dombit waited in a side room, alone. He knew that General Klarot was being held by a marshal in another room. The remaining accused consisted of military officers in one holding room and Great Dragon bishops in another. The audio part of the proceedings was brought into the rooms so the accused could hear the entire proceeding.

The choice of whom to accuse was difficult. Dombit had participated behind the scenes, and he suggested charging the bishops with Lizard Rights abuses once he learned about their treatment of the Arcan girls.

After speaking with Katengi and Boszut, Prosecutor Groklet put Dombit on the stand first. A marshal came for him and escorted him into the Hall and to the accused dock. He climbed the steps and entered the dock. The marshal locked the door behind him. He was surrounded by bullet-proof material. A speaker brought him the outside sounds. An adjustable mike rose in front of him. Earlier, someone had instructed him on its use.

"State your name and position," Prosecutor Judhee Groklet said.

"Teynal Dombit, Major, Geroptic Dragon Army," Dombit answered.

"You are charged as follows: Count one, materially assisting General Klarot in his overthrow of the legitimate government of The Geroptic Nation. Count two, materially assisting General Klarot in his unprovoked invasions of Amred and Ceffid. Count three, materially assisting General Klarot in his failed attempt to detonate nuclear weapons over Amred City and Ceffidia."

A gasp went up from the crowd. Chief Judge Olkklot Vulorn rapped his gavel and said, "Order in the tribunal!"

The crowd quieted down.

The prosecutor asked Dombit, "How do you plead?"

Dombit came to full attention and said, "I plead guilty with mitigating circumstances to counts one and two, and not guilty to count three."

"Do you wish to state your mitigating circumstances for charges one and two?" the prosecutor asked.

"I do."

Dombit then recited to the court the same narrative he had presented to both presidents and the Humans Torpe and Butler. In his mind, his participation was naïve, and he had followed orders without giving them much thought.

Dombit finished by saying, "I was following the orders of my superior officer in routine military movements, setting up local communications and local portals General Klarot received from the offworlder Orlov. I also delivered modern weapons to the military posts that came from the offworlder Orlov. I did not know about any private arrangements General Klarot may have made with the offworlder. I was working in the same capacity that any other senior staff officer would have worked. None of my personal actions were directed at either Amred or Ceffid. I was unaware of the general's invasion plans, perhaps naively so, but unaware. Finally, however, I did facilitate General Klarot's invasion plans. This is why I plead guilty with mitigating circumstances."

"You have pled not guilty to count three. Do you wish to make a statement?" the prosecutor asked.

"I do. I was aghast when I realized that General Klarot wanted nuclear-tipped missiles to hit every major city in Amred and Ceffid. When the offworlder denied his request, I was relieved, but then they decided to hit both capitals. I had no way to disable either the nukes or missiles, but I had heard that in its war with Ceffid, Amred fighter craft had completely disabled Ceffid's missiles and nukes. So, I had confidence the missiles would not be a threat. The first two were destroyed as I had expected. Then we discovered that the nukes in the second set of missiles were somehow disabled. I thought that would end the general's nuclear ambitions. By this time, I realized what all the earlier troop movements were about. I was ashamed of the unwitting role I had played, but I could do nothing about the past. Then General Klarot and the offworlder designed a way to move small nukes directly from the offworld warehouse to the Dragon Compound and then directly through another portal to chosen spots in Amred City and Ceffidia. General Klarot assigned me to facilitate the transfer, just like I had done for the other weapons. And this was my opportunity. We had only a few seconds to move the nukes from their arrival spot through portals to Amred City and Ceffidia. I prepared carefully and disabled each nuke as it was sliding through the portal by cutting a wire. I figured that every wire in the metal cage had a purpose, and that cutting even one would disable the detonation. I was correct, because the bombs did not detonate. Later, Astronaut Kenred Zlaxiz informed me he and Astronaut Jocara Porovik had disabled the nukes from above, but then landed to inspect them and found that both had already been disabled. He told me I had saved the lives of millions of lizards."

"Thank you," the prosecutor said. "Our protocol calls for me to present the people's case against you for each of the charges. Instead, I will allow you to call any witnesses who can verify what you have said here."

"I call Astronaut Kenred Zlaxiz."

Kenred approached the witness stand, mounted the steps, and entered the stand. After swearing in Kenred and identifying him, the prosecutor let Dombit question his witness.

"Please tell the Court how you and Astronaut Jocara Porovik disabled the nukes in Amred City and Ceffidia, and what you found when you landed and inspected the nukes."

Kenred responded. "Astronaut Jocara Porovik and I were assigned holding stations over both capitals, she over Ceffidia. When our onboard detectors picked up an opening portal through which we believed live nukes would be shoved, we disabled the suspected nukes with our neutrino beam weapons. When we then landed to inspect the nukes and remove them, we both found that someone at the Dragon Compound had already disabled the nukes. We found out after that the accused, Major Teynal Dombit, had courageously risked his life to disable the nukes. Had he not done this, I believe they would have detonated before Astronaut Porovik and I could have disabled them. This lizard should not be accused, but should be celebrated as a hero!"

The Chief Judge spoke up. "Astronaut Zlaxiz, why do you believe your disabling actions would have been ineffective?"

"Your Honor, normally, nukes reside in specific fixed locations or are in a moving missile. In either case, our equipment has time to identify the nuke, set a sharp focus, and disable it. Here, the offworld port delivered the nukes to the Dragon Compound, where they were immediately moved through portals to the capital cities. We had no detector stationed over the compound, and the time was too short, anyway. In reviewing the matter after the fact, only one moment existed where the nukes could have been disabled, and Major Teynal Dombit did the only thing that could have been done to save the capital cities from utter destruction."

One of the other judges spoke up. "Major Dombit, how did it feel to betray your country?"

"I did not betray my country, your Honor. I acted to protect my country from a dangerous lizard who had usurped its legitimate government and was undertaking a wrongful invasion of Amred and

Ceffid. I did what I could and regret that I could not prevent the deaths of so many soldiers on all three sides."

Another judge asked, "Astronaut Zlaxiz, what is your personal opinion of the accused?"

Kenred responded, "Major Teynal Dombit is the bravest individual I know. I use the word *individual*, because I know well offworlders who are Human, Asterian, and Oort, and I include these acquaintances in my evaluation of the major's courageous valor."

The prosecutor said, "If it please the Court, I wish to move to the witness stand."

"You may," the Chief Judge said.

The prosecutor descended from his stand and mounted the witness stand. The Chief Judge swore him in and identified him.

"For three generations, I have taught the lizards of Cordan math, science, technology, and the classics in violation of Dragon School requirements. I did this because I believed that the Geroptic lizards had a right to know about the universe in which we live. I had contacts in Amred who kept me informed of the world outside The Geroptic Nation. As the war got underway, my contact told me that someone at Dragon HQ was working against General Klarot and his plans. I arranged to contact that lizard, who turned out to be Major Teynal Dombit. Through me, he communicated vital information that materially shortened the conflict. He did this at extreme risk to himself, but never wavered in his resolve to stop the war and save lives."

"Why have you brought charges against Major Teynal Dombit?"

"The major did, as he admitted, materially assist General Klarot's war efforts. Bringing him before this tribunal on serious charges and allowing him and his witnesses to tell his story, seemed the best way to exonerate him."

"Isn't this a conflict of interest on your part?" another judge asked.

"I don't think so, your Honor. My staff and I researched each accused and assembled a portfolio on each. As prosecutor, I presented this tribunal with the case we had assembled against Major Teynal Dombit. That case was assembled without reference to my experience or personal bias."

"What is your conclusion?" the Chief Judge asked.

"As prosecutor, I would dismiss all charges, but in this case, I believe it is up to your judges' council to decide."

The Chief Judge looked left and right. "Do we need to meet in private to deicide?" he asked. When no one answered, he said, "Are we amind?" He looked at each judge, receiving a slight nod from each.

Then the Chief Judge spoke to Dombit. "Major Teynal Dombit, face the Tribunal. After hearing the charges and the evidence, we find you not guilty on all counts. I thank you for voluntarily appearing at this tribunal, and especially for your extraordinary service to this country. You are free to go, and may the Great Dragon go with you."

The Tribunal Hall, Colonel Blozok Garlan—Dragon Temple, Dragon City, The Geroptic Nation, Planet Arcan

Next up were the twelve post commanders. They would be brought to the dock one at a time. Colonel Blozok Garlan was first in the dock. He wore his full-dress uniform with medals. The court would not allow him to wear his ceremonial sword. He walked stiffly to the dock and came to attention after the marshal locked the door.

After swearing him in, Prosecutor Judhee Groklet said, "State your name and position."

"I am Colonel Blozok Garlan, Commander of the Ramden Military Post."

"You are charged as follows: Count one, materially assisting General Klarot in his invasions of Amred and Ceffid. Count two, enabling the abuse of young female Geroptic citizens by Great Dragon Bishop Klophut Gebala in the Ramden sector."

The crowd uttered a quiet gasp.

The prosecutor continued, "Count three, crimes against lizardkind."

The prosecutor asked, "How do you plead?"

"I plead not guilty on all three counts."

"Do you wish to make a statement before I present the evidence against you?" the prosecutor asked.

Colonel Garlan came to attention. "I am a decorated commissioned officer in the Geroptic Dragon Army. I fall under the jurisdiction of the *Military Justice Code.* This tribunal does not have jurisdiction over me."

Chief Judge Olkklot Vulorn appeared surprised, his scales turning pale yellow. He appeared to be looking at something on his computer screen, and then pressed a finger to his ear, apparently listening to someone talking in his earwig. The visitors in the Hall, of course, were unaware of any of this. Dombit watched in fascination as the Chief Judge consulted with an off-scene advisor. Then he looked up at the colonel.

"My ruling is that this tribunal has full jurisdiction over you, given the nature of these proceedings and the events that led up to it." He dropped his gavel against the sound block, sending an amplified sound through the Hall that woke several dozing citizens.

"You may continue," the Chief Judge said.

"I officially object to these proceedings. I give my testimony under protest. To simplify my testimony going forward, my objection applies to every answer and response I may give."

The Chief Judge responded, "I acknowledge that your testimony and any answers and responses are under protest. I remind you that there is no appeal from these proceedings, and that sentences will be carried out immediately."

Colonel Garlan said, "I have always followed orders from my superior officers. In this matter, my superior officer was General Klarot, who was also the designated Prophet, the leader of my country. I have done no wrong. And as I stated earlier, this should be adjudicated under the *Military Justice Code*. Regarding the second charge, I have no control over nor any connection to Bishop Klophut Gebala. I cannot be held responsible for what he may or may not have done. As to charge three, on its face it's ridiculous. In all my life, I have respected my kind and have never undertaken any act that could be considered a crime against lizardkind. I am outraged by the very application of this charge to me." The colonel relaxed his stance in the dock.

The prosecutor then presented his evidence for charge one. It consisted of documentation of the colonel's troop movements, their training for the portal, his modifications as problems arose, and his interactions with Major Dombit. Then, he called Dombit to the Witness Stand.

Chief Judge Olkklot Vulorn swore him in, and then the prosecutor said, "State your full name and position."

"Major Teynal Dombit, formerly Aide-de-Camp to General Nirurian Klarot."

"How did you interact with Colonel Garlan?" the prosecutor asked.

"I set up a portal comm system with his staff and portal transportation between his post and Dragon HQ. I supervised the weapons transfer from the offworlder warehouse to his location. I inspected his troop readiness for the invasion, and I specifically looked at his archers' ability to loose their arrows below the portal top."

"Major Dombit," the Chief Judge said, "you have described routine actions a commander would take whether or not an attack was imminent. Did any of Colonel Garlan's behavior show his active support of General Klarot's intentions?"

"Your Honor, you ask me to look into Colonel Garlan's thoughts. I cannot do that, Sir, but I can tell you this. The colonel was briefed about the invasion by General Klarot, along with the other commanders, and diligently trained his troops for his part of the invasion. When the order came, Colonel Garlan enthusiastically sent his troops through his portal."

"Thank you, Major Dombit, for your testimony. You may step down."

"Colonel Garlan, have you any witnesses to call?" the prosecutor asked.

The colonel called several junior officers from his command who testified as to the colonel's faithfulness and adherence to orders from above. Dombit thought they were fair witnesses. They didn't hurt the colonel.

To his surprise, the colonel called him to the witness stand.

"Point of order," the prosecutor said. "Can a witness serve as both a prosecution and a defense witness?"

Once again, the Chief Judge seemed to consult an off-scene entity and then checked his computer screen. After several moments, he looked up.

"Major Teynal Dombit may testify on behalf of the accused."

Dombit entered the witness stand.

"I remind you that you are still under oath," the Chief Judge told him.

"Major Dombit, in our interactions, did I ever object to an order or not follow an order?" the colonel asked.

"On several occasions, you clarified an order through me, but I never saw you disobey an order."

"Describe to the tribunal your opinion of me as an officer in the Geroptic Dragon Army."

"You are an excellent officer for whom I have great respect."

"Thank you, Major."

"I have no further witnesses," the colonel said.

"We will now take up charge two, enabling the abuse of young female Geroptic citizens by Great Dragon Bishop Klophut Gebala in the Ramden sector."

The prosecutor brought forth two witnesses who stated that they had seen the colonel socializing with Bishop Klophut Gebala in a Ramden nightclub. When the colonel questioned them, they were adamant that they had seen him. One witness even described what drink each was drinking. Another witness said she was a working girl in a Ramden social club and had seen the colonel with a girl supplied by the bishop.

The colonel vehemently denied the testimony of all three witnesses and requested a short recess while an aide located and brought in two witnesses on his behalf.

Chief Judge Olkklot Vulorn granted a two-hour break. Dombit took advantage of the break to refresh himself and grab a bite to eat. He was back in his seat on the front row a few minutes before the end of the break.

Colonel Garlan called his first witness, the manager of the nightclub in question. After the witness was sworn in and identified, the colonel questioned him.

"To the best of your knowledge, have I ever visited your establishment?"

"No, Sir, I have never seen you there," the witness answered.

"Have you ever seen Bishop Klophut Gebala at your establishment?"

"No, Sir, I have never seen Bishop Klophut Gebala there," the witness answered.

Colonel Garlan then called his second witness. After she was sworn in and identified, he asked, "Exactly what do you do every day?"

"I work in Bishop Klophut Gebala's palace every day. I arrive in the morning and depart in the evening after all activities cease."

"What do you mean by 'After all activities cease'?" the colonel asked.

The young female lizard looked around the Hall fearfully. When she did not see a bishop present, she took a deep breath as her scales turned deep red with fear. "The bishop hosts parties for friends and dignitaries several times a week," she said. "Nubile females are available for anyone who wishes to partake."

"To the best of your knowledge," the colonel asked, "do any of these young females ever leave the premises?"

"No, never!" the witness exclaimed forcefully. "They never leave, never!"

"Thank you," the colonel said. He turned to the Chief Judge. "I rest my defense on this charge."

One of the other judges asked, "Colonel Garlan, do I understand correctly that after General Klarot assumed control of the Geroptic government, he specifically put each sector military commander in direct control of the sector bishop?"

Colonel Garlan registered surprise at this question, his scales rippling yellow. He answered carefully.

"I suppose that is true, but at least in my case, I did not actually have any control over the bishop's activities."

"Why is that?" the same judge asked. "You were given total control."

"I considered it unseemly to interfere with the Dragon Church's activities," the colonel responded.

Another judge asked, "Were you aware of Bishop Klophut Gebala's extracurricular activities?"

"I heard rumors," the colonel said, "but I never took them seriously. They seemed too outlandish."

"So, you never investigated the rumors?" the judge asked.

"I did not, your Honor," the colonel answered, drooping his shoulders, his scales rippling pink.

"We will now take up charge three, crimes against lizardkind," the prosecutor said.

He called a witness Dombit did not know, a civilian working for the military who testified that Colonel Garlan had prosecuted the invasion with great enthusiasm and said on many occasions how much he looked forward to his troops running through the portal and smashing the enemy troops.

The prosecutor called on Dombit again.

He asked Dombit a single question, "Major Dombit, from your personal knowledge, did Colonel Garlan send his troops through a portal?"

"He did," Dombit answered.

The crowd in the Hall, having heard the evidence, had a collective sense of where this case was going. A murmur rose from the crowd as Dombit stepped down from the witness stand.

The Chief Judge rapped his gavel twice.

One of the judges spoke up. "Colonel Garlan, in your testimony, have you been totally honest and open, without guile or spin, without subterfuge of any kind? I caution you that you are under oath."

The colonel did not respond immediately. He appeared to be in thought.

"Colonel?" the Judge said with a questioning voice.

"You put me on the spot here," the colonel finally said.

"No, Sir!" the judge snapped. "You put yourself on the spot. Now answer my question."

"I, uh, answered truthfully, but as anyone would, I tried to put things in a positive light for me."

"So, you were not totally honest and open, without guile or spin, without subterfuge of any kind?" The judge's voice sounded angry to Dombit and his scales reflected this, rippling bright orange. "Do you wish to change any of your testimony?"

The colonel sighed deeply, his scales turning light red with apprehension. "I am well acquainted with Bishop Gebala, and we have, in fact, visited that nightclub together."

"So, was your witness lying?" The judge's scales remained orange with anger.

"Yes, your Honor, I paid for his testimony."

The witness, who was sitting in the front row, jumped to his feet and ran toward an exit.

"Stop that lizard!" the Chief Judge ordered. "Hold him for questioning."

The judge continued his questioning. "As for your second witness, your question, and her answer implied that since none of the girls ever left the premises, you could not have been seen with one of the bishop's girls somewhere else."

The Chief Judge turned to the prosecutor. "Bring Colonel Garlan's second witness back to the stand."

The female lizard returned to the stand, scales bright red with fear. The questioning judge turned to her.

"Please remember that you are under oath. Who brought you to the tribunal?"

The girl, flushed with fear, told the judge that he was a military officer and gave his name.

The Chief Judge ordered, "Locate that lizard immediately and take him into custody. Let me know when you have him." The Chief Judge turned to the witness.

"Did he threaten you?"

"Yes, your Honor, he said he would kill my daughter if I said anything about the colonel's presence at the bishop's mansion." Chief Judge Olkklot Vulorn turned to the judge who had been doing the questioning. That judge turned to the witness.

"Did you ever see Colonel Garlan at Bishop Gebala's mansion?"

"Yes."

"Did Colonel Garlan ever use one of the girls at Bishop Gebala's mansion?"

"Yes."

"Thank you. Does anyone else have questions?"

"Did he ever abuse you?" another judge asked.

"No, your Honor. I was not one of the play girls."

After a brief pause, the Chief Judge said, "Thank you for your testimony. You may step down. A marshal will escort you to your daughter. She is in a back room waiting for you. You both are safe now, I promise." He turned to the questioning judge.

"I will ask you again," the questioning judge said, "were you ever a guest at Bishop Gebala's mansion and did you ever participate in any activities with his *play girls?*"

The colonel's scales displayed several colors as he hung his head and answered softly, "Yes."

"Speak up and into the microphone," the judge demanded.

Colonel Garlan spoke into the mike, "Yes, I am guilty."

The crowd gasped, and the Chief Judge rapped his gavel.

"You are dismissed," the prosecutor said.

The colonel stepped down from the dock and was escorted out by two marshals.

The Chief Judge announced, "The tribunal will be in recess for three hours while we deliberate this case. If we see it will take longer, the clerk will notify the Hall."

✳

Three hours later, the judges returned to the bench. Dombit had taken the time to ensure for himself that the witness and her daughter were safe. He felt a powerful anger at how this case had gone, focused on what Colonel Garlan had turned out to be. When the tribunal commenced, he was confident that the field commanders would be exonerated. Now he was no longer so certain. Obviously, Colonel Garland was going down. Now he had his doubts about the others. He took his seat and looked at the bench expectantly. Six minutes later, the judges returned and took their seats. Chief Judge Olkklot Vulorn banged his gavel, and the crowd quieted.

"The tribunal is in session," the Chief Judge intoned. "Bring the accused, Colonel Blozok Garlan, to the dock."

Several minutes later, two marshals brought the colonel to the dock. He entered the dock, and the marshals remained standing at the dock steps. The Chief Judge turned to face the colonel, who came to rigid attention.

"Colonel Blozok Garlan, on count one, materially assisting General Klarot in his invasions of Amred and Ceffid, this tribunal finds you guilty but with extenuating circumstances. Judgment is waived. On count two, enabling the abuse of young female Geroptic citizens by Great Dragon Bishop Klophut Gebala in the Ramden sector, this tribunal finds you guilty and sentences you to twenty years' incarceration. On count three, crimes against lizardkind, this tribunal finds you guilty and sentences you as follows: One, you are stripped of your rank as colonel and are reduced to the rank of private. Two, you are dishonorably discharged from the military without benefits. Three, you will be incarcerated for ten years to run concurrently with the earlier sentence."

Colonel Garlan stood in the dock in complete shock. His scales turned orange and then red, expressing his anger and fear.

"Remove the colonel's rank insignia," the Chief Judge ordered.

The marshals mounted the stairs into the dock, shackled Garlan, and ripped the insignia from his uniform.

"Remove the private and execute the rest of the sentence," the Chief Judge ordered, followed by, "May the Great Dragon have mercy on your soul."

✳

Dombit left the Tribunal Hall with a heavy heart. The evidence was clear; Colonel Garlan was guilty. But Dombit couldn't shake the feeling that he, himself, had gotten off too easily. As he thought about it, the only real difference between his testimony and the colonel's regarding their work with General Klarot was that Garlan had twisted things to his favor while Dombit had simply told it as it was, without spin. That, he concluded, was the difference. The crimes against lizardkind charge was for sending his troops through the portal. The colonel did that, there was no question. *I guess*, Dombit thought as he walked along the street in the cool evening, *he could have refused. Had they all refused, a lot of lives would have been saved. I guess that's what I did with the nukes—refused to let them detonate.*

Dombit relaxed a bit as he walked in the cool evening air. *I did the right thing. They didn't.*

✳

Five of the other field commanders were found to have participated in their bishop's extracurricular activities, and were each sentenced to ten years' incarceration. The six commanders who did not take part in the bishops' extracurricular activities were found, nevertheless, to have facilitated their activities by doing nothing to stop them, and were each sentenced to five years' incarceration. All nine other field commanders who sent their troops through the portals received the same punishment as Garlan, stripped to private, dishonorably discharged, and sentenced to ten years' incarceration. The two commanders who had their portals appropriated for the nukes had not participated in their bishops' extracurricular activities, and so received five-year sentences. Like Garlan, the other eleven commanders were found guilty of materially assisting General Klarot in his invasions of Amred and Ceffid, but with extenuating circumstances. As with Garlan, judgment was waived.

The Tribunal Hall, Bishop Klophut Gebala—Dragon Temple, Dragon City, The Geroptic Nation, Planet Arcan

Chief Judge Olkklot Vulorn intoned, "The tribunal is in session," and rapped his gavel twice, as the crowd quieted. "Today, we try twelve bishops from the twelve sectors of The Geroptic Nation. Bring the first accused to the dock."

Marshals escorted Bishop Klophut Gebala, dressed in his black robes of office, who mounted the steps and entered the dock. After swearing him in, Prosecutor Judhee Groklet said, "State your name and position."

"I am Bishop Klophut Gebala, Bishop of the Ramden Sector. This tribunal has no jurisdiction over me or any other bishops. We are governed by the Great Dragon's law as codified in *The Book of the Great Dragon*. I repeat, you have no jurisdiction!"

The prosecutor turned to the Chief Judge, who didn't even check his screen. "This tribunal determined before proceedings commenced that it had full jurisdiction over Geroptic clergy, including the bishops, their lower-level people, and the Prophet himself. The accused's objection is overruled."

The prosecutor turned back to Bishop Gebala. "You are charged as follows: Count one, the kidnap and sexual abuse of young female Geroptic citizens. Count two, the forced abortive removal of fertilized eggs from young female Geroptic citizens. Count three, forcing young female Geroptic citizens to become religious acolytes or die. Count four, killing those young female Geroptic citizens who refused to become acolytes."

A loud gasp rose from the crowd, followed by three sharp raps from the Chief Judge's gavel.

After the crowd quieted, the prosecutor continued. "How do you plead?"

The bishop hissed, "I reiterate, this tribunal has no jurisdiction over me or any other bishop." He drew himself to his tallest height and planted his tail firmly, while his scales went from pale orange to deep orange—irritation to anger.

The prosecutor looked at the Chief Judge again. The Chief Judge intoned, "The Bench enters 'Not guilty on all counts' for the accused." He rapped his gavel once.

Again, the prosecutor turned to the bishop. "Do you wish to make a statement before we proceed?"

"I repeat," the bishop hissed, "you have no jurisdiction over me!"

"I remind you, Sir," the prosecutor said evenly, "there is no appeal from this proceeding."

"Then do what you must do," the bishop hissed, his scales flashing bright orange.

The prosecutor turned again to the Chief Judge. He responded, "Continue as best you can."

The prosecutor read the first count, the kidnap and sexual abuse of young female Geroptic citizens, and then one by one laid out the evidence against the bishop. A dozen witnesses testified about the bishop's parties and the young females he made available to his guests. Two female witnesses were former bishop play girls who had escaped. The evidence was overwhelming.

At the end of his presentation, the prosecutor asked, "Bishop Klophut Gebala, do you wish to respond to this count and the evidence presented?"

The bishop stiffened his stance and hissed, "No jurisdiction!" His scales remained orange.

After glancing at the Chief Judge again, the prosecutor continued his presentation with the second count, the forced abortive removal of fertilized eggs from young female Geroptic citizens. He meticulously presented the evidence, including preserved fertilized eggs that had been recovered outside the bishop's mansion following one incident. Twelve witnesses detailed how eggs were forcibly removed from young female pouches. As with the first count, the evidence was overwhelming.

At the end of his presentation of count two, the prosecutor asked, "Bishop Klophut Gebala, do you wish to respond to the count two evidence?"

The bishop shook his head slightly while hissing quietly, "No jurisdiction!" His scales remained orange.

The prosecutor continued with count three, forcing young female Geroptic citizens to become religious acolytes or die. Again, the evidence the prosecutor presented, including the testimony of seven witnesses, overwhelmingly demonstrated that young Geroptic girls who had just had their fertilized eggs forcibly removed were offered the choice of becoming an acolyte or death.

Twice, the Chief Judge had to quiet the crowd before the prosecutor could continue.

When the crowd quieted, the prosecutor asked, "Bishop Klophut Gebala, will you respond to count three evidence?"

The bishop remained immobile with orange scales, hissing quietly, "No jurisdiction!"

The prosecutor looked down at his papers and then launched into count four, killing those young female Geroptic citizens who refused to become acolytes. As with the three previous counts, the evidence was overwhelming. Ten witnesses testified they had observed the disposal of young female bodies, and four witnesses testified they were forced to escort young females to their execution by the bishop's security forces. By the end of this testimony, the crowd was beside itself. The Chief Judge finally called a brief recess to bring the crowd under control.

When the tribunal resumed a half hour later, the prosecutor asked, "You have refused to answer the previous counts, Sir. Bishop Klophut Gebala, will you respond to count four evidence? I caution you that this is the most serious count that carries the most severe penalty. You really should respond, Sir."

"You have no jurisdiction, Prosecutor Judhee Groklet," the bishop hissed, "and I remind you we know where you live."

The crowd erupted in shouts and boos, oblivious to the Chief Judge's attempts to quiet it down. Perhaps fearing total loss of control, the Chief Judge ordered the removal of the accused and retirement of the judges until marshals could restore order.

As a key witness in further proceedings, Dombit was moved out of the Hall with the judges, prosecutor, and the clerk recording the proceedings. He spent a few minutes chatting with Prosecutor Judhee Groklet.

"It's good to meet you personally," Dombit told the Cordan teacher.

"Likewise," Groklet responded. "It's too bad this isn't under better circumstances."

"How does it feel, being prosecutor at this tribunal?"

Groklet's scales rippled pink. "I am sad it came to this," he said. "All this could have been avoided."

A loudspeaker, something with which not everyone was familiar, called everyone back to the Great Hall. Dombit returned to his seat. The marshals had installed a barrier behind the third row that, Dombit hoped, would hold back the crowd sufficiently long for lizards in front of the barrier to escape. Groklet told him that marshals had been dispatched by portal to protect Cordan and its inhabitants from any action by the bishop's security forces, and furthermore, the bishop's security forces were being rounded up for prosecution.

With order reestablished in the Great Hall, the prosecutor spoke to the bishop, who was now shackled inside the dock.

"Bishop Klophut Gebala, you have refused to respond to counts one, two, three, and four, and, on the record, you have threatened me and my family. I offer you one final opportunity to respond to the charges."

The bishop stood stoically and silently in the dock.

"I offer you a chance to retract your threat against me and my family."

"You and yours will pay the price," the bishop shouted.

The prosecutor turned to the Chief Judge. "The prosecution rests, Your Honor."

The Chief Judge rapped his gavel three times. "This tribunal is in recess while we deliberate this case."

※

One hour later, Chief Judge Olkklot Vulorn reconvened the tribunal after the twelve other judges filed onto the dais and took their seats. He banged his gavel twice, and when the crowd quieted, he commenced the proceedings.

"Bishop Klophut Gebala, on count one, the kidnap and sexual abuse of young female Geroptic citizens, this tribunal finds you guilty and sentences you to incarceration for life without parole. On count two, the forced abortive removal of fertilized eggs from young female Geroptic citizens, this tribunal finds you guilty and sentences you to twenty years' incarceration to run concurrently with your life sentence. On count three, forcing young female Geroptic citizens to become religious acolytes or die, this tribunal finds you guilty and sentences you to incarceration for life without parole. On count four, killing those young female Geroptic citizens who refused to become acolytes, this tribunal finds you guilty and sentences you to death by firing squad, to be carried out no later than sunset today."

Marshals removed the bishop from the dock, stoic and unrelenting.

※

Eleven more bishops stood before the tribunal facing similar charges. All but one were executed for their roles in the abuse and death of young females. The Bishop of Dragon City convinced the tribunal that he and his staff did not sexually abuse or kill young females. The tribunal found him guilty of abusing his position as Bishop and sentenced him to twenty years of incarceration with possibility of parole in ten years.

※

As Ran dropped below the oceanic horizon west of Dragon City, twelve rifles newly issued to twelve Geroptic soldiers who had been practicing all week sounded as one in the courtyard at Dragon Headquarters.

CHAPTER TWENTY-TWO

The Great Assembly Hall, General Nirurian Klarot—Dragon Temple, Dragon City, The Geroptic Nation, Planet Arcan

General Nirurian Klarot had been held incommunicado since his capture. He was held in humane conditions, but not allowed any contact with the outside world. He reacted with total outrage when he awakened from his EMD-imposed unconscious state several hours following his capture.

From Klarot's perspective, one moment he was hunkered down in his troop carrier, and the next he was shackled hand and foot in a small, windowless room. He had no idea how he got there or what had happened, but he wasted no time in demanding outside help once he understood a tribunal loomed in his immediate future. He would be representing himself, he was told, and he could call witnesses. He prepared a list of potential witnesses and asked for pen and paper on which he outlined his career and wrote notes he planned to use for his defense.

On the day of Klarot's appearance before the tribunal, the Great Hall seats were filled early. Dombit, who had a reserved seat in the front row, waited as long as he could. On one hand, Ran was bright in a clear, cloudless, blue sky, and he was enjoying the out-of-doors. On the other, he wanted to avoid eye contact with his former boss as long as possible. Not that he feared Klarot; the general's time was over. But he still felt pangs of conscience at the steps he had felt compelled to take—his sabotage of Klarot and his military intentions.

Dombit took his seat, and shortly thereafter, the thirteen judges filed across the dais. Chief Judge Olkklot Vulorn took his seat and gaveled the tribunal to order.

Two marshals brought out General Klarot, clothed in his full-dress uniform minus his ceremonial sword. Dombit thought he looked rather resplendent despite the shackles on his hands and feet. The marshals placed him in the dock and shackled his hands to the bar. Because of his military stature, the marshals had taken extra precautions. Armed marshals stood outside the main entrance and every side entrance of the Hall. Additional armed marshals stood at locations throughout the Hall. While Chief Judge Olkklot Vulorn didn't expect any trouble—in fact, the military had cooperated fully—he was taking no chances. He nodded at Prosecutor Judhee Groklet.

"State your name and position," the prosecutor said.

"I am General Nirurian Klarot, head of the Geroptic Military, Chief Executive Officer of The Geroptic Nation, and the Designated Prophet of the Great Dragon." He spoke slowly, with dignity. "I am compelled to protest this proceeding. As Head of State and Designated Prophet, I am subject to the jurisdiction of the Great Dragon according to the rules within *The Book of the Great Dragon*. As a decorated commissioned officer in the Geroptic Dragon Army and Head of the Geroptic Military, I am subject to the jurisdiction of the *Military Justice Code*. I demand that my trial be moved to one of these venues."

Chief Judge Olkklot Vulorn had already dealt with the military side of the jurisdiction issue and had researched the religious side. He paused for several seconds and then said, "My ruling is that this tribunal has full jurisdiction over you, given the nature of these proceedings and the events that led up to it." He rapped his gavel against the sound block.

"You may continue," the Chief Judge said.

"I officially object to these proceedings. I give my testimony under protest, and my objection applies to every answer and response I may give."

The Chief Judge responded, "I acknowledge that your further testimony is under protest. I remind you that there is no appeal from these proceedings, and that sentences will be carried out immediately." He turned to the prosecutor. "Please continue, Prosecutor Judhee Groklet."

"You are charged as follows," the prosecutor said. "Count one, the overthrow of the legitimate government of The Geroptic Nation. Count two, the unprovoked invasions of Amred and Ceffid—a crime against lizardkind. Count three, attempting on three occasions to detonate nuclear weapons over or in Amred City and Ceffidia—a crime against lizardkind." Prosecutor Judhee Groklet looked directly at General Klarot. "How do you plead?"

General Klarot looked right back at the prosecutor. "Under protest, I plead not guilty to all counts, and I specifically object to your use of the phrase 'Crime against lizardkind'."

✳

Prosecutor Judhee Groklet meticulously and carefully laid out the evidence for count one, the overthrow of the legitimate government of The Geroptic Nation. He relied heavily on the testimony of the Dragon City Bishop and Major Dombit. The capstone of his presentation was Dombit's description of Klarot's deceptive removal of Prophet Vrokhun and his assumption of power.

When Groklet had finished his presentation of the evidence for count one, Chief Judge Olkklot Vulorn asked, "Where is Prophet Vrokhun?"

Klarot answered, "I don't know."

"Carry on," the Chief Judge said to Prosecutor Groklet.

Groklet laid out the evidence for count two, the unprovoked invasions of Amred and Ceffid—a crime against lizardkind, in the same careful manner as for count one. Several of the field commanders were called to testify, which they did, under protest as hostile witnesses. Dombit's testimony rounded out the evidence as he detailed the careful work that went into planning the invasions, and the role he played against his wishes.

After he completed presenting his evidence for count two, Groklet said, "May it please the Court, I wish to expound on why this count is characterized as a crime against lizardkind."

"Proceed," the Chief Judge said.

"These invasions were entirely unprovoked. There was no economic justification, because both Amred and Ceffid were eager to trade with The Geroptic Nation. There was no threat from either nation; there was no external reason at all for the invasions. Major Dombit has testified that General Klarot wanted to rule the world, to place both Amred and Ceffid under his personal control. While Prophet Vrokhun had vague aspirations to bring the entire globe under the Great Dragon, in actuality, this was nothing more than empty words. General Klarot used the inspiration of the Great Dragon with his troops to turn them into fanatical warriors bent on subjugating the world. Thus, the designation of a crime against lizardkind."

"Have you anything to say in response?" Chief Judge Vulorn asked.

"I do, your Honor. Wanting to bring the primitive Geroptics into the modern world, and then uniting the nations of Arcan against the offworlders, is not a crime, but something deserving of high praise."

The crowd's reaction to Klarot's comments made it clear this was something the tribunal observers had not considered. Modernizing The Geroptic Nation was a good thing. Uniting against the offworlders was a new thought.

The Chief Judge's gavel brought the crowd's focus back to the tribunal.

Prosecutor Groklet picked up his folder for count three. "As for count three, attempting on three occasions to detonate nuclear weapons over or in Amred City and Ceffidia—a crime against lizardkind…" He ruffled the papers in the folder. His scales turned bright orange for a moment before gradually returning to green.

"Your Honor," he finally said, "may we have a short recess while I compose myself?"

Chief Judge Vulorn said quietly, "This tribunal is in recess for eighteen minutes," and rapped his gavel.

When the tribunal reconvened, Groklet said, "Major Teynal Dombit, please take the witness stand."

Dombit mounted the steps and faced the Chief Judge. "I remind you that you are still under oath. Proceed, Prosecutor Groklet."

"Major Dombit, please amplify your earlier testimony about General Klarot's conversation with the offworlder Orlov concerning nuclear-tipped missiles."

Dombit knew where this questioning was going and, frankly, wanted to see it play out. "While I was present, General Klarot and the offworlder Orlov discussed the possibility of the offworlder supplying the general with nuclear-tipped missiles. General Klarot specifically requested sufficient missiles to hit every major city in Amred and Ceffid. Orlov refused, telling General Klarot he had no idea of the destructive power of these weapons. Instead, Orlov suggested one nuke for each capital. General Klarot acquiesced."

"Now describe the launching of the missiles."

"First, I should explain that General Klarot requested and received four nuclear-tipped missiles, two for backup. Orlov delivered the missiles by portal from a warehouse somewhere in the Solar System. I was responsible for bringing the missiles to the Dragon City HQ compound. I supervised troops digging water-filled channels to vector the rocket exhaust away from the compound. I did not know enough to sabotage the rockets, and the nukes were hidden away at the top of the missiles. I had to rely on the information I had received about the Ceffid nukes somehow being deactivated by the offworlders. Perhaps they could do it here as well. The missiles exploded over the water. General Klarot ordered me to ready the backup missiles, but I thought their warheads may have been deactivated by the offworlders, so I suggested to the general that he request a check from Orlov's technicians. The backup nukes turned out to be duds. General Klarot then requested small nukes that could be moved by portal from Orlov's warehouse to the compound and immediately by portal to the two capitals. I have already testified about those nukes and how I deactivated them a second before shoving them through the portals."

"Thank you, Major," Prosecutor Groklet said.

Dombit returned to his front row seat.

One of the judges spoke up. "General Klarot, when the offworlder Orlov told you about the horrific destruction a nuclear device causes, why did you continue to pursue using nukes?"

"Once Orlov explained the power of nukes, I decided only a single nuke for each capital would suffice for my purpose. I thought if I decapitated command and control for both Amred and Ceffid in one stroke, that and the accompanying civilian casualties would bring both nations to their knees, and the war would be over."

With yellow scales, the judge asked, "Didn't you consider the awful lizard toll, the millions who would suffer and die?"

"We call them 'collateral damage'," the general answered, "unfortunate, but necessary."

The crowd gasped as he said this. Chief Judge Vulorn rapped his gavel twice.

"Your Honor," Groklet said, "I wish to wrap up this matter."

"Proceed," Chief Judge Vulorn said.

"We have shown that Nirurian Klarot actively sought to procure a sufficient quantity of nukes to demolish every major city and their lizard populations in Amred and Ceffid. When this failed, he procured four nuke-tipped missiles that, but for the intervention of the offworlders, he would have used to destroy Amred City and Ceffidia. Then he procured two more nukes that he intended to transport to the capitals in a manner unseen by the offworlders. He was stopped by the heroic efforts of Major Teynal Dombit. I can think of no act that more completely fits the definition of a crime against lizardkind than this."

Chief Judge Vulorn banged his gavel and announced, "This tribunal is in recess for three hours."

✳

Three hours later, the clerk called out over the announcing system, "All rise for Chief Judge Olkklot Vulorn and his twelve junior judges," as the judges filed across the dais to the bench. The Chief Judge took his seat and banged his gavel.

"This tribunal is in session."

The crowd sat with a quiet hum of anticipation.

Two marshals brought General Klarot to the dock and shackled him to the bar.

The Chief Judge banged his gavel again.

"General Nirurian Klarot, on count one, the overthrow of the legitimate government of The Geroptic Nation, this tribunal finds you guilty and sentences you to incarceration for twenty years without parole. On count two, the unprovoked invasions of Amred and Ceffid—a crime against lizardkind, this tribunal finds you guilty and sentences you to incarceration for life without parole and banishment outside the Ran system, never to return. On count three, attempting on three occasions to detonate nuclear weapons over or in Amred City and Ceffidia—a crime against lizardkind, this tribunal finds you guilty and sentences you to incarceration for life without parole to run concurrently with the previous sentence, and banishment outside the Ran system, never to return."

Chief Judge Olkklot Vulorn rapped his gavel. "Remove the prisoner and execute the sentence."

As General Klarot descended to the tribunal floor and shuffled toward the exit, the Chief Judge said, "May the Great Dragon have mercy on your soul."

The Great Assembly Hall—Dragon Temple, Dragon City, The Geroptic Nation, Planet Arcan

The tribunal was over, the guilty were judged, and it was time to create a civil Geroptic government. Former Cordan mayor and tribunal Chief Judge Olkklot Vulorn played a major role. The lizard who laid the groundwork for everything that happened post Holy War, teacher Judhee Groklet, worked with Vulorn to create a national constitutional convention. Local communities across the country elected delegates to meet at the Great Assembly Hall to form a self-governing nation free from religious coercion.

The delegates welcomed advice from Amred and Ceffid and even the offworlders, and in a month crafted a constitution that served the needs of a nation newly emerging into the modern world while dropping the chains of religious despotism.

Their first task as a newly minted nation was to select a president. Judhee Groklet took to the floor to nominate Teynal Dombit. Olkklot Vulorn seconded, and a great cry rose from the delegates filling the Great Assembly Hall: *Dombit!...Dombit!... Dombit!...*

EPILOG

Federation Headquarters—Oort Cloud, Solar System

Prophet Dudengi Vrokhun awakened in a small windowless room with gravity somewhat greater than normal. He got to his feet as two offworlders entered the room; one of them he knew, the Human Orlov. Vrokhun was ignorant of Human body language, but to him it seemed that Orlov deferred to the other Human. The last thing Vrokhun remembered was passing through some kind of door into an apparently gravity-free environment—and then waking up here.

The Human stranger spoke to him in perfect Geroptic, while his words were presumably translated into the language the Human Orlov spoke.

"I am John Butler, Chairman of the Oort Federation, the largest governing unit in the Solar System around the star you know as Rodal. While I understand your country still believes that your sun is a god, the Great Dragon, I will assume that you are more sophisticated than that."

Orlov interrupted, his words being translated into Geroptic.

"Chairman Butler, allow me to explain how I come to have Prophet Vrokhun in my custody. I was negotiating with General Klarot from The Geroptic Nation when our negotiations went south.

General Klarot dumped the Prophet into my vessel and cut off all communications."

"Thank you, Isidor Orlov. I note your version of the events. I ask you to leave now, before I find a reason to detain you."

※

"John Butler," Prophet Vrokhun said, "the story told by the Human Orlov is not true."

"I know that, Prophet Vrokhun. Much has changed in your country since you were abducted. Your country lost a major war perpetrated by General Klarot. Progressive elements in your country have taken over and displaced the theocracy over which you presided. They have established a new government run by representatives of the people. All but one of your bishops was executed for perverse sexual crimes and murder. General Klarot has been banished from the Ran star system."

Vrokhun shook his head in dismay. "What am I to do?" he asked.

John Butler's face split horizontally, a facial gesture Vrokhun would learn was a Human smile. "May I offer you sanctuary while you educate yourself on the modern universe? You have much to learn, and I am willing to assist your education."

Federation Detention Facility—Federation HQ, Oort Cloud, Solar System

General Nirurian Klarot awakened on the floor in a windowless room with greater than normal gravity, and no knowledge of how he got there.

"The Great Dragon take it," he muttered, "I hate waking up like this." He assessed his surroundings as memories returned. The tribunal…the guilty verdicts…the sentencing…he was alive. At that moment, being alive was all that mattered. He got to his feet and looked at himself. His uniform was gone, replaced by an orange jumpsuit, but he was no longer shackled. He saw that as an advantage, small, but positive.

A chair appeared from nowhere—a portal, Klarot deduced. He sat. Then a Human appeared sitting in a chair with a facial expression Klarot knew was a smile. Another portal.

Speaking perfect Geroptic, the Human said, "I am John Butler, Chairman of the Oort Federation, the largest governing unit in the Solar System, around the star you call Rodan. You were sentenced to incarceration for life without parole and banished from the Ran star system."

The Human Butler stopped talking and sat quietly, looking at Klarot. Then he continued. "I have agreed to host your banishment in this incarceration facility." He smiled again.

Klarot saw an opportunity that might not come again. The Human was distracted. Klarot lunged.

Had Klarot been able to see outside himself, he would have seen a silvery sphere encase his body, followed by two Humans dressed in silvery suits entering the sphere, shackling him to a chair, and collapsing the sphere. From his perspective, one moment he was lunging through the air, the next, he was bound hand and foot, and shackled to his chair. He had experienced no sense of the passage of time between the two events. The Human Butler sat opposite him, unperturbed.

"Must we do that again?" Butler asked. "This room is surrounded by the vacuum of space. The only way in or out is by portal. I personally hold the only hyper-disks—what you knew as larger hyper-bricks. This is the most secure detention facility in three star systems. You cannot escape." The Human smiled again. It was beginning to annoy Klarot.

"If I give you my parole as a general in the Geroptic Dragon Army, will you remove my shackles?" *It is worth a try*, he thought.

"I'll give you a couple of days to think about it," Butler said. "Then we'll address the subject again."

✳

Several days later, Klarot sat across a table from Butler. Butler was outlining things Klarot could do to wile away his time.

"This will be your home until you die," Butler said. "I have reviewed every word of the tribunal. I find it was fair and generous toward you and the other accused." He smiled.

There, that awful facial expression, Klarot thought. I will kill him if I ever get the chance.

Butler continued, "I believe you are fortunate to be alive." He smiled again while Klarot dropped his head so he didn't have to see the smile.

We will grow closer, Klarot thought, until I can get close enough to grab him. Then…

Phoenix Starship Andromeda—Bridge

Phoenix Starship Andromeda dropped out of nullspace loop, appearing majestically in the sky beyond Lodan. Five M-Class fighters piloted by SPC pilots danced around the starship like fireflies around a flame.

Presidents Katengi, Boszut, and Dombit stood on the Bridge, awestruck by a machine larger than anything they had ever seen.

"Is *Andromeda* the largest structure ever built by sapient beings," Dombit asked no one in particular.

"Actually, no," Thorpe answered. "Back in the day on Earth, we built space launch loops to get into space. Typically, they were two thousand klicks long—way bigger than this."

"We built them on Rogan, too," Holon Mavik said.

"There is something very much bigger that a sapient civilization night build," Thorpe said, "a Dyson Sphere. When a civilization needs to capture all the energy its star produces, they might construct a sphere entirely encasing their sun to capture all the energy—a concept developed by Physicist Freeman Dyson long ago on Earth."

"Now, that's what I would call a large structure, no, an enormous structure," Mavic said.

"How about ginormous?" somebody across the Bridge quipped.

✳

"All M-Class craft return to the hangar bay," Thorpe announced over All Call, so it was heard throughout *Andromeda* and on the fighters. "All visitors depart the ship."

He bid farewell to his Bridge guests, and they departed by portal to their respective capitals. Several minutes later, Thorpe's Link indicated the M-Class craft were secure in the hangar bay, all visitors had departed, and *Andromeda* was ready to depart.

                    Robert G. Williscroft

Thorpe took his seat at the Control Console. To his left sat Kenred Zlaxiz and Jocara Porovik. Daphne O'Bryan, *Andromeda's* Chief Scientist, sat to his right as his First Officer. The spacious Bridge had sufficient room for a group of senior crew members who had nothing better to do.

Thorpe called up an image on the holoscreens of their ultimate destination, the Cold Spot in the Cosmic Microwave Background—the CMB. "Listen up, people," Thorpe said. This is our ultimate destination in the constellation of Eridanus. We'll be making several stops along the way. Ran was the first. The second is the triple-star system Keid, also called forty Eridani, about seven lightyears distant." He turned to Jocara.

"Jocara," he said, "take us to Keid."

❋❋❋

Please Post a Review for
RAN: A Civilization in Hiding

Authors rely on reviews, so I really appreciate your posting a review on Amazon and Goodreads. To post a review, scan the pertinent QR code below and follow the prompts. You will be prompted to log onto the platform. If you are not a member, you will need to sign up. It's free. Amazon will require a minimum $50 purchase volume during the past twelve months. Goodreads has no requirement. Thank you very much for going through this effort!

Scan to review on Amazon

Scan to review on Goodreads

CHAPTER ONE

Phoenix Starship Andromeda—Underway for Keid

Thorpe sat at the Bridge control console deep inside Andromeda's central disk. A large holoscreen surrounding the Bridge presented him outside views from the massive vessel and presented data to individual operators around the Bridge. To his left sat Kenred Zlaxiz and Jocara Porovik, the Saurian astronauts from the planet Arcan around the star Ran—their immediate departure point. Daphne O'Bryan, Andromeda's Chief Scientist, sat to his right as his First Officer. The spacious Bridge had sufficient room for a group of senior crew members who had nothing better to do.

Andromeda was an FTL (Faster Than Light) ship powered by MERT portals—a Casimir field that contained a stable wormhole.

"Listen up, everybody," Thorpe said as the background chatter died away. "Our destination is the triple-star system Keid, also known as Forty Eridani, just six lightyears distant. Those of you who are classic American film buffs will recognize this star as the sun of the planet Vulcan in the classic Star Trek television series. That's right, Spock's home planet. Back in the early twenty-first century on Earth, astronomers actually thought they had discovered an Earth-like planet around Keid-A. After the excitement died down, it turned out they were wrong. We're gonna find out what's really there."

Thorpe turned to Kenred with a grin. "This is a bit different from your circum-Lodan capsule."

"That's an understatement. The difference between our two-person capsule and this huge starship is almost beyond description." Kenred turned to Jocara, his female fellow astronaut on the first trip around their moon, Lodan. "Could you have imagined this two years ago?"

Blinking eyes wide open, the Arcan equivalent of a Human grin, she shook her head in amazement, and then turned to Thorpe. "Are you really going to let us do the honors?" Jocara asked, her scales rippling dark blue with excitement.

"You two are the only true astronauts in our entire ten thousand crew," Thorpe answered. "Oh, we've got fighter pilots, marines, scientists, bureaucrats, tabby cats, and even guys like me, but we have only two astronauts."

Kenred looked at Jocara, eyes wide open and blinking. "You do it, Girl! Be the first Arcan to pilot a starship between stars!"

✳

"Mother, she said, addressing the ship's resident AI, transit to the star Keid-A, jump interval six picoseconds, specific destination, the outer edge of Keid's life zone." Jocara gave the order in the Amred language in which Mother, *Andromeda's* central processor, was fluent. Her scales slowly returned to their normal light green.

Phoenix Starship Andromeda—Keid-A System

There was no indication of anything except the holoscreen turned a uniform speckled gray. One minute and eight seconds later, Jocara blinked as a blazing orange star with an apparent width wider than Ran as seen from Arcan filled the holoscreen center. A bright white star and a less bright reddish-orange star appeared close together off to the right. Even though she knew Andromeda was an FTL ship, and the MERT portal technology had been explained to her, it was still hard to believe that they had traveled six lightyears in just over a minute! Her scales rippled from the blue of excitement to lavender, showing her pure joy at the experience.

"Time to scan for planets," Thorpe said in his matter-of-fact manner. He turned to the control room visitors. "This doesn't work like in the holovision plays. We're on the outer edge of the life zone on Keid-A's ecliptic, about one hundred sixty-five million klicks from the star. Light takes about ten minutes to reach us from Keid. We find an inner planet by observing its transit across Keid. Mother can measure the orbital perturbations of any inner planets we find to calculate the presence and location of any larger outer planets. All this takes time, lots of time. We can drive our way around Keid much faster than the orbital period of four hundred sixty-four days at our distance." He checked a calculation on his internal Link. "If we travel at five thousand klicks per second, it'll take us two and a half days for the survey, and Mother should be able to pick up any inner planets."

Kenred looked at Jocara. "This must be pretty exciting for someone who studied astrophysics."

She responded by opening her eyes and blinking, while her scales rippled blue again.

✳

Thorpe watched carefully as the Saurian astronaut guided *Andromeda* onto the scanning flight path. She accomplished it flawlessly. He was amused at the almost childlike joy the two Arcans took in maneuvering the massive vessel. He had to remind himself that when he found them, their technology was at about the *Apollo* stage in Earth's spaceflight history. The Arcan Space Push Consortium had definitely chosen their astronauts well.

✳

Daphne had grown close to the female Saurian during *Andromeda's* sojourn around Arcan. Despite their physical differences, they had become good friends. Daphne had learned how to interpret Jocara's scale colors and understand her facial expressions and gestures. Each had a Human equivalent.

As she watched Jocara bring *Andromeda* onto the survey track, she took genuine pride in her friend's demonstrated expertise.

"Can you imagine," she said quietly to Thorpe, "how one of our Apollo astronauts would have reacted in a similar scenario? Do you think they would have handled it as well as the Arcans?"

She got up and walked over to Jocara, putting a hand on her shoulder. "It never gets old," she said quietly, "never."

✳

A day later, Mother announced acquisition of an Earth-size planet in an orbit 0.6 AU from Keid-A, which put it near the inner edge of the life zone. By the end of the survey, Mother added two more planets to the list, both much closer to Keid and far too hot for life.

Once again, Thorpe allowed Jocara to bring *Andromeda* into orbit around the new planet. He put the name for this planet up for a vote by ship's company. The Asterians knew nothing about *Star Trek* and so declined to vote, as did the Arcans. The Oort, who had downloaded into Human form before the voyage commenced, were well acquainted with the old television series and chose to vote.

By a very lopsided count, the result was *Vulcan*.

Phoenix Starship Andromeda—Orbiting Vulcan

"Vulcan seems to be very much like Arcan," Jocara told Daphne. "Or like Earth," Daphne said back. "Except I don't see any evidence of plant life."

They sat on the Bridge looking at the holodisplay of Vulcan and the surrounding skies.

"It's an Arcan-size planet—a bit smaller," Jocara said.

"Yeah, much like Earth," Daphne added. "Look," she pointed, "four continents, oceans, and polar ice caps."

"Can't tell from here if there's anything of interest down there or not," Jocara said.

"We have a bunch of people examining every detail visible from orbit," Daphne said. "Once they're done, you and I will take my craft down to the surface and give it some personal attention."

"You can just do that? Don't you need permission?"

"We don't do things that way, Jocara. First, as Chief Scientist, I set my schedule. But beyond that, I notify Thorpe when I will be away from the ship. If he needs me, he'll let me know. We all have specific jobs to do, but only a few of us regularly leave the ship."

"Sounds a bit like Amred, Kenred's home country. My home, Ceffid, was more structured—still is, for that matter. Kenred and I are still getting used to your freewheeling ways."

"We just received a preliminary atmosphere report," Daphne said, pointing to a holoscreen, "…nitrogen, low oxygen, high CO_2. Pressure is only a half bar."

"We're going to need pressure suits," Jocara said. "I've never even been on our moon, Lodan. I've never set foot on any planet but Arcan. This will be exciting for me." Her scales rippled blue.

"Drones first," said Daphne. "I think they're launching them now."

❋

The drones were invisible on the Bridge holoscreen.

"We launched about a thousand," Daphne told Jocara. "That's not very much for a planet, but they can hit the important points and confirm our orbital assessment of the atmosphere."

Kenred entered the Bridge, sweeping his tail aside as he sat next to Jocara. "Are we going to the surface?" he asked Daphne.

"Do you feel up to piloting an M-Class starship yourselves?" Daphne asked, glancing at both of them.

Both their scales rippled blue.

"Without a doubt," Jocara answered for them both.

"I want each of you to pilot a craft," Daphne said. "eDaphne will accompany you, Jocara, in a matrix onboard your craft, and eBraxton will accompany you, Kenred. Are you both okay with this arrangement?"

"Are you kidding?" Jocara nuzzled her snout against Daphne's cheek, her scales rippling bright lavender with joy. "This is wonderful!"

Kenred sat quietly, his eyes wide open, blinking slowly. Like Jocara, his scales rippled lavender.

"When do we leave?" he asked.

"We'll stage tomorrow morning," Daphne said. "I'll meet you in the vehicle bay."

❋

Daphne and Thorpe sat on the Bridge, sharing coffee and watching the vast expanse of Vulcan on the holoscreen as it passed below *Andromeda*.

"I've assigned Jocara and Kenred each to a personal M-Class," Daphne said. "As you pointed out, they're our only genuine astronauts."

Her eyes twinkled. "They're both excellent pilots, and they earned their chops in the Holy War on Arcan. eDaphne will ride with Jocara and eBraxton will ride with Kenred, but I anticipate no problems. These guys are as good as they get."

"When are you staging?" Thorpe asked.

"Tomorrow morning. We'll get the drone results and analyze them overnight. This will give the M-Class pilots definite destinations. If they find anything interesting, we'll open a portal and send a team through. They'll wear pressure suits, like what you wore on Mars, with Moxie Automated Breathing Units."

"I have to believe," Thorpe said, "that we have significantly improved the MABUs since my Mars days."

"Matter of fact," Daphne said. "Given sufficient power, which we supply through a small portal, if the atmosphere contains over ten percent carbon dioxide, our MABUs can supply oxygen indefinitely."

"I think I need to get out more," Thorpe said with a wry grin.

You have just been reading from Chapter One of Robert G. Williscroft's exciting Science Fiction novel, RAN: A Civilization in Hiding, *the thied book in* The Oort Chronicles. *Download a copy of* RAN *or order a hard or softbound copy or an audio version from your favorite online bookseller.*

About the Author

Dr. Robert G. Williscroft is a retired submarine officer, deep-sea and saturation diver, scientist, author, and a lifelong adventurer. He spent twenty-two months underwater, a year in the equatorial Pacific, three years in the Arctic ice pack, and a year at the Geographic South Pole. He holds degrees in Marine Physics and Meteorology and a doctorate for developing a system to protect scuba divers in contaminated water. A prolific author of both non-fiction, submarine technothrillers, and hard science fiction, he lives in Centennial, Colorado.

Dr. Williscroft is a member of Colorado Author's League, Independent Association of Science Fiction & Fantasy Authors, Science Fiction & Fantasy Writers Association, Libertarian Futurist Society, Los Angeles Adventurers' Club, Mensa, Military Officer's Association, U.S. Sub Vets, American Legion, and the NRA, and now spends most of his time writing his next book, speaking to various regional groups, and hanging out with the girl of his dreams, Jill, and her two cats.

Scan for more information: 

Other Works by this Author 

Please visit RobertWilliscroft.com to discover other books by Robert Williscroft. Scan for more information.

Current Events:
> *The Chicken Little Agenda: Debunking "Experts'" Lies*

Children's Books:
> The Starman Jones Series:
>> *Starman Jones: A Relativity Birthday Present*
>> *Starman Jones Goes to the Dogs (2026)*

Biographies:
> *Mission Possible* (by Gladys L. Williscroft)
> *Submarine-ër* (by Jerry Pait; compiled by Robert G. Williscroft)

Short Stories:
> *Reality Hack*
> *First Contact*
> *The Cold Spot*
> *The Virus*

Novels:
> Mac McDowell Missions:
>> *Operation Ivy Bells*
>> *Operation Ice Breaker*
>> *Operation Arctic Sting*
>> *Operation White Out*
>> *Operation Vela Redux*
>> *Operation Alfa Rogue* (2026)
>
> The Starchild Saga:
>> *Slingshot*
>> *The Daedalus Files*
>> *The Starchild Compact*
>> *The Iapetus Federation*
>
> The Oort Chronicles:
>> *Icicle: A Tensor Matrix*
>> *The Oort Federation: To the Stars*
>> *RAN: A Civilization in Hiding*
>> *KEID: A Lost Civilization*
>> *Beyond the Beyond (2025)*

Connect with the Author

I really appreciate you reading my book! Here are my social media coordinates:

Facebook: *https://www.facebook.com/robert.williscroft*
X/Twitter: *@RGWilliscroft*
Amazon author page: *https://buff.ly/2N5ZnlG*
Blog: *https://ThrawnRickle.com*
LinkedIn: *https://www.linkedin.com/in/argee/*
Book website: *https://RobertWilliscroft.com*
Newsletter: *https://eepurl.com/guZ5uv*

Glossary for
RAN: A Civilization in Hiding

ABO Drive—Alcubierre-Broeck-Orlov Drive, based upon the pioneering work of Mexican theoretical physicist Miguel Alcubierre and Belgian theoretician Chris Van Den Broeck, as developed by Isidor Orlov's team.

AI—The resident Artificial Intelligence unit built into every *M-Class* ship. Called *Mother*.

Amred—(1) A country on the planet *Arcan*, in the *Ran* star system. (2) A citizen from the planet *Arcan*.

Amred City—The capital city of *Amred*.

Andromeda—*Phoenix Starship Andromeda*, a half-kilometer thick circular disk five kilometers across with an elaborate cityscape on one surface and an upside-down pastoral landscape on the other, complete with mountains, meadows, and streams. Transparent domes cover both sides. An artificial mini black hole inside the central disk supplies artificial gravity and powers the craft.

Arcan, Arcans— (1) A planet in the *Ran* star system populated by an incipient spacefaring *Saurian* species. (2) The *Saurian* species living on *Arcan*.

Aster, Aster System—A star eighty-four lightyears from Sol in the constellation Aries. It has two Earth-like planets in its life zone.

Asterian— (1) An individual from one of the planets around the star *Aster*. (2) The common language spoken by all *Asterians*.

Casimir field—In quantum field theory, the Casimir field is the physical force arising from a quantized field. It is named after the Dutch physicist Hendrik Casimir, who predicted them in 1948.

Ceffid, Ceffids— (1) One of three major nations on *Arcan*. (2) Citizens of *Ceffid*.

Ceffidia, Ceffidian— (1) The capital city of *Ceffid*. (2) A citizen of *Ceffidia*.

Cislodan—The space surrounding *Arcan* and its moon *Lodan*.

Cosmic Microwave Background (CMB)—A type of electromagnetic radiation that fills the observable universe. The CMB is the cooled remnant of the first light that could travel freely throughout the universe. It's the furthest that any telescope can see.

Cold Spot—A section of the *CMB* in the constellation of Eridanus that is cooler than the rest. The most exciting explanation for the Cold Spot is that it is the intersection of two parallel universes—ours and another universe.

Cordan, Cordans— (1) A village in the southeastern corner of *The Geroptic Nation*. (2) Citizens of *Cordan*.

Dark Forest Theory—An explanation of the Fermi Paradox— why we have not heard from any interstellar civilization— proposed by Chinese science fiction writer Cixin Liu. The universe is a dark forest. Every civilization is an armed hunter stalking through the trees like a ghost, being careful, because everywhere in the forest are stealthy hunters like him. If he finds another life, there's only one thing he can do—open fire and eliminate it. And when one civilization becomes a killer species, it will scour the galaxy, eliminating all rivals.

Databank—An electronic or digital repository for data.

Donker—The *Arcan* equivalent of a Human horse.

Dragon City—The capital city of *The Geroptic Nation*.

Dyson Sphere— A hypothetical megastructure that encompasses a star and captures a large percentage of its solar power output. The concept attempts to imagine how a spacefaring civilization would meet its energy requirements once they exceed what can be generated from the home planet's resources alone. Because only a tiny fraction of a star's energy emissions reaches the surface of any orbiting planet, building structures encircling a star would enable a civilization to harvest far more energy. Physicist Freeman Dyson in his 1960 paper "Search for Artificial Stellar Sources of Infrared Radiation," speculated that such structures would be the logical consequence of the escalating energy needs of a technological civilization and would be a necessity for its long-term survival. A signature of such spheres detected in astronomical searches could be an indicator of extraterrestrial life.

Dytom— The *Arcan* name for the *Aster* star system.

E-disk—(Escape-Hyper-Disk) A specially designed *hyper-disk* that senses the holder's environment and will open a portal and whisk the holder to safety when conditions warrant.

EMD stun weapon—An Electro-Muscular-Disruptor stun weapon, much like a Taser.

Einstein-Rosen Bridge—(Also called a *wormhole*.) A theoretical passage through spacetime that could create shortcuts for long journeys across the universe. Imagine space-time as a two-dimensional sheet: if you fold that sheet so two distant points touch, an Einstein-Rosen Bridge or wormhole would be the tunnel connecting those points. Based on a special solution of the Einstein field equations proposed by Albert Einstein and Nathan Rosen in 1939.

Entangled-Particle Detector (EPD)—Entangled particles are physically separated, and one element of trillions of these pairs is projected in an expanding sphere around the source. When these particles encounter an object, the entangled partner signals are instantly presented in a holographic sphere called an Entangled-Particle Detector.

Frohlic—The original planet of the *Asterians*. It orbits closest to *Aster* in the life zone.

Frohlican—(1) An individual from *Frohlic*. (2) The language spoken by all *Frohlicans*.

FTL—Faster Than Light.

GEO—Geosynchronous Earth Orbit (pronounced geo or G-E-O).

Geroptic Nation, The, Geroptic(s)— (1) One of three major nations on *Arcan*. It is governed by a heavy-handed, primitive theocratic rule. (2) Citizens of *The Geroptic Nation*.

GlobalNet—A planet-wide information system using optical cables and satellites.

Holocam—A holographic camera.

Holocast—A holographic, 3-D, broadcast.

Holodisplay—A holographic display that produces a three-dimensional color holographic image.

Holoimage—A three-dimensional color holographic image.

Holoscreen—A holographic screen that produces a three-dimensional color holographic image.

Hyper-brick—A two-kilogram elongated cube used as a portable portal activation device developed by *Udachny Enterprises* similar to *Phoenix's* hyper-disc.

Hyper-disk—A 5-cm disk with a dull metallic side and a deep black side connected to a portal *Locus* through *nullspace*. Rubbing the metallic side activates the portal.

Icicle—The original uploaded Braxton Thorpe in *The Oort Chronicles* volume one, *Icicle—A Tensor Matrix*.

Kuiper Belt—A circumstellar disc in the outer Solar System, extending from the orbit of Neptune to approximately 50 AU from the Sun. Contains many comets, asteroids, and other small bodies made largely of ice.

Lagrange points—In celestial mechanics, the five points near two large bodies where the smaller orbits the larger, where the balance of gravitational forces allows a much smaller object to maintain its position relative to the large bodies. L1 is between the two large bodies, close to the smaller one. L2 is on the far side of the smaller of the two large bodies. L3 is on the far side of the larger of the two bodies. L4 leads the smaller body in its orbit around the larger body. L5 trails the smaller body in its orbit around the larger body. These are named after the 18th-century Italian astronomer and mathematician Joseph-Louis Lagrange, who first determined their existence.

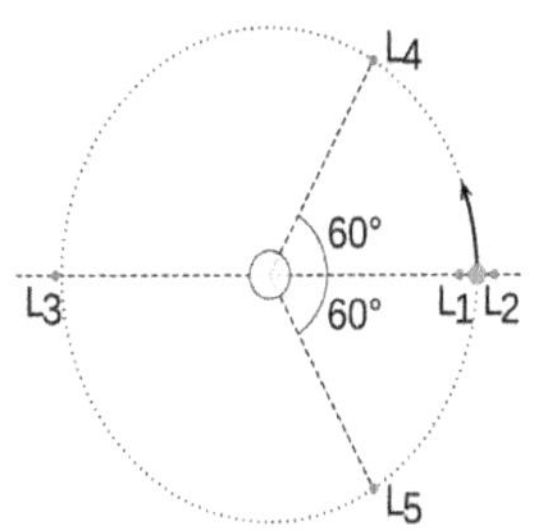

Lagrange L1 point—The *Lagrange point* between the larger and smaller body in a system. In the Earth-Luna and *Arcan-Lodan* systems, about 60,000 km toward the planet from the moon.

Lagrange L2 point—The *Lagrange point* beyond the smaller body in a system. In the Earth-Luna and *Arcan-Lodan* systems, about 60,000 km beyond the moon.

Lagrange L3 point—The *Lagrange point* beyond the larger body in a system. In the Earth-Luna and *Arcan-Lodan* systems, about 400 thousand km beyond Earth or Ran in the moon's orbit on the other side of the planet.

Lagrange L4 point—The *Lagrange point* in the orbit of the smaller body leading the smaller body in a system. In the Earth-Luna and *Arcan-Lodan* systems, about 400 thousand km from the planet and moon, leading moon in moon's orbit.

Lagrange L5 point—The *Lagrange point* in the orbit of the smaller body trailing the smaller body in a system. In the Earth-Luna and *Arcan-Lodan* systems, about 400 thousand km from the planet and moon, trailing moon in moon's orbit.

LANR—Lattice Assisted Nuclear Reaction. Formerly called cold-fusion.

Launch loop—A method for launching human and freight payloads into space without using rockets. Constructing the World's first *Space Launch Loop* is the theme of *Slingshot*, the first novel in *The Starchild Saga*.

LEO—Low Earth Orbit (pronounced L-E-O).

Link—An electronic device for hooking up to the *GlobalNet*. It has various configurations, from a wristband, to a piece of apparel, to a surgically implanted device. It has both aural and holographic displays.

Lodan—Moon of the planet *Arcan* in *Ran* star system.

Locus—See *Portal Locus*.

Matrix—(1) Within the framework of this novel, a box shaped to fit into an electronics rack that contains complex electronics that can form its own electrical pathways over time. It contains the self-aware essence of an uploaded individual (or cat). Plural herein is matrixes.

(2) a mathematical expression of n dimensions (where n > one) whose elements are tensors with n-1 dimensions. For example, a two-dimensional matrix with columns and rows has one-dimensional tensor elements that are the point intersections of each column and row. Plural herein is matrices.

MBH Drive—A *subluminal* spacecraft with a rapidly rotating Mini Black Hole (MBH) at its core. It has a circular plasma path lined with 100-Tesla electromagnets surrounding the MBH. A dense plasma focus generates a plasma stream in the ring. The magnets accelerate the stream to near light speed and bend it into a circle. Upon reaching terminal velocity, the plasma stream splits off continuous particle pairs. As each pair passes a designated drop point, one of the particles drops into the MBH event horizon. Governed by the Penrose process, the MBH loses a minuscule amount of angular momentum, while the remaining particle gains that angular momentum plus an additional 27 percent. This continuous process develops an enormous amount of energy that powers the extraction process and supplies all the power needed to drive the spacecraft.

M-Class Craft—A type of smaller starship combining the *MBH Drive* with the *MERT Drive*. Typically used for planetary exploration and as a combat fighter.

MERT Drive—An *FTL* drive consisting of passing one MERT Portal through another, and then the second through the first, and so on, to leapfrog quickly through normal space.

MERT Portal—MERT=Morris-Einstein-Rosen-Thorne. A *Casimir field* that contains a stable wormhole with the ability to position one end of the wormhole manually.

Microbiome—The total of all the trillions of microorganisms inside a living being.

Mother—The name of the controlling *AI* for MERT Drive ships.

Nanobot—Nano-size robots controlled by programs generated by the *Nanocosm*.

Nanocosm—A device capable of translating simple English directions into highly complex, wide-ranging instruction sets to *nanobot* swarms that build whatever the original instructions dictated.

Nullspace—Within the framework of this novel, stands for non-space. The interior of a *wormhole* or a series of connected *wormholes*.

Ogden Enterprises—The company founded by Daphne O'Bryan and Kimberly Deveraux that handles all upload and life-extension activities throughout the Solar System.

Oort—Collective name for all the uploaded individuals dwelling in the *Oort Cloud*.

Oort Cloud—An extended shell of icy objects that exist in the outermost reaches of the Solar System at distances ranging from 10,000 to 100,000 AU. Named after astronomer Jan Oort, who first theorized its existence.

OptiComm—The *Ceffid* government optical communication network.

Phoenix— Originally called Denver Revive Labs in Los Angeles, it is where Braxton Thorpe, the Icicle from the *First Oort Chronicle*, was revived and uploaded as an electronic entity—a Tensor Matrix. Upon moving to Denver, it was renamed Phoenix Labs, and as operations extended throughout the Solar System, it became just Phoenix.

Phoenixes—The blockchain digital coin (Φ), nearly universal anywhere in the Solar System except Earth.

Portal Locus—The origin end of a *MERT portal*.

PS—Phoenix Starship

Q-carbon—A carbon phase that is harder than diamond, ferromagnetic, glows when exposed to energy, and back-converts to diamond with a simple melting process.

Ramden—The southernmost city in *The Geroptic Nation*.

Rodal—The *Arcan* name for the Human Solar System.

Rogan—The planet orbiting *Aster* at the outer edge of the life zone. *Frohlic* colonized Rogan long ago.

Roganian—(1) An individual from *Rogan*. (2) The language spoken by Roganians.

Saurian—Reptilian.

Schwarzschild radius—The radius defining the event horizon of a Schwarzschild black hole. It is a characteristic radius associated with any quantity of mass. Named after the German astronomer Karl Schwarzschild, who calculated this exact solution for the theory of general relativity in 1916.

Sogard—The third-largest city in *The Geroptic Nation* located in the southeastern corner, several dozen km south of *Cordan.*

Space launch loop—See *launch loop.*

Subluminal—Slower than lightspeed.

Superluminal—Faster than lightspeed.

Udachny Enterprises—The Solar System business established and owned by Isidor Orlov.

UKK—Udachnyy Kosmicheskiy Korabl—Udachny Spaceship.

UZ—Udachnyy Zvezdolet—Udachny Starship

VASIMR engine—The Variable Specific Impulse Magnetoplasma Rocket is an electrothermal thruster that uses radio waves to ionize and heat an inert propellant, then a magnetic field to accelerate the resulting plasma, generating thrust.

Wormhole: See *Einstein-Rosen Bridge.*